MURDER
ON
SKIATHOS

by Margaret Addison

A Rose Simpson Mystery

Rose Simpson Mysteries (in order)

Murder at Ashgrove House
Murder at Dareswick Hall
Murder at Sedgwick Court
Murder at Renard's
Murder in the Servants' Hall
Murder on Bonfire Night
Murder in the Folly
Murder on Skiathos

Chapter One

'Rose, darling, what in the world possessed you and Ceddie to choose this place of all places to take a holiday?' complained Lady Lavinia Sedgwick, wrinkling up her nose as if she had suddenly become conscious of some unpleasant vapour. The action caused her brow to crease, the combined effect marring, for a moment, the young woman's beauty. There next followed a pout, which complemented rather admirably the petulant tone in which she had spoken. Indeed, it brought to the mind of the woman being addressed, the image of a child who had received a present which had fallen far short of its expectations.

With the memory of the resemblance to the spoilt child still in mind, Rose shifted in her seat and regarded her sister-in-law with a somewhat practised eye. Lavinia had, until that moment, been reclining rather listlessly on a bentwood and wickerwork chaise, her elegant figure artfully posed and stretched out under a lace-embroidered parasol. Having spoken so disparagingly of their surroundings, however, she had now made languid efforts to raise herself into a sitting position. This she did with the aid of her elbow and the adjustable back of the sun lounger. An exquisitely manicured hand was thrown out in an expressive gesture. The purpose of which was to indicate that, in the unlikely event that there remained any doubt, her sentiments encompassed not only the hotel terrace on which the two women were seated, but also embraced the beach below and, indeed, everything as far as the eye could see.

It might reasonably have been supposed that the young woman's companion would display signs of being ruffled or upset by such a forthright condemnation of her choice of holiday venue. Of this, however, there was little evidence. Instead, Rose, Countess of Belvedere, appeared to take such comments in her stride, as if such declarations were neither infrequent, nor wholly unexpected. Certainly, she made no attempt to appease her friend or concur with the view expressed. Rather, the expression on her face was one of barely concealed amusement as she turned her gaze to the hotel terrace, with its scrubbed, irregular paving stones, edged in white paint, gleaming in the afternoon sun, and to the well-tended lawns, little oases of green in the parched, dry earth. She looked beyond these towards the edge of the cliff, on which the hotel was built, noting the thick clumps of vegetation that fought for purchase on the rock and decorated the crag's mantle of pebbles and small stones.

From her current vantage point, seated on the terrace, Rose could not see, without rising to her feet, the cliff's sheer drop, though she was conscious of its ominous existence. For, more than once during her stay at the hotel, she had ventured out to stand on the cliff edge so that she might appraise the view it offered. She had peered down at the tiny beach below, which was little more than a cove bordered on three sides by rock face, its fourth side flanked by the Aegean Sea, whose waves lapped at the shore enticingly. Despite the relatively modest dimensions of the beach, its sands were golden, and it was almost unpopulated, for it had the honour of being reserved exclusively for the hotel's patrons.

As she contemplated her immediate surroundings, it was clear from her bright, upturned face and contented intake of breath that Rose did not share Lavinia's unfavourable opinion of Hotel Hemera, or its beach, or indeed the Greek island of Skiathos on which they were situated. Instead, she laughed, a light sound that caught the breeze that came in from the sea and appeared to linger there.

'Well, I think,' Rose said finally, feeling the warmth of the sun on her face and conscious of the sea beneath the cliff which surely must sparkle and glisten temptingly in the afternoon sun, 'that it is all quite heavenly.'

'Well, *you* would,' said Lavinia rudely, but not without humour, a grudging smile turning up the corners of her lovely mouth. 'I should have known better than to ask you that question. I daresay you don't mind if everything is deathly dull; but I do. It's not what I'm used to after London, I can tell you. I mean to say, what is there to do in a place like this other than stare out at the sea and count the waves?'

'There is plenty to do if you have a mind to look,' retorted Rose briskly. 'You could go for a swim or organise a tennis party or catch up with your correspondence. I, for one,' she added, idly flicking over the pages of her copy of *The Lady* magazine, 'am quite content to sit here in the sun for a while and read.'

Lavinia pulled a face and paused for a moment to adjust her outfit. She was dressed in a rather becoming black and white swimsuit with matching silk cape. 'It is all very well for you,' she continued, rearranging the cape about her shoulders to prevent her porcelain skin from burning in the afternoon sun. 'You haven't had to refuse a dozen invitations to come here. When I think what I might have been doing … well, it doesn't bear thinking about.' She turned her head and gazed forlornly out to sea, as if she hoped that something on the horizon might grab her attention.

'Nonsense!' said Rose, not deceived by this display of boredom. 'I believe you are enjoying this holiday as much as I am.'

'As I said, it's all very well for you,' continued Lavinia, peevishly. 'You are used to living in the country –'

'Where not much happens?' suggested Rose, with a wry smile, discarding her magazine in order that she might look pointedly at her sister-in-law. 'Really Lavinia, I don't know how you can possibly say that. You love Sedgwick Court with a passion; you know you do. And as to it being quiet and uneventful in the country, have you quite forgotten what occurred in the folly?'

'Well, no,' said Lavinia, frowning rather sheepishly. 'I hadn't forgotten *that*.'

Rose had meant her words to be no more than a gentle rebuke. Certainly, she did not intend them to upset the peace and tranquillity in which she was presently basking. They had initially brought a smile to her own lips, but almost immediately her mood became sombre. For her mind had drifted back unbidden to the tragic events that had occurred so recently in the grounds of the Belvederes' country estate. She reminded herself sternly that murder was not a subject for merriment, and inwardly she admonished herself severely for alluding to it in so flippant a manner.

Rose had dropped her head in contemplation; now, she turned her gaze and followed Lavinia's example of looking out to sea. Dozing pleasantly in the hot Mediterranean sunshine, she supposed she might almost be forgiven for forgetting that a darker, more complicated world existed beyond the isle's pleasant shores. For here in the calm and serenity of the Greek island, it was all too easy to believe that the recent death at Sedgwick Court was little more than a figment of her own vivid imagination.

Inwardly, she sighed. For it had struck her in that same moment that it was not uncommon to become accustomed to things which initially appeared shocking or strange. Eventually she knew they would barely register, much in the same way as the strange haunting song of the cicadas, which had at first sounded deafening to her English ears, was now as familiar to her as the British dawn chorus.

'I was about to say,' said Lavinia, continuing in the same vein as before, despite Rose's scolding, 'that it is not so much that there is little to do here, more that there is no one to do it with.'

'I can't think what you mean by that,' said Rose, somewhat surprised as her mind drifted on to more pleasant things, in particular, to reflect on the hotel's other patrons. 'I would have said there were quite a few people here given the circumstances. I wouldn't have been at all surprised if we had been the only guests here. You know, Hotel Hemera opened its doors for the first time just last week. We missed the opening ceremony by a few days.'

'What I mean,' said Lavinia, frowning at the need to provide further explanation, 'is that there is no society to speak of. This hotel is all very well, but there is no one of any standing here. Oh, I daresay you will disagree,' she hurried on, as her companion made to protest. 'You will point to that dull vicar and his daughter, or to the dreadful Misses Trimble, or even to that rather strange young man who is some sort of private courier. But really, they are hardly our sort of people.'

'*Your* sort,' corrected Rose, a trifle coldly, 'and by that I suppose you mean they are not of your class. Have you forgotten that I once worked in a dress shop?'

'Hardly,' said Lavinia, rolling her eyes in an exaggerated fashion. 'But you are quite different, darling. From the usual shop girl, I mean. And besides, I worked there too for a time, if you remember?'

Rose did remember, and the recollection caused her to smile in spite of herself. For Lavinia was referring to a time when she had been fulfilling a bet made with her brother that she could not earn her own living for six months. It had been purely by chance that she had chosen to work in the same, rather obscure, London dress shop in which Rose herself was employed. An unlikely friendship had developed between the two girls despite their very different backgrounds, and Rose's marriage to Lavinia's only sibling, Cedric, Earl of Belvedere, had further cemented the bond that existed between the two girls.

'Anyway, you're not a bit like that,' continued Lavinia. 'If you were like the other guests ... and besides, you are married to my brother and

...'

'You needn't explain,' said Rose with a laugh, recovering a little of her sense of humour. 'I know you don't mean half the things you say.'

Lavinia made a face which suggested that perhaps on this occasion she had meant every word. Indeed, she opened her mouth as if in readiness to emphasise this very point, and no doubt would have done, had not the two women that very minute been hailed by one of the other hotel guests.

'Lady Belvedere; Lady Lavinia. How very fortunate,' cried a rather timid voice that nevertheless seemed to penetrate the summer air as effectively as any yell or shout. 'I am so glad to have found you. I rather thought you might be on the beach. And really, it is far too hot to go down those awful little steps. I can't tell you how dangerous I think they are, cut into the rock like that ... so very steep when one is my age ...'

The voice trailed off as the speaker focused her efforts on crossing the hotel terrace while keeping one hand firmly on her hat lest it be blown off in the breeze, and the other clutching a large and rather shabby leather bag which Rose knew contained, among other things, a pair of knitting needles and three balls of wool. Thus encumbered, the owner of the voice made something of a comical picture. Being barely five feet tall and fighting with a hat whose brim was far too big for the small face it shielded, it seemed that both the hat and the ungainly bag engulfed the tiny figure. Her movements too were strange, being a mixture of hesitant steps and quick little skips, so that her progress across the terrace appeared erratic and disjointed. Certainly, she reminded Rose of a little bird picking at, and worrying, a scrap of food, reluctant to forsake it, but ever cautious of the possibility of the presence of a predator.

'Good afternoon, Miss Hyacinth,' greeted Rose with a welcoming smile. Lavinia, by contrast, immediately looked about her for a means of escape. Seeing there was none, unless she wished to appear frightfully rude by scurrying across the terrace and retreating into the relative safety of the hotel, a ruse which would appear too obvious even to the genial Miss Hyacinth, she slumped back on to the sun lounger and toyed with her hat, as if she thought it might serve as a mask or veil.

If Miss Hyacinth Trimble was aware of the measures taken by Lavinia to avoid conversing with her, she made no sign of it as she made her way towards them, other than to give a quick glance in the girl's direction. Lavinia, by this stage, had half-hidden her face beneath her sun hat and gave every appearance of being asleep. Certainly, Miss Hyacinth, as she approached, directed her conversation to the countess, panting slightly from her exertions.

'I have some very exciting news.'

'You have discovered what we are being served for dinner,' mumbled Lavinia, from beneath her hat.

Rose threw her sister-in-law a reproachful look, fervently hoping that Miss Hyacinth had not heard her muttered words. A quick glance at the newcomer did nothing to allay her fears, for a confused look had appeared on Miss Hyacinth's face. Evidently, the older woman was aware that Lavinia had spoken. Rose's only hope was that she had been unable to make out her actual words.

'And what is that, Miss Hyacinth?' enquired Rose pleasantly, feeling that she must atone for her friend's rudeness by giving an exaggerated display of interest. 'Please, won't you take a seat?'

'That is very kind of you, your ladyship; I'm sure I don't mind if I do,' muttered the rather flustered Miss Hyacinth, mopping at her forehead with an over-sized handkerchief as she perched herself carefully on the edge of a loom wicker chair. 'It's the heat, you see. I doubt whether my sister and I would have come if we had realised how very hot it would be at this time of year. Very silly of us, I am sure. But then, as you know, my sister and I are not frequent travellers. We are used to a more inclement climate …' Miss Hyacinth paused and, after a brief rummage in her bag, produced a paper fan, which she employed in earnest. 'Oh dear,' she said, stopping for a moment as if it had suddenly dawned on her that she was creating rather a spectacle. 'I suppose I must appear a frightful sight?'

'Not at all,' Rose replied politely, though somewhat mendaciously given the woman's lobster-red cheeks and the large strands of hair that were escaping from under Miss Hyacinth's straw hat, which rather gave her the appearance of a wilting flower.

'Now, what was I saying?' said Miss Hyacinth, returning the fan to the confines of her bag.

'Nothing at all,' murmured Lavinia, under her breath.

'You said you had something to tell us,' Rose prompted helpfully. 'I daresay it is to do with the excursion Father Adler is planning to the monastery?'

6

'The Holy Monastery of the Annunciation?' enquired Miss Hyacinth, a trifle vaguely, almost as if she had forgotten its very existence. A moment later, she was as a student being recalled to the subject by an officious governess, the words tripping off her tongue in parrot fashion. 'Or Evangelistria, as it is commonly referred to here on the island ...' she said, remembering the passage about the holy building she had read in the vicar's guide book. Though she had yet to see the church, it sprung up in her imagination, resplendent in all its Byzantine architecture. Indeed, for a moment she could almost feel the stone walls beneath her fingers. 'No, it is not that ... though I daresay it will be most interesting. Indeed, I cannot tell you how much Peony and I are looking forward to it. When I think how our dear father ... oh, but I digress,' she added hastily, perhaps conscious that Lavinia had stifled a sigh, and even Rose seemed a little restive. 'How very silly of me,' she continued, appearing a little flustered. 'We are not used to having company, my sister and me. And such esteemed company at that! You see, it was only ever just the two of us and father –'

'You had something to tell us,' Lavinia said rather curtly, her platinum curls emerging from under her sun hat, and her eyes squinting in the bright sunlight. With an ill-concealed show of resignation, she sat up and all but scowled at the unfortunate Miss Hyacinth, who gave a start, almost as if she had forgotten the other girl was there.

Rose, for her part, winced at Lavinia's rudeness. However, the interruption had served its purpose. Miss Hyacinth's manner became less hesitant and confused, and she ceased to ramble. Instead, her cheeks became flushed with excitement. She leaned forward in her chair, tapped the side of Lavinia's sun lounger with the brim of her hat for emphasis, and said:

'You will never guess what I have heard, Lady Lavinia. Mr Vickers was just after telling me –'

'Oh, I shouldn't believe a word that Old Vickers says, if I were you,' retorted Lavinia, before Miss Hyacinth had an opportunity to complete her sentence. 'The man is a first rate bore, if you ask me. He'll talk about anything if you give him half the chance. Why just yesterday –'

'Lavinia!' exclaimed Rose. 'Pray, do continue with what you were saying, Miss Hyacinth,' she said, turning her back to her friend and giving the older woman a nod of encouragement to continue with her story.

'Well, I suppose it's not very exciting; for young women such as yourselves, I mean,' conceded Miss Hyacinth. 'But you will understand my sister and I live such a very quiet existence. Very little happens in Clyst Birch.' She paused a moment as her mind drifted back to her birthplace. 'It is a very little village, you see, little more than a hamlet really.' Her eyes glistened as she battled with a tear, overcome with a sudden wave of homesickness. 'Our dear father was the clergyman there.'

'Yes. You told us on the first day we made your acquaintance,' said Lavinia rather unkindly, tiring of making any pretence that she was not thoroughly bored with the conversation. Indeed, having abandoned any semblance to civility, she rose and made as if to leave. 'If you will excuse me –'

'Oh, but Lady Lavinia,' cried Miss Hyacinth, stretching out her hand as if to pull at the young woman's cloak to detain her. 'You have not heard my news.'

'You have just said ...' began Lavinia, before catching Rose's eye. She sighed and resumed her seat, a look of resignation on her face.

Miss Hyacinth, aware that she now had her companions' attention, decided to play her advantage without further delay. 'It concerns one of the hotel guests,' she said quickly. 'That's to say, a guest that is yet to arrive.' Out of the corner of her eye, she saw Lavinia roll her eyes at Rose. 'Mr Vickers,' she continued hurriedly, 'has it on good authority that they chartered a boat in Athens and are making their way here to the island. I believe they should arrive any minute.'

'Who chartered a boat?' asked Rose, with renewed interest. She had been watching Miss Hyacinth keenly from the moment the woman had mentioned there was to be an additional guest. Unlike Lavinia, she was not bored with the hotel's clientele, and her curiosity was roused. Miss Hyacinth, always timid and deferential, appeared strangely agitated, as if she were in two minds whether to speak out or not. Indeed, she hesitated a moment before replying, permitting an awkward silence to fill the terrace, disturbed only by the noise of the cicadas.

'I have had quite enough of all this intrigue,' declared Lavinia rising. 'No, it's no good,' she added, as Rose made to protest. 'Miss Hyacinth, you have had your chance,' she continued, addressing the older woman. 'I'm afraid I haven't all day to sit and gossip. I daresay our mysterious guest will present themselves at dinner.'

With that, Lavinia set off across the terrace, her little striped cloak billowing out behind her in the breeze. She had only walked a few feet, however, when her ears caught Miss Hyacinth's next words, though they were uttered to Rose in a loud whisper.

'It's the … Duchess of Grismere.'

Rose, who had been watching Lavinia's retreating figure, dismayed by her friend's rudeness to Miss Hyacinth, was surprised to witness the girl halt abruptly, almost as if she had turned to stone. The next moment she had turned to face them, the sun hat that had been clutched in her hand falling to the ground abandoned. It was not this, however, that intrigued Rose as much as the expression on Lavinia's face. It was one of incredulity. With a stab of something akin to foreboding, Rose realised that it was the first time during their stay on the island that her friend had appeared animated, her face lit up with barely concealed excitement.

Chapter Two

'The Duchess of Grismere?' queried Rose, as soon as Miss Hyacinth, having imparted her news, had scurried into the hotel. Except for a servant sweeping away fallen leaves, the two girls were quite alone on the terrace.

'Yes,' cried Lavinia, dashing back to her chaise, and throwing herself down upon it in so reckless a fashion that the wickerwork groaned loudly in protest. 'It's frightfully exciting, don't you think?' Her eyes, Rose noticed, were very bright; gone was the glazed look of boredom that had been so prevalent before.

Rose pondered her friend's question and did not reply immediately. The name sounded familiar, yet she could not remember the context in which she had heard it mentioned before.

'The newspapers have been full of nothing else,' Lavinia said, a touch reproachfully, feeling that some of the wind had been taken out of her sails by Rose's continuing silence.

She threw her sun hat down on to the floor beside her and regarded her companion meditatively. She could hardly believe Rose was ignorant of the rumours to which she referred, and yet her lack of response suggested otherwise.

'I'm afraid I haven't the faintest idea what you are talking about,' admitted Rose. 'Having said that, I do feel that I have heard the name before, though I am certain I have never met the duchess, or the duke, come to that.'

'I should think you have!' Lavinia snorted in something of an unladylike fashion. 'Really, Rose, you are quite impossible,' she said, her look incredulous. 'I daresay,' she sighed, 'it is not your fault. I suppose you just read all the wrong sorts of papers. The village gazettes and all that. Why, I bet you busy yourself with reading the Parish magazine; who had the prize marrow at the Sedgwick village fete, that sort of thing.'

'I do nothing of the sort,' exclaimed Rose, suppressing a giggle. 'That's to say, I do, but I read other things too. But not the scandal sheets and gossip columns if that's what you mean?'

'Is there anything else worth reading?' enquired Lavinia, making a face, though there was a gleam in her eye. She leaned forward suddenly and grabbed the other girl's hand. 'No, but seriously, Rose, you must have read all about it in the papers? Why, Ceddie must have spoken to you about it. After all, the Duke of Grismere is a member of his club.'

At the mention of her husband, Lavinia noticed that her sister-in-law's face suddenly looked flushed. 'Is everything all right?' she enquired. 'With you and Ceddie, I mean? You have both been very quiet. Indeed, you hardly speak to each other at dinner, and when you do you are frightfully polite –'

'The Duchess of Grismere?' Rose prompted hurriedly, hoping fervently that Lavinia would not pry any further into the relations between her brother and his spouse. Lavinia gave her an odd sort of look but continued to talk obligingly on the subject of the duchess.

'She's vanished!

''The Disappearing Duchess!'' exclaimed Rose, recalling some headline or other that she had glanced at. 'I say, is that her?'

'Yes, of course it is,' said Lavinia, a note of exasperation in her voice. 'How many duchesses do you think have vanished? No, don't answer that,' she continued hurriedly. 'It's all jolly mysterious. One evening the duchess was at a ball, and the next minute she had disappeared. A bit like Cinderella, though of course she was already married to her prince. If you can call the duke that. He's frightfully dour and heaps older than her and –'

'What do you mean by disappeared?' asked Rose, interested in spite of herself.

'She hasn't been seen since that fateful night.'

'I take it by that you mean, she has not been seen out in society? Is that so very odd? Very likely she's ill. I mean to say, surely the duke knows where she is?'

'That's just it,' Lavinia said. 'No one thinks he does. The duchess hasn't been seen for weeks. Not by anyone, if one believes what one reads in the papers. Not by her servants, or even her closest friends. I can't tell you the amount of gossip there is doing the rounds in London. It is all anyone talks about. And,' she added, tightening her grip on the other girl's arm so that Rose winced, 'the old duke has kept himself to himself, which is not a bit like him. He is rather a one for hosting lavish parties, you see. But, of late, he has become something of a recluse, hardly venturing out and, when he does, he won't talk to anyone. He just skulks about as if he had something dreadful to hide. And they say he has aged terribly. Why, Ceddie barely recognised him when he came across him at his club the other day. Didn't he tell you?' She did not wait for an answer but hurried on. 'Rumour has it that the duke spends all day shut away in one of the turrets at Grismere Castle. He just sits there and broods.' Lavinia sighed reflectively. 'I suppose grief hits one like that. It's frightfully sad. Everyone is saying that he's dying of a broken heart.'

'Indeed?' said Rose, eyeing her friend rather cynically. To her ears it sounded a highly improbable tale, which she thought Lavinia enjoyed telling a little too much for her liking. However, though it was obvious that the narrative had been highly embroidered and exaggerated, she was, nevertheless, sufficiently moved and interested by it to enquire whether or not the police had been called in to investigate the duchess' sudden disappearance.

'Or you yourself, come to that,' said Lavinia. 'After all, you would have been the obvious choice given your reputation for being something of an amateur sleuth. But no, you see, that's just it. The duke hasn't contacted anyone, which is what is causing all the speculation and gossip.'

'Surely that would suggest that the duke *does* know what has happened to his wife?'

'It's difficult to say,' said Lavinia. 'It's all frightfully mysterious.'

'In a minute you will be telling me that the duke has done away with the duchess!'

'Murdered her, do you mean?' exclaimed Lavinia. 'Oh, I hadn't thought of that.' Her eyes brimmed with excitement and her mouth fell open as a thought suddenly struck her. 'I say, do you think she could be buried beneath the floorboards in that turret of his?'

'I do not,' said Rose, picking up her discarded magazine and glancing through its pages, aware that she had almost permitted her thoughts to become as fanciful as Lavinia's. 'Not if what Miss Hyacinth says is true, and the duchess is about to arrive here by boat.'

By common accord, the two girls remained on the terrace until it was time to dress for dinner, each absorbed in their own thoughts concerning the missing duchess. At each gust of wind, or sound of voices carried to them on the breeze, they looked up as if half expecting the missing woman to appear before them, having climbed the steep steps up from the beach. In this, however, they were to be disappointed, and it was with a growing feeling of despondency that they retired to their rooms to dress for dinner.

When they came down to dinner that evening, it struck Rose immediately that the atmosphere was different. There was an unmistakeable tension in the air that had not been present on the previous evenings. She gazed about her trying to determine the cause, aware only that everyone appeared to be on edge, as if waiting in anticipation for something to happen.

Certainly, most of the guests appeared restive; even little Miss Hyacinth Trimble's actions seemed particularly pernickety and erratic that evening, as she dabbed at her cheeks with her handkerchief and adjusted the position of her wire-rimmed spectacles for the umpteenth time. It was almost as if she feared that something might escape her notice if they were not lodged firmly on the bridge of her nose.

Her sister, Miss Peony, naturally reticent due to her deafness, sat looking about her eagerly, her two-piece Bakelite ear trumpet, reminiscent of an oversized pipe, peeping out from under her napkin in case it should be required later. The very fact that it was present in the dining room and not hidden in her room was a sign that Miss Peony was greatly excited, for she was usually loath to be seen using the device in public, preferring it seemed to remain deaf and ignorant to the conversations taking place about her rather than produce the ugly instrument. Instead, she was obliged presumably to content herself with nodding and smiling blindly, pretending she could decipher what was being said to her when really it was as if those about her were speaking in some foreign tongue that she alone could not understand.

During Rose's study of the Misses Trimble, Mr Vickers had entered the dining room, and it was with some amusement that she noted that Miss Hyacinth was making discreet efforts to catch his eye. Having succeeded in this mission, Mr Vickers, the resident hotel bore, as Lavinia had so aptly described him, weaved his way on unsteady feet towards the Trimbles' table. It was no coincidence, Rose thought, that the man seemed to spend the majority of his time propping up the hotel bar. His jacket looked creased and his bow tie was inexpertly tied, so that he gave the overall impression of being dishevelled and unkempt.

'The man's three sheets to the wind,' Rose heard Lavinia declare loudly in her ear. 'They'll never get rid of him,' she added, looking in the direction of the Trimble sisters. 'Not that I suppose it matters very much if he talks a lot of rot. Miss Peony won't hear a word he says. She'll just nod and smile politely. It's Miss Hyacinth I feel sorry for. I suppose she wants to hear what has happened to the duchess, not that Old Vickers will know. I don't know why she encourages him; one can't believe a word he says.'

Despite her fine words, Lavinia, Rose noticed, studied Mr Vickers intently, as if he was in possession of the key to the Duchess of Grismere's disappearance. The two girls caught only the odd unsatisfactory word as it drifted towards their table. Any moment now, Rose thought, the hotel band will strike up, and all will be lost. The same thought had obviously occurred to Lavinia who, after a moment's hesitation, made her way towards the sisters' table. Not for the first time did it occur to Rose that the hotel, and indeed the island itself, was a great leveller in respect of class. In England, Lavinia would have had little to do with the Misses Trimbles of the world. Socially, they were her inferior, and in her opinion barely worthy of a glance being bestowed in their direction. But here on Skiathos, due to the scarcity of hotel guests, their presence was more conspicuous and, though Lavinia might pretend to view them with something approaching contempt, she was not opposed to engaging them in conversation for her own ends.

Rose looked on in some amusement as Lavinia interrogated Mr Vickers, while Miss Hyacinth listened intently at Lavinia's shoulder, smiling in a deferential fashion. Alone at her table, Rose smiled contentedly and breathed in the warm night air. The floor-length windows remained open, permitting the night air to drift in and mingle with the hazy scents of perfume and herbs. Later, as the evening progressed, the windows would be pulled shut and the curtains drawn, and they might almost be in an English drawing room, save for the wickerwork chairs and tables, the potted herbs of thyme and basil, and the grape vines that sprouted out from scattered plant pots and grew up to the ceiling.

Rose studied her menu card and threw a surreptitious glance at the door. There was no sign of her husband, who had spent the afternoon fishing with the local fishermen and, with Lavinia deeply engrossed in conversation at the next table, she suddenly felt strangely alone. She was reminded of her sister-in-law's remark that something appeared to be wrong between Rose and her brother, an observation that she had hastily brushed aside, but which now filled her thoughts. She bit her lip as she contemplated the chasm that had sprung up between them since the awful event that had occurred in the folly. Inwardly, she cursed herself for allowing the doubt and suspicion in her mind to bear fruit and grow and linger, so that it seemed to taint her every thought. She stared before her, her vision blurred. Tonight, she resolved to have it out with Cedric. She would not continue on this path of mistrust and uncertainty. She must know the truth; however awful it might prove to be.

With this thought uppermost in her mind, she looked up and caught sight of her husband making his way across the floor to their table. Despite the fact that he was dressed for dinner, his white tie and tails strangely out of place in the hot Mediterranean surroundings, she was reminded of the impression he had made on her when she had first laid eyes on him at Ashgrove House. He was tall and slender with chiselled features to rival those of any *matinée* idol. His skin, usually a golden brown, had darkened in the Greek sun, and there was a vitality about him that he had brought in with him from the sea. His blond hair, commonly worn slicked back from a side parting, was slightly ruffled, as if it still bore traces of being tousled about by the wind. Rose noted with a pang that he cut something of a dashing figure as he crossed the room. The observation made her rather pity poor Mr Vickers and his sorry entrance. It made her conscious too of her own ordinary looks. For a moment she caught Cedric's eye, and it is possible that she might have held his gaze had they not both been distracted by a high-pitched laugh emanating from the Trimbles' table. Lavinia, it appeared, was in full flow, her features animated, her *lamé* gown accentuating her willowy frame and delicate, aristocratic features.

'I must speak with you,' Cedric said quietly, seating himself beside his wife. 'We can't go on like this.' Had they been alone, he might have taken her hand. Instead, he gave her an imploring look. 'Darling, I ...' he began and faltered, for Lavinia had returned to their table, a vision in gold, and was regarding them with ill-concealed curiosity.

'Oh, don't mind me,' she said rather flippantly, realising the conversation between husband and wife was unlikely to resume in her presence. Indeed, both parties appeared to be struck dumb, and were now staring down rather blindly at the tablecloth, as if for each it held some peculiar fascination.

'I have just been talking with that awful Mr Vickers and –'

'Ssh Lavinia! He'll hear you,' snapped her brother, casting a furtive glance in the man's direction.

'I don't care if he does,' Lavinia declared petulantly. 'It would serve him jolly well right. Besides,' she added hurriedly, as Cedric made to protest, 'he's half cut. I wonder he's capable of hearing anything.'

'Lavinia!'

'Well, he is, and it's no good your looking at me like that, Ceddie. I don't know how the Trimbles can stand him, breathing his whisky fumes over them like that. Still,' she said, taking her seat, 'I suppose they'll suggest he returns to his own table in a minute. He had nothing more to tell us, after all. He denies everything, you know.'

'What do you mean?' asked Rose. Her voice sounded strange, even to her own ears, for her thoughts remained focused on her husband. She wondered what he had been about to say to her before they had been interrupted.

'Vickers says he never mentioned the duchess, let alone that she was arriving here. In fact, he got frightfully upset when I asked him about it.'

'Oh?' said Rose, her interest piqued, in spite of herself. 'Surely he's not suggesting Miss Hyacinth made up the story?'

'What story?' asked Cedric, only half listening, his mind patently elsewhere as he toyed with his fork.

'Why, the one about the Duchess of Grismere, of course,' said Lavinia. 'Surely Rose told you about it?' she added, looking at her sister-in-law reproachfully. 'Really, what do you married people talk about?'

'Not about disappearing duchesses,' said Cedric abruptly. 'But, I say, are you telling me that she is expected here at the hotel?' His feigned interest in the tablecloth and cutlery had quite disappeared.

'According to Mr Vickers, she is,' said Lavinia. 'Well, at least that's what he told Miss Hyacinth this afternoon. I daresay he was only trying to impress her. She's the only one in this hotel who gives him the time of day.'

'Oh dear,' said Rose, glancing at the Trimbles' table. 'Miss Hyacinth is looking terribly upset. I do hope Mr Vickers wasn't rude to her.'

16

As one, they watched as the man in question made his way back to his own table. There was an ugly, sullen look on his face, which did not bode well. Rose turned her attention to Hyacinth Trimble, whose pale, white face contrasted sharply with Mr Vickers' flushed red one. She was just wondering whether she ought to go over and comfort the older woman when a disturbance of sorts caused her attention to return to Mr Vickers. It appeared that, somewhat worse for drink, he had collided with Ron Thurlow, the private courier, who had not long returned from one of his tours of the island and was hurrying to his table before the soup was served.

'I say, look where you're going, Vickers, won't you?' said the young man, affably enough, given the circumstances. 'You almost made me walk into that table.'

Mr Vickers' only reply was to mutter something under his breath and push his way rudely past the young man.

'I say,' said Ron Thurlow, to nobody in particular, 'what's up with him?'

He did not wait for a reply but glanced instead at the Adlers' table, where he bestowed a discreet smile on the vicar's daughter, Mabel, before making his way towards his own table. He had only walked a few steps, however, when Cedric accosted him.

'I say, Thurlow, you're employed by a travel company, aren't you? That's to say, you arrange escorted tours and that sort of thing?'

'Yes, my lord, for individual travellers and private parties.' Ron Thurlow said, strolling over. He approached the Belvederes' table and drew himself up to his full height, adding with a chuckle, as if he were reading from a page: 'My role is to supervise the general arrangements of a tour, relieving the individual traveller or party of all troubles as to details.'

'I say,' said Cedric, 'that does sound grand. I don't suppose you have been asked to charter a boat?'

'To go to the mainland?'

'No. To come here to Skiathos from Athens.'

'No, my lord. Is the hotel expecting further guests?' The young man looked surprised. 'I thought we were to be the only ones, what with it being Hotel Hemera's inaugural season. I've still to submit my report to my travel company, you know, to advise them whether I consider it a suitable hotel for our clientele. Of course,' he added confidentially, 'between you and me this hotel is far too grand for our usual type of customer. Their purses won't stretch to this, but –'

'What my brother is trying to ask you,' interjected Lavinia impatiently, 'is have you been engaged by the Duchess of Grismere?'

'The Duchess of Grismere?' said Ron, visibly surprised. Rose wondered whether it was her imagination that his hand shook a little. Before she could think any further on the matter, however, their conversation was interrupted once again.

'Oh, Lord Belvedere; Lady Belvedere,' cried a voice, and Miss Hyacinth Trimble was upon them appearing flustered. 'I really don't know what to say. I thought Mr Vickers said the Duchess … but you see, I must have been mistaken. I have just spoken with the proprietor, Mr Kettering, who assures me that though two guests are indeed expected, neither one of them is the Duchess of Grismere. Oh, I feel such a fool, I can't tell you, and yet I was certain that Mr Vickers said … Oh, dear; how silly of me.' She gave them a rather foolish smile. 'Apparently they are a Mr Dewhurst and his sister, Miss Dewhurst.' She giggled nervously.

Much to everyone's relief, the hotel band began to play and for a few minutes the attention of all those present was drawn to the stage and the musicians battling with their instruments in the heat. They struck up a delightful tune, and the thoughts of some had drifted to the dancing that would take place after dinner. Even Mr Vickers seemed to be appreciating the music, swaying in his seat to the melody.

The stage on which the band performed was set at one end of the room, flanked on each side by a large pair of French windows which, like the other windows, had been left open, the thin curtains that adorned them billowing gently in the breeze. The windows themselves looked out upon the terrace that skirted the perimeter of the hotel building, and which was now in darkness except for the glow cast by the chandeliers inside the room. One tune had just finished, and another was starting, when a commotion of sorts could be heard outside one of the windows. It was loud enough to render the musicians silent as they turned, with instruments in their hands, to ascertain the cause of the disturbance. Behind her shoulder, Rose heard a sharp intake of breath as a young man emerged from the shadows and came into the room through the open

18

window. He was tall and dark, and his evening clothes, which were exquisitely cut, fitted him to perfection. He stared at the upturned faces of the hotel guests and the vague, bewildered looks of the musicians and smiled. It was obvious from his expression that he was delighted by the reaction his unorthodox entrance had caused. The same could not be said, however, of his companion, a woman, who, in the silence that followed, could be heard calling to him in hushed tones.

'Brother, darling, do come here.'

Rose was conscious that her husband started at the sound of the voice. The young man being addressed, meanwhile, pretended not to have heard his companion and ventured further into the room. The movement caused the woman to appear at the window and peer into the room, while keeping herself mostly in the shadows. It was evident that this furtive action had annoyed the young man for, before she could prevent him, he had seized the woman by the hand and all but dragged her into the room.

'Come, there is no need to be shy … sister,' he said, laughing.

The woman pulled herself away from his grasp, clinging vaguely at the thin curtain, as if she wished to use it as a veil of sorts to conceal her identity. The gesture was too late, however, for the harm had been done.

'Good lord!' exclaimed Cedric. 'It *is* the duchess!'

Chapter Three

The woman by the window froze, almost as if she were a statue. She was too far away to have heard the earl's muffled exclamation, but some hidden instinct caused her to glance round the room. Her eyes alighted at once on the Belvederes' table, and she gave a visible start, her hand going up to her mouth, as if to stifle a cry. For a moment, she seemed to hover on uncertain feet, swaying slightly in the evening breeze that wafted through the window. Then she turned and groped almost blindly back through the curtains, her hand outstretched to push aside the fabric and escape. The next second, she had disappeared. Her companion, meanwhile, looked somewhat taken aback by this turn of events, and not a little put out. He remained standing where he was for a few minutes, as if he half expected the woman to reappear. When it became evident that she would not, he shrugged his shoulders at the assembled crowd and followed the woman's example, retracing his steps back on to the terrace and out into the night.

Rose, who was seated next to Cedric, looked about her surreptitiously, wondering if anyone else had heard her husband's startled cry of recognition. A quick glance at his face had been enough to reveal that the words had escaped unbidden from his lips, such had been his surprise. She did not doubt that he fervently regretted his outburst. Looking about her, however, it appeared that his words had fallen on deaf ears. For what had intrigued the hotel patrons the most was not so much the identity of the newcomers, but their unusual entrance and departure.

'Well, I say, how very odd!' declared Miss Hyacinth. 'I suppose they must be members of the band to just appear at the window like that? I thought the man was about to march on to the stage and start singing, didn't you?'

This question was not directed at anyone in particular, but at the room at large. Among them all, it was only Lavinia who chose to respond.

'He looked the sort,' she agreed conversationally. 'I must say, there was something awfully familiar about the woman. I daresay I've seen her perform somewhere, though it's difficult to tell, what with her being wrapped up like that.'

'Fancy her wearing what she was, Lady Lavinia,' continued Miss Hyacinth, in her element. 'I mean to say, who would wear a fur coat in this weather?'

'Yes, it is a trifle odd. And rather a good one at that. The coat, I mean. Silver fox, I'd say.'

'She seemed a poor nervous little thing,' said Miss Hyacinth, 'clinging on to the curtain like that. Performers often are shy, or so I've been told. Oh,' she added, 'here's Mr Kettering now. Let me ask him. I say, Mr Kettering ...'

They did not hear the remainder of her sentence, for she had scurried across the floor to accost the hotel proprietor before anyone could stop her. They all watched her idly, for her enthusiasm to undertake the task seemed almost comical. However, without what Lavinia termed Miss Hyacinth's endless prattle, the room seemed strangely quiet. Even the band still appeared distracted by the odd encounter, for they were yet to strike up another tune.

Rose, growing bored with the spectacle of Miss Hyacinth dramatically gesturing towards the window, and Mr Kettering nodding politely in response, took the opportunity to study the other occupants of the room. It was with some surprise that she found Ron Thurlow still staring intently at the window through which the man and woman had appeared. It was then that she remembered hearing a sharp intake of breath, and she regarded the young man curiously. It was possible that he, in turn, felt her eyes upon him, for he turned to her and smiled.

'It's certainly one way to make an entrance, your ladyship' he said. 'Next time, I'll think about coming in that way myself.' His tone was jovial enough as he cast a look in the direction of the vicar's daughter, which appeared reciprocated, yet Rose had the odd impression there was something rather forced about his humour.

It was only when Ron Thurlow had returned to his own table and Lavinia, impatient as ever, had joined Miss Hyacinth to interrogate the poor hotel proprietor that Rose turned to address her husband.

'Was that woman really the duchess?' she said, her voice barely above a whisper.

Cedric gave an involuntary start. 'You heard what I said?' He passed a hand through his hair, alarm clouding his handsome features. 'Gosh, I hope the others didn't.'

'I shouldn't think they did; you spoke very quietly.'

'But *you* heard me,' Cedric pointed out.

Rose might have said that in a sea of voices she would have distinguished his, that however quietly he had spoken she would have heard his words. Instead, she said:

'Yes … well, I was sitting next to you.' She picked up her napkin and stared at it, as if she found something about its fabric that enthralled her.

'Darling –' began her husband.

'Was that really the missing duchess?' Rose repeated sharply, as if she feared her husband's talk would stray on to other topics.

'Yes,' said Cedric, glancing at his wife in a resigned fashion, and interpreting her mood correctly. 'That's to say, I think so. I only caught a glimpse of the woman, but it looked awfully like her.'

'I wonder what she is doing here on Skiathos?' mused Rose.

'I don't know. It's quite a coincidence her turning up like this.'

'Yes. I suppose she quite reasonably assumed she wouldn't meet anyone who knew her on this island, certainly no one in society.' Rose gave her husband a sidelong glance. 'It was just unfortunate for her that your secretary's brother had chosen to open a hotel here, and that we should be among his first guests.'

'I'd say. I don't suppose we should have come here otherwise. Though it really is the most delightful island.'

'It is,' murmured Rose, her thoughts elsewhere, for she was remembering the woman's frightened gasp. 'Of course, she recognised you too; the duchess, I mean. I suppose you know that, don't you?'

'I say, do you think so?' Cedric frowned. 'I thought she did, though I hoped I'd been mistaken. We've only met on a few occasions and I thought it quite possible she wouldn't remember me.'

'It would only have been a matter of time before she discovered you were staying here,' pointed out his wife.' I imagine she would have enquired of the proprietor about the other guests.'

'Yes, and now she knows I'm here, I suppose she'll keep to her rooms. Of course,' Cedric added, his forehead furrowed, 'it puts me in a dashed awkward position.'

'Oh?'

'The duke is a member of my club. We're not closely acquainted or anything like that, but we know one another. We pass the time of day, that sort of thing.' He leaned forward, lowering his voice to a whisper. 'But I happen to know from some of the other chaps that he's awfully cut up about this business. He goes about with a long face, and I can't tell you how he's aged in the last few weeks.'

'Because of the duchess' disappearance, you mean? Do you think he knows she's here on Skiathos?'

'I very much doubt it, though she left him a letter, by all accounts.'

'Before she vanished?' enquired Rose, considerably intrigued.

'Yes. She gave it to one of the servants at the ball with the request that he hand it to her husband later that evening. Rumour has it in the club that she asked the duke not to look for her. You know the sort of thing? She was dreadfully sorry and all that, but he must try to forget her.'

'And he has complied with her wishes?'

'I shouldn't think so. He's dashed worried about her. One only has to look at him to know that. Besides, he's not the sort of man to not do anything. He'll be searching for her all right, though he won't make a song and dance about it.'

Both fell silent for a moment and Rose took the opportunity to study her husband's face, as if searching for a clue to his thoughts.

'You're not proposing to write to the duke, are you?'

'I'm not sure what to do for the best,' admitted Cedric. 'It would seem pretty underhand and of course really it is none of my business …'

'But you feel it your duty nevertheless?'

'You should have seen him, darling. The duke, I mean. The other day in my club. He looked so wan and frail, a shadow of his former self.'

'I don't think it would be right or very fair to the duchess to do anything without speaking to her first,' Rose said firmly. 'As you've said, it's none of our business.' She regarded her husband's troubled face. 'Why don't you request an interview with her? I daresay she's anxious to speak with you, if only to ask you to keep her presence on this island a secret.' Cedric made as if to protest, but Rose hurried on. 'You could take the opportunity to tell her that you are worried about her husband's health and that you would feel awkward keeping him in the dark concerning her whereabouts.'

'I say, that's an idea,' said Cedric, brightening considerably, 'I might suggest that she write to him herself.' His face clouded again. 'I didn't much like the look of that fellow she was with, did you? There was something damned impertinent about his manner.'

Rose hesitated a moment and then said: 'Did you hear how she referred to him? Is he really her brother, do you think?'

Cedric snorted. 'I don't think that very likely, do you?'

'No,' Rose admitted, a little reluctantly. 'There would have been no need for secrecy if she were just visiting a relative. I suppose you think that –'

'She has run off with this chap?' Cedric said, finishing his wife's sentence. 'Yes, I do. What else can one think? Though I'm more than a little surprised. I always thought the duke and duchess were a most devoted couple.' He sighed. 'But I suppose one can never tell what goes on inside other people's marriages.'

'No,' said Rose, crumpling the napkin between her fingers. 'I daresay one can't.'

The note of bitterness in her voice caused her husband to look up. He regarded the pained expression on her face, and for a moment did not speak. For he did not need to be any kind of a genius to realise that his wife was no longer referring to the Duke and Duchess of Grismere. Inwardly, he groaned, and yet he felt a lightening of his mood, for it seemed an age since they had talked liked this. He had grown too used to polite, forced conversation and monosyllabic answers.

'Rose –'

'I say,' said Lavinia, bounding up to their table, 'you two do look glum. Have you had a falling out?' She did not wait for them to reply but hurried on, a force to be reckoned with. 'They're called Dewhurst. The new guests. Brother and sister, though I thought she looked a lot older than him, didn't you? Mr Kettering says she's something of an invalid, which must make it dreadfully dull for her poor brother. I expect she's just the sort to keep to her room and expect him to wait on her and pander to her needs. You know the sort, fetch and carry for her, like a servant.'

'She reminds me a bit of you,' said Cedric, attempting to lighten the atmosphere.

Lavinia made a face, and even Rose was persuaded to smile.

'Poor man,' said Lavinia. 'He's frightfully handsome, don't you think, Rose?'

'Your Mr Dewhurst, or me?' asked her brother flippantly.

'Oh, Mr Dewhurst, of course,' Lavinia replied, 'though I suppose you are quite good-looking in your way.'

'Well, your Mr Dewhurst doesn't look the sort to fetch and carry,' retorted her brother. 'He seemed an arrogant sort of fellow to me.'

'I think you're being dreadfully unfair,' said Lavinia. 'I knew you'd take against him, and you don't even know him.'

'Well, I wouldn't lose your head over him, if I were you,' said Cedric, a serious note creeping into his voice for the first time. 'He didn't strike me as the sort of fellow who'd play fair.'

'Really, Ceddie, you do talk the most awful rot. I'm not a hothouse flower, you know.'

Rose, who shared her husband's reservations concerning the duchess' companion, wondered whether they should take Lavinia into their confidence. As she watched the siblings spar, however, it occurred to her that Lavinia was well able to look after herself and hold her own. Besides, she reasoned, Lavinia was not one to hold her tongue, and the fewer people who were aware of the duchess' real identity, the better.

Just as these thoughts were passing through her mind, Ron Thurlow sauntered back to their table, his hands thrust nonchalantly in his pockets.

'I say, any news on our newcomers? Are they musicians or guests?'

'Guests,' replied Cedric, rather abruptly.

'Jolly good,' said Ron. 'They looked the sort of people for whom I might arrange a tour. I say, my employer will be glad. Perhaps I should go and introduce myself. I wonder if they will be staying long?'

'They're a brother and sister by the name of Dewhurst,' said Lavinia helpfully.

'Oh?'

Was it Rose's imagination or was the courier visibly shaken by this piece of information? Certainly, a puzzled frown had creased his forehead, and again she caught him staring meditatively at the window through which the newcomers had made their entrance. Aware suddenly that she had been regarding him for a while, she turned away and surveyed the rest of the room. It was with something of a jolt that she discovered that Ron Thurlow was not the only person to be fixated by the fateful window. For Mr Vickers was also casting furtive looks in its direction, as if seemingly under its spell. She studied him with a growing feeling of repulsion, for his sly and shifty manner, coupled with his habit of licking his dry, fleshy lips, did little to enhance the man's already shabby appearance and general air of desolation.

With a shudder she returned her gaze to her immediate companions. Though the room was warm, bordering on humid, she suddenly felt cold and suppressed a shiver. She took a sip of water, keen to steady her nerves and regain her equilibrium. Cedric, she noticed, was watching her closely, and continued to do so during dinner, while Lavinia prattled on about nothing in particular, oblivious to the fact that her audience was inattentive and subdued.

'I say, darling, are you all right? enquired her husband in a concerned fashion, as soon as the meal was over.

Rose did not reply immediately. Lavinia had left their table and so ostensibly she and Cedric were alone, though the hotel band had struck up a jaunty tune to remind them that they were still in the crowded hotel dining room. As if to emphasise this point, odd fragments and snatches of conversation from the neighbouring tables drifted over to them.

Rose turned to look at her husband, aware that she must appear agitated. Had there not been that awful gulf between them, she might have taken his hand and clasped it tightly. Instead, she merely shook her head and said: 'I'm frightened. I daresay it is very silly of me, but I have an awful feeling that something dreadful is going to happen.'

Chapter Four

Later in the evening, Rose wondered whether she had imagined the odd sense of foreboding that had entered the room the very moment the man and woman had stepped in through the window. The atmosphere had certainly altered with their entrance, though whether this was because the newcomers were viewed as trespassers rippling the comfortable familiarity and accord that had struck up between the hotel guests, or was in fact something more sinister, it was hard to tell. All Rose could say, if asked, was that the air felt charged, as if there were a tension in the room that had not been there before.

As much for something to do, as for reassurance, she surveyed the room, stopping at each table in turn to note the diners. Had she been requested to do so, she would have been able to say where each guest would be seated without looking. For, at the commencement of their stay, each had been assigned a particular table at which to take their meals. Only Ron Thurlow had shown any inclination to stray from his allotted place to take coffee at the Adlers' table, where he would ostensibly converse politely with the vicar. The young man's attention, however, as Lavinia would readily point out, to anyone who would listen, appeared exclusively focused on Miss Mabel Adler, who would bestow on him the odd encouraging smile while her father talked.

'It's a great pity,' Lavinia was wont to say, 'that the poor girl's mother is dead. If only she were here to occupy the vicar, Mr Thurlow and Miss Adler might manage to get a moment or two to themselves. As it is, her father quite refuses to take the hint.' Following which, Lavinia would address her brother. 'Can't you pretend that you are interested in religious artefacts or something, Ceddie?' she would plead. 'To lure the vicar away, I mean. Of course,' she would sigh, 'I suppose I could organise a tennis party, but really, it is far too hot to play.'

Mr Vickers kept to himself, except when inebriated at the end of the night when he was apt to stagger inadvertently into another table and mumble a slurred apology. As oft as not, it was the Misses Trimble who suffered this indignity. Rose had noticed that Miss Hyacinth was in the habit of smiling and pretending the fault was hers, while her sister, Miss

Peony, deaf to Mr Vickers' feeble efforts at an apology, would bestow on that gentleman a look which could curdle eggs. Mr Vickers, apparently oblivious or indifferent to the fact that he had caused any offence, would then stumble away to his room.

On this particular evening, Rose was conscious only of the stifling heat in the dining room, despite the open windows and the efforts of the Hunter ceiling fans, with their beechwood blades and black enamelled, cast iron frames. Indeed, the almost unbearable warmth, coupled with the noise of the band, produced a heady mix which suddenly made her feel rather giddy.

'Darling, are you all right?'

Rose stared almost blindly at her husband, fighting back the tears that threatened to come unbidden. For she was acutely aware that tonight the awful gulf that had sprung up so sharply and suddenly between them had seemed to lessen and diminish. Of course, it was quite possible that this thawing, or truce, of sorts, was just temporary, yet she felt the need to grasp at it with open hands. She was reminded also of her intention that tonight on this Greek island, far from her husband's ancestral home and the responsibilities and duties of his estate, she had resolved to speak with him to determine the fate of their marriage.

It was with something of a heavy heart, yet coupled also with a faint flame of hope and optimism, that she rose from her chair. Her husband mirrored her actions, his face a picture of concern and bewilderment. She swayed for a moment, suddenly feeling light-headed, clutching at the starched linen tablecloth to steady herself, much as if she had been the intoxicated Mr Vickers stumbling his way out of the room. The comparison brought a smile to her lips. Had it not, she might have been tempted to sit down again and permit the distance to resume between herself and her husband, for there was a part of her which did not wish to know the truth. Instead, the comic image of Mr Vickers, conjured up in her mind's eye, gave her the impetus she needed to draw the situation to a head.

Aloud, she said: 'I am feeling a little faint. It is very hot in here; I need some air.' She fumbled with the clasp of her evening bag, withdrew from it a handkerchief, and put it up to her flaming cheeks. 'Will you come out with me on to the terrace?' she added in a voice which sounded strange even to her own ears. She dared not look at her husband in case he refused. Indeed, she was on the point of leaving without receiving a reply to her question, the prospect of being left to stand foolishly and dejectedly at the table being too awful to comprehend, when Cedric muttered a few words.

'Yes,' he said. 'Of course.'

Almost before she was aware of what was happening, he had taken her by the arm and was steering her between the tables towards the open window. Though she was in something of a daze, she was vaguely aware that Lavinia was staring after them, a thoughtful look, for once, on her beautiful face.

'We need to leave here at once,' cried the woman who had appeared at the dining room window.

She was standing in the Dewhursts' private sitting room, which overlooked the terrace. Her focus had initially been drawn to the window which, though concealed by heavy linen drapes, stood partially open, allowing the music from the band to drift in and remind her all too readily of her recent humiliation. With something of a shudder and following a last despairing glance in the direction of the dining room, she closed the window and retreated into the room, her attention now drawn to her companion, who was reclining full length on a sofa in stockinged feet.

'Eh?' the young man remarked absently, seemingly unperturbed by her comment.

'I said we need to leave here at once. I daresay we can't leave the island until tomorrow morning, but surely there must be another hotel or similar establishment. Our cases are yet to be unpacked. The hotel manager, I am certain, would help us to find alternative accommodation if we were to ask …'

The woman allowed her sentence to falter. It was patently evident, even to the most casual observer, that the young man was preoccupied not on what she was saying, but with the contents of the newspaper he was reading.

'Oberon …'

'Hello?'

The woman had been fidgeting with a button on her dress. Now she gave a reproachful glance at the newspaper, which so effectively hid her companion's face from view. She advanced a step or two closer. This time, when she spoke, there was a note of urgency in her voice.

'Oberon …'

'Well, what is it?' The young man lowered his paper a fraction but made no effort to raise himself into a sitting position. Instead, he regarded the woman before him in something of a bored fashion. 'Not still worrying about the Belvederes, are you?' The woman nodded, her hand pulling at the light fabric of her dress. The young man gave her a dispassionate look and said with unexpected fierceness: 'I've no intention of leaving, I can tell you. It took an age to get here. Why we couldn't have stayed in Athens –'

'Lord Belvedere is an acquaintance of my husband's,' cried the woman. 'He recognised me, Oberon. I am sure of it. He is certain to write –'

'He will have far better things to do than write to your husband,' said the young man, somewhat irritably, 'and I say, do stop calling me Oberon. I can't stand the name; never could.'

Something akin to a gasp escaped from the woman's lips. 'Can't you?' She quickly collected herself, however, and said: 'I suppose it is a little old-fashioned, but I rather like it.'

'I should say it is!'

'I think,' she continued, as if she had not heard him, 'it is rather a romantic name.'

'Do you? I'd much rather be called Alec.'

'Alec?' said the woman, with a look of disdain.

'Yes. There is nothing wrong with Alec. It's a good solid name,' said the young man, warming to the subject. 'Alec.' He rolled his tongue around the name.

'Alec?'

'Yes. After all, no self-respecting chap wants to be named after the king of the fairies.'

'But –'

'I know what you're about to say. It's your favourite play of Shakespeare's. Something about a dream. I'm keen on Shakespeare myself, but I prefer Caliban or Iago for a name. They have a little more substance to them, don't you agree?'

30

'No, I don't. I think,' said the woman slowly, and with feeling, 'that Oberon is a lovely name.'

The young man cast her a quick sideways glance, as if suddenly conscious that he had offended her.

'Yes, of course it is. I daresay I'm tired, that's all,' he said hurriedly. 'As it happens, I'm rather proud of my name. But,' he continued, choosing his words with care, 'it would be much better if you called me Alec while we're here.' He held up his hand as the woman made to protest. 'Oberon is a very … a very distinctive name. It is the sort of name people remember. And we don't want people to remember us, do we?'

'No … I suppose you are right,' agreed the woman, with some reluctance. 'I shall call you Alec when we are in company.'

'You might forget if you were to call me by two different names,' replied the young man, eyeing her closely. 'And the servants might talk if they happened to hear you call me Oberon. We wouldn't want that.'

'Very well,' said the woman in a resigned sort of voice. 'I'll call you Alec if you wish.'

'I do.' The young man smiled and sat up, regarding the woman before him. Despite the heat and the sun, he thought she looked rather pale. The colour had quite gone from her cheeks and he thought that he could detect strands of grey in her hair that had not been there when he had first made her acquaintance. She was still a fine figure of a woman, but she looked older. Inwardly, he sighed. He found her endless fretting and dithering irritating; her restive streak annoyed him. The smile left his lips, and he said rather cruelly: 'I was just reading something about you in the paper. Do you know that they are calling you the 'Disappearing Duchess'? It has quite a ring to it, don't you think?'

An anguished cry left the woman's lips and she tore at the newspaper, snatching it from the young man's grasp.

'I say, Sophia,' said the young man, rather taken aback. 'There's no need for all that. I'd be quite happy to read the article to you, you know. You have only to ask.'

The woman ignored him, clutching the newspaper to her as if it were some favoured possession. She moved to a bookcase, on which a candle was burning, and scoured the sheets of paper until she had found the offending article. With a sharp intake of breath, she read the commentary. The colour had returned in a bright flush to her cheeks, and her bottom lip was trembling. All the while, the young man watched her, fascinated and not a little perplexed.

'It's caused quite a stir, hasn't it? Your vanishing like that, I mean,' he said, conversationally.

Again, she ignored him, her eyes riveted on the page. She stared, almost transfixed at the photograph which accompanied the article. It had been taken earlier that year at a May Ball she had attended. She had just emerged from a car and had turned to face the photographer, a bright smile on her well made up face. She was wearing a beautifully cut chiffon dress of the palest yellow, and her neck was covered in diamonds, which seemed to sparkle and dazzle even in the black and white print. Instinctively, her hand went up to her throat, which seemed strangely naked and bare. She stared at her gloved hand in the photograph. It appeared to be clutching at some object. Something stirred in her memory. Her husband, who had not been included in the photograph, had accompanied her to the ball and it was his arm, she recalled, that she had taken to steady herself as she got out of the car. It was the fabric of his jacket which she was clutching so tightly ...

She turned and regarded her companion, the newspaper falling from her hand.

'What is it?' demanded the young man, somewhat alarmed by her expression.

'I was just remembering how it was ...' she said, in a voice that was barely audible, her voice tailing off before she had finished her sentence.

'Before I came into your life?' suggested the young man. 'I say, that's rather galling. A chap could take offence. I suppose you'll be telling me next that you wish you'd never laid eyes on me.'

'I should never say that!' cried the woman. In one swift movement she was seated beside him on the sofa and took his hands in hers. 'You mustn't say that, even in jest. It's ... it's very unfair.'

'Is it?' enquired the young man, retrieving his hands. There was a challenge in his eyes, and she shrank back from him, twisting her hands together in something of a pathetic, helpless manner.

'Don't. Please don't, I couldn't bear it if ...' she said.

There was a strong possibility that she was about to weep, and the young man, aware that he had gained the upper hand, took measures to

32

stem the flow of tears that threatened to fall.

'What's a fellow to think?' he said in a lightly mocking voice. 'Blowed if I know.' His voice softened, and he said in rather an insincere voice: 'My dear, I don't like to see you looking miserable.'

'I'm not miserable,' said his companion quickly. 'Really I'm not. You mustn't think that. It's just my husband ...' She paused to pick up the newspaper. 'It says here,' she continued, jabbing at the page with a finger that trembled, 'that he's hardly been seen out in society. He missed Lady Setter's ball, and it's not at all like him to do that. I'm afraid I've made him desperately unhappy.' She bowed her head and said despondently: 'I had no wish to hurt him.'

'Well, it's a bit late for all that, isn't it?' replied Oberon Dewhurst rather nastily, returning to form. 'You made your choice and you chose me. It's no use regretting it now.'

'I'm not regretting my choice.'

'Aren't you? It sounded to me as if you were. I wonder if the old codger would welcome the return of his prodigal wife.'

The duchess visibly started at the insult directed towards her husband, but she made no move to curtail the young man's vicious tongue.

Instead, she clenched her fists until her knuckles became white. 'I love you,' she said, returning to the curtained window. 'There isn't anything I wouldn't do for you.'

'Good,' said Oberon, returning to his perusal of the newspaper in the mistaken belief that all was well.

Chapter Five

The Earl and Countess of Belvedere emerged on to the terrace leaving the music and chatter behind them. The pale glow cast by the chandeliers from the dining room lit up areas of the promenade, leaving other parts in darkness. As if by agreement, they kept to the shadows and continued walking in silence, past the formal lawns with their sunken urns, and the seldom-used tennis courts which bordered the gardens, out on towards the cliff edge. They hardly glanced at their surroundings, for each was deep in their own thoughts; the only sound was their footsteps partly muffled by the undergrowth as they negotiated their way to the edge of the cliff.

When they had reached their destination, they stopped and stared out at the black sea, as if transfixed by the way it shimmered faintly in the sparse moonlight. It was still warm, though the blackness seemed to disguise the heat and Rose shivered, pulling her silk shawl more tightly around her shoulders, as if there was indeed a chill in the air. It was a moment or two before either of them dared speak, and then when they did, emboldened by the darkness, their words came tumbling out abruptly, all in a rush, speaking over each other.

'Darling, I –'

'It's no use –'

There was a moment of awkward silence, and then Cedric said hoarsely:

'What is no use?'

Despite the dim light, Rose could feel her husband's eyes on her, searching her face for a clue to her ominous words. She withdrew a step or two, wringing her hands as she went, trying to summon up the necessary courage to give voice to the thoughts that had haunted her. After a while, conscious of her husband's growing impatience, she said simply: 'I can't go on like this.'

'Like what?' demanded Cedric.

Rose wondered idly if he was being deliberately obtuse.

'Like this.' She threw out her hands in something of a dramatic gesture that seemed to encompass the cliff on which they stood, the air above and the dark sea below. 'This not talking to one other. Oh,' she cried hurriedly, sensing that Cedric was about to argue, 'you will say we do talk, and we do, but just about silly, trivial things. We're frightfully polite to each other, but it's all wrong. I daresay even our servants must sense something ... We ... we might very well be strangers!'

Now that she had spoken, Rose found to her dismay that it was very difficult to stop. What was more, with each passing second, she felt the bitterness that she had kept so closely bottled up inside her, creep out and taint her words. She turned to face her husband, barely making out his features in the darkness.

'What I am trying to say is that we don't *really* talk, do we? That's to say, not like we used to. We were so happy, and now...' She allowed her sentence to falter, afraid to finish it.

Cedric did not appear to share her reservations, however, for he said sharply: 'And now we're not. Is that what you were going to say?'

'Yes,' she said quietly. She waited for what seemed an age to see how he would respond to such an assertion. As the seconds passed, she felt a lump forming uncomfortably in her throat. When it appeared that he was unwilling to say anything further, she added miserably, if only to break the awful silence that engulfed them: 'I'm not happy.'

'No, I can see that,' Cedric said, a note of bitterness in his own voice. He turned his gaze from her face to look out at the sea below. 'Of course, what you really mean is that *I* don't make you happy.'

The finality of his words caught her, and she was aware of her own sharp intake of breath. She said hurriedly: 'You did make me happy once; very happy. I would be happy again if I thought you still cared for me.'

'Well, of course I still care for you,' exclaimed Cedric, turning towards his wife and taking her by the shoulders. There was a touch of anger in his voice now, as well as an odd sense of bewilderment. Rather unexpectedly, Rose felt her heart surge. She had feared apathy, had dreaded indifference even. Certainly, she had not expected this display of emotion. She had little time to reflect on what it might mean, however, for she was conscious that, having spoken, she must continue to voice her thoughts before she lost her nerve. Aloud, she said:

'If you do care for me as you claim to do, why are you never at Sedgwick? I hardly see you; you spend all your days in London and all your evenings at ... at your club.'

'I thought you preferred it that way.'

Rose started: 'What ... what do you mean by that?'

'Simply that I thought you wished to be alone,' said Cedric slowly, a touch of weariness in his voice. To avoid any ambiguity, he added: 'By that, I mean, I was under the impression that my presence at Sedgwick distressed you.'

Put starkly like that, the effect of his words on his listener was pronounced. In the immediate silence that followed, both heard the shocked gasp that escaped unbidden from Rose's lips. For the words had struck her as forcibly as if she had been slapped. She put a hand up to her cheek, feeling the colour drain from it despite the heat. She might have stumbled, had her husband not put out a hand to steady her. As it was, she took a few moments to collect herself and regain her composure, all the while unable to rid her mind of how dreadful it all was. Her husband thought she disliked him, despised him even! How had they reached this impasse? How had they sunk to these awful depths? Even as she put the questions to herself, she knew the answer. It assailed her like a wave. Aloud, she said:

'I thought you had tired of me. I was under the impression,' she continued, adopting his words, 'that ...' Here she hesitated for a moment before continuing, knowing that what she said now, once uttered, could not be unsaid. 'I thought ... I was awfully afraid you were in love with someone else.'

'Someone else?' In the dark, Cedric sounded perplexed, and not a little surprised; then enlightenment apparently dawned on him, for he said: 'I suppose by someone else you mean Miriam Belmore?'

'Yes.' Now she had given voice to her fears, Rose was sorely tempted to turn tail and disappear into the darkness though, conversely, she also felt an odd sense of relief.

'After barely a year of marriage you thought I had tired of you and fallen for someone else?' Cedric sounded both angry and incredulous.

'Yes,' reiterated Rose dully, vaguely conscious that her husband's reaction might suggest otherwise. Indeed, put into words, the notion that her husband had been unfaithful sounded ludicrous, even to her own ears. Had she not remembered the way in which Cedric had staunchly proclaimed Miriam's innocence regarding the murder in the folly or, more particularly, his seemingly furtive telephone conversations with Miriam, both of which had contributed to the awful gulf between them, she might have been tempted to mumble an apology. Instead, she held firm, doggedly pursuing the path she had chosen. Holding her head up high, she said:

'Men of your class often do have mistresses, don't they? I daresay you would like me to turn a blind eye, but I'm afraid ...' She suddenly felt herself close to tears and added rather pathetically: 'I'm not made that way.'

'I'm jolly glad to hear it, for I should hate it like poison if you were,' retorted Cedric. 'It would mean that you didn't really love me, and I couldn't bear that.'

His words slowly penetrated her consciousness, and her mood lightened, as if a veil had been lifted. She said:

'Are you saying you aren't having an affair with Miriam?'

'Well, of course I'm not. What a ridiculous idea. Miriam is not, nor ever has been, my mistress. I can't for the life of me think what put the notion in your head that she was.'

'Lavinia said –'

'Oh, I shouldn't believe a word of what my sister tells you, if I were you,' said Cedric dismissively, unable to suppress a chuckle despite the tension that hung in the air between them. 'She has always had the most ridiculous notion that every eligible girl in the land must be in love with me, and that they only have to flutter their eyelids for me to return the favour!'

This statement fitted so well with Rose's image of Lavinia's character, and the siblings' relationship, that fleetingly it even brought a smile to her own lips. Her mood soon darkened, however, and she said:

'That is all very well, but you defended her like anything when she was suspected of murder.' She held up her hand as Cedric made to protest. 'It's not just that, of course. By itself, it wouldn't mean anything, but then there were the telephone calls too. Surely you won't deny that you have been in the habit of telephoning her.'

Even in the dark, she sensed her husband start; she could almost hear his mind working frantically.

'I do not deny that,' said Cedric eventually, speaking slowly, and rather formally, she thought.

'And you are so very secretive about it,' continued Rose, her fears fast returning. 'If you had nothing to hide, why –'

'I did not say I had nothing to hide.'

Cedric's statement cut her to the quick, and yet her brain seemed strangely dull and unresponsive as she played over his words in her mind. An awkward silence threatened to ensue; it was Cedric who finally broke it.

'By that, I mean that I do have something to hide,' he said slowly, choosing his words with care. 'But it is not what it seems. That's to say, it is not what you think I am hiding.'

'What exactly do you mean by that?' demanded Rose, regaining both her voice and her feeling of righteous indignation. 'What you are saying does not make any sense. You are talking in riddles. Are you, or are you not, in love with Miriam Belmore?'

'I have already told you I am not.'

'But what you are hiding, this secret it –'

'It has something to do with Miss Belmore; yes.'

'I see!' cried Rose, turning away from him.

'No, you do not see at all! I daresay I am putting it very badly, but it has nothing to do with me and you.'

In one swift movement, Cedric had turned her to face him, gripping her firmly by the shoulders so that she almost winced with the pain. In the darkness she could not make out his features, though she felt his breath on her face.

'It does not mean what you think it means,' he repeated. 'I suppose one might say it is a secret of sorts, but,' here he paused and held her very tenderly, 'it is not *my* secret.'

'It's Miriam Belmore's?' enquired Rose sharply.

'I can't say any more,' replied Cedric despondently. 'As it is, I've probably said far too much.' It is possible that he sensed her frustration, for he added hurriedly: 'The thing is, I was told something in confidence. You would think very little of me if I were the sort of chap who betrayed a confidence.'

'Would I?' queried Rose, though, even as she uttered the words, she thought she might.

'Yes. You wouldn't consider it very honourable of me, and you would be quite right.' He took her in his arms, and she sensed that he was regarding her keenly. 'Will you trust me? You must know how much I adore you. There has never been any other girl for me, but you.'

Rose felt her heart soar, yet the existence of a secret, to which her husband and Miriam Belmore were a party and from which she was excluded, still troubled her. 'It is an awful lot to ask of me,' she replied.

'Yes, but if it has nothing to do with our marriage, or our relationship?' implored Cedric.

'Why would Miss Belmore seek to confide in you?' countered Rose. 'May I not know what your business is with her?'

'There is a reason why she should choose to confide in me,' admitted her husband. 'I am, however,' he continued, rather cryptically, 'not at liberty to disclose it.'

Rose stared at him open mouthed, her mind working furiously. A vague idea as to what he might refer had formed in her mind, yet it seemed so ludicrous and far-fetched that she was almost tempted to dismiss it immediately. But what else, she wondered, would explain both her husband's natural reticence to discuss the matter, and the connection that evidently existed between himself and Miriam? It was useless, she knew, to probe any further into the nature of the secret that lay beyond her reach. Instead, she said simply, feeling much depended on her husband's answer:

'Will you ever be able to tell me what this secret is?'

There was a momentary silence, while Cedric considered his answer. To Rose's heightened senses everything seemed unbearably quiet and still; even the breeze had subsided, and there was no sound from the cicadas.

'Yes,' he said finally, 'though goodness knows when that will be.'

Rose turned and stared out to sea. She supposed it was an answer of sorts. Had her husband said no, she knew she would have left him standing on the cliff top, their marriage in tatters. Now she was at a loss what to do.

'I daresay I have no right,' said Cedric, 'but I ask that you trust me.'

The words seemed to spring up out of the darkness and she started. There was something about the manner in which they had been uttered that suggested sincerity. She swayed slightly, conscious of the cliff edge and the sheer drop beneath. It occurred to her suddenly that it mirrored her marriage. She was teetering on the brink of a precipice; one false move and all would be lost.

She put out a hand to steady herself. Before she could stop him, Cedric grabbed her arm and pulled her towards him. She did not resist for already she felt a rise in her spirits, coupled with a sudden strange urge to laugh.

'All right,' she said, staring up at his face, which was masked by the darkness, 'I will.'

As they retraced their steps back to the hotel, though the secret still existed between them, she felt an odd sense of relief. It was almost as if a weight had been lifted from her shoulders, though she remained in ignorance concerning her husband's connection with Miriam Belmore. She was conscious that she had faced a crossroads of sorts; the way ahead had been obscured and unclear, but she felt, rightly or wrongly, that she had emerged intact. For, whether rational or not, she felt certain that she had chosen the right path. That evening she had been reminded of her husband's true character. He was what she knew him to be, a man of integrity. He had also shown that his feelings for her had not diminished; they were as deep and robust as ever. With a contented sigh, she rested her head on her husband's shoulder, breathing in his scent, conscious only of his arms wrapped tightly around her.

Chapter Six

'Well, Peony, dear, this is all most exciting,' declared Miss Hyacinth to her sister, as soon as they had retired to their room for the night.

She did not wait for, nor apparently expect, her observation to elicit a comment from her sibling. Instead, she busied herself with the task of folding their Chinese silk-embroidered shawls and stacking them neatly on a shelf in the wardrobe. She then turned her attention to brushing their velvet evening shoes, dabbing at the toe of one with a damp cloth to remove a particularly stubborn mark. It would have been quite futile for anyone to have suggested to her that the hotel maid, assigned to them for the duration of their stay, was quite capable of undertaking such chores. For Hyacinth Trimble had always kept house for her father and sister, and the thought of some strange servant undertaking such intimate tasks, or rummaging among their things, would have been quite abhorrent to her. Indeed, as far as she was concerned, the duties of servants were confined to cooking and heavy work. She was more than capable of a bit of light dusting and, as she was wont to tell those of her acquaintance who would listen, a little housework never did anyone any harm.

However, if any of those same acquaintances were to enquire if Miss Peony was similarly employed, they were met with a frown and a look of reproach. 'Miss Peony,' Miss Hyacinth would whisper, careful that her words should not reach her sister's ears, 'is not very strong. She is something of an invalid, don't you know.' If those same observers then took it upon themselves to glance at the elder Miss Trimble, it is possible that they might have questioned the validity of this statement. For Miss Peony, a little larger in build than her sister, and quietly confident in the sanctuary of her own rooms, looked remarkably robust.

That evening, however, there was no one present to observe the sisters. Only Miss Peony, seated in a high-backed chair, was there to regard her sister's activities. She watched as her sibling fussed and fretted over the state of their evening clothes, once or twice stopping to remark that the dust had played havoc with the velvet, and was it a wonder the silk had been ruined by the heat?

The minutes ticked on while Miss Hyacinth prattled on to herself, content in her employment and her sister's presence, but requiring no more from Miss Peony than that she be there to observe her efforts. For Miss Hyacinth was quite accustomed to talking to herself. Her sister's deafness and their lack of society in the village of Clyst Birch had rather made this inevitable, similarly the habit she had adopted of asking questions and answering them herself.

'The Dewhursts ... it reminds one of the morning or the spring, doesn't it? Such a nice name. Of course, we are very honoured to have Lord and Lady Belvedere among our fellow guests, and dear Lady Lavinia, too. Who would have thought we should be staying in the same hotel as members of the aristocracy? But they are all rather young, though still quite charming ... Mr Thurlow too, though of course he's not gentry. But as I was saying to you only yesterday, dear, he has very charming manners ... But Miss Dewhurst. She's nearer our own age, and rather delicate. Such an elegant creature from what little one could see of her. Rather shy too, hiding her face in all that fur. I suppose she must feel the cold to be muffled up like that. I wonder if I should pay her a visit tomorrow? What do you think, dear? I feel it would be our Christian duty, don't you? She looked rather timid to me, as if she could do with a friend. She reminded me awfully of the squire's wife, didn't she you, dear? But, of course, Mrs Clement suffered with her nerves, poor thing. Really, the more I think it over, the more I really think it would be rather remiss of us if I didn't pay her a call.'

'Stuff and nonsense!' replied Miss Peony rather bad-temperedly, from her position in the chair. 'You do talk a great deal of rot, Hyacinth; you always did, even as a child.'

'Well, really, Peony!' exclaimed Miss Hyacinth, dropping the handkerchief she was holding, in her surprise.

What had startled her most, however, rather than the actual words spoken, had been the sound of her sister's voice. For Peony Trimble had a tendency to act as if she were mute as well as deaf, a circumstance that had initially arisen due to her fear that her deafness might lead her to speak too loudly in public. She had an abhorrence of being stared at, or worse, of making a spectacle of herself, something she was secretly of the opinion her sister did every time she opened her mouth. And having adopted this rather unenviable position, she had found that when in company she was very often ignored; certainly, she appeared invisible in large gatherings. Had she been her sister, Hyacinth, Peony Trimble might well have been distressed by this discovery. Instead, she thrived for she found to her delight that it enabled her to freely eavesdrop on conversations. Due to her reported deafness and the insipid creature she presented in public, very few people bothered to lower their voices in her presence, and indeed frequently spoke quite candidly in front of her under the misapprehension that she was present only in body, not in mind. She had, therefore, gleaned many a piece of gossip or fascinating fact of which she would otherwise have been quite ignorant.

This did not explain, of course, why she should remain silent when she was alone with her sister, who's good opinion she did not seek. Miss Hyacinth, if asked, would have explained, again in a lowered voice, that her sister had quite got out of the habit of speaking. Miss Peony, however, would have explained it quite differently. 'Hyacinth,' she would have said, 'requires no encouragement. She speaks quite enough for the two of us, and what she does say isn't worth listening to.'

Miss Hyacinth was, therefore, rather taken aback that her sister should deem it necessary to contribute to the conversation on this occasion. After mopping her brow with the handkerchief that she had retrieved from the floor, she gave her sister a particularly reproachful stare.

'There's no use your looking at me like that, Hyacinth. It doesn't do anything for you. And you do talk stuff and nonsense,' continued Miss Peony, in the rather gruff voice she adopted when addressing her sister, which was reminiscent of a cough. 'You'd do well to follow my example. Now how does the saying go? Something about it being better to keep quiet and be thought stupid, than to open one's mouth and remove all doubt.' The elder Miss Trimble threw her head back and roared with laughter; the noise reminded Miss Hyacinth of a croaking frog.

'Peony!'

'I'm sorry, Hyacinth,' said her sister, mopping her eyes with a large gentleman's handkerchief that had once belonged to her father, 'but really you have only yourself to blame.'

'Father always said –'

'I don't know why you're always spouting Father. He was a miserable old miser, who never did anything for anyone.'

'What a dreadful thing to say!' objected Miss Hyacinth, looking a little flustered. 'Really, Peony, dear, it is not a bit kind to speak of Father in that way.'

'I don't mean to be kind,' retorted Miss Peony, completely unruffled by her sister's words of reproach. 'Father may have been a vicar, but he behaved like a despot.'

Miss Hyacinth pursed her lips and said rather primly: 'I see you are in one of your moods. It is not the slightest bit of use my talking to you when you are in one of your moods.'

For the next few minutes she pointedly ignored her sibling, occupying herself instead with straightening the sheets on the beds and rearranging the flowers in the vase on the washstand. Having completed these few domestic tasks, she seated herself at her dressing table, her back turned purposely towards her sister, and began applying cold cream to her face.

Miss Peony knitted her brows in a restive manner and regarded her sister's reflection in the mirror. Hyacinth really was too much. Why, she often wondered, did her sister have to be such a sensitive soul? She sighed, for she had realised, rather belatedly, that she had played her hand all wrong. It was not in her character to apologise, nor to attempt to smooth any ruffled feathers caused by her curt tongue. On this occasion, however, she was tempted to intervene. If she did not, Hyacinth was likely to sulk for hours and, really, she could not be expected to keep her bit of news to herself.

'Mr Vickers was quite right,' she said intriguingly.

Hyacinth Trimble, who was engrossed in the act of applying cold cream to her forehead, did not reply immediately.

'Mr Vickers was quite right about the 'Disappearing Duchess',' continued Peony, with growing asperity.

'Was he?' said Hyacinth, sounding not even vaguely interested in what her sister had to say.

It was time, Peony thought, to take decisive action. She rose from her chair, crossed the room, and extracted a newspaper from her travel bag. Out of the corner of her eye she was encouraged to see that Hyacinth was watching her movements in the mirror. Quickly, she scoured the pages of the newspaper until she had found the article she was looking for.

'Ah!' With a note of triumph, she crossed the room and banged the newspaper down on the dressing table, almost upsetting the pot of cold cream. 'There,' she said, jabbing her finger at a photograph underneath which was written: 'The Duchess of Grismere'. Now, tell me that isn't your Miss Dewhurst!'

Mr Vickers coughed and spluttered and stumbled into his room. His throat, as was usual at this time of night, felt parched and, with unfocused eyes, he surveyed the room in vain for a tumbler of water. Swaying slightly, he put a hand up to his scrawny neck and clutched at his limp bow tie, which came undone all too readily in his hand. He regarded it with distaste, as if it were some foreign object, and flung it on to a chair. The creased jacket followed shortly, abandoned unceremoniously in a crumpled heap on the floor. On something of a roll, Mr Vickers next discarded his shoes, without first untying the laces. He tottered unsteadily around the room in stockinged feet, managing to stub his toe on the leg of the bedstead.

With a savage oath, he sprawled himself, fully clothed, on to the bed. A few strands of hair stuck unbecomingly to his damp forehead. He passed a tongue over his dry lips. He did not make a very pleasing spectacle, looking in every respect the reprobate he undoubtedly was.

God, he hated this place. Full of toffs and gentry, it was, and them as thought they were better than everyone else, when, really, they were worse. He'd seen the way they'd looked at him, turning up their noses and averting their gaze whenever he came into view, as if he were something dragged up from the gutter, no better than a sewer rat. Well, he'd show them, all right. They might give themselves airs and graces and talk all lardy dardy, but they weren't no better than him. He supposed that Thurlow chap was all right at a push. At least he worked proper; this was no holiday for him. Pleasant enough young fellow he was too. Happy enough to give him, Vickers, the time of day as long as Miss Mabel weren't there. Everyone could see the chap had it bad, though why he should set his sights on a vicar's daughter, he didn't know. Well, good luck to him, that's what he said. He supposed the Misses Trimble were all right in their way. At least the younger one was, though she wouldn't stop her chattering. It would be enough to drive a man to drink. He didn't think much of the other one. The looks she could give a chap could turn him to stone, they could. If she could talk, he bet she'd have a vicious tongue, just like his Aunt Em, who could screech like a fish wife when she put her mind to it.

No, it was the proper gentry he didn't like. That Lady Lavinia, now, she was a one. A looker, he'd give her that, but the way she looked at him, wrinkling up her nose, as if he were an unpleasant smell. The cheek of it. It could give a man a chip on his shoulder, it could. He had as much right as anyone else to be there, he had, and he'd been tempted once or twice to tell her to her face. Now, whether he'd have chosen this hotel for himself, if it weren't to do with work, was another thing. Of course, by rights, it shouldn't have been him as came. Frank, now he'd have been much better at it, would old Frank. He'd have blended in just fine, what with his fancy ways and his handsome looks. He wouldn't have bought a dinner jacket from a pawnbroker that was two sizes too big for him, he wouldn't; not Frank. But Frank had gone and broken his leg, and what else could Jameson do but give him, Vickers, the job? Not that he had wanted to, of course. You could tell by the look on his face that he'd rather do anything but that. But needs must, as his good old mother would have said, and it was worth a pretty penny. 'Now, don't you let me down, Alfie,' Jameson had said, glowering at him as if Frank's broken leg was all his fault. 'You'll need to smarten yourself up, you will. It's no use you going about the place looking like you've just been pulled through a hedge backwards; else, you'll stick out like a sore thumb. This isn't just any old job, you know. If we do this one right …' He'd regarded Vickers' poor, emaciated physique with more than a critical eye. 'And don't you go drinking,' he'd warned him. 'It ain't food, you know. You look half starved. You'd do better putting a bit of steak and kidney pudding in your stomach than a whisky.' He'd leant forward then and pointed his finger at Vickers. 'You're to remember you're on a job, my boy. None of your larking around that'd make a man half your age blush. You'll need to keep your wits about you. That's to say, what little wits you have, which isn't saying much.'

Vickers sighed, as he remembered his instructions. Jameson had a mean way about him, all right. He'd been in half a mind to tell him what to do with his job and all, only jobs weren't so easy to come by, not nowadays. And it was all very well for Jameson to utter commands in that disagreeable way of his, but it wasn't him as was here on what felt like the other side of the world, among people he could not fathom, and who made

46

it all too obvious they detested him. Look at the way the hotel proprietor had looked him up and down as if he'd answered an advertisement for a position on the hotel staff. Kettering hadn't wanted to give him a room; his face had said as much as clear as day. As it was, he'd been allocated a room that was little more than a broom cupboard. And he'd had nothing to do for the most part but twiddle his thumbs and prop up the hotel bar. He might have liked it well enough if it hadn't been so hot and if he'd had someone proper to talk to, someone to share a pint of beer with. He might have thought of it as a holiday if he hadn't had to stuff himself into a boiled shirt every evening and eat those fancy meals that played havoc with his stomach. He'd never felt so conspicuous or lonely, not even when the wife had left him to take up with that chap in the haberdashers. What else could a chap do in such circumstances, but drink? Especially when someone else was paying. It would have been rude to have abstained; the temperance movement held little attraction to him. What man in his position would have refrained from drinking? Save for Frank, who always was something of a stickler for the rules.

Minutes passed as Vickers lay on his back regarding the ceiling and cursing his lot in life. Gradually, however, his memory cleared. He sat up with a jerk, and his mind became more focused. A vague recollection of the events of the evening had come back to him, and with them a smile appeared on his cracked lips. Though his head was throbbing, he scrambled off the bed with an energy hitherto unknown to him. He made a rapid search of the pockets of the dinner jacket that had been so carelessly tossed aside. After a moment, he found what he was looking for, and extracted a photograph, which he studied carefully.

'That's her, all right,' he declared to himself. 'I'd swear a month's wages on it being her.' He gave a sly grin, though there was no one present to witness his sudden jubilation. 'She's no better that she ought to be, though like as not she considers herself my better.' He laughed mirthlessly at his joke and jabbed the photograph with a grimy finger. 'I'll not be put in my place by the likes of you,' he said savagely.

Mr Vickers was not the only guest to return to his rooms that night in something of a befuddled state. Ron Thurlow was his fellow in this regard, though his condition was not the result of an overindulgence in liquor. Rather, it owed its cause to a severe shock or, to be more precise, to two harsh shocks, that seemed to tear at his very innards, so that for a few minutes he was rendered uncomfortably helpless.

'Well, I'll be blowed!' he said at last, recovering some of his usual good humour. 'Now, what are the odds of that happening to a chap?' His face soon darkened, however, as he somewhat reluctantly acknowledged the peril in which his present predicament placed him. Painful memories rose unbidden to the surface. 'Damn the lot of them!' he exclaimed. He was used to carrying his various secrets bottled up inside him and, by the ordinary way of things, he'd have been all right. The past was the past and could be buried; in time, memory and knowledge of it would be diminished. The likelihood that the various secrets of his existence should threaten to surface, become entwined and be exposed by the same hand, was incredulous. Yet, this was the future that awaited him, a ruin of sorts on a Greek island far removed from the England he had left behind him. He had thought himself to be safe here, and in this he had been mistaken. What a stupid fool he'd been.

He cursed himself severely and began to pace the room, all feelings of tiredness having left him. If he had not been afraid of bumping into Vickers, he might have retired to the hotel bar for a last whisky and cigarette and a chance to contemplate his future. Instead, he ventured out for a stroll, his steps taking him towards the cliff edge where, unbeknown to him, he narrowly missed coming upon the Earl and the Countess of Belvedere on their homeward journey.

The very act of walking, coupled with the night air on his face, proved restorative. He was able to consider the matters troubling him in a more reasoned manner. It was true that he felt agitated still, yet he was relieved to find that the awful sense of dread that had initially filled him had subsided. Instead, he felt intrigued, as if he held a puzzle in his hand.

'But it's an odd old business, just the same,' he acknowledged, the words escaping from his lips before he could retrieve them. Humming softly to himself, he returned to his rooms. What, he wondered, was the worst that could happen? If all else failed, he reasoned, he could escape the island, though he felt tolerably certain that it would not come to that. It did not occur to him then that events might take a far worse turn.

Chapter Seven

'I thought I'd find this island dreadfully dull,' remarked Ron Thurlow to Mabel Adler, the following morning.

They were climbing the steep cliff path that wound its way up from the beach. It was little more than a stony, meandering track, on one side of which the hotel had erected a crude wooden handrail to aid the ascent. It was still a tiring climb, however, and required a degree of concentration and effort. The conversation between the two hotel guests, therefore, was sporadic and uttered between panted breaths.

'And isn't it?' teased Mabel, continuing the thread of her companion's observation. 'Dull, I mean?' she added, when he looked puzzled. She was slightly ahead of Ron on the path and paused for a moment to gaze down at him, conscious of her elevated position.

'Far from it,' answered Ron at last, as they emerged at the top of the cliff somewhat out of breath, though both were laughing, as if they shared some private joke. 'The younger Miss Trimble is a frightfully good sort. She's full of the most useful information. I can't tell you how much I've learned about Clyst Birch. Of course, I've never been to the village myself, but I feel I know it quite as well as any denizen. In fact, I'm thinking of arranging an escorted tour there one of these days.' He grinned at her. 'I say, do you fancy coming?'

Though pleased by the invitation, Miss Adler ignored the question, and instead asked one of her own. 'Are the Trimbles the only reason you don't find this place dull?'

'Oh, rather! I mean to say, one can say the most frightful things to the older Miss Trimble and she won't take offence because of her being as deaf as a doorpost.'

'I don't believe a word of it,' declared Mabel, but not without humour. 'That you say anything frightful, I mean. Why, I've never heard you say an unkind word to anyone.'

'That's because I view everyone as a potential client and am always on my very best behaviour. Though, there's always a first time.' He paused a moment to give Miss Adler a meaningful look. 'Of course, I'd never utter an unkind word to you.'

'I should think not,' retorted Mabel, blushing fetchingly. With crimson cheeks, she turned her gaze to look back out to sea. Apparently unwilling to forsake the subject, she said, still looking into the distance: 'Is it just the Trimbles' company you find amusing?'

'Oh, hardly. Mr Vickers is quite a hoot. It's –'

'Oh,' said Mabel, turning to face him, a deliberate note of disappointment in her voice.

'Of course,' said Ron hurriedly, 'none of them is a patch on you.'

'Aren't they?' enquired Mabel, rather breathlessly.

'No,' said Ron, with feeling.

Mabel felt her stomach give a little flutter. 'We shall be returning home soon,' she said, giving her companion a sideways glance. 'Father and I, I mean.' She permitted herself to look a little crestfallen.

'I say, will you really?' exclaimed Ron, disappointment very much evident on his own face. 'How rotten for you.'

'Yes.' There was a long pause, and then Mabel said rather timidly, almost as if she were plucking up the courage to ask the question: 'Do you ever return to England, Mr Thurlow?' She averted her gaze while she waited for him to answer, smoothing the fabric of her dress and removing from it an invisible thread. 'I suppose,' she added quickly, perhaps afraid of his answer, 'that you travel a great deal on the Continent for your tour company?'

'Yes, I do. That's to say, there has been very little reason for me to return to England until now.'

The emphasis that Ron placed on the last two words was not lost on Mabel. She said hurriedly, before she lost her nerve: 'And now there is?'

'I should say there is! Look here, I do wish you'd call me Ron.' He moved towards her and, with something of an awkward gesture, took her hand in his. 'Mabel, you must know … oh, dash it all!' He let go her hand abruptly and glared in the direction of the hotel. 'There's someone coming.'

'Is there? I didn't hear anything,' said Mabel startled, reluctant to let the conversation falter, yet moving a step or two back so that a respectable gap existed between the two of them.

'Yes. That's to say, I thought I heard footsteps and someone whistling. I can hardly believe I imagined it. Yes, look … I was right. There *is* someone coming.'

The figure of a young man dressed in a single-breasted jacket and white flannel trousers came sharply into view. Mabel was vaguely aware that her companion gave a start, while the newcomer appeared equally surprised to find them on the cliff path at such an early hour of the morning. Indeed, for a fleeting moment it looked as if he might retrace his steps rather than encroach on their privacy. He appeared to think better of it, however, and quickened his pace, now apparently intent on making their acquaintance. Mabel turned to Ron in order that he might make their introductions, yet that gentleman remained resolutely silent, his lips pursed. She was conscious suddenly that they must appear a rude pair, and that it was up to her alone to make amends.

'Mr Dewhurst,' she said hastily, recognising the newcomer as the stranger of the night before. 'How do you do? This is Mr Thurlow,' she turned to indicate Ron, who made no move to step forward and shake hands, 'and I am Miss Adler. We are fellow guests.'

'How do you do, Miss Adler, Mr Thurlow.' The young man gave each of them a shrewd look, taking in the scene. With a half-smile, he said: 'I do hope I am not intruding.'

'Oh, no,' cried Mabel, far too quickly, clearly flustered. She added hurriedly, keen to change the subject: 'Tell me, Mr Dewhurst, how is your sister? I understand she is something of an invalid. She must have found the crossing from Athens rather tiresome?'

'My sister? Ah … yes. You are quite right, Miss Adler. Sophia did find it somewhat tiring.' He turned, somewhat abruptly, to address Ron. 'I beg your pardon, I did not quite catch your name, Mr …'

There was an awkward silence. 'Thurlow,' said Mabel, when it became painfully evident that Ron had no intention of supplying his name.

'Thurlow,' Alec Dewhurst repeated contemplatively.

'Yes,' said Mabel, inwardly furious to be placed in such an excruciating position. For she was all too conscious that Ron was resolutely, and annoyingly, silent, and that Mr Dewhurst in contrast made rather a pleasing picture with his engaging manners and his dark good looks. His physical appearance was at sharp variance with Ron's straw-coloured hair and freckled complexion. In her eyes, it led to an unfavourable comparison as far as the courier was concerned. It occurred to her then, rather belatedly, that she had been staring at Mr Dewhurst for rather a long time. It was possible that he read her thoughts, for the smile he gave her, as he bid them farewell and proceeded with his walk down towards the beach, was particularly disarming.

Annoyed as much by her own transparency of feeling, as with her companion's insolent manner towards their fellow guest, she turned to Ron and said rather curtly: 'You were awfully rude to Mr Dewhurst. Whatever can he have thought? Really, I can't think what has got into you.'

Ron shook his head and said. 'Nothing has got into me. I just didn't take to the fellow, that's all.'

'Well, I doubt whether he took to you,' said Mabel crossly. 'Come on, my father will be wondering where I've got to.'

With that, she set off at a pace towards the hotel, Ron following miserably in her wake. There was no light-hearted banter this time as they made their way towards the terrace. In fact, Mabel barely gave Ron a second glance. Certainly, the easy camaraderie that had existed between them minutes before seemed to have evaporated. It was no longer a moment for confidences or declarations. The time had passed and Ron Thurlow, as he watched Mabel's furious, retreating back and heard her hurrying footsteps, had the odd feeling that the moment was lost forever, never to return. For him the day was ruined and he cursed himself severely, for he knew the reason for this was as much to do with his own bad temper as with Alec Dewhurst's ill-timed interruption.

'Well, I must say, you two are getting along,' remarked Lavinia to her sister-in-law over breakfast. They were seated at their allotted table in the hotel dining room. A smile played across her lips, as she turned her gaze from Rose towards her brother, who was standing before the sideboard, helping himself to another portion of poached eggs.

'Well, of course we're getting along,' replied Rose, rather brusquely, somewhat embarrassed by this observation. Lavinia raised a questioning eyebrow, and Rose added, rather flippantly: 'He *is* my husband.'

'I don't put much store by that,' retorted Lavinia, regarding her keenly. 'In my experience, women very soon bore of their husbands, and husbands of their wives. I'm quite sure I would soon bore of my husband if I were married.'

'Then perhaps it is just as well you're not!'

Lavinia made a face; there was mischief in her eyes. Rose felt, on reflection, that she could hardly blame her friend for noticing that Rose's relations with her brother were no longer strained, indeed, that during the course of the night they had undergone rather a remarkable transformation. She had no wish, however, for Lavinia to pry any further into the matter of her marriage. Seeking to distract her, she looked desperately about her for some object or other to divert Lavinia's interest. Settling on one, she said:

'I do believe the Trimble sisters are actually having a proper conversation.'

'What do you mean by that?' enquired Lavinia, displaying little interest in this observation, certainly not bothering even to turn her head.

'That they are talking to one another. In the ordinary way of things, Miss Hyacinth does all the talking and Miss Peony doesn't utter a word.'

'That's hardly surprising is it?' muttered Lavinia, a trifle bored with the topic of their conversation. 'That Miss Peony seldom says anything, I mean. I doubt she manages to get a word in edgeways when Miss Hyacinth's talking; I know I don't. And besides, she's deaf, which can't help matters.'

'Well, they definitely seem to be discussing something this morning,' said Rose. 'I don't think I have ever seen either of them look so animated.'

With a shrug, Lavinia turned in her seat to regard Miss Peony who, commonly being silent and undemonstrative, had never held much fascination for her. 'They look to me,' she said, 'as if they are having some sort of argument.'

'Don't make it obvious that you are staring at them,' Rose whispered hurriedly, clutching at Lavinia's arm, rather regretting that she had ever drawn the Trimbles' activities to her friend's attention. For Lavinia, whose curiosity had at last been roused, was now craning her neck in a very blatant fashion to look at the two older women.

'They're poring over something,' Lavinia reported, her bored manner quite forsaken. 'Yes … Why, I do believe it's a newspaper.'

'Oh?' said Rose, with a degree of foreboding as various photographs she had seen of the Disappearing Duchess in the society pages flashed before her in her mind's eye. She peeped cautiously at the other table. The sisters' manner did little to alleviate her growing anxiety for, if anything, they appeared strangely furtive in their actions, casting nervous glances around the room, and half concealing under a napkin the newspaper they were so closely scrutinising.

'They're definitely hiding something,' declared Lavinia, evidently now intrigued by the women's odd behaviour. 'I wonder what it is they are looking at in that paper?'' She surveyed the room and gave a little laugh. 'I wonder if they've put something in the water. Everyone seems to be acting a little strangely this morning, don't you think? First, there were you and Ceddie, hanging on each other's every word, then the Misses Trimble acting in the most suspicious manner, and now even Miss Adler and Mr Thurlow are behaving a little oddly.'

'Are they?' said Rose, interested in spite of herself. 'I can't say I've noticed.'

'Well, you wouldn't,' replied her sister-in-law, rather rudely. 'I don't think you would notice anyone but my brother this morning. But they are; acting oddly, I mean. Mr Thurlow has been trying this last half hour to catch Miss Adler's eye, and she has been very pointedly ignoring him.' Lavinia sighed wistfully. 'I suppose they must have had some sort of a falling out.'

Unobtrusively, Rose looked across to where Ron Thurlow was sitting at his solitary table. She was careful not to catch his eye, for she had no wish to be caught spying and thereby adding to the young man's misery. She noticed that he was picking rather listlessly at a piece of bread and, now that she observed him more closely, she thought he made a dejected figure. Before she had an opportunity to study Mabel Adler's demeanour, while also trying to steer Lavinia's conversation on to more general topics, she saw Alec Dewhurst wander into the dining room.

The young man's arrival caused something of a minor sensation, following on as it did from his odd entrance the night before. Alec Dewhurst's dark good looks, which had been most becoming in the forgiving light cast by the chandeliers, still held a certain charm in the harsher light of day.

Not until that moment when a hush fell over the hotel guests, was Rose aware that before there had been a general hum of voices. Now, however, the room had become unnaturally silent, and she was conscious, even without looking about her, that all eyes were turned in the direction of the newcomer. Certainly, Lavinia was distracted by the young man's entrance, all thoughts of the other hotel guests' odd behaviour clearly forgotten. Mabel Adler, too, was apparently affected by the young man's arrival, a spark of recognition lighting up her grey eyes. Rose saw Cedric stiffen, plate in hand. This movement was mirrored by Ron Thurlow, arrested in the act of picking at his bread, which he crumbled with uncalled for savagery between his fingers. Father Adler beamed rather blandly at Alec Dewhurst, his thoughts obviously still with the monasteries he hoped to visit. Mr Vickers, for once sober and alert, stared at the stranger with undisguised interest, as did the Trimble sisters, who surreptitiously covered the newspaper they were studying with a nest of napkins.

Alec Dewhurst looked about him and grinned. There was a confidence about him that suggested the art of making an entrance was not foreign to him. Certainly, he looked unruffled by such avid scrutiny as was bestowed on him by the hotel patrons. Indeed, if anything, he seemed rather to bask in it, as if it was the sun that blazed so brightly outside the window. He surveyed the room in an unhurried manner. A servant stepped forward, presumably to direct him to one of the unoccupied tables. Miss Adler, however, seemed to have other ideas. For, out of the corner of her eye, Rose saw the girl tap her father on the arm and mutter something hurriedly in his ear. The vicar, for whom his daughter was a being to be indulged and acquiesced to, nevertheless raised an eyebrow in surprise. Though rather taken aback that Mabel should be so insistent, he was nevertheless quite prepared to acquiesce to her request, considering it to be his Christian duty to welcome a stranger to Hotel Hemera. Alec Dewhurst was watching the exchange between father and daughter with a degree of amusement. Indeed, his smile was sardonic now, and there was a gleam in his eye which suggested that he had won some private victory. As the vicar stood up and beckoned to the young man to join them at the Adlers' table, instructing the servant to lay another place, Rose noted both Alec Dewhurst and Miss Adler threw a glance in the direction of Ron Thurlow. That gentleman, his face white, was sitting quietly fuming at his table, his piece of bread now little more than a pile of crumbs.

Cedric returned to the Belvederes' table scowling, his own face a mixture of emotions.

'What's the matter with you?' demanded Lavinia.

Cedric ignored his sister and spoke in an undertone to Rose.

'The gall of the fellow!'

'Ssh!' His wife gave him a warning look, but it was too late, for Lavinia had evidently heard the exchange and was regarding them closely, clearly puzzled.

'Why do you say that?' she queried.

'Never you mind,' her brother replied curtly.

'Well, I do,' objected Lavinia. 'I think it beastly of you to say what you did. It is hardly Mr Dewhurst's fault if we all stared at him when he came into the room. If anything, it is us who were rude. Why, I've a good mind to go over and introduce myself to him.'

'Don't you dare!' said Cedric.

The note of anger in her brother's voice was not lost on Lavinia and she stared at him, slightly taken aback, for she was not used to him speaking to her in such a manner, nor seeing him so evidently riled.

'What's the matter?' she persisted and then, when Cedric declined to answer, she turned to Rose and said again: 'What is the matter? You know, don't you? Won't you tell me?'

'I think we should,' said Rose quietly, conscious that Lavinia's fascination with the young man was unlikely to wane, and that her friend's voice carried at the best of times, and particularly when she was excited or agitated, as she was now. Indeed, she could hardly believe that Alec Dewhurst was not at that very moment staring at them. She gave a surreptitious glance in the direction of his table and was somewhat relieved to discover that the vicar's party was in fact leaving the room, having chosen to take breakfast out on the terrace.

With their departure, there was every sign that the previous idle chatter that had existed in the dining room would resume, with Lavinia contemplating aloud how they should spend their day. Indeed, Rose was just on the point of inwardly breathing a sigh of relief, an awkward moment and explanation having been at least temporarily postponed, when she was aware of a presence at her shoulder. Unbeknown to her, Miss Hyacinth Trimble had sidled up to their table, and a quick look was sufficient to tell her that the ominous newspaper was clutched tightly in the woman's hand.

Chapter Eight

'Miss Hyacinth,' said Cedric, with undue sincerity. He was presumably thanking providence for the woman's timely appearance which in effect put an end to Lavinia's persistent questioning. 'What may we do for you?'

Miss Hyacinth, who until that minute had been rather hesitant in her actions, no doubt afraid that she was intruding on a family affair, beamed at them all, considerably relieved at her welcome. A moment later, however, and she was colouring slightly at the news she had to impart, uncertain whether it could be classed as gossip, something of which her father had heartily disapproved.

All the while, Rose looked on with an awful fascination, consumed by a feeling of helplessness to stop the events that were about to unfold. For a fleeting moment, she wondered whether there was anything she could do to prevent the inevitable revelations concerning Miss Dewhurst's identity. A quick glance about her, however, soon dashed any hopes that might have lingered. For something of Miss Hyacinth's excitement had been caught up by the others. It was not only Cedric who was giving the woman his full attention, but also Lavinia, who eyed Miss Hyacinth somewhat warily, words of protest directed at her brother frozen on her lips. Even Ron Thurlow and Mr Vickers did not appear immune to what was happening at the Belvederes' table, each edging forward a little and craning their necks so that they might catch Miss Hyacinth's news.

'Well, really,' began Miss Hyacinth, suddenly flustered. 'I hardly know if I should say anything. It was my dear sister who noticed the resemblance ...' She paused and looked rather helplessly back at her sister, who at that moment appeared engrossed in looking out of the window, and so did not catch her eye. 'Well,' continued Miss Hyacinth pluckily, resigned to not receiving any aid from that quarter, 'it is uncanny but ... well, we may be quite wrong, and if we are, well, I do feel I should never forgive myself. I mean to say, to take away someone's good character ... to cast aspersions which may well prove quite unfounded ... My poor, dear father would be quite appalled; he would turn in his grave. I –'

'What are you talking about?' asked Lavinia, clearly losing patience with the older woman. Even Cedric was looking a little bemused by the woman's ramblings.

Miss Hyacinth, no doubt fearful that she was about to lose her attentive audience, suddenly thrust the newspaper she was holding down on the table and pointed at a photograph that occupied a corner of one page. Rose stared down at it with growing trepidation. Her heart sank. If she had hoped that the image would be blurred or taken from a distance where a positive identification would prove difficult, she was to be disappointed. For it was a studio photograph, which showed all too clearly the features of the handsome woman it depicted. Worse still, both the pose and the costume adopted by the woman pictured were so reminiscent of the stranger who had appeared the night before in the dining room that any doubt that might have existed in Rose's mind regarding the accuracy of her husband's identification of the woman as the missing duchess soon evaporated. Indeed, peering at the newspaper more closely, she thought it was quite possible that the silver fox coat, draped in such a nonchalant fashion around the shoulders of the woman in the image, was the very same fur that had partially shrouded the face of Miss Dewhurst from observers the previous evening. Instinctively, she felt a pang of pity for the woman who had appeared so reluctantly at the window of the dining room, remembering the way she had clung nervously at the curtain, only to be dragged rather unceremoniously into the room by her companion.

She was abruptly roused from her musings by Lavinia, who gave a surprised gasp. 'Why, it's Miss Dewhurst!'

'It was my dear sister who recognised her from the photograph,' began Miss Hyacinth, a trifle apologetically, suddenly aware that her actions might have certain ramifications. Indeed, there was a part of her that wished she had not produced the newspaper for all to see. As it was, she was uncomfortably aware that Mr Vickers was taking an uncommon interest in the photograph. Indeed, he had gone so far as to advance on them and grasp hold of one edge of the newspaper, pulling it towards him in a most insolent manner. Miss Hyacinth pursed her lips and frowned. Really, she thought, the man is becoming insufferable. Why, the page had been in very real danger of being torn. It was with a certain smugness, therefore, that she noted that Mr Vickers' discourteous actions had elicited a glare from Mr Thurlow. Such a nice young man, she thought. Had she been Rose, she might have noticed that the courier was himself eyeing the photograph in rather a peculiar manner. Unlike the others, he did not appear inclined to step forward and peer at the newspaper; if anything, he seemed disposed to recoil from it, taking a step or two backwards, which unfortunately resulted in him colliding with a chair which he sent toppling over. The subsequent clatter brought him sharply to his senses, though his face remained pale under its tan.

'It *is* Miss Dewhurst, isn't it?' continued Lavinia, persistent in her questioning as ever, though there was a note of incredulity in her voice. The question, rather than being addressed to Miss Hyacinth, was directed to her brother. 'You have met her, haven't you, the Duchess of Grismere, I mean?'

After a moment's deliberation, Cedric said: 'On a couple of occasions. There is a resemblance, certainly, but ...' he faltered, unsure how to continue, aware that all eyes were now turned on him.

'You think it's her, all right, don't you, your lordship?' chirped in Mr Vickers, with an unnatural eagerness, which made those present wonder whether he had already been at the spirits notwithstanding the earliness of the hour. 'You don't think it right or proper to tell us, and very decent of you to be sure, seeing as how you're trying to protect her ladyship's reputation and all, but the truth will out, and it's better as how we know.'

'Mr Vickers!' exclaimed Miss Hyacinth, visibly appalled by the man's speech, which seemed to her as uneducated as it was repulsive. These sentiments appeared to be shared by the young earl, who regarded the man coldly.

'No,' said Cedric mendaciously. 'I admit there is a certain likeness, but –'

'How can you deny it?' cried Lavinia, apparently oblivious to all else but seeking out the truth. 'Miss Dewhurst is the Duchess of Grismere, you know she is.' Her voice had risen rather shrilly, and Rose wondered whether her words could be heard out on the terrace where Mr Dewhurst and the Adlers were breakfasting. A fleeting look in their direction, however, reassured her that they were quite ignorant of the discussion taking place in the dining room. Rather, Mr Dewhurst and Miss Adler appeared deep in conversation, with the vicar looking on as a benevolent spectator.

'I say,' continued Lavinia, turning to address her sister-in-law, 'that is what the two of you were whispering about, isn't it? Cedric recognised the duchess and was discussing with you whether or not you should tell me.'

'Do be quiet, Lavinia, there's a good egg,' said Cedric, with an attempt at flippancy, which failed rather dismally.

'I wonder,' continued his sister as if he had not spoken, 'what possessed her to come to this island?'

'We do not know for certain that it is the duchess,' said Rose hurriedly, sharing some of her husband's reservations over the fact becoming common knowledge. Certainly, she did not like the way Mr Vickers' bottom lip was quivering with emotion, or his manner of staring at her with eager anticipation, as if he thought she might be persuaded to divulge something incriminating.

Lavinia pouted and said stubbornly: 'Well, Ceddie has met the Duchess of Grismere and ...' She did not finish her sentence, for she had caught her brother's eye and interpreted correctly his look of warning. She flushed rather prettily and with obvious reluctance continued with her breakfast.

There was an awkward silence. Miss Hyacinth, possibly realising that she had overstepped the mark, or that nothing further could be elicited from the Belvederes' table, withdrew tactfully to join her sister, the offending newspaper clutched under her arm. Meanwhile, Ron Thurlow remained standing where he was for a few seconds, gazing into the distance. For a fleeting moment, a peculiar expression appeared on his face which Rose, watching him closely, found difficult to interpret. It seemed to her a strange mixture of emotions ranging from wonder to horror. What was painfully evident, however, was that something had shocked the young man. Before she could dwell on the matter any further, Ron, recollecting his surroundings, looked about him quickly, caught her eye and smiled somewhat ruefully. After nodding briefly at those seated at the Belvederes' table, he returned to his own, clearly in deep meditation; though this time, Rose noticed, he took steps to conceal his thoughts from prying eyes.

It was not Ron Thurlow's demeanour, however, that caused Rose most speculation, or indeed, cause for concern. Rather, it was Mr Vickers'. At the best of times she found that gentleman's presence objectionable.

However, this morning there had been something particularly insulting in his behaviour, not least in the way that he had addressed her husband with offensive familiarity, prying and probing to scent out a fragment of scandal like an officious bloodhound on the track of some wild boar. She stole a furtive glance towards his table and her heart sank. For there was a gleam in his eye and his face was flushed red, for once with excitement rather than with whisky. Indeed, the man could barely contain his emotions. What was more, it was evident that he intended to make a hurried breakfast. On this occasion, Rose thought it unlikely that the lure of the hotel bar was the reason for his quickened steps, rather, she thought, he was driven by a much stronger influence.

It was then that the thought struck Rose forcefully, causing her to catch her breath and clutch at the tablecloth, as if to steady herself. How very dense and stupid they had all been. They had dismissed Vickers as the hotel bore and frowned rather condescendingly at his dishevelled appearance and partiality to liquor. Yet to the Duchess of Grismere, with a reputation that hung so precariously in the balance, he was of much greater significance than that. For, unless Rose was very much mistaken, of all of them he could do her the greatest harm. With these thoughts uppermost in her mind, Rose watched as the man in question licked his lips, passing his tongue over teeth that only now she noticed were discoloured and yellow. She grabbed at her husband's arm, pulling at the fabric of his sleeve in her urgency. Somewhat taken aback, Cedric bent his head towards her so that she could whisper in his ear.

'Quick!' Rose said. 'We must warn the duchess!'

'Well, of course it's the duchess,' declared Miss Peony vehemently, as soon as the Trimble sisters had retired to their room to gather their things in readiness for the day ahead. 'You only had to look at the earl and the countess' faces to see it was. Why they didn't just admit it and get it over and done with, I don't know. They must take us for fools. Still,' she sniffed, and added rather disparagingly, 'I suppose Lord Belvedere's just trying to protect her character, not that she deserves it, duchess or no duchess.' She paused to run a finger over the top surface of the tallboy, searching for dust. Tutting, she said: 'Of course, it's more than likely that it's that husband of hers he's trying to shield.' She made a noise that sounded suspiciously like a snort. 'Them lot stick together.'

'Which lot, dear?' enquired Miss Hyacinth, only half listening.

'Toffs,' replied her sister with relish.

'Really, Peony dear,' said Miss Hyacinth, with a note of disapproval in her voice. Sometimes she despaired of her sister, she really did. She returned her gaze pointedly to the dressing table mirror, before which she sat adjusting her straw hat. It did not prevent her from being uncomfortably conscious that her sibling sat regarding her with a sardonic smile. Ordinarily, she would have pretended not to notice and indeed taken measures not to antagonise her sister; today, however, she had a growing conviction that they had been in the wrong. Her back towards her sibling, she began rather tentatively: 'I do rather think we ought not to have done it. No,' she added hurriedly, aware that her sister was very likely to protest, 'I daresay we are quite right in believing Miss Dewhurst to be the Duchess of Grismere, but to say so ... so openly in front of all the other hotel guests ... well, I think we made a grave mistake. I blame myself entirely.'

'And so you should,' retorted her sister, somewhat unexpectedly. 'It was your idea, not mine, to go marching over to the earl's table and thrust that newspaper in his face like some sort of town crier.' Something of a malicious gleam came into the older woman's eyes. 'Father would have been disgusted by such behaviour, and rightly so. He'd have considered it common and beneath you.'

'As if you ever cared what dear Father thought, Peony,' Miss Hyacinth replied with spirit, though her face visibly crumbled at mention of doing anything of which her late, revered parent would have disapproved. In the ordinary course of events, it was likely to reduce her to a fit of weeping. Possibly fearing this, Miss Peony sniffed and, relenting somewhat, said rather begrudgingly: 'There, there, don't go on so. I daresay they'll think you're just a silly old woman who hasn't got anything better to do than spread gossip.' Aside to herself in a voice barely audible, she added: 'And they wouldn't be far wrong, neither!'

Fortunately, Miss Hyacinth did not hear this part of her sister's speech. She turned around in her chair, however, and addressed her sibling with an imploring look. 'Oh dear ... oh dear me. What must they think of me? I wouldn't have shown them, of course, only I caught Lady Belvedere looking at us in such a curious manner, and I suppose we must have looked rather suspicious. Really, I can't think what possessed me to bring the newspaper in to breakfast, and then to hide it under the napkins and take peeks at it as if we were a couple of giggling schoolgirls ...'

Miss Peony gave her croak of a laugh. 'You should have seen their faces. I could study them closely from where I was sitting without being observed because, of course, no one gives me the time of day. Ha-ha, his lordship looked horrified.'

'Oh dear,' said Miss Hyacinth again, a favourite expression of hers when she was unsure what to say. After a moment's reflection, however, she rallied a little. 'I still think as how it was right what I did. After all, they were all bound to find out and the duchess' young man ... I suppose it is just possible,' she continued, sounding doubtful, 'that he really is her brother?'

'Pah! If he's her brother, I'll eat my hat!' retorted her sibling. 'She's run away with him, that's what she's done, and her a married woman and all. Well, she'll rue the day, Hyacinth, if she hasn't already, you mark my words,' said the older woman, wagging her finger at her sister.

It was with a degree of satisfaction that she noted the horrified look on her sibling's face. It was only too easy to shock Hyacinth, she reflected. She supposed it was due to their sheltered upbringing, though she herself had tried to rise above it, and if it hadn't been for her awful deafness she might have succeeded and made a bit of a life for herself. Of course, she could hardly blame Hyacinth for that, yet it aroused in her certain feelings of animosity towards her sister. It also inclined her to bouts of vindictiveness, which she was later apt to regret. Staring at Hyacinth's face now, pale under its sunburn, and all but dwarfed under the brim of the ridiculous straw hat she would insist on wearing, Peony felt the inevitable stirrings within her to be malevolent.

She gave her a sly look. 'That vicar of yours, you think so highly of, had better look out,' she said maliciously. She was rewarded by her sister giving her a worried look of surprise.

'I don't suppose you noticed how that young man of the duchess' was all over the vicar's daughter? That Adler girl has not a brain in her head, and she's no better than she ought to be, fluttering her eyes at any chap who shows the slightest bit of interest in her.' Miss Peony, getting into her stride, gave a malevolent smile. 'Last week it was that travel company fellow she lost her head over. Well, I'll say this for him, he seems a decent sort and not the type to take advantage, so I suppose there was no harm done. But you can't say the same about that other fellow. He doesn't mind carrying on with one woman if she'll keep him, while dallying with another just for the fun of it –'

'Peony!' exclaimed Miss Hyacinth, palpably appalled by her sister's vulgar rhetoric and spitefulness. 'That will do. If you say one more word on the matter, I shall walk out of this room and leave you here.' Miss Peony, possibly aware that she had been particularly ferocious in her criticism, or afraid that her sister would indeed carry out her threat, had the grace to look a little sheepish, which gave Miss Hyacinth the encouragement she needed to proceed with her reprimand. 'Really, dear, at times you can be most unfair. Miss Adler was just showing Mr Dewhurst some Christian kindness by inviting him to join her and her father for breakfast.'

'You didn't see the way he looked at her, or she at him,' muttered her sister, 'to say nothing of the looks Mr Thurlow was giving him. Daggers – ' She stopped abruptly, aware that she had tried her sister's patience to its limit. Deciding to change tack, she took a step forward and lowered her voice. 'You keep an eye out for that girl, Hyacinth, or she'll come to no good.'

Chapter Nine

'Are you saying that Vickers is working for the penny press?' asked Cedric, clearly appalled by the suggestion. Like the Trimbles, the Bevelderes had returned to their rooms to don their apparel for the day ahead. In the earl's case, this consisted of tennis flannels and a cotton shirt.

'It is just a thought I had,' said Rose, smoothing down the skirt of her summer dress and standing before the dressing table mirror to put on her sun hat. She had waited until they had returned to their rooms to express her view, anxious to ensure that they were out of the hearing of the other hotel guests. 'It would explain why Mr Vickers was so very keen that you identify Miss Dewhurst as the duchess.'

'I can't say I took to the fellow myself. And if what you say is correct ...well, it's a rum go, all right.' Cedric pondered the matter a little longer before he spoke again. 'It was Vickers who suggested that the duchess would be coming here to this island, to this very hotel, wasn't it?' he said. 'Didn't you say he said as much to Miss Hyacinth?'

'Yes, though he denied it all later. In fact, if you remember,' said Rose, warming to the subject, 'he was frightfully rude to her when she raised the matter with him at dinner.'

'I suppose he cursed himself for having spoken so freely. I mean to say, a chap like that would need to keep his cards close to his chest if he were after a scoop,' said her husband, beginning to pace the room. 'He wouldn't want Miss Hyacinth going about letting the cat out of the bag and telling all and sundry.' He chuckled in spite of himself. 'I can't for the life of me think why he thought the woman would hold her tongue. I suppose he was somewhat inebriated at the time.'

'It would also explain what he is doing staying in this hotel,' mused Rose, continuing her train of thought. 'I have always thought it rather odd his being here.'

'Yes. He doesn't look the sort of chap who could rub two pennies together, let alone afford to stay in a place like this.'

Rose suppressed a smile at her husband's unconscious snobbery. Aloud, she said: 'What I meant was that he rather gave me the impression that he despised us all; his fellow guests, I mean.'

'He certainly has a tendency to keep himself to himself,' concurred Cedric.

'I confess I was rather curious about him,' admitted Rose, blushing slightly in light of what she was about to divulge. 'In fact, I asked Mr Kettering this morning if he knew what Mr Vickers did to earn his living.'

'Ho, you did, did you?' said her husband, evidently amused.

'Yes. Mr Kettering said he wasn't certain, but he thought Mr Vickers was some sort of commercial traveller.'

Cedric made a face. 'I daresay at a stretch I could just about picture Vickers donned in a bowler hat and a large overcoat, though of the faded and crumpled variety, of course. Not that I can imagine him selling anything to anyone.'

'Which is all the more reason to suppose I was right in the first place,' said Rose. 'Mr Vickers is really a journalist.'

'In which case,' said Cedric with a tightening of the lips, all attempt at frivolity and flippancy forsaken, 'we must, as you say, warn the duchess to be on her guard. If common-sense prevails, she'll keep to her rooms. If not, it'll be in all the papers how she's run off with a man young enough to be the duke's grandson!'

As had become his custom of late, after breakfasting that morning, Ron Thurlow withdrew hurriedly to his own modest room where he lay down wearily on his bed, conscious that his meal sat heavy on his stomach. It had also left a bitter after taste in his mouth. For one fleeting moment, earlier, he had been tempted to join the party that gathered each morning on the terrace, if only to overhear their conversation. Mabel who, until that fateful day when they had first encountered Alec Dewhurst on the cliff path, had encouraged Ron's attentions, had greeted him that morning with a look which could be best described as ambivalent. It had not been the girl's expression, however, which had stayed Ron's steps, but rather the sardonic grin from her companion, whose dark eyes had gleamed with malicious intent. Ron had hesitated, wavering between facing the danger head on, and recoiling in defeat. He had chosen the latter, and now, stretched out on his bed in the relative safety of his room, he cursed his own cowardice.

The evening would be worse still, he knew, for it was now Alec Dewhurst, not he, who was in the habit of taking coffee with the Adlers after dinner. Surely it was only a matter of time, Ron reflected miserably, before Alec Dewhurst accompanied the vicar and his daughter on the various excursions they made of the island.

Ron gave a cursory glance at the pile of papers on his desk, aware that recently he had become rather neglectful of his duties. There were reports to write detailing his impressions of the island and notes to jot down of his various conversations with the local tavernkeepers and fishermen. Yet he knew that, even if he should sit at his desk this very instant, he would be unable to focus on his work. For his mind still dwelt on Mabel's face and, more precisely, on Alec Dewhurst's ever mocking smile.

He sighed and picked up his hat which lay discarded on a chair. Notwithstanding the heat, he had a sudden longing to be outside. He was vaguely hopeful that the vivid sunshine would restore his mood and banish his feelings of melancholy. With this end in mind, the young man set off at a brisk pace, giving little thought to the direction in which his feet were taking him. He did not realise, therefore, until he felt the light, summer breeze on his cheeks, that he was making for the cliff. It was too late to change course. Somewhat reluctantly he proceeded on his way, stopping only to look out to sea. As he did so, he sighed and gave a rueful smile. The last time he had taken in this view, Mabel had been by his side, and the air had been filled with their laughter.

With a heavy heart, he was in the very act of turning around, intending to retrace his steps back to the hotel, when he was arrested by the sound of a voice surprisingly close at hand.

'I thought I'd find you here.' The words were uttered in an assured way, as if the talker was certain of his ground.

Ron started violently, though it took him but a second to identify the speaker. 'What do you want?' he said curtly.

'I say, that's no way to greet an old friend,' replied the newcomer advancing. If he was disappointed by his lacklustre reception, he did not show it; if anything, he grinned.

'What are you doing here?' demanded Ron.

'I might well ask you the same question,' Alec Dewhurst replied. 'I wasn't certain it was you at first. I didn't recognise the name and you look a little different from when I saw you last. You've filled out a bit. Th-ur-

67

low.' He rolled the word on his tongue. 'Is that the name you go by now? I say, it sounds dashed respectable.'

'And Dewhurst,' Ron countered, 'I can't say I've heard you called by that name before.'

'It's rather good, don't you think?' the man calling himself Alec Dewhurst said, with a nonchalant air. 'It has a certain ring to it.'

'It has nothing of the sort,' retorted Ron. Unable to keep his temper, he grew bellicose and raised his voice. 'You haven't answered my question. What the devil are you doing here?'

'I would have thought that was pretty obvious,' replied his companion. 'I say,' he added, watching Ron keenly, 'that proprietor fellow told me you were some sort of private courier working for a travel company.'

'What if I am? It's no business of yours.'

'No?' said Alec, a flash of triumph in his eyes. 'I daresay they don't know you've been to prison. I rather think it my duty to tell them, don't you?' He paused a moment and made what he considered to be a lucky shot. 'I wonder what Miss Adler would say if she –'

'You can go to the devil!' cried Ron, clenching his fists.

'Ah, I've hit a nerve, I see.' An unpleasant smile contorted Alec Dewhurst's handsome features. 'I rather thought you were fond of her. She's a pretty little thing, I'll admit, but not the sort of girl to break one's heart over.'

'Why, you –'

'Yes, yes,' said Alec, with a dismissive gesture. 'I only wanted to know the lie of the land.'

'There's many a thing I could tell Miss Adler about you –'

'There is,' agreed Alec, 'but you won't, not if you know what's good for you.' The last vestiges of humour had left his voice. He glared at Ron. 'You'll hold your tongue.'

There was a moment's awkward silence, as each man glowered at the other.

At last, Ron said: 'Your … sister …'

'Oh, she's hardly that,' replied Alec, somewhat flippantly. 'But, of course, you know that already. That's why I'm calling myself Dewhurst. I mean to say, when a chap's living with another man's wife, he'd be a fool to use his own name. The lady in question doesn't even know it.'

'They say she's the Duchess of Grismere, this woman pretending to be your sister.'

Was it Ron's imagination, or did the other man start? Certainly, to Ron's untrained eye the other gave every appearance of being startled.

'Do they, indeed?' said Alec, recovering a little of his equanimity. 'What a lot of rot. It's not like you to listen to servants' gossip. I would have thought you were above such things.'

He made as if to go, but Ron clutched at his sleeve to detain him, his nails digging painfully into the other man's arm. 'It was Lord Belvedere who recognised her.' He felt Alec Dewhurst stiffen under his grasp. 'Tell me,' Ron said rather breathlessly, 'is it true?'

'Of course not. He's quite wrong. There is a bit of a resemblance, I agree, but that's all. I mean to say, what would the Duchess of Grismere see in a chap like me?'

'Very little, I'd have thought,' replied Ron coldly.

Alec Dewhurst glared and wrestled his arm free from the other man's grip. He set off purposefully and bristling towards the hotel leaving Ron to look after his retreating figure, a look of utter contempt on his face. There was another expression there also. Even the most casual observer would have concluded that the courier was considerably agitated. He seemed perplexed too. Indeed, he was the perfect study of a man in deep contemplation, who was also suffering from some form of extreme mental anxiety.

As it happened, there was no casual observer in the vicinity. But there was an interested one. The two young men had been too engrossed in their argument to give any consideration to their surroundings. Had they not been so intent on glowering at one another, they might have noticed that they were not alone. They had been standing on the very edge of the cliff, but neither had thought to look down and ascertain if anyone was on the cliff path that weaved its way down to the beach. Had they done so, they would have noticed a figure perched a few yards below the cliff edge. A fellow hotel guest, in fact. That in itself might not have caused them undue alarm, had it not been for the way in which the breeze was blowing, which had caused their voices to be carried out to sea. Indeed, had the young men seen fit to glance down at the figure, they would have seen the interested look on its face. It is quite possible that it might have dawned on them then that the onlooker had heard every word of the argument that had passed between them.

It was all very well to decide in theory to warn the duchess of the ominous presence of the journalist on the island, but to put it into practice, Rose soon discovered, was quite another thing. The chief difficulty lay in the fact that the duchess rarely, if ever, left her rooms.

In stark contrast, Alec Dewhurst soon became something of a regular fixture on both the hotel terrace and the private beach. Indeed, so often was he seen about the hotel and surrounds without his companion that it was tempting to forget that he had been accompanied on his travels by another, who presumably languished lonely and abandoned in their rooms. As if to further illustrate this peculiar fact, Miss Hyacinth was apt to remark, to anyone who would listen, that, had she not witnessed the Dewhursts' arrival with her own eyes, she would quite readily have believed the young man to be travelling alone.

'His dear sister must be at quite a loss without his company,' she had remarked rather tentatively to the vicar one afternoon, while watching Alec Dewhurst and Mabel Adler engaged in playing a game of tennis. Since her worrying conversation with Miss Peony, she was given to studying Alec Dewhurst's conduct closely for any signs of an inappropriate dalliance. 'Such a shame that she is obliged to keep to her rooms. I say, Mr Dewhurst,' she said, raising her voice to attract the attention of the young man playing tennis, 'how is Miss Dewhurst feeling today? I do hope she is a little better. Do you think she will feel up to taking dinner in the dining room this evening? It would be so nice to make her acquaintance.'

The interruption caused Alec Dewhurst to miss his serve and a scowl appeared fleetingly on his face, momentarily marring his handsome features. It was replaced almost immediately by a charming smile and words to the effect that Miss Hyacinth was very kind to ask after his poor sister but, alas, she was not very strong, and any form of company was likely to exhaust her. Still, he was hopeful that the Mediterranean air might yet prove to be the tonic she needed to return her to health.

'If only the poor woman would see fit to step outside her rooms,' Miss Hyacinth remarked rather cattily to the vicar, 'she might breathe in some of that restorative air of which Mr Dewhurst speaks so fondly. Let us hope that at least the windows of her rooms are kept wide open.'

'Now, now, Miss Hyacinth,' said the vicar soothingly. 'I'm sure Mr Dewhurst knows what's best for his sister's health.'

Miss Hyacinth was not so certain. She regarded the vicar's kindly face and bestowed on him something of an incredulous look. It was true, she reminded herself, that Father Adler had not been present when she had produced the offending newspaper article and commented on the likeness between Miss Dewhurst and the Duchess of Grismere. He had not heard Lady Lavinia's assertion that the two women must be one, nor heard Lord Belvedere's vehement, but quite unbelievable, denial. Poor Father Adler, she thought. He does not doubt for one moment that Mr Dewhurst is exactly whom he purports to be; a young man of considerable wealth and charm, accompanying an invalid sister on her travels.

Inevitably her eyes were drawn back to the game of tennis being played out before her. She studied Alec Dewhurst and Mabel Adler closely, conscious of every exchange between them, each nod of the head, each laugh, each coy adjustment of a wayward curl by Miss Adler. While thus engaged, the game finished abruptly, and the players advanced towards the net and shook hands. Miss Hyacinth continued to watch avidly, aware that the two young people remained by the net, hands still clasped, heads bent together. To Miss Hyacinth's attuned ear, there was a great deal of whispering. She stole a sideward glance at her companion, but the vicar appeared deeply engrossed in the reading of a sermon that he had composed that morning. She sighed thinking that there were none so blind as those who did not care to see what was happening in front of them. For, unless she had given way to imaginings, she felt certain of a growing intimacy developing between Mr Dewhurst and Miss Adler, of which the vicar appeared entirely ignorant.

It was at the very moment she was thinking such thoughts that the vicar chanced to look up from his pocketbook and cast an affectionate glance in the direction of his daughter. It said much for his indulgence towards his offspring that he neither blinked rapidly nor drew in a sharp intake of breath at the intimate picture she presented with Alec Dewhurst.

'Such a charming young man,' her father remarked rather abstractedly, much in the same vague tones he had previously spoken of Ron Thurlow. 'I suppose,' he added rather hesitantly, 'one ought to enquire after his family ...'

Miss Hyacinth shot him a bewildered glance. It had not occurred to her that the vicar would seek to encourage his daughter's infatuation with the young man, or still yet that he envisaged a satisfactory outcome. In a state of considerable apprehension, she removed her straw hat and used it to fan her flushed cheeks.

'I suppose,' Father Adler was saying, 'he is a young man of independent means ...'

'Oh dear,' cried Miss Hyacinth, the knowledge she possessed gnawing at her conscience. In her mind's eye, she saw the wretched photograph that she had waved so triumphantly in the faces of the Belvederes; she heard again her sister's cackle of laughter at her own naivety in suggesting that Alec Dewhurst might in fact be the Duchess of Grismere's sibling.

She wondered later what she would have done had Mabel Adler not looked up at that very instant, caught her father's eye and smiled. This act had done nothing to allay Miss Hyacinth's fears. If anything, it had strengthened them, for she realised with a sharp stab of horror that the girl was as trusting as her father. Even then, all might have been well had she not spied the gleam of mischief in the young man's eyes. Had his expression been benign, might she not have looked away and held her tongue, deeming it none of her business? Instead, she had opened her mouth and spoken. If asked afterwards, all she could say was that she was suddenly conscious of the presence of evil. Danger lurked half concealed in the Mediterranean air. She was faced in that moment with two opposing paths that seemed to loom up in front of her. She almost felt her dead father's presence guiding her hand to choose the right course, and for once she knew that Peony, for all her vulgar outspokenness, would concur with her choice.

Bending forward a little in her chair, she took a deep breath and said in a lowered voice: 'Oh dear. It is a rather delicate matter, and of course, really, one hardly knows how to begin, but I feel that it is my Christian duty to tell you ...'

Chapter Ten

'I say,' said Alec Dewhurst, entering the private sitting room he shared with his companion, his cheeks flushed in rather a becoming fashion following his recent exertions on the tennis court. 'It's frightfully hot out. All one wants to do on a day like this is go down to the beach and swim.'

The Duchess of Grismere's greeting was hardly encouraging. She had been awaiting the young man's return impatiently and had spent the better part of the afternoon anxiously pacing the room and casting quick, furtive glances out of the window at the terrace beyond, careful always not to be observed. In the ordinary course of events, she might have remained silent, if a little cold and terse in her manner towards him. This afternoon, however, she felt disinclined to be tolerant. It might have been that she felt oppressed and suffocated by the heat, magnified by being cooped up in her rooms, or the realisation that her companion's absences were becoming more frequent. Whatever the reason, it had the effect of loosening her tongue, and words of reproach escaped from her lips before she could recall them.

'I've been by myself for ages. Where have you been? I thought something awful had happened to you.'

The sentences had come tumbling out on top of each other with hardly a breath in between. Even to the duchess' own ears her voice sounded shrill and unreasonably petulant. She took a step back, as if to distance herself from her words, and clenched her fists. The damage, however, was done. She was all too conscious of the sneer that had crept on to her companion's face. The dark eyes flashed at her, barely concealing a look of irritation and another emotion, which she could not interpret but she feared might be contempt.

'I was playing tennis,' Alec Dewhurst answered curtly. He had entered the room in a jovial mood, but now he sounded put out. 'Of course, it was quite the wrong time of day to play, but Miss Adler insisted.'

'Miss Adler? The vicar's daughter?'

'That's her. Rather a pretty little thing, if a bit dull. Still,' Alec paused for a moment, as if to ascertain her reaction, 'it helps to pass the time of day while we're holed up in this wretched spot.'

A wave of repulsion washed over the woman. She knitted her hands together in an odd gesture that was peculiar to her in times of anguish. Not for the first time, she stared at Alec Dewhurst feeling rather dazed and disgusted. Her head throbbed painfully from worry and a lack of fresh air. The unpleasant thought lingered in her mind that this was the man for whom she had ruined her life. Despite his good looks and transient charm, he seemed to her now rather a sorry specimen of a creature. For she now knew him to be sly, manipulative and fickle. If only she had suspected before that his air of respectability was no more than a cheap veneer. Yet, even now, despite these deficiencies, she felt the same raw tenderness towards him that she had experienced during their initial acquaintance. Averting her gaze, she said rather miserably:

'Must you be so very cruel?'

'Cruel?' Alec feigned a look of surprise. 'I would hardly call it that.' He tossed his tennis racquet carelessly on to a convenient chair. 'I wouldn't say as much to her face, of course. About her being dull and ordinary, I mean, if that's what you're getting at?'

His companion remained silent, turning her gaze instead to the window. It was this action, and not the words of admonishment that preceded it, that had the effect of angering the young man. Interpreting the gesture as a form of dismissal, he glared at her.

'How you have the audacity to call *me* cruel,' he said, his temper rising.

He had no need to elaborate, for his words had the desired effect. The woman spun round, her hand clutched to her breast, her face pale despite the heat.

'Don't,' she cried. 'Please don't. I know you can never forgive me.' Her words were met with a resolute silence. Undeterred, she continued valiantly, though her voice faltered a little and her hands clenched and unclenched. 'I know I don't deserve your forgiveness. If only you knew how very wretched I have been ...' Her sentence died in her throat. Her eyes searched the young man's face.

Alec Dewhurst, in his turn, regarded the duchess with a mixture of scorn and disdain. How easy it was to bring her to heel, he thought. He had only to play on the shame that consumed her. He was half tempted to persist with this form of ill-treatment. On reflection, however, and for no

74

other reason than to further his own ends, he concluded that it might be wise to show a small degree of compassion. After all, these aristocratic types required careful handling. It would not suit his purpose should the wretched woman get it into her head to take to her bed in a fit of sobbing. An unexpected fit of impetuousness and devilment, however, made him suddenly act recklessly.

'The other guests have been enquiring after you. They think it jolly odd that you keep to your rooms. It is causing a great deal of speculation, I can tell you.'

His companion started and said rather helplessly: 'What else can I do?'

'You could join me for dinner this evening.'

The duchess put her hand up to her mouth, as if to stifle a scream. 'But Lord Belvedere –'

'Will keep your secret,' said Alec firmly. 'I can't imagine he'll be anything but civil to you in public.' He noted the look on her face and laughed; it was not a pleasant sound. 'He won't denounce you in front of everyone, if that's what you're worried about.' With a note of contempt, he said: 'I've been studying our dear young earl and he seems a decent sort.'

'You can't ask –'

'Oh, but I do!' cried Alec Dewhurst, a note of urgency creeping into his voice. Met with a face frozen with horror, he decided to change tack, as was his habit with her, and adopt a more gentle approach. 'Look here, don't you see how your continued absence does nothing but draw attention to us? Surely that is not what you want?' She shook her head rather grudgingly. 'I am thinking only of you and your reputation,' he said, putting as much tenderness into his voice as he could muster. He looked at her reaction, sensing he was gaining ground. 'Really, there is nothing to fear. I will introduce you; as my sister, of course. You need only remain a short while. You can retire early feigning a headache or some such ailment.' He held out his hand to her, but she remained where she was by the window. 'Surely you can see that it is for the best?'

Despite his best efforts, he was conscious that the wretched woman was still wavering, drifting between a desire to comply with his wishes and the urge to resist this particular request. He appealed to her vanity.

'I daresay you'll soon have the vicar eating out of your hand, and the Trimble biddy will be quite beside herself that you have deigned to talk to her.'

Still her resistance remained. He could sense its presence as readily as any tangible object. He bit his lip and tried to hide his impatience. Inwardly, he was seething, though outwardly he managed to arrange his features into a pleasant expression. His face ached with the effort, so at odds with his natural feelings. Damn the woman, he thought. He felt the anger surging up inside him. Afraid that it would erupt before he could rein in his temper, he played the card that he always kept up his sleeve for just such contingencies.

'You are ashamed of me. I daresay I could hardly expect anything less and yet ...' He paused a moment, lowering his gaze and adopting a woeful manner. 'You must return to your husband. I doubt any real damage has been done.'

'No!' The Duchess of Grismere sprung forward like some unleashed animal. With wild abandonment, she clutched at his arm. 'You must never say such things. I could no more leave you than ... You know that there is nothing I would not do for you.'

'Very well,' replied Alec Dewhurst, slightly louder than was strictly necessary. He gently disentangled himself from her grasp. 'Join me at dinner tonight.' He phrased the sentence as a statement, rather than a question, now that he was sure of his ground.

His companion remained silent. This fact did not bother him too much, for he knew from her demeanour that he had won this particular battle. And, as was her habit, she would no doubt insist he accept a gold trinket from her. A small token of her affection, as she always called such things. It was rather amusing, when one thought about it, that such gifts should follow a quarrel. It had become something of a ritual. Still, he must be cautious not to overplay his hand. He did not wish her to ask too many questions which might prove awkward to answer, or pry too deeply into his private affairs. That would never do. He gave an involuntary shudder, aware too late that the duchess was eyeing him curiously. He bestowed on her a disarming smile, which had the desired effect. She lowered her guard and some colour returned to her cheeks. Nevertheless, Alec thought, he must tread carefully. With this object in mind, he focused his thoughts on the fortune he was slowly amassing. It produced in him a genuine smile, which was reciprocated by his companion.

He picked up his discarded tennis racquet and, swinging it idly by one hand, made his way leisurely to his bedroom to change. It struck him then how clever he had been. Not for one minute had it occurred to the duchess that he might have had an ulterior motive for requiring her presence at dinner that evening. It had all been accomplished most satisfactorily, and he was just in the act of congratulating himself when he heard a scream.

It came from the sitting room and it was a matter of a few seconds for him to retrace his steps and throw open the door. The spectacle that greeted his eyes rendered him momentarily speechless. When he had left the room only a few moments earlier, the duchess had been perched on the end of the sofa contemplating the ordeal that lay ahead. During his absence, she had apparently leapt up from her seat and was now cowering against the wall furthest from the window, her hands behind her, her fingers pressed hard against the wall. It was obvious, even to the most nonchalant observer, that she was recoiling from some hidden terror. That it lurked outside the building was evident, for her eyes were drawn to the window as if transfixed by some awful apparition.

Alec, following her gaze, ran up to the window, threw open the casement and peered outside. Somewhat to his disappointment, the view afforded him revealed nothing more sinister than the terrace, empty of everything save a scattering of wrought iron tables and chairs. He turned and regarded his companion with something of a quizzical look. She was still staring at the window, her arm outstretched as if she were pointing at some ominous presence.

'There was a man ... I saw his face; it was horrible ...' As Alec took a step forward, as if to comfort her, she added, her lip trembling: 'He ... he had a camera. He ... he was spying on us!'

Chapter Eleven

There was an air of anticipation in the dining room that evening, which infected each guest in turn, like a creeping miasma, as they entered the room. The fact that Alec Dewhurst had not appeared at his usual hour had not gone unnoticed and served only to add to the palpable tension. Perhaps not surprisingly, the first person to comment on the young man's absence was Mabel Adler. Having consulted her wristwatch rather fretfully several times, while adjusting, with one hand, the new pearl earrings that were screwed fetchingly, but rather painfully, to her ears, she declared to her father that the young man was late. Five minutes followed, and then another, and in that time the girl had asked a good seven times: 'What has happened to Mr Dewhurst?'

To begin with, her parent had given this question the due attention it deserved and mumbled a reply which expressed suitable bewilderment. On the eighth time of asking, however, Father Adler's patience had most definitely run out, though he gave no outward sign of this fact. If he appeared a little quieter and reflective that evening, it can hardly be wondered, for Miss Hyacinth's warning was still fresh in his ears. Indeed, he was still reeling from the revelation that Mr Dewhurst was not the respectable young man of wealthy means whom his manners and appearance suggested him to be.

'What –'

'My dear,' said the vicar hastily, fearing that the same question was about to be put to him for the ninth time, 'can we not talk about something else? I am sure that Mr Dewhurst has a perfectly good reason for not being here. Perhaps he is feeling unwell, or his sister has had one of her turns and he is reluctant to leave her by herself.'

'But he promised,' Mabel said petulantly. Even her over indulgent father was reminded of a spoilt child who had failed to get its own way.

'Oh, Vicar,' cried Miss Hyacinth from her table, 'and Mabel, dear, are you quite recovered from your tennis? If you don't mind my saying, you do still look a little flushed. Of course, you must have got frightfully hot playing your game, and really it is quite stifling in here.' She turned to smile fleetingly at Miss Peony. 'I was only saying to my sister that we could do with some more ceiling fans.' She cast a look around the room. 'No Mr Dewhurst this evening, I see?' She looked questioningly at Mabel, but the girl remained silent. She caught the vicar's eye, gave him a meaningful look, and said in a lowered voice which was nevertheless clearly audible: 'Well, I daresay it's for the best.'

'What exactly do you mean by that?' demanded Mabel, scowling, for the exchange of looks between her parent and Miss Hyacinth had not gone unnoticed. Indeed, it had aroused in her a feeling of indignation.

'Oh, nothing, dear,' said Miss Hyacinth hurriedly, fearing a scene in which she would be forced to play a principal part. 'Ah, Lady Lavinia, what a very beautiful dress. Tell me, is that what people call beaded net?' With that, she floated away to the Belvederes' table to examine the gown in question, much to that young woman's delight.

Mabel Adler and Miss Hyacinth were not the only ones to query Alec Dewhurst's absence. Rose had spotted that his table was vacant as soon as she had entered the dining room and had remarked on the fact to her husband.

'I say, do you think they have taken it upon themselves to leave the island?' Cedric asked hopefully, careful to lower his voice so as not to be overhead by Lavinia and Miss Hyacinth, who were still at the table discussing the younger woman's gown. 'Hello? Where's old Vickers? It's not like him not to be here. I suppose he's still in the next room, propping up the hotel bar. I don't know why Kettering … Good lord!'

From Alec Dewhurst's perspective the evening had not begun agreeably. Ever present in the back of his mind was the knowledge that it was only a matter of time before Fleet Street, or her various representatives, descended upon them, and then the game would surely be up. That in itself did not cause him undue anxiety. For one thing, he was rather bored of it all and, for another, it was this evening that mattered to him. What happened after that was almost irrelevant. Besides, if indeed a photograph had been taken, he was safe in the knowledge that it had not captured his image. No, it was not the Peeping Toms of the press that caused him concern as such. More, it was the effect that the sudden appearance of the man at the window had produced on his companion, whose nerves were already on edge.

For such was the duchess' fear of discovery that she had immediately reverted to her original position of refusing to accompany him to dinner. A series of cajoling had followed, predominantly of a bullying nature. And when finally the woman had relented, from sheer exhaustion at Alec's persistent and clumsy efforts to persuade her, as much as for any other reason, she had collapsed resigned on to the sofa, her demeanour very much that of an animal at bay.

Alec Dewhurst eyed her apprehensively, fearing her mood did not bode well for the evening ahead. He glanced impatiently at his gold full hunter pocket watch, one of the many gifts the duchess had given him, his initials engraved flamboyantly on its outer casing. He frowned, for it was later than he had thought. In all likelihood, the other guests would already be seated in the dining room. Above all else, he had not wanted to make a spectacular entrance. Inwardly, he seethed, alternating between cursing what he viewed as the duchess' unreasonable mulishness, and reviling the shadowy figure of the photographer for his ill-timed intervention, which had caused all the consternation.

This exclamation was sufficient to cause Rose to turn in her seat and follow her husband's gaze. Alec Dewhurst had finally appeared in the doorway to the dining room, looking uncommonly agitated. It was not the young man's rattled demeanour or his late entrance, however, that had caused the earl to give a startled cry. Rather, it was the arrival of his companion that had precipitated the exclamation. Rose did not doubt for a moment that it was the duchess, not Miss Dewhurst, who clung rather nervously to Alec Dewhurst's arm, looking for all the world as if the last thing she wanted to do was enter a room full of guests. To Rose's way of thinking, it was a remarkably odd thing for her to do. The woman was either very blasé or very brave, yet her rather pathetic demeanour suggested otherwise. Whatever the reason for her sudden appearance, it afforded Rose an opportunity to study the woman closely, though she took considerable pains not to appear as if she was staring. A quick glance at Lavinia revealed her sister-in-law to have no such qualms, for she was positively gaping at the duchess. Rose cast her a reproachful look which the girl very pointedly ignored. Rose returned her gaze to the duchess. She was a tall, well-groomed woman who appeared to be in her early forties. While she looked remarkably distinguished and had the same fragile, aristocratic beauty that Lavinia possessed, to Rose's eye, she and Alec Dewhurst made an odd couple. It was not just the disparity in ages, but rather that there was something rather flamboyant and gaudy about the young man which was at odds with the reserved and refined creature who clung timorously to his sleeve.

Rose surveyed her fellow diners, careful not to catch Lavinia's eye. She wondered how many of the other guests were staring at the newcomer completely enthralled, doing little to hide their curiosity. Most, she noted, were having difficulty concealing their surprise. The vicar and Miss Hyacinth were staring rather stupidly, their mouths wide open, while Miss Peony was frozen in the act of raising a fork of food to her mouth. Even Ron Thurlow looked rather taken aback by the course of events. Rose felt a stab of pity for the duchess. While it could be argued that she had brought it upon herself, the woman could hardly be oblivious to the fact that her appearance had caused a sudden hush to fall over the room. It occurred to Rose then that, had she taken a revolver from her bag and fired it, the effect could not have been more devastating.

It was Mabel Adler who was the first to recover her wits, possibly for the reason that she alone was ignorant of the woman's real identity. Indeed, if she was aware that an odd silence had befallen the room, then she betrayed no sign. Rather, she gave the impression of having been too deeply absorbed in her own thoughts to notice what happened about her, and it was Alec's appearance, not the duchess', that piqued her interest. Instead of astonishment on observing Alec Dewhurst's companion, the expression on her face was one of mild acceptance. While the other guests merely stared, surprised into a stunned silence, she leapt up from her chair and came forward, her hand outstretched towards the duchess, as if she had every intention of coaxing her to come into the room.

'I can't tell you how much I have been looking forward to meeting you,' said Mabel, with enthusiasm. The woman she addressed merely looked bewildered, as if she had just awoken from a strange dream. It is quite possible, in her eagerness, that the vicar's daughter did not notice her dubious reception, or possibly she did, and that was why she spoke hurriedly. 'Your brother has told me so much about you.' Was she aware that the woman visibly started at this piece of information or that she cast an anxious look at the young man at her side?

'Alec,' Mabel continued, 'pray, won't you introduce us?'

'My dear,' said Alec to the duchess, a little amused by Mabel's enthusiasm, 'may I introduce Miss Adler? Miss Adler ... ,' this followed by a sweeping gesture towards the duchess, 'may I introduce my sister, Miss Dewhurst?'

The introduction, while blatantly false to everyone but Mabel, had the effect of diminishing some of the high tension in the room. For, by introducing the duchess as his sister, Alec Dewhurst had taken the wind out of the sails of those minded to gossip. While it was a pretence, it was at least a palatable one, suggesting as it did that there was no need for any unpleasantness or awkwardness providing everyone saw fit to play the game.

The hotel guests, on the whole, were quite happy to do so, and breathed a collective sigh of relief. They turned to their neighbours and resumed their various conversations. The odd, furtive glance was still cast in the duchess' direction, but there was no accompanying commentary. Even the Misses Trimble were at pains not to be seen to be whispering or pointing, with Miss Hyacinth making quite a performance of reading the menu loudly to her sister.

Rose glanced at her husband. His face was pale under his tan, but even he looked as if he had been given a temporary reprieve from a tricky situation. Lavinia, as was her nature, was bursting with curiosity, though she was evidently trying hard to disguise the fact, her fingers absentmindedly playing with one of her gold filigree earrings. The vicar, it was true, looked a little uncomfortable, like one suffering from indigestion. Mabel had insisted that Alec Dewhurst and the duchess join them at their table for dinner, and it was evident, even to a casual observer, that her father was deliberating on the propriety of the situation, while attempting to make polite conversation.

It was Ron Thurlow's conduct, however, that aroused Rose's interest the most. The young man was as pale as a corpse and was staring down at his plate with a rigid fascination, as if nothing would tempt him to lift his gaze from the crockery. For a moment, she wondered if he were merely deep in thought, and so unconscious of his surroundings. A minute or two later, and she had the distinct and unsettling impression that he was almost afraid to lift his head. Whether this was because he feared being seen or dreaded what he might see she was unable to determine. What was patently obvious, however, was that the young man wished above all else not to be there in the dining room while Alec Dewhurst and the duchess were present.

A sudden laugh, high and a little affected, drew Rose's attention back to the Adlers' table. She turned in her chair to catch Mabel chattering happily to the duchess, very much in the manner of one speaking to an old friend rather than to a new acquaintance. In contrast, the duchess, she noted with interest, was saying very little, allowing the younger woman to lead the conversation, while she nodded in a listless fashion, which suggested that either the subject being discussed was of little interest to her, or she was barely listening to what was being said. Like Ron, she gave the impression of wishing to be elsewhere, her cheeks white save for two spots of vivid scarlet, her fingers worrying at her rings. Every so often, she gave a surreptitious little look in Cedric's direction, careful not to catch his eye, worried perhaps, despite Alec Dewhurst's fine and confident introduction, that the earl meant to denounce her.

Had she seen fit to enquire, Rose would have told her that she had nothing to fear with regard to her husband. Cedric was not a mean-spirited young man. He had no wish to cause the woman offence or embarrassment; he had no intention of humiliating her. Even so, Rose fervently hoped that Alec Dewhurst would not see fit to insist on extending the introductions and introducing the duchess to the Belvederes as his sister. She did not doubt that Cedric was quite capable of carrying off the deception, though it would be awkward for all concerned. Rather, it was how Lavinia would manage the charade. Knowing the girl as she did, she doubted her capable of maintaining a straight face. More than likely, Lavinia would dissolve into a fit of the giggles.

It rather amused her to see that Miss Hyacinth, at the urgent persuasion of Miss Peony, was gingerly edging her way towards the Adlers' table, presumably either in search of an introduction to the imposter, or to obtain a better look at the duchess.

'What a beautiful pocket watch, Mr Dewhurst,' exclaimed Mabel. Only a minute before Alec had withdrawn the gold watch from his pocket and made a great show of consulting it. In so doing, he had caught Mabel's eye and smiled. She had stretched out her hand towards the object, much in the manner of an inquisitive child, determined on examining it. Her eyes had widened appreciatively as she had studied the watch, which was encrusted with diamonds that glittered in the candlelight.

Was it Rose's imagination, or did Miss Peony make a quick move to draw her sister back? Certainly, an odd expression crossed the older woman's face. Miss Hyacinth, however, was not to be deterred in her mission. Somewhat fascinated, Rose watched Mabel turn the pocket watch over in her hand, apparently counting the diamonds. 'Five, six …' began Mabel. The duchess was sufficiently vexed by this action to say by way of protest: 'Oberon –'

She was met with a steely glare of such ferocity from Alec that she did not finish her sentence, but instead seemed to withdraw stung, back into her chair. Mabel, looking up at that moment, caught something of the exchange of looks between the two. It is possible that she was merely taken by surprise, or perhaps on reflection she thought her actions had been too forward or over familiar, that the picking up of the watch and studying it with such relish had been vulgar and gauche. Whatever the reason, something persuaded her that she should return it at once to Alec's possession. In fact, that nothing was more important than that she do so. Clearly flustered, and hurrying in her efforts, her actions consequently were clumsy. It was hardly a surprise then when the pocket watch slipped from her fingers and rolled on to the floor.

There followed a shocked silence, and then something of a mad scramble to retrieve it, as if everyone wished to know the worst in respect of any damage. Miss Hyacinth, who was standing not far from the watch, made a grab for it. Ron Thurlow, however, proved too quick for her, for he was out of his chair and had pounced on it before she had moved a couple of steps. Every eye was on him as he turned the watch over in his hand. Not a breath could be heard as he examined the watch's outer casing. Meanwhile, the other hotel guests calculated the likely destruction. There had been no sound of breaking glass, and the watch had fallen on to the woven rug rather than on to the marble floor.

'No harm's been done,' declared Ron. However, he made no move to return the pocket watch. Instead, he continued studying it as if it held for him a particular fascination.

'If I might have it back, there's a good chap,' said Alec, rising from his seat, a note of coldness in his voice.

Ron did not stir. With one quick movement, Alec snatched the watch from Ron's grasp.

'Did you check the movement?' asked Father Adler rather timidly, no doubt afraid that his daughter would be held liable for any damage.'

'It looks fine,' replied Alec rather brusquely, giving the watch a cursory glance before stuffing it without ceremony into his pocket.

'I say, I'm awfully sorry,' said Mabel, her face a deep shade of crimson. 'I can't think what's the matter with me, I seem to be all fingers and thumbs.'

Alec turned and bestowed on her a smile of such sweet intensity that the girl blushed afresh. 'There's no harm done,' he said softly, repeating Ron's words.

Was it Rose's imagination, or did his fingers touch Mabel's and linger on them for a moment? She could hardly believe that they did. For Alec Dewhurst did not strike her as a foolish young man. In certain circumstances she could imagine he might be reckless, daring even. Indeed, had he not acted rashly in eloping with the duchess? But to make so intimate a gesture towards another woman in his lover's presence … why, surely it was an act close to madness? And yet, she had not been mistaken. Mabel's animated face, with its dewy eyes and chin jutted up at an angle so that she might better study her suitor, was clue enough. It revealed to Rose that the girl, at least, held Alec Dewhurst in high affectionate regard.

She turned her gaze next towards the vicar and the duchess. It was quite inconceivable that the actions and displays of affection had gone unnoticed by either of them. To her fanciful mind, the duchess appeared pale and agitated, while Father Adler looked decidedly ill at ease, as if something were troubling him.

The hotel guests had all but forgotten Mr Vickers. His absence had initially been commented upon vaguely, as an observation rather than as a matter of interest. Indeed, his vacant table had generated very few glances. The general view of those seated in the dining room was that he was a most disagreeable fellow and dinner was immeasurably improved by his not being present. It was, therefore, quite likely that his late appearance in the dining room would not have been particularly noted or remarked upon had the man in question not stumbled into a chair and sent it flying. The resounding clatter of the wooden chair on the marble floor caused all eyes to be turned on him momentarily. A servant ran to right the chair as Mr Vickers staggered to his table, apparently oblivious to the reproving frowns and reproachful looks cast in his direction.

It was evident to all those present that the man was inebriated. Even his physical appearance that evening looked particularly dishevelled, as if he had rushed his toilet in his eagerness to assault the hotel bar. Bleary eyed and unkempt, he made a sorry picture, and the hotel guests soon wrinkled their noses and averted their gaze, as if the man were some unpleasant vapour. It seemed only Rose stared at him perplexed. For it occurred to her that, while his slovenly outward appearance suggested otherwise, a light had suddenly entered the unfocused eyes. He had paused in the act of sitting down and looked about him, all at once alert, as if he had caught a fleeting whiff of something more intoxicating than liquor. Certainly, she could not be mistaken that there was something furtive and surreptitious about his movements now. Instinctively, Rose glanced towards the duchess. A quick look back at Mr Vickers was enough to show her that the woman was also in his sights.

Afterwards, she wondered if the duchess felt their eyes upon her, for in that instant the woman turned and, caught somewhat unawares by Mr Vickers' penetrating stare, she let out a startled scream.

'That's him!' she cried, clutching at Alec's sleeve. Met with a bewildered gaze from her companion, she added for clarity: 'That's the man. The one who was peering in at my window!'

Chapter Twelve

'Was it by Jove!' said Alec, advancing on Mr Vickers in a dramatic fashion. It is possible that he had thought the face at the window was no more than a figment of his companion's vivid imagination. Now it appeared there was some substance behind the notion that they were being spied upon. He felt himself possessed by a feeling of righteous anger. It did not help matters that he had never taken to Mr Vickers, whom he had readily dismissed as insignificant.

'Well, and what have you to say for yourself, my man?' he demanded, towering over the scrawny figure. Mr Vickers made no attempt to answer him. Instead, he blinked very rapidly and took a great gulp of air. 'What, has the cat got your tongue?' Alec said unpleasantly. It was apparent that he was finding the little man's continuing silence infuriating for he proceeded to prod Mr Vickers painfully in the chest. Mr Vickers winced and emitted a pitiful cry. 'Answer me, you sorry specimen of a man,' continued Alec, between breaths, his hands now about Mr Vickers' collar, as if he had in mind to shake the truth from him. 'Why, you pathetic little —'

'That will do, Dewhurst,' said Cedric, himself advancing on to the scene. 'There are women present.' He looked first at Mr Vickers and then glared at Alec. 'Can't you see the man's frightened half to death?'

'It serves him right if he is. It's no more than he deserves,' replied Alec savagely, though he loosened his grip on the man's collar. Mr Vickers, taking advantage of this temporary reprieve, withdrew a few steps and toppled in to a table.

'Eh, what are you playing at?' he complained, feeling his neck tenderly. 'Can't a man come in here and get his dinner without being set upon?'

'Be quiet,' said Cedric quickly, fearing the man's words would only seek to fan the flames and drive Alec Dewhurst to a further display of violence. 'Is it true what her ... her ...', he paused awkwardly, 'Miss Dewhurst says?'

'No, it ain't,' declared Mr Vickers, all traces of class and breeding having left his speech. 'It's a dirty lie, that's what it is.'

'The man's a Peeping Tom,' said Alec. 'Why, I've a good mind to –'

'Are you a pressman?' demanded Cedric.

Was it Rose's imagination, or did the little man look genuinely surprised at the question? Certainly, his: 'No I ain't, my lord,' was uttered with considerable conviction.

'A journalist?' cried the duchess, putting a hand up to her mouth as if to stifle another scream. She rose from the table, hurried forward, and clutched again at the young man's sleeve. 'Ober ... Alec, I believe he had a camera ... of course, I might have imagined it, but if he had ...' For one awful moment, she looked as if she might crumple and faint, but at the last minute she managed to compose herself.

'Well, 'said Cedric, turning to Mr Vickers, 'do you have a camera?'

The little man made no reply, but merely scowled. Some of the colour had left his flushed cheeks, and he appeared more sober now, but for the fact that he swayed a little on his feet, though whether from fear or liquor, it was hard to tell.

'Answer him, damn you!' cried Alec Dewhurst. He took a step forward and made as if to grab the man's shirt. Mr Vickers instinctively took a step back and crouched behind the earl's tall, reassuring form. An ugly smile appeared on Alec's face and he raised his hand as if he had it in mind to strike the man. Miss Hyacinth shrieked and Mr Vickers cowered even further behind Cedric.

'I've a good mind to –' began Alec Dewhurst.

'That's enough, Dewhurst,' Cedric said hastily, making sure that he was standing firmly between the two men to form an effective barrier. 'Let me speak to Kettering and find out which is this man's room. I'll get him to open the door and I'll have a look for the camera myself. 'No,' he said firmly, as Alec made to follow him. 'You stay here. And you,' he said, turning to address Mr Vickers, 'had better come with me.' He lowered his voice a little before adding: 'If only for your own safety.'

Alec glared at the young earl and made to protest, but evidently thought better of it. At the back of his mind it occurred to him that he had made rather a spectacle of himself. A quick glance at Mabel informed him that the girl had been somewhat shocked by the vulgar nature of his performance, and indeed her father was making efforts to encourage his daughter to retire to their rooms. All his efforts were about to come undone, and though there was a part of him that was tempted to stand his ground and even land a punch on the little man's wretched cheek, he forced himself to turn his back on Mr Vickers and resume his seat, his splendid mask in place and his features set in a smile, if a little strained.

With the young man's withdrawal from the scene, Mr Vickers seemed to gain some confidence. 'You ain't got nothing on me, you haven't, my lord,' he informed Cedric, in a whiny voice, as the younger man steered him by the arm towards the door. 'I can have a camera just the same as the next man. And I'm blowed if I'll let you take it from me. A present it was, from my missus, and mighty riled she'll be if I come home without it.' He bowed his head towards the earl and, in something of a genuflecting fashion which Cedric found repulsive, said: 'And that's not all. There's a thing or two I could tell you about that one, I could.' He jerked his head towards Alec Dewhurst as he spoke, who was engaged in conversation with Miss Adler. 'Dewhurst ain't his name, I can tell you that.'

'I never thought it was,' said Cedric, somewhat brusquely, attempting to take some of the wind out of the older man's sails.

'No, I doubt you did,' admitted Mr Vickers, somewhat grudgingly, before brightening and saying with a leer: 'Still, I'll wager you can't guess his surname.' He looked eagerly at Cedric, but it was evident from the young man's expression that he had no intention of participating in such a game. 'Well, I'll tell you anyway,' continued Mr Vickers, determined to say his full pennyworth. 'Goodfellow, that's what it is, and if a man weren't more unlike his name, I haven't met him.' Not receiving the response he desired from the earl, he repeated the surname, this time speaking more loudly and with greater emphasis: 'Goodfellow.'

'Do shut up, there's a good chap,' Cedric said hurriedly, rather afraid that Mr Vickers' voice had carried to the Adlers' table, not to mention to the Trimble sisters, whom he knew would be staring agog.

A furtive, backward glance at Alec Dewhurst confirmed Cedric's worst fears. The young man had evidently been in the act of sipping from his wine glass when Mr Vickers' 'Goodfellow' had caught him unawares and caused him to make a sudden, involuntary movement. The sound of ringing glass could be distinctly heard. For Alec's glass had slipped from his fingers and fallen, clattering noisily on to his plate. The young man had been quick to correct the oversight, picking up the glass and signalling to a servant to attend to the spilt wine. Neither glass nor crockery had been broken and, but for the slight trembling of Alec's hand, it appeared to a casual observer that not very much damage had been done. But Cedric was anything but an uninterested observer. A vivid red wine stain had appeared on the white table linen which had an uncanny resemblance to a bloodstain. For a fleeting moment, Alec Dewhurst had regarded it, as if transfixed. Even the duchess had appeared intrigued by it. A frown creased her lovely forehead, marring the aristocratic beauty and causing her features, though illuminated by candlelight, to pale.

Even for Cedric, frogmarching Mr Vickers to the door, the wine stain had held a strange fascination, and, while speaking to the hotel proprietor on the matter of the camera, he was surprised to find that a vision of the spoiled tablecloth lingered in his mind. He was not to know then that the image was destined to haunt him in the days to come. Had he done so, there was no doubt he would have averted his gaze.

To Rose, impatiently awaiting her husband's return, the evening seemed to evolve with a dogged slowness. With the somewhat unceremonious departure of Mr Vickers, the evening had followed its habitual form, culminating in the usual music and dancing. The duchess' unexpected appearance in the dining room, while at the outset causing some interest, had soon been all but forgotten, for the woman in question had withdrawn as soon as her meal was over, citing a headache.

Even Lavinia, after initially displaying much interest in the duchess, had soon become bored with the woman, for it had become evident that the duchess would not be drawn into making an exhibition of herself, even though the majority of those present thought she would be justified given the very blatant displays of affection between Mabel Adler and Alec Dewhurst. That the duchess preferred to withdraw into herself, and all but fade into the background, rather diminished her as an object of interest to the other guests, as if she were not the same woman who had graced the society pages or been the subject of national speculation.

It was a warm night and, despite the French windows being thrown open to admit the night air, the atmosphere within the dining room, a giddy mix of artificial light, music and alcohol, was, to Rose's mind at least, stifling. She gazed impatiently at her wristwatch, wondering when Cedric would return. A quick glance at the dance floor informed her that

Lavinia was occupied in dancing with Ron Thurlow, with whom even Lavinia had felt some sympathy. Indeed, it had caused the aristocrat to put aside any considerations of class, enabling her to dance with him as an equal partner. A smile passed Rose's lips. Knowing her friend as she did, she could never imagine such a scenario happening in England where Lavinia would be happily ensconced with people of her own class.

To Rose, with her relatively humble beginnings, the relaxed atmosphere of Skiathos with respect to society, proved refreshing. The thought occurred to her then that the duchess might find it equally so. This was not an island on which her conduct would be judged too harshly, and where she might associate freely with a man who was so obviously from a lower class than herself. With this in mind and satisfying herself that she would not be missed should she take a brief stroll out on the terrace, Rose gathered her oriental silk shawl about her shoulders and ventured outside.

What struck her at first was how still and quiet it was. The noise of the cicadas made no impression on her; for they were now so familiar to her and as much a part of the Greek island as the waves that lapped the shore. Away from the music and chatter, the island loomed up before her as a calm, still sanctuary. The knowledge that it would be quieter still beyond the terrace persuaded her to venture further afield despite the darkness. Never had the island felt threatening to her, even now as she left the safety of the hotel building and moved in the semi darkness through the formal gardens towards the tennis courts. She was vaguely aware of the rustle of the wind in the leaves or the odd twig being snapped by a bird or small animal as they set out on their nocturnal journeys.

It certainly never occurred to her that she might have been followed, that her departure from the dining room had been observed and acted upon. It was, therefore, a little while before she became aware of the sound of footsteps behind her, quiet and hurried, like some scuttling animal afraid of being detected by its prey. The idea that she was not alone crept up on her slowly, until it gathered momentum. It caused her to stop and turn around half afraid of what she might discover. Indeed, it was while she was still considering why anyone should wish to stalk her in so furtive a manner that a figure loomed up out of the darkness. It was all she could do to stifle the scream that leapt so readily to her lips, as she gathered her shawl about her as if it were a shield capable of warding off danger.

'Please forgive me, your ladyship. I didn't mean to startle you.'

Rose had never heard the voice before, and yet, though the figure was still partially concealed by the shadows that edged the path, she knew instinctively to whom the voice belonged. The speaker's deferential words might suggest otherwise, yet to be accosted in so direct a manner suggested a confidence prevalent in the higher ranks of society. There was no doubt in Rose's mind, therefore, that the person who addressed her in so subservient yet self-assured a fashion was none other than the duchess. The woman was her social superior and yet it appeared, at least from her initial words, that she intended to continue the charade of being plain Miss Dewhurst.

When considering her own behaviour afterwards, Rose justified it to herself reasoning that she had not wished to be complicit in playing the duchess' childish game. In addition she had found the notion of being spied upon rather repugnant, incurring in her as it had done a momentary sense of fear and indignation in equal measure. Before she could stop herself, therefore, or consider the consequences, she had found herself addressing the woman by her true title and with undue abruptness.

'How do you do, your grace?'

The woman started visibly. Had Rose struck her physically, the effect of her words could not have been more shattering. For even in the darkness, Rose was aware that one of the woman's hands flew to her mouth, while the other clutched at her heart in a gesture which Rose considered, at the time, to be overly dramatic.

'Then ... then you know who I am?' the woman stuttered as soon as she could find the words to express her disbelief.

'My husband recognised you the night you appeared at the window with your ... companion,' Rose replied, a trifle awkwardly, aware that she had acted rather clumsily, but also of the view that the woman was being unnecessarily theatrical. 'You recognised him too, I think, the Earl of Belvedere?'

'Yes ... yes, of course,' the woman admitted quietly, and a trifle reluctantly, as if she found the recollection of her arrival at the hotel distasteful. 'It was only that I hoped, indeed thought ... he would keep my secret. I daresay it was frightfully naïve of me, but –'

'You were not wrong in supposing that he would,' said Rose,

somewhat coldly, resenting the woman's implication that Cedric's conduct had fallen short of her expectations. 'He has told no one but myself.' The woman made no comment concerning this act of chivalry and, in her indignation, Rose added, somewhat angrily: 'In fact, my husband has been at great pains to persuade the other guests that you are *not* the Duchess of Grismere when it is so obvious to everyone that you are. Really, I can't tell you what a fruitless task it has been given that your photograph has appeared in every newspaper!'

Her anger died as quickly as it had flared up, and immediately she felt ashamed of her behaviour. She had allowed herself to be riled by the duchess' haughty manner, which even now she felt was in evidence despite the darkness which acted as an effective camouflage. Still, her outburst had shown her in a poor light and, being naturally kind hearted and of a charitable disposition, she had no wish to cause offence. Before Rose could make amends, however, the duchess spoke in a low voice full of contrition.

'You were quite right to admonish me,' she said. 'Oh dear. I fear that we have started off on the wrong foot. Do you think it possible that we might begin again?'

'I don't see why not,' said Rose, though there was still something about the woman's manner that she found irksome. Later, on reflection, she thought it was the older woman's certainty that she would comply with her wishes. 'Perhaps you would tell me why you were following me? Did you wish to ask me about anything in particular?'

The directness of Rose's question seemed to startle the woman. Instead of becoming annoyed, however, she appeared flustered, knitting her hands together in that odd gesture that was peculiar to her in times of anguish.

'No ... Yes ... By that, I mean, I had decided to take a stroll before retiring to bed, when I happened to notice you on the path leading past the tennis courts. I thought it would be a good opportunity to speak with you without the risk of being observed.'

'By your companion or by the other guests?' asked Rose, before she could stop herself.

'By the other guests, of course. Why should it matter if Oberon ... Alec, sees me talking to you?'

'Not at all, I should imagine,' said Rose, interested in the duchess' slip of the tongue, though having no desire to pursue it at that moment. For, if truth be told, she was keen to end this strange, unsettling interview as soon as possible and return to the populated dining room and to Cedric, who even now was no doubt wondering where she was. Her curiosity, however, suddenly got the better of her and she asked hurriedly, before she could change her mind:

'Why did you wish to speak with me?'

'I was wondering if his lordship had any news of my husband? By that, I mean, does he know if he's ... he's well?'

Whatever Rose had expected the duchess to say, it had not been this. Caught unawares, she spoke more bluntly than she had intended. 'You would like to know how he is bearing up?'

'Yes, I suppose I do. It sounds rather awful when one puts it like that, doesn't it? Of course, it never occurred to me that my disappearing as I did would cause such a great scandal.'

'Didn't it?' said Rose, not totally convinced by the woman's words, though admittedly she sounded fairly earnest.

'No,' said the duchess firmly, perhaps sensing some of the other woman's cynicism. 'I thought my husband would say I was ... I was just visiting friends. I can't tell you how I wish he had.'

'And yet it is your husband, rather than the scandal, that concerns you the most?'

'Well, of course it is. What sort of a person do you take me for? No, don't answer that,' said the duchess, a flash of anger in her voice. 'You have made up your mind what sort of a woman I am, and you will not help me.'

'Why should you require me to help you?' asked Rose, somewhat perplexed by the woman's odd behaviour.

'Can't you see how wretched I am?'

It seemed such an odd thing for the duchess to say that there followed an awkward silence.

'If you are upset,' said Rose at last, finding something rather repulsive in the woman's self-pity, 'then really you have only yourself to blame.'

'Indeed?' Again there was that odd flash of anger.

'By that I mean how did you expect the society pages to react to your vanishing like that?' Fearing another uncomfortable silence, or worse, open hostility, she added; 'Rather than feeling sorry for yourself, you should give a thought to your husband. From what I hear, he has aged dreadfully. Indeed, Lady Lavinia Sedgwick informs me he is little more than a recluse. Really, if anyone has a right to feel wretched, it is your husband!'

Chapter Thirteen

As soon as the words had left her mouth, Rose cursed herself for having been so outspoken, yet there was something in the duchess' manner that piqued her. Still, she had not meant to speak so unkindly, and she felt it was up to her to extend the olive branch and put an end to this strange animosity that had sprung up so oddly between them. It did not make her feel any better about her handling of the situation to realise that the reason for the continuing silence was that the duchess was crying bitterly.

'I'm sorry,' Rose said gently, taking a step forward.

She fumbled in the darkness and took the other woman's hand in hers. Their nearness meant that she could now distinguish the duchess' features clearly. For the first time, she became a real flesh and blood person. The woman's beauty, if there had ever been any, was extinguished by the strained expression on her face and the dark smudges underneath her eyes, which emphasised the fine lines around her eyes and lips. They seemed to age her together with the ashen pallor of her skin.

'That was beastly of me,' said Rose, conscious that she had only contributed to the duchess' wan appearance. 'I had no right to upset you like that. I don't know what came over me and made me behave as I did.'

The duchess sniffed and a tear trickled down her cheek. She said: 'Is my husband really ill?'

'I'm afraid I can't say for certain. Though I believe he has taken your leaving him rather badly,' admitted Rose, fearing another batch of tears. 'Indeed, my husband hardly recognised him when he met him at his club the other day. I believe he misses you dreadfully.' The detective in her got the upper hand and she said: 'My husband says you left him a note.'

'Yes, I did,' said the duchess, drying her tears with the edge of a lace handkerchief. 'But it was so difficult to know what exactly to write. By that, I mean, I could hardly tell him the truth.'

'Couldn't you?' said Rose. 'Wouldn't it have been kinder to hear the truth from you instead of reading a scandalised version of it in the penny press?'

The duchess' eyes widened in fear. 'There is no reason for the press to know anything about it unless …' Her sentence trailed off, incomplete.

'My husband and I refuse to keep quiet?' supplied Rose. 'Is that what you were about to say?'

'I should not have put it as crudely as that,' said the duchess, rallying a little of her spirit.

'No,' said Rose, 'but it is what you meant, all the same.'

It seemed to her that they were going around in circles and lashing out at one another in a dreadful fashion. Why did this woman infuriate her so? Was it because she seemed intent on perpetuating her own unhappiness? Rose, recognising that it was up to her to take herself in hand, took a deep breath and said:

'Look here, it is most unfortunate that we have come across one another like this. Neither Lord Belvedere nor I are out to cause you any harm, but you must understand that the Duke of Grismere is by way of being an acquaintance of my husband. It places his lordship in a difficult position. He will see it as his duty to inform the duke that we encountered you during our travels.'

'Will he see it as his duty to tell him about … Mr Dewhurst?'

'If pressed,' said Rose, choosing her words carefully, 'I think he will feel obliged to tell your husband that you had a companion.'

'I see.' There was something rather pathetic in the way the duchess said these two words, as if the fight had quite gone out of her, and she was now resigned to leading a life of melancholy.

'Look here,' said Rose. 'It is quite obvious to me that you still care for your husband. It would be much better if you told him what you have done rather than that he hear it from someone else, particularly from the scandal sheets. Why not write to him?'

The duchess shuddered. 'I … I should rather die than do that. My husband is a very proud man. He would never forgive me.'

'Very probably,' said Rose, losing some of her patience, 'but it does not mean that you have to remain here with … with your companion, does it? If you feel quite wretched, as you say you do, why don't you leave him? You needn't return home to England if you'd rather not. You could stay on the Continent.'

'Leave Alec?' The duchess sounded horrified. Indeed, she uttered the words with such passion that Rose was rather taken aback by this raw display of emotion. That the woman truly loved Alec Dewhurst had not occurred to her, and yet why should she find it so surprising? Why else would the duchess have left a supposedly happy marriage and privileged existence to form a liaison with a rather worthless young man who seemed to lack any sense of integrity? The more she thought about it, the more bewildering it seemed. She could not imagine that Alec Dewhurst could hold any more than a fleeting attraction for the duchess. Certainly, he did not seem the type of man a woman such as the Duchess of Grismere would lose her head over. It was then that another thought occurred to her.

'Are you afraid that he might stoop to blackmail?' she asked quietly. 'Are there … letters?'

'Letters?' For a moment the duchess appeared startled. A minute later, and she had regained some of her composure. 'Of course there are letters,' she said, rather angrily, Rose thought. 'A great many of them as it happens. But Mr Dewhurst would never lower himself to that. You … you have no right to think such a thing of him.'

It appeared to Rose that she had every right to suppose such a thing, particularly in light of the way Alec Dewhurst was carrying on with Mabel Adler under their very noses. Indeed, she was sorely tempted to say something to that effect, but on reflection thought better of it. An uneasy silence prevailed as each woman wondered in her own way how their strange, rather candid conversation would end. It was while they were deep in their own thoughts that they became aware, in the same instant, that they no longer had the darkness to themselves.

It was the laughter that they heard first, quickly followed by words uttered in urgent whispers, and accompanied by hurried footsteps. Rose did not need to see the faces of the newcomers to know that Alec Dewhurst and Mabel Adler were approaching. She cast a worried look in the direction of the duchess, wondering how the woman would react to the situation. The growing darkness obscured the duchess' features, but even so Rose had the impression that the woman tensed, as if all her senses were sharpened for the awful revelation that the man she loved was no more than a common cad. Indeed, Rose herself waited with almost bated breath, as if the inevitable discovery of betrayal was as much her own tragedy as it was the duchess'.

The inevitable moment came when Alec Dewhurst took the young woman in his arms. Rose felt the duchess stiffen beside her, but she heard no cry of anguish or sharp intake of breath. Indeed, it was almost as if the duchess had become a wax effigy, so lifeless did she seem. Before Rose could think quite what to do for the best, the situation resolved itself in a way by Alec Dewhurst and Mabel Adler, oblivious to the two women's presence, rushing past them towards the cliff.

As the two women stood reeling, Rose wondered which one of them would be the first to speak. It now seemed to her unnecessary to describe to the duchess the sort of man she thought the woman's lover to be. There would be no need for her to urge the duchess to leave her companion, for the woman had witnessed with her own eyes his fickle, disreputable nature. That the duchess might be in a state of acute agitation, she did not doubt. While she might well have harboured vague suspicions concerning her lover's character, to have his flaws paraded before her in no uncertain terms was beyond the pale. It occurred to Rose then that the kindest course of action might be to squeeze the woman's hand sympathetically and slip away, leaving the duchess to her own contemplations. She was quite unprepared, therefore, for the words that sprung defiantly from the lips of her companion.

'I shall never leave him,' the duchess said quietly, but with such an intensity of feeling it almost took Rose's breath away. Perhaps fearing opposition, she added, almost as an afterthought: 'The girl does not mean anything to him. It will come to nothing.'

'You may well be right,' said Rose, regaining some of her composure but with incipient anger, 'yet does it not bother you that Mr Dewhurst is willing to humiliate you in front of the other guests for his own ends?'

Her words were met with a mulish silence that she found infuriating. It was almost as if the duchess had wrapped herself in a cocoon and was refusing to see the truth that was staring so blatantly at her. It occurred to Rose that if all else failed she might appeal to the woman's pride. Yet, like Miss Hyacinth, she was reminded of the old proverb that there were none so blind as those who would not see. On reflection, therefore, she decided to change tack.

'If you will not think of yourself, then at least have a care for Miss Adler.'

'Miss Adler? Do you mean that girl?'

'Yes. Miss Adler is under the impression that you are Mr Dewhurst's sister. Indeed, your … your companion has made a point of introducing you to her as such. She is unworldly and does not know the type of man he is. No doubt she has some romantic notion that –'

'What of it?' said the duchess. 'What is it to me?'

The woman's tone was dismissive, verging on indifference. Rose's focus, however, was only on the duchess' apparent selfishness. At no time during their conversation had the woman shown herself to consider anyone but herself. Even when she spoke of Alec Dewhurst, it was only in terms of her feelings for him rather than of the man himself. It seemed to Rose, regarding the woman in the darkness, that she was intent on wallowing in a pit of self-imposed disenchantment. Indeed, it was patently obvious that she intended to do nothing to aid her own plight or that of anyone else affected by the actions of Alec Dewhurst. This sudden realisation produced in Rose a feeling of righteous anger, the effect of which was that she was induced to speak more freely and harshly than she intended, all her pent-up frustration with the woman exploding in a torrent from her lips.

'Must you think only of yourself?' she demanded, her voice raised. 'Would you have him ruin the poor girl's reputation as he has ruined your own?'

Apart from a sharp intake of breath, her words were met with an angry silence. Even in the darkness, Rose was aware that the duchess blinked at her rapidly, her face taut. Rose admonished herself for having spoken so harshly. It was not helped by the stillness that followed which she felt certain both women were finding unbearable, punctuated as it was only by the faint sound of the waves lapping the shore in the distance and the ever-persistent humming of the cicadas.

'I'm sorry,' said Rose. 'I should not have spoken as I did.'

'You do not understand,' said the duchess, at last. The haughtiness had returned to her voice and some of the colour to her face. 'I am not quite the awful woman you suppose me to be, and Alec … Alec is not the man you think he is. You judge us both too harshly. If you only knew the truth …' Her words faltered, as if she was overcome by a sudden tiredness, or was half afraid to continue her sentence. Indeed, Rose had the odd impression that she was trembling, though whether from fear or from emotion, she could not tell.

Fearing another wretched silence, Rose said quickly; 'Then why don't you tell it to me, the truth I mean? It's possible that I can help you. It's obvious that you are miserable, why –'

'Oh, what does it matter anyway?' the duchess said, clearly bored by the conversation, though a note of desperation had crept into her voice. 'You have made up your mind about me. No, please don't say another word. There is nothing you can do. There is nothing anyone can do.'

She broke off from what she was saying, for again there was the sound of footsteps. This time the two women instinctively drew apart so that only Rose was visible on the path, the duchess having retreated to the relative safety of the shadows cast by the bushes.

'Ah, darling, there you are,' came the welcome sound of Cedric's voice. 'I wondered where you'd got to. Lavinia didn't see you leave. I thought it unlikely you'd have retired for the night without telling her.'

Rose gave a quick, furtive glance at the bushes. She could no longer make out the figure of the duchess in the darkness. It was possible, she supposed, that the woman, fearing the awkwardness of meeting the earl under such strained circumstances, had decided to disappear further into the bushes to await their departure.

'I'm sorry I've been an age,' Cedric was saying, He had taken Rose's arm and was steering her back towards the hotel. Rose had a sudden vision of the duchess crouching in the dark, miserable and wretched. It occurred to her then that if she and Cedric made a short detour and walked instead in the direction of the tennis courts, and perhaps lingered there for a moment or two to take in the night air, the duchess would have an opportunity to make her way back to her own rooms unobserved. Quite oblivious to his wife's musings, Cedric allowed himself to be propelled unceremoniously, and without objection, towards the tennis courts.

'That Vickers fellow,' he said, 'is a querulous sort. He talks the most frightful rot, I can tell you. Kept telling me that Dewhurst is a petty thief who goes by the name of Goodfellow. Of course, I didn't believe a word of it and I told him as much. Anyway, Kettering's given him his marching orders. He's to leave the hotel first thing tomorrow after breakfast.'

'Did you find his camera?' enquired Rose.

'Oh yes, it was there all right. Kettering's put it in a sort of safe. Our man Vickers made quite a fuss about it, I can tell you. He's an unpleasant sort, and no mistake. The sooner he's left the hotel, the better.'

They retraced their steps to the terrace and the dining room loomed in front of them, lit up by its giant chandeliers. The hotel band was still playing and the music drifted out to them enticingly. Had she been in a different mood, Rose would not have given the duchess another thought but drifted into the room and danced. But the odd encounter among the shadows had affected her, and she could not rid herself of the feeling that she had, to some extent, been at fault. The duchess had reached out to her and she had done very little to alleviate the woman's suffering. If anything, she had only made matters worse. She wondered what it was about the woman that had antagonised her so.

Later, it occurred to her that had she acted differently, events might have taken a different turn, and the old proverb was to return to taunt her. For she was to realise too late that, of all of them gathered at Hotel Hemera, the one that had been truly blind had been herself.

Chapter Fourteen

The figure made its way stealthily across the hotel terrace. It was pitch black but he was familiar with the route and, though he was forced to grope his way blindly, he did not stumble. Rather, the darkness was his ally, cloaking him in a sheet of black. Even those hotel guests who kept late hours and might happen to glance sleepily out of their windows before retiring for the night would be ignorant of the fact that he was there. Of course, he had not chanced entirely to luck; that was not his way. He had made a point of studying the route in the daylight so that he might tread it easily at night when he was encumbered not only by the darkness but by his various treasured possessions, which, while small and light in themselves, seemed oddly to weigh him down heavily as if they were a manacle around his neck. Was it guilt, he wondered, that hung in the air about him? Was it what remained of his tattered conscience reminding him that what he had accrued had been achieved by deception?

It was only when he had cleared the terrace that it occurred to him that had he thought it all out properly, as he was wont to do, he would have packed up all his things in advance and had them sent down secretly to the boat, for he did not doubt for a moment that some of the servants could be bribed. Still, it was no use thinking about that now. What was done, was done and he must look forward. To a certain extent, things had gone to plan, if matters had to be rushed and hurried somewhat, so be it.

Somewhere, a few feet away, a twig snapped. In the ordinary course of things such an occurrence would barely have registered in his consciousness, but tonight for some odd reason he felt strangely apprehensive and jumpy. There was no reason why he should feel alarmed and yet he sensed that danger lay waiting for him as distinctly as if it had tapped him on the shoulder and called out his name. Such a notion was ridiculous, of course. He was not usually given to flights of fancy, and the thought that he was in the grip of some irrational fear annoyed him. He did not see it as a sign that something was amiss. His senses were heightened and yet he cursed the fact, as if it were some wretched inconvenience. Still, the broken twig had unnerved him and, despite himself, he quickened his pace. More to occupy his mind than anything else, he endeavoured to engage his thoughts on the task at hand.

He passed the formal gardens and the tennis courts and strode out purposefully towards the cliff. It had not occurred to him before that it was a considerable walk. The darkness and being alone seemed to accentuate the distance, so that for one awful moment he wondered whether he had taken a wrong turn. Despite his good intentions, he found that he had become distracted. His head had been preoccupied with thoughts of a sinister kind so that he became disorientated. All of a sudden he found himself on the cliff edge. It rattled him to think that a step or two more and he might have found himself falling to the beach below. He took a deep breath and straightened, scouring the area for the path. It would be something of a perilous descent in the dark, and one that he did not particularly relish. Still, he could not stay where he was and he dared not return to the hotel. There was nothing to be done but spend the night on the beach as he had originally intended. It meant a treacherous climb down but it had to be done, and the sooner it was accomplished, the better.

He had been badly frightened, not by the sheer drop that faced him but by the multitude of angry words exchanged that evening that had made him instigate a change to his carefully laid plans. It was a crying shame, but he must make the best of it and take with him what he could salvage. Utmost in his mind was the conviction that he must disappear before his absence was noted. He did not wish to become a subject of common gossip for he knew himself to be in a precarious position.

He halted abruptly, frozen in the act of putting one foot before the other. He'd heard another twig snap, and this time it had sounded very near indeed; a few steps away at most. In all probability it was just some nocturnal island animal, and yet he felt what he could best describe as an affliction of the nerves. He was tempted to turn around and stare in the direction from where the noise had come, and yet he felt strangely afraid to do so, almost as if he thought that some strange apparition would rise out of the darkness and strike him, as penance for his numerous misdeeds.

He took a deep breath and admonished himself severely for letting his nerves get the better of him. He'd do far better to focus his attention instead on finding the path that led down to the beach, and then he would be thoroughly occupied, for he knew it would take all his concentration to descend it in the dark. It was difficult to get his bearings, yet he was pretty certain that if he walked a little way to the right he'd come across the path. Yes ... there it was, complete with the old, gnarled handrail. Now all he had to do was grab the rail and watch his footing. He hadn't remembered it being so steep. He'd have to edge his way along it gingerly, a step at a time. There was no need to rush ...

When the blow came, he had all but forgotten about the broken twig. In the brief seconds between consciousness and oblivion, it came to him as a memory, almost as if in a hazy dream. He was vaguely aware also of a dull pain and a thundering in his ears, and above all else of the eerie sensation of falling. In that moment, before the darkness consumed him, he knew himself to be crashing down towards the beach below and to his ultimate death.

'Peony, where have you been?'

The head that emerged from beneath the bed covers was all but hidden by the mob cap that swamped the grizzled curls beneath, giving the speaker the odd appearance of a baby roused unceremoniously from its sleep.

'Go back to sleep, Hyacinth,' said her sister a little harshly, her voice strangely hoarse.

Instead of complying, however, Miss Hyacinth sat up, propping her back against her pillows and lit the candle on the little wooden table that was positioned next to her bed. She regarded her sibling with open curiosity in the flickering candlelight which, to her fanciful mind, gave a rather ghostly glow to the proceedings. Indeed, studying her sister closely, she thought Miss Peony gave a very good impersonation of a beleaguered witch. If nothing else, she was dressed from head to foot in black, the stiff old-fashioned Victorian silk rustling as she moved.

'Where have you been?' she asked again. 'And why are you dressed like that? Wasn't that gown you are wearing Mother's?' Her gaze moved to the clock on the mantelpiece and she started. 'It's half past two in the morning!' she exclaimed, her eyes wide open.

'I couldn't sleep,' said Miss Peony, somewhat gruffly, careful not to catch her sibling's eye. 'I thought I'd just take a turn around the hotel grounds, that's all. I daresay I should have done it before turning in.'

Miss Hyacinth's hand leapt to her mouth as an awful thought occurred to her. 'You didn't –'

'No, I didn't,' said Miss Peony, sharply. 'Now, go back to sleep, Hyacinth. I can't do with all your talking, not at this time of the night. I'm tired.'

Miss Hyacinth blew out the candle and settled down once more in her bed among the pillows, arranging the covers about her. A few minutes elapsed during which neither woman spoke. When Miss Peony next cast a cursory glance in her sibling's direction, she was relieved that her sister gave every appearance of being asleep. Yet, if she had looked more closely, she would have seen that Miss Hyacinth was in fact wide awake and regarding her sister surreptitiously from behind her cotton sheets. Even in the darkness, it occurred to Miss Hyacinth that her sister appeared strangely agitated. For her sibling fumbled clumsily with the buttons of her gown, as if she could hardly muster the energy to undo them. Miss Hyacinth had the odd and disconcerting feeling that something dreadful had happened. It may have been just an odd fancy on her part, but she knew her sister well enough to conclude that at the very least something had unsettled her badly. The brusqueness of her manner and her clipped sentences said as much. And as for her taking walks after dark … well, she'd never heard anything like it. But it was not this that held her attention or troubled her. Rather it was Miss Peony's hands. Strong, capable hands, she had always thought them, though they belonged to an invalid. But they didn't look like that now. For, as Miss Peony paused to take off her wristwatch, Miss Hyacinth noticed with something akin to horror that her sister's hands were trembling.

The Misses Trimble were not the only women to be awake that night. Mabel Adler joined their ranks, sitting forlornly in front of her dressing table, staring dejectedly at her tear-stained face, only too aware that a severe bout of crying did very little to accentuate one's beauty.

It was her habit to brush her hair before climbing into bed each night and instinctively she reached out for her hairbrush, hardly aware of what she was doing until it dawned on her that it was not in its usual place beside her mirror. The recollection of where it was, packed neatly in her bag, brought on a fresh bout of tears, and this time she noted her red-rimmed eyes with a dark gratification, a testament to her desolate mood.

Tomorrow, she would look dreadful and it would serve him jolly well right to witness the misery he had caused in the person he claimed to love above all others. Miss Hyacinth was certain to comment on her wretched appearance, flitting about her in that way of hers like an over indulgent mother hen, which Mabel, unused to a mother's ministrations, usually found so infuriating. Tomorrow, however, she would indulge the woman. Indeed, she would get a grim satisfaction in seeing the horrified look on Miss Hyacinth's face when she told the woman her woeful tale. And what would *he* do while she was telling it, she wondered? Would his ears burn with the shame of it all, or would he scurry off and hide his head among his sermons and pretend that he was not the subject of shocked whispers?

She had known her father to be rather set in his ways, had recognised him to be jovial and tolerant and somewhat absent-minded in a way most people found quite charming and endearing. It was what they sought for in a man of the cloth. But never before had she had occasion to glimpse flashes of the latent anger which lay beneath the pleasant exterior waiting to be ignited. It was as foreign to her as disease or abject poverty, and because of that all the more terrifying. She stifled a sob as she remembered her father's face, livid with emotion. As she laid down the hairbrush retrieved from her case, marvelling, in spite of everything, at the richness of her fine blond curls, it occurred to her to wonder whether that was not in fact what had upset her the most. She was so used to wrapping her father around her little finger that, not for a moment, had it ever occurred to her that she would not always get her own way. Her parent might harbour various misgivings about her proposed endeavours, but she had always been confident before that, with a very little effort, he could be persuaded to her way of thinking. For the first time in her rather spoilt young life, she could no longer be certain of her father's unconditional subservience.

But it was not merely this fact, terrifying though it was, or that her carefully laid plans had been so unceremoniously broken that she found most distressing. It was that for the first time in her life she had been afraid; dreadfully afraid. It was only then that the thought struck her, so forcefully that for a few seconds she could do little more than gaze rather helplessly at her reflection in the mirror and take a deep breath. The question that had lingered at the back of her mind and had now succeeded in fighting its way to the fore was awful by the nature of its very simplicity. For whom had she been afraid? It hadn't been for herself, not really. Her father would never lay a finger on her, but ... She shuddered violently and passed a hand across her face, obliterating her view of the room with the neatly packed case standing waiting. Try as she might, she could not rid herself of the vision of her father's face as it had looked that evening, full of hidden menace.

It was Ralph Kettering's habit to go for an early morning swim when the tide was right. As proprietor of Hotel Hemera, the majority of his day was naturally enough spent attending to the needs of his guests. The few moments he could snatch to devote to his own wants were therefore extremely precious to him. At six o'clock in the morning, while the day was just beginning for his servants and the heavy wooden shutters barring the windows of his guests' rooms were still resolutely shut, he was at one with the world. That time of day, from his point of view, was still his own and he embraced it with the enthusiasm of a schoolboy. This morning was no exception and, with his beach towel rolled up under his arm, he sauntered towards the cliff with a definite spring in his step. Indeed, he vaguely remembered afterwards that he had even been whistling a jaunty tune, so untroubled were his thoughts at that time of the morning. Even his dress, though decidedly casual, retained an air of smartness about it, consisting as it did of tennis flannels and shirt. Only later would he be required to don his lounge suit, the thick fabric of which he found stifling and uncomfortable in the Mediterranean heat.

Almost before realising it, he came to the edge of the cliff and scoured the edge for the start of the path, which he quickly located with a practised eye. It struck him now, as it had occurred to him often, that it might be prudent to erect a fence around the edge of the cliff to ensure the safety of his patrons. As on previous occasions, he dismissed the thought as soon as it had entered his head. To do so would undoubtedly spoil the view, and it was not as if he actively encouraged his guests to visit the cliff after dark. While he knew that for some of his clientele it held an irresistible, romantic fascination, he was always careful to warn his guests of the perils when they first arrived. And though he had been sorely tempted to do so, he refrained from lighting the path with torches. If his guests decided not to heed his advice and visited the cliff edge in the hours of darkness, he could very well argue that they did so at their own risk.

108

He descended the path quickly, familiar with its various twists and turns, and each loose stone which might seek to hinder his progress. He did not look down at the beach, rather his gaze was directed at the sea beyond which twinkled and glistened in the early morning sun most invitingly. Having reached the sand, he disrobed in a matter of minutes and it was only when he had folded up his clothes neatly and was looking for a place to stow them on the beach, that he became aware of an unfamiliar object lying a little way from the bottom of the cliff.

His first impression was that it was a collection of old hessian sacks which had been carelessly discarded by some slovenly fisherman. Indeed, he was in the very act of making a mental note that he would instruct one of his servants to dispose of them as soon as he returned to the hotel after his swim, when something about the bundle piqued his curiosity. He edged a step or two nearer and concluded that, on second glance, they did not appear to be made of the usual dense woven fabric normally associated with hessian sacks. For, unless he was mistaken, the material was black in colour rather than the usual light brown. Of course, it was quite possible that the material had become dirty and discoloured, particularly if it had spent the majority of its life at the bottom of a fishing boat, but, even so, something struck him as being not quite right.

It was with some misgivings that he turned his back on the sea and set off down the beach towards the discarded pile. A moment or two later and he found himself running towards it, his breath laboured by a growing sense of urgency. It was not, however, until he was standing beside it that he could fully comprehend the spectacle that greeted his horrified eyes. It was not a pile of old sacking that was strewn on the beach as he had first supposed. Rather, it was the body of a man clothed in evening dress.

Ralph Kettering knelt down gingerly beside the body and stretched out a hand to feel for a pulse. It was an unnecessary act, for a glance was sufficient to inform him that the life that had once inhabited this inanimate object was now extinct. Having satisfied himself that he was indeed looking at a corpse and that any help he could have offered before was now futile, he steeled himself to turn the body over so that he might have a look at its face. Afterwards, he wondered whether, notwithstanding the clothes in which the corpse was dressed, he had been expecting to see the gnarled, weather-beaten face of a fisherman. To find himself staring into the face of a man for whom manual toil and the external elements had been distinctly foreign was therefore something of a surprise. It was not this, however, that caused him to recoil and stumble to his feet in one quick, jerky movement. Neither was it the reason why a strangled cry sprung involuntarily from his lips. He had thought that nothing could shock him more than the discovery of a corpse on this stretch of beach. In this, however, he had been gravely mistaken. What drained the colour from his face and made his body tremble was the sudden, dreadful realisation that in life the corpse had been one of his hotel guests.

Chapter Fifteen

In the brief period between sleep and wakefulness, when her senses were still dulled by her dreams, Rose had the vague impression of sudden activity unfolding outside her bedroom window. The thud of hurrying feet on the terrace and the echo of harsh whispers floated to her ears from the other side of the heavy wooden shutters. In her stupefied state, she imagined that the sun and the shade were alternately casting their light and shadow across the bright, whitewashed walls. However, it was the low but persistent knocking on the main outer door to their rooms which gradually brought her to her senses.

She heard the bolts being slowly drawn back and the sound of a muffled exclamation from their servant. A second later and the newcomer had evidently been admitted to the little room which served as an entrance hall. There was again the sound of muted footsteps, this time the servant departing in search of his master because there shortly followed something of a hurried exchange. Rose listened carefully and, though the words spoken were inaudible, emanating as they did from behind solid walls, she thought she recognised her husband's voice, slightly raised in surprise. A glance at the clock on her bedside table informed her that it was a little after a quarter past seven. It struck her as a very early hour for a visitor to call and instinctively she grabbed her *negligée*. Her maid servant entered her room requesting, ever so politely, that if she would be so good as to get dressed as quickly as possible and join the gentlemen in the sitting room, it would be much appreciated.

Rose, full of curiosity, readily obliged. It was a matter of only a few minutes before she made her way across the hall and opened the door to the sitting room. Two men, who had waited for her impatiently, rose to their feet to greet her. Cedric, dressed in pyjamas, over which had been hastily thrown a silk dressing gown, gave her a rueful smile. The other man, in contrast, was impeccably dressed in an outfit more suited to a London office than to the Mediterranean climate. To Rose's keen eye, he gave the impression of being ill at ease, as if he feared that he had committed some awful *faux-pas* by descending on them at so untimely an hour.

As if to confirm her thoughts, the first words uttered by the man were: 'Your ladyship, it is very good of you to receive me at this hour.'

'Good morning, Mr Kettering,' said Rose, observing the hotel proprietor appeared rattled, though he was making a valiant effort to appear otherwise. In light of the man's agitated state, she concluded that it would be best to dispense with the usual pleasantries and ascertain at once the reason for his visit. With this in mind, she asked, a little abruptly: 'What may we do for you?'

For a moment, the hotel proprietor appeared flustered, as if he did not know quite how to respond to such a direct question. Cedric, noting his confusion, was quick to come to his aid.

'I think it would be better, Kettering, if you were to begin at the beginning,' he said, 'and give the particulars to her ladyship, just as you told them to me.'

'Very good, my lord,' said the hotel proprietor. 'No', he said, as Cedric indicated a chair, 'that's very kind of you, but I'd prefer to stand if you don't mind; it helps me to think. Begin at the beginning, you say? Well, that would be this morning; about six o'clock. I was just telling his lordship, your ladyship, how it is my habit to go for an early morning swim. I find it most refreshing. I am firmly of the view that it clears the head and sets one up for the day.' Rose smiled and nodded at him encouragingly, wondering where the story would lead. 'Today was no exception. I went for my swim,' continued Mr Kettering, growing in confidence as he got into his stride. 'It looked a fine morning … it still does, of course, as far as the weather is concerned. Anyway, there was nothing to indicate that anything was amiss. I suppose it is worth mentioning at this juncture that I didn't pass anyone as I made my way towards the cliff.' He coughed self-consciously. 'You will see the relevance of such a statement later on in my tale.'

'I am certain of it,' said Rose politely, somewhat intrigued.

'I like to consider myself an observant sort of a fellow,' continued the hotel proprietor, 'but, as I say, I didn't notice anything out of the ordinary. It was only when I was looking for a large stone or piece of driftwood under which I could stow my clothes while I was swimming that I noticed what I took to be a pile of old hessian sacking located not far from the bottom of the cliff.'

'Only it wasn't,' said Cedric, rather tiring of hearing the story for the second time. 'Old sacking, I mean. It was a body.'

'A body?' Rose's eyes widened. Whatever she had been expecting to hear, it had not been this.

'That's right,' concurred Mr Kettering, apparently relieved that Cedric had taken it upon himself to recount some of his tale. 'At first I thought it must be the corpse of a fisherman. It certainly never occurred to me that it might be the body of one of my guests.'

'One of your guests?' exclaimed Rose. 'Are you saying one of them toppled off the edge of the cliff?'

'Yes. That's to say in a manner of speaking.'

In her mind's eye Rose saw Mr Vickers, staggering drunkenly across the dining room floor. She imagined him stumbling towards the cliff edge, waving wildly, a whisky bottle clutched in his hand. It didn't take much imagination to fancy him tottering to the very edge of the cliff and swaying dangerously. It would only require one wrong foot or sudden gust of wind to send him hurtling down to the beach below.

'Vickers. The body was that of Mr Vickers?' Rose murmured. She posed the sentence more as a statement than as a question, so vivid was the picture she had conjured up in her imagination.

'Vickers?' said Ralph Kettering. He sounded surprised. 'It wasn't Vickers' body I found on the sand. It was Mr Dewhurst's.'

'Alec Dewhurst's?'

'Yes.'

For a moment there was a brief silence, punctuated only by the ticking of the clock on the mantelpiece. Then Rose said: 'Are you quite certain? That it is Mr Dewhurst's body, I mean?'

Even as she asked the question, she knew it was absurd to think otherwise. There was no reason why the hotel proprietor should have made a mistake. In physical appearance, Alec Dewhurst had resembled none of the other guests at the hotel. His handsome, dark looks had set him apart. The emaciated and scrawny figure that was Mr Vickers could certainly never be mistaken for Alec Dewhurst's, even in death.

'It was Mr Dewhurst's, all right,' said Mr Kettering, pushing his horn-rimmed spectacles further up his nose.

'Are you wanting me to tell the … his sister?' said Rose. 'Is that why you are here?'

113

Mr Kettering coughed. 'That is not exactly why I am here, your ladyship, though it would be most kind of you ...' He faltered. For the first time during the interview the hotel proprietor took no pains to conceal his obvious distress. Cedric looked at him with interest. It was obvious that Kettering had not mentioned to him why he had sought them out.

'Oh dear,' said Mr Kettering, regaining some of his composure. 'The matter is a most delicate one. One hardly knows where to begin, or what precisely to say. As you suggest, my lord, one should begin at the beginning, but in a matter of such delicacy as this ...'

'You would like our advice concerning Miss Dewhurst?' Rose suggested. 'You are aware that Miss Dewhurst is not really Miss Dewhurst? By that I mean you know her to be the Duchess of Grismere?'

For a moment Mr Kettering looked decidedly shocked. Then he mumbled: 'His lordship may have mentioned something of the sort last night when we were dealing with ... the business concerning Mr Vickers' camera. But,' he added quickly, as if he feared further scandalous suggestions, or indeed merely wished to get the matter off his chest, 'the reason I have sought you out at this odd hour is that Mr Dewhurst's death is not what it first appeared to be. That is to say, what I took at first glance to be an unfortunate accident may well in fact prove to be a murder.'

This sentence was greeted by a shocked silence, and an exchange of horrified glances between husband and wife. If the hotel proprietor had said that the building was on fire and that they should run for their lives, the effect of his words could not have been more devastating to his audience. While the Earl and the Countess of Belvedere were well accustomed to violent death, here among the scorching sun and the olive groves, the sunken urns and the rugged cliffs, they had thought themselves to be immune from that particular evil in society. In this assumption they had evidently been wrong, for even here on the island of Skiathos, with its vibrant beauty, located as it was across the sea but still in the shadow of Athens and the classical gods, it appeared they could not escape the vile motives and actions of others that seemed to shape their almost monthly existence.

Rose gave a heartfelt sigh. She had long been of the belief that in England murder actively sought her out. Due to the unquestionable fact

114

that she had, purely by circumstance, become something of an amateur expert in the field, murder was drawn to her as absolutely, and irresistibly, as a wasp to a bottle of sweet lemonade. It was as if she held for it an awful fascination.

'Dewhurst was murdered?'

It was Cedric who spoke, his face visibly strained and pale beneath his tan. He sounded as if he had forced the words out against his better judgment. It is possible he thought that, if he remained silent, it might all turn out to be some sort of a horrid dream. Ralph Kettering, however, quick to dispel any such notion, picked up the cue thrown him with undue eagerness. It was evident to both his listeners that he was anxious to unburden himself of the awful knowledge of which, until a few moments ago, only he, a couple of trusted servants and the island doctor were in possession.

'Unfortunate though it is, my lord, it would appear that he was. Of course, I can assure you the thought never crossed my mind when I first discovered his body. It was beneath the cliff, you see, so I just assumed …' The hotel proprietor gave a shudder. 'You see, I have never been overly fond of the sight of blood,' he continued apologetically, as if he considered this a great failing on his part. 'I didn't study his … his injuries very closely. I just assumed that they were consistent with a fall from the cliff.'

'You said just now that Mr Dewhurst *had* toppled over the edge of the cliff,' said Rose, finding her voice at last. She had sat down on an old wooden chair positioned next to the wall. She had a hand held up to her mouth, as if she thought it might help her to draw breath and digest what she was being told.

'If you recall, your ladyship, I said he had done in a manner of speaking,' said Mr Kettering, a little diffidently, as if he half feared he was speaking out of turn. 'That's to say, Mr Dewhurst had undoubtedly fallen from the cliff but only, it would seem, as the result of a hard blow being struck to the back of his head.'

'Oh?' said Cedric, clearly interested in this new piece of information. 'And how do you know that? Has a doctor examined the body?'

'Yes, indeed. My first action on finding the body was, of course, to summon a doctor. Or should I say my second? My first task was to arrange for the body to be moved. I had it taken to one of the basement rooms in the hotel.' Noting Cedric's raised eyebrows, the hotel proprietor hurried on, as if he felt compelled to justify his actions. 'The notion that the poor man had been murdered never occurred to me or I would of course have left the body where I found it. I thought it was an accident, a tragic one, yes, but an accident nevertheless. My overriding concern was that none of my guests should see the body. I had one of my servants summon Dr Costas. He is only an island doctor but, I should mention, of the first rate. I instructed him to examine the body, merely as a matter of form, you understand. It never occurred to me ...' At this point the hotel proprietor paused for a moment to mop his forehead with a large, white handkerchief. 'It never occurred to me that he would say there was anything suspicious about the man's death. If I am quite truthful, it has always been rather a worry of mine that one of my guests might take a wrong turn in the dark and topple over the cliff. I don't encourage it, of course. Guests walking to the edge of the cliff in the dark, I mean, not taking wrong turns. But it is only human nature, I suppose ... Why, even this morning before I found the body, I was wondering whether I should erect a fence. But of course, it would spoil the view and –'

'I say, I suppose this doctor of yours couldn't be mistaken?' said Cedric interrupting, without ceremony, Mr Kettering's somewhat rambling speech. 'About the blow to the back of the head occurring before death, rather than as being the result of the fall, I mean?' He began to pace the room and continued speaking without waiting for the answers to his questions. 'Could the poor fellow not have struck his head during his fall? I don't suppose,' he added, though he sounded somewhat dubious, 'he might have stumbled or slipped on something at the top of the cliff which caused him to fall?'

'No, I put a similar question to Dr Costas. He is of the very firm belief that Mr Dewhurst was struck hard by a blunt instrument. Very particular about it, he was. The injury was not something he felt that the deceased could have inflicted upon himself, either by accident or design. The position of the blow and the force used suggested to him otherwise.'

'I see,' said Cedric. Resigned now to the fact that the circumstances of the death were indeed suspicious, he ceased pacing the room. 'Has this doctor of yours any idea as to the exact time of death? That's to say, is there any reason to believe that it happened after dark, or is that just idle speculation? Mayn't it have happened this morning, just before you yourself went down to the beach?'

'No,' said Mr Kettering, as if he were some all-knowing oracle. 'Mr Dewhurst had been dead a number of hours when I found him, by Dr Costas' reckoning rather than by my own, I might add. When I asked the good doctor to hazard a guess as to the time of death, he thought death was likely to have occurred sometime between ten o'clock last night and three o'clock this morning. I am afraid that he refused to be any more precise, though I pressed him.'

'Between ten o'clock last night and two o'clock this morning?' reflected Cedric. His face brightened a little. 'Perhaps we can be a little more exact than that. After all, the poor fellow dined in the dining room last night. Why, I saw him myself. He supped at the Adlers' table, as was his habit. And afterwards, no doubt, he danced. I didn't see him do so myself, as I was otherwise engaged in dealing with that awful Vickers chap. But you, my dear,' he said, glancing at his wife, who he thought looked unusually pale, 'must have seen him dancing?'

'Yes,' said Rose, rather dully. 'He danced all right. First with Miss Adler and then with ... the duchess. He made quite a show of it. If I recall correctly, he even danced with Miss Hyacinth.'

'Did he, indeed?' said Cedric. 'I should have liked to have seen that.'

'I saw him later that evening, as well,' said Rose. 'Outside. He was making his way towards the cliff ...' She hesitated, remembering the precise circumstances in which she had seen him. She had been standing in the shadows with the duchess and Alec Dewhurst had come running past, hand in hand with Mabel Adler, making his jubilant way towards the cliff edge ... She looked up and was aware that the hotel proprietor was studying her keenly. The thought occurred to her then that what she said next might well determine someone's fate, or at least cause them to be seen in a prejudiced light. Aloud, she said quickly: 'I don't think we should say any more. It would be most unwise. Besides, there is no use speculating as to what might have happened, or ... whom might be responsible. It would be much better if we just waited for the police to arrive.'

She caught her husband's eye, and it seemed to her that he had detected the feeling of dread that had so suddenly overcome her, for quickly he nodded, though it was obvious, even to the most casual of observers, that her words had intrigued him. It was the hotel proprietor who spoke, somewhat hesitant in his manner, as if he feared a violent quarrel or rebuke.

'I am afraid it will be quite a long wait. You see, they have yet to be informed of what has happened.'

Chapter Sixteen

This statement was met with a look of such incredulity by his listeners that Mr Kettering was himself almost inclined to follow Cedric's example and pace the room, so keen was he not to meet their gaze. Instead, he swallowed hard and held his ground, tempted though he was to recoil a little under their penetrating stares.

'If I might be permitted to explain?'

'Please do,' said Cedric, a trifle gruffly.

Aware that his companions regarded him with a great deal of curiosity, the hotel proprietor removed his horn-rimmed spectacles and polished them rapidly with his handkerchief. He said:

'The police here on the island have not been advised of what has happened, and what is more, it is not my intention to inform them.' He held up his hand as Cedric made to protest. 'If this were merely a matter of illegal gambling or theft, then, yes, I should summon the local Gendarmerie without delay. But it is not. It is a matter of great delicacy and must be handled as such. If you will permit me to speak candidly, your ladyship, the man we presume to be …' he paused to give a little embarrassed cough before lowering his voice. 'That's to say, the man we assume to be a … um … a particular friend of the Duchess of Grismere has been found dead in the most suspicious of circumstances. The lady herself is here, and the reputations of both the duchess and my hotel are at considerable risk of being ruined.'

'Yes?'

'I do not wish Hotel Hemera to become the subject of gossip mongers,' said Mr Kettering firmly. 'I do not want boat loads of macabre sightseers flocking to my hotel to see the exact spot where Mr Dewhurst was murdered. Hotel Hemera is a respectable establishment. I should like it to remain as such.'

'What do you propose?' asked Cedric.

He had visons of the awful headlines that would appear in the penny press. It would be a ghastly scandal all right, but it did not seem to him that there was anything much that could be done about it. As it was, he could hardly bring himself to imagine how the Duke of Grismere would take the news. His wife's disappearance had already had a shattering effect on the peer. He was not a young man to begin with and had become increasingly frail. Why, Cedric had witnessed it with his own eyes. To be informed of his wife's antics was awful enough, but then to know that a lurid account of it appeared in every newspaper column as a subject to be dissected and commented upon, by everyone from the lowest scullery maid to his fellow peers, would surely be too much for any man to endure. It was in that moment that Cedric pitied the old duke as he had pitied few men before. It made him inclined to despise the duchess, or at least think very little of her. It was true that she was likely to be distraught at the news of her lover's death. But he thought rather harshly that it would be no more than she deserved. She had brought the catastrophe upon herself, and now she must deal with the consequences.

'I propose that I contact an acquaintance of mine who happens to hold a senior position in the civilian city police force in Athens.'

'Athens!' exclaimed Cedric.

'I have not sent for him yet, and of course there will be a considerable delay in his coming here. I do not doubt that it will take him a few days to arrive. He is very busy, what with the affairs of the capital and –'

'My dear fellow!' protested Cedric, clearly appalled by the suggestion.

'I think, my lord, you will agree with me that it is for the best. I know Marangos to be the most discreet of fellows and as a policeman I hold him in the very highest of esteem. He will understand that this is a delicate matter, that it needs to be handled carefully and with a certain degree of discretion.'

'And what is it that you propose we do in the meantime?' asked Cedric, sounding exasperated. He took a deep breath and said: 'Look here, Kettering, it really won't do, you know. A matter like this cannot be withheld from the local police. It is our duty to inform them; surely you must understand that? And even if we were to go along with this ridiculous plan of yours, vital evidence will be lost. False alibis will be concocted, and the murderer will have the opportunity to flee or, at the very least, to hide his tracks.'

'It is most unusual, I admit, my lord, but I would not call it ridiculous,' said the hotel proprietor, sounding a little offended by Cedric's tone. 'I do not propose that we wait, as you suggest. I am of the opinion instead that we take the matter into our own hands, as it were.'

There was a sharp intake of breath and both men turned at once to regard the woman who had given it, and who was sitting so quietly on her chair that both men had almost forgotten that she was there. Rose, who had all the while been listening to this interesting exchange with a degree of incredulity, rose to her feet and said:

'You do not propose that we wait and do nothing, do you, Mr Kettering? You would like me to investigate this case on your behalf. That is it, is it not? You should like to be in a position to present the case to your friend as a *fait accompli*, as it were. The crime and the murderer all neatly bundled up and handed to him on a plate.'

'That is it exactly!' cried the hotel proprietor, clapping his hands together, such was his sense of relief that here, at least, was one person who followed his line of reasoning. In the ordinary course of events, he was not given to such dramatic demonstrations, which he considered decidedly foreign. Indeed, if anything he was the most composed and restrained of figures; reserved, he would have called it, if he had thought to give it a name. But here, faced with a series of objections from the earl and a very real possibility that his wishes would be disregarded, he was given to a more visual display of expression.

'You understand my way of thinking very well, your ladyship, if I may say so,' he said, bowing to her in a slightly obsequious fashion. 'You have a reputation for being something of an amateur sleuth. A great reputation, I should say. My brother, your secretary, my lord,' he added, pausing to give a look in Cedric's direction, 'speaks very highly of your abilities, your ladyship. Why, I believe even Scotland Yard have, on occasion, consulted you on a number of cases?'

Rose was unable to suppress the smile that had leapt so readily to her lips at Mr Kettering's flattering words. In spite of the troubling situation in which they found themselves, it was hard not to imagine the outraged expression on Detective Inspector Bramwell's face should he have happened to overhear the hotel proprietor's words regarding Scotland Yard's supposed reliance on her detecting skills.

Mistaking Rose's smile to be one of acquiescence, Mr Kettering continued detailing his approach to dealing with the problem facing them with a growing sense of confidence.

'I shall accompany your ladyship in your investigations,' he said. 'I shall be the sergeant to your inspector, as it were. We shall gather the guests together and I shall inform them what has happened. I shall announce that, while we are waiting for the police to arrive from the mainland, I, in my capacity as hotel proprietor, have engaged your ladyship to undertake a private investigation into Mr Dewhurst's death. You will be acting on my behalf.'

'It is quite possible,' said Rose quietly, 'that one or two of your guests shall refuse to answer any questions that I put to them. I have no authority, after all, to do such a thing. One could hardly blame them if they did. In fact, they would be acting quite properly.'

Her thoughts had drifted, as she spoke, to the Duchess of Grismere. The woman's haughty manner still riled her, and she was reminded also of the strange feeling of animosity that had sprung up between them on such a short acquaintance. She blushed at the recollection, for she had neglected to mention last night's encounter with the duchess to her husband, feeling, as she did, rather ashamed of herself, that in some way she had ill-judged the situation and played her hand badly. She knew that, had Cedric been an observer, he would have been rather disappointed in the way she had managed the confrontation. There was a part of her also that wished it had been he, not she, who had come across the duchess in the shadows, for she felt certain that he would have handled the matter in a far more competent fashion.

'In that case, I would tell them that it would be extremely unwise for them to do such a thing,' Mr Kettering was saying. 'That it would be far better for them to be interviewed by you than by the local Gendarmerie.'

'Unless, of course, they happened to be the murderer,' said Cedric, a touch of mischief in his voice.

'Ah … yes, indeed,' agreed the hotel proprietor, unsure how to respond to what he felt was an inappropriate show of frivolity given the situation. Rose, comprehending her husband's character, knew full well that Cedric's attempt to sound flippant was merely a way of trying to dispel the horror and gloom that hung about the room in equal measure.

'I do not think they will demur,' continued Mr Kettering, keen to get back to the matter in hand. 'If you don't mind my saying, your ladyship, they will be as familiar with your reputation as an amateur sleuth, as I am myself. They will welcome your interest in this dreadful matter for, if I may be so bold as to suggest it, they will regard you in the same way as they would regard a friend. One might say, you would be doing them a great kindness; a familiar face among the horror.'

The poetic eloquence of the hotel proprietor's words brought a smile to Rose's lips, which she took pains to conceal. She caught Cedric's eye and saw that he too was attempting to stifle a grin.

'It would be highly irregular,' she said, feeling herself waver. She did not really feel herself torn for she knew with an awful certainty that she would comply with his wishes. The detecting instinct in her was too strong to resist such an opportunity. Even without the hotel proprietor's blessing, she knew she would feel compelled to investigate. It is possible that Mr Kettering saw it too, for his face instantly relaxed. The worried frown that had creased and puckered his forehead became less pronounced. Indeed, a fleeting smile crossed his face.

'It would be a little irregular,' he admitted. 'Certainly it would be informal. But if I gave you my word that I would take full responsibility for the … the decision, would that do? I will say, if questioned, that it was all my fault; that I had refused to summon the local Gendarmerie. You could say that you did not know what else to do but aid me in my investigations.'

Still, Rose hesitated. She felt the room swim before her, as if she was being offered something exquisitely tantalising, yet a little beyond her capabilities. Never before had she been required, or asked, to lead a murder investigation. At best she had been an auxiliary helper, somewhat grudgingly tolerated by the police. This would be different. She would be taking on her shoulders a great deal of responsibility. It would be up to her to determine the best way to proceed, which avenues of inquiry should be pursued, and which should be discarded. It was quite possible that vital evidence might be lost on her watch.

'I am confident,' continued Mr Kettering, in his most persuasive voice, 'that it won't come to that. My having to defend my decision, I mean. Besides, it is not as if I have refused to inform the police, merely that I have chosen to notify the civilian city police force, who really are more suited to this type of inquiry than their island compatriots.'

'Very well,' said Rose, taking a deep breath, her eyes looking at Cedric and receiving a grin, accompanied by a nod of approval. 'I shall do what I can. The first thing to be done is to take certain measures to gather and preserve the evidence.'

They made their way towards the cliff path, a little procession of four. Mr Kettering led the way, with Rose quick on his heels. Cedric followed her with Dr Costas bringing up the rear. He was a slightly built man, of very few words, dressed in a rather shabby black suit that had obviously seen better days, and which helped to give a funereal air to the proceedings. This impression was further accentuated by the doctor's sombre expression, and the fact that no one felt inclined to speak.

Rose, perhaps shrinking a little from the obligation to inform the duchess of her lover's death, had deferred this task, reasoning quite properly that, given the hour, the majority of the hotel's guests would still be asleep. She was also keen to be better informed about what had occurred and, therefore, deemed that her first courses of action must be to inspect the crime scene and interrogate the island doctor on his findings, following his cursory examination of the corpse.

'I found the body over there,' said the hotel proprietor, peering over the edge of the cliff and pointing to an area on the beach marked by a yard of stiff black fabric, which had been weighed down securely at each end by a number of rocks. 'Before I arranged for the body to be removed to the hotel, I thought it prudent to mark the place where I had found it with my towel,' he explained. 'Of course, when Dr Costas informed me that it was, in all probability, a case of murder, I took more robust steps to mark the spot.'

'That was very good of you,' said Rose. 'Would it be possible for you to arrange also for some photographs to be taken? From this spot here, I think, as well as from down on the beach itself?'

'But, of course,' said Mr Kettering. 'I happen to be something of an amateur photographer. I will take them myself.' He gave a small, diffident cough. 'I have also made a rough sketch of the body. That's to say, how I remember finding it lying on the beach, which I have given to Dr Costas.'

'It is consistent with Mr Dewhurst's injuries,' the doctor informed them in a strong accent. 'The body, I do not think it was moved after death.'

Both Rose and Cedric looked at the doctor in surprise. It had not occurred to either that he might speak English.

124

'You are surprised, I think,' he said, giving a chuckle, 'that I speak a little English? It would surprise you too, I think, to know that I have studied a little in England?'

'I say,' said Cedric, good-humouredly, 'you do put us to shame. Do you think Mr Dewhurst was standing on the edge of the cliff when he was struck?'

'It is quite possible,' agreed the doctor. 'The wound, it was at the back of the head. Here.' He touched a place on the back of the hotel proprietor's head to demonstrate. Mr Kettering, who happened to be looking out to sea at the time, started. 'It was a heavy blow,' continued the doctor, apparently oblivious to the hotel proprietor's discomfort. 'Done with a blunt object, yes?'

'A heavy blow, you say?' said Cedric, looking interested. 'You don't think that it could have been done by a woman then?'

'But of course!' exclaimed the doctor. 'I did not say it could, or could not, be a woman. Mr Dewhurst, if he was going down the path at the time … Mr Kettering, if you please, I will show you. Mr Kettering, you are the unfortunate Mr Dewhurst. You are going down to the beach. You take a few steps down the path. Yes, you may stop now. There is no need to tremble. I will not really hit you, I just pretend, yes? I am the woman. I am not very tall, so I can be the woman. You have your back to me. I, I raise my arm like this. It gives me the swing, the necessary force … Bang. I have hit you on the head. You fall to the beach, or I give you a little push like this. Mr Kettering, stand still. I will not really push you. I just pretend to do so.' The doctor turned to face Cedric and Rose, his hand positioned as if he were still holding the imaginary blunt instrument. Mr Kettering, meanwhile, had scrambled back up the path to the relative safety of the cliff edge.

'So our murderer might have been either a man or a woman,' said Cedric. 'It would not have been a very difficult task for our murderer, not if Mr Dewhurst was just descending the path to the beach at the time, as you suggest. It would have been easy enough for our murderer to have crept up behind him and delivered the blow.'

'Yes,' agreed Rose. 'Mr Dewhurst's attention at the time would, in all probability, have been focused on walking down the path. It would have been quite a feat to accomplish in the dark even with the aid of the handrail. He would have been afraid of slipping.'

As she spoke, she took a few steps down the path, attempting to put herself in the place of Alec Dewhurst, negotiating the dust and the small stones that made up the path while an unknown assailant crept up behind him brandishing a weapon … She shuddered, hoping fervently that Alec Dewhurst had been unaware of the peril he was in, that he had been struck before he was conscious of his murderer's presence, and had fallen unknowingly to the ground below.

Despite the warm sunshine, she shivered. How strange and unreal it all seemed. She stood staring out to sea, watching as the water glistened and sparkled in the sun's rays like jewels in a treasure chest. She lowered her gaze to take in the beach below with its pale golden sands, which cushioned bare feet while simultaneously scalding their soles. It occurred to her then how quiet it was at this time in the morning without the presence of the hotel guests on the beach. There was no soft murmur of voices or the sound of Miss Hyacinth's knitting needles clicking rhythmically in the heat while she sat with her sister, engaged in some one-sided conversation consisting exclusively of Miss Hyacinth's observations and thoughts. There was no splash of the waves as Cedric dived into the sea. Instead, there was an eerie silence, with the piece of black cloth stretched out on the beach like a shroud.

She shivered again and averted her eyes, instead looking down at her feet, counting the little pebbles … It was then that something caught her eye. Something gleaming and brilliant that had fallen in the dust yet had retained some of its sparkle. For a moment, she stood staring at the object, which looked so delicate and slight. Had she not been surveying that bit of ground she would almost certainly have missed it, as Mr Kettering had done when he had taken part in the doctor's reconstruction of the crime.

It had taken her only a moment to recognise what the object was and, more importantly, to whom it belonged. Aware that her heart was beating, she stole a quick, furtive glance towards the others. The three men were standing on the edge of the cliff with their backs towards her, looking in the direction of the hotel and engaged in what appeared to be rather an intense conversation. She knew she must act quickly. Any moment now one of them might turn around to see what had detained her. She took a deep breath. It was only a matter of seconds to crouch down on the path and scoop up the object in her handkerchief, before stuffing it hastily into her pocket. A hurried look towards the others informed her that her actions had not been observed. Quickly, she scrambled up the path to join them, almost stumbling on the stones in her haste, her cheeks flushed. She was conscious, however, of nothing but the presence of the earring in her pocket, which lay there like some ominous weight.

Chapter Seventeen

They remained at the cliff edge for another half an hour. Together, Mr Kettering and Rose undertook a thorough examination of both the path and the spot on the beach below where Alec Dewhurst's body had been found. Despite their best efforts, their search unearthed no further clues to speak of. Certainly, there was no sign of the murder weapon, which they concluded in all probability had been tossed into the sea and was lost forever. Rose was conscious all the while of the scorching heat. For the sun shone down on them relentlessly, as if it were intent on discouraging them from undertaking their grim task. It was, therefore, with a certain amount of relief that they eventually retraced their steps, winding their way up the steep, uneven cliff path, until they had reached the top, hot and out of breath.

At the doctor's insistence, Cedric had, somewhat reluctantly, visited the makeshift morgue and examined the wound inflicted to Alec Dewhurst's head. Rose herself had no desire to see the body. The sight of a corpse, while not unfamiliar to her, held little attraction. She was content to accept the doctor's testimony with regard to the cause of death or, at least, that there had indeed been foul play. A brief glance at Cedric's face when he emerged from the hotel basement told her that she had made the right decision.

'It was perfectly appalling seeing the fellow stretched out like that,' said her husband, mopping his forehead with a handkerchief. 'He didn't look a bit like he did in life. I suppose death does that to one, and, of course, his clothes were all torn and dishevelled from the fall, to saying nothing of his face. I never took to the fellow, as you know, but even I could see that in life he held a certain physical attraction for some women.' He gave an involuntary shudder. 'If they could see him now, the duchess and Miss Adler ... well, all I can say is that it is best they don't.'

'There is no doubt in your mind about the blow to the head having contributed to his death?' inquired Rose.

'None at all, more's the pity. Someone undoubtedly struck the poor fellow on the back of the head. I won't describe the wound to you, but it was pretty ghastly. All I'll say is it was there, all right, just as the doctor stated. I suppose it does not matter whether it killed Dewhurst outright, or made him lose consciousness and topple over the edge of the cliff. The intention was the same. Whoever delivered that blow intended to cause his death.'

'Yes,' said Rose, picturing Alec Dewhurst as she had seen him last with his dark good looks and clothed in immaculate evening dress. She could hardly imagine the picture of him that her husband had described, macabre and ragged, covered in dirt and sand and ...

'I say, are you all right?' asked Cedric, giving her a concerned look and putting an arm around her shoulders. 'Of course, it's absolutely beastly for you being asked to investigate his death like this. If you refused, I wouldn't think any the less of you, you know. After all, when all is said and done, we are on holiday and it's a shocking affair and likely to become even more unpleasant. There's the duchess, for one thing –'

'Yes, the duchess,' murmured Rose. It was as if she were coming back from somewhere far away, so engrossed had she been in her own thoughts. 'I suppose I really ought to speak to her. She'll be frightfully upset, and I shouldn't like her to hear the news from one of the servants.'

'Will she?' Cedric made a face. 'Be upset, I mean? I know one ought not to speak ill of the dead but, given the way Dewhurst was carrying on with Miss Adler, I shouldn't have thought the duchess will shed too many tears at his demise.'

'I wonder,' said Rose, thinking back to her conversation with the woman in question. She recalled that, even in the shadows and the darkness, she had been aware of the fierce intensity of feelings the duchess had displayed towards the dead man. Even Alec Dewhurst's dalliance with the vicar's daughter, played out before their eyes, had not seemed to dampen the duchess' ardour for him. If anything, it had seemed to strengthen it and make her more resolved than ever to remain with him, as if she were some desperate seaman clinging to the hull of a sinking ship.

Rose sighed. 'I had the impression that she cared for him very much. Besides, she would hardly have abandoned her husband to be with him if she hadn't loved him dreadfully.'

'Well, she doesn't strike me as the sort of woman to go to pieces.'

Rose was not so certain, for only now did she remember how the woman had appeared to tremble when she spoke of the young man. 'I will never leave him,' she had said, with a quiet passion which was all the more deadly for its apparent calm. It struck Rose then that it was possible that what the duchess had actually meant was that she would not let him abandon her. She had lost too much because of him to surrender without a fight.

With such thoughts uppermost in her mind, it was, therefore, with a feeling of growing trepidation that she made her way to the duchess' rooms.

It became apparent as soon as Rose approached the Dewhursts' rooms that the duchess was not an early riser. The windows were still shuttered, and there was little, if any, sign of life behind the wood. Rose, apprehensive of the forthcoming interview, found herself becoming fanciful. She had the odd impression that the rooms behind the shutters had lain dark and undisturbed for years. Long abandoned, she imagined she would find nothing within the four walls but furniture draped in heavy muslin sheets, covered in dust and rubble.

She gave herself a severe talking to for, while the rooms gave every appearance of being uninhabited, she knew it not to be the case. Unless, of course, a little voice said inside her head, the duchess had seen fit to make a hasty departure following Alec Dewhurst's untimely death.

In the very act of lifting a hand to tap on the outer door, she was rescued from her contemplations by being hailed abruptly.

'And what might you be doing, may I ask?' said a brusque voice.

Rose started, as if she had been caught undertaking some dubious or unlawful act.

'I don't know,' continued the owner of the voice, aware that it had the advantage. 'Disturbing those that haven't even had their morning cup of tea. Shame on you.' The speaker huffed and positioned her hands comfortably on her hips, all the while addressing Rose's back. 'I suppose you're the new girl as has been taken on? Well, don't you go banging on doors making a nuisance of yourself. You can make the beds later, aye, and turn them down again. I've a good mind to complain to the hotel proprietor, I have.'

There was a slight pause in the flow of words and Rose took the opportunity to turn around. She found herself facing a tall, thin woman, dressed from head to toe in black. The only bit of relief to the sombre colour of her dress was a meagre collar of white lace attached to what appeared to be a frock made from a material akin to artificial silk.

It took Rose a moment to gather her thoughts and compose her words, so startled was she by the vision standing before her. For the woman looked in all appearance to be some form of inferior lady's maid, more suited to an English village setting than to a Grecian island.

The woman herself seemed somewhat taken aback by Rose's own apparel. Certainly, Rose was conscious of her clothes being quickly appraised by a practised eye, which had no doubt noted the expensive fabric of her summer dress and the tailored cut of her bodice.

'I'm not the new girl,' said Rose quickly, fearing the woman would be embarrassed by her mistake, 'but I have been engaged by the hotel to act on its behalf. I should like to speak to … to Miss Dewhurst. I'm afraid I am in possession of some rather distressing news regarding her brother, Mr Dewhurst.'

'Oh?' said the maid, obviously intrigued, but still showing no inclination to allow the visitor to enter the Dewhursts' rooms.

'Yes. Have you a key? Will you let me in? It is dreadfully important. I really have the most frightful news. I shouldn't wish Miss Dewhurst to hear it from anyone else.'

The servant gave her a long, penetrating stare and Rose was conscious of being scrutinised from head to toe. Much to her relief, it appeared that she had passed muster, the servant having presumably concluded that the newcomer was unlikely to steal the Dewhurst silver. She fumbled in her pocket for a key and Rose was shown into a hall very like her own.

'I'll have to go and wake my mistress. Who should I say has called?' The maid gave Rose a suspicious look. 'You did say how it was urgent, didn't you? I wouldn't want to bother my mistress over a mere trifle.'

'Yes, it's terribly urgent. You see,' said Rose, bending her head towards the servant to indicate that she was about to divulge some information of a confidential and delicate nature, 'it's some rather ghastly news concerning her brother. I'm … I'm afraid there's been a dreadful accident.' She paused a moment before adding: 'Mr Dewhurst is dead.'

For a fleeting moment the servant was speechless. Her eyes fluttered and she seemed to gulp at the air rather like a fish. She put a hand on her chest and said: 'Well, I never! What's the world coming to, I ask you?'

Her eyes widened with a look of horror. 'The mistress will be that upset. Awful fond of her brother, she was.'

'Was she?' said Rose, quickly concluding the servant might prove to be a useful source of information. 'I wondered how she would take the news. I don't know her very well. We hardly saw Miss Dewhurst, you see. Any of us.'

'No, well, you wouldn't, seeing as how she is something of an invalid and keeps to her rooms. She only has me and her brother for company, and seeing as he is gone … well, it don't bear thinking about, do it? Poor thing. She'll be that lonely, and in a nasty, foreign country too.'

'At least she'll have you, Miss …'

'Calder,' supplied the servant, a trifle self-consciously, fiddling with the lace about her throat.

'It will be a blessing for her to have you here, Miss Calder,' said Rose, wondering how she might prolong the interview with the servant, who seemed to her the sort of woman who liked to talk about her employers given modest encouragement. 'Tell me, have you been in the employ of Miss Dewhurst for very long?'

'For about a month, give or take a day or two. Before that, I was working for a Mrs Moore for nigh on nine years. I came with her to Athens, but when she got it into her head to go to India I decided I'd stay put. I had it in mind to return to England, of course, but not before I'd had a bit of a look at Athens, what with all its ancient columns and temples. And then, before I knew where I was, I found I'd spent the money I had kept aside to pay for my passage back home.'

'How awful for you,' exclaimed Rose. 'What did you do?'

'Well, there was nothing for it but to contact an employment agency for a bit of work. A reputable one, mind. I wasn't going to work for just anyone,' said Miss Calder, basking in the unexpected interest in her particulars shown by this well-dressed stranger.

'I should think not,' agreed Rose. 'Is that how you came to be employed by Miss Dewhurst? Through the agency?'

'Yes, that's right. She wanted a proper lady's maid, she did, and very pleased I was to get the job, I can tell you.' She bent her head towards Rose and lowered her voice. 'I could tell as soon as I laid eyes on her, she had breeding. She's not one of those women that gives herself airs and graces for no reason. She don't need to. That's not to say that she's not very particular or demanding, because she is. Not that I mind. I'd rather have them sort than the other, and you know what they say, if a job's worth doing, it's worth doing well.'

By this stage they had crossed the hall and Miss Calder was opening the door to a room which appeared to be some sort of annex to the sitting room.

'What was it you said you did?' she enquired vaguely of her visitor, possibly rather mindful that she had permitted her tongue to run away with her without first establishing her visitor's position. Fortunately, Rose was not required to provide an answer, for the woman's mind was already focusing on what she might do to alleviate her mistress' distress on being informed of her brother's death. 'Mr Dewhurst, God rest his soul, was in the habit of using this room as a sort of study, and –'

The maid had crossed to the window and thrown open the shutters to allow the morning sun to penetrate the room. She had not bothered to glance about her, and it was only when she had returned to the door to bid Rose to enter that she took in her surroundings. She gave a stifled exclamation and released the door knob, as if it had suddenly become unbearably hot. Rose, who had remained in the hall, pushed her way forward past the woman to ascertain what had startled her. It took her only a moment to determine the cause.

The annex room was in a condition of considerable disarray. To Rose's astonished eyes, it gave the general impression of having been ransacked. A large oak desk, positioned in the middle of the room, had evidently been rifled, for all its drawers had been pulled out and the majority of their contents emptied on to the floor. The papers on top of the desk had also been scattered, a few solitary pages clinging doggedly on to the blotter. The chair which was usually positioned behind the desk had been upturned and now lay on its side. A similar fate had befallen the wicker waste paper basket, with its assortment of pieces of paper crushed into balls tumbling out of it. Even the bookcase at the end of the room had not gone unscathed. Books had been pulled out from the shelves and lay open on one of the occasional tables. A quick glance at them revealed that some of the pages had been creased or torn, and even a couple of the spines broken, as if someone had turned over the pages in a hurried and careless fashion.

Miss Calder ushered Rose quickly out of the room and closed the door behind her.

'I don't want the mistress to see that, not on top of the news about her poor brother. She'll have a turn, see if she don't. Now, you stay here,' she added, 'and don't you go saying a word about it to her. The poor mite will have enough on her mind.'

Though Rose's inclination was to return to the annex room, she did as she was bid, realising that to protest would prove fruitless; Miss Calder was on a mission to protect her mistress and would not be thwarted. She would not welcome prying eyes into the apparent chaos that existed in the Dewhursts' rooms. Besides, Rose was reluctant to do anything that would put a stop to their colloquy. They had spoken only in passing of Alec Dewhurst and she was keen to obtain the maid's opinion of the young man. She therefore refrained from commenting on the state of the study, instead giving every appearance of examining one of the watercolours which hung on the wall.

'Chalk and cheese, the mistress and Mr Dewhurst are ... were. She likes to keep her things ever so nice, while he ... well, as I say, you ought not to speak ill of the dead, but his manners could be awful shocking sometimes, to say nothing of all his comings and goings and the way he talked to his poor sister.'

'Mr Dewhurst did not have a manservant who did for him, then?' enquired Rose.

'No, he didn't. He didn't like his things touched. Very particular about it, he was. Of course, they had a maid who came in to do the dusting and the heavy work, but you should have heard him grumble if she tried to clean that there study of his. And now I see why, of course –'

'You had not been in that room before?' asked Rose, somewhat sharply.

'No, I hadn't,' said Miss Calder, making a face. 'And I shan't go in there again neither, save to put it straight. Not allowed, I wasn't, and besides I had no cause to go into the room, being as it was never used by the mistress.'

'Miss Dewhurst never went into that room either?' asked Rose curiously.

'No. Her brother was awful strict about it. Her not going into his room,

134

I mean. And, what with her being the sort of woman she is, she didn't like doing anything to upset him. That fond of him, she was.' Miss Calder gave a sniff. 'Not that I think he deserved it, of course, but I'm not one for gossiping.'

'Why did you show me into that room?'

'Well, there's no harm in it now, is there? Mr Dewhurst's not here to give me a talking to, and besides,' the lady's maid added, colouring slightly, 'it's not as if I could show you into the mistress' sitting room, not with you just being one of the hotel staff, if you'll forgive me for saying. What was your name? I'd better tell my mistress, and I don't think as how you told me?' She looked at the girl enquiringly.

Rose knew that it was only a matter of minutes before her identity was revealed, by the Duchess of Grismere if not by herself. It would surely spell the end to Miss Calder gossiping to her in that easy, unguarded fashion of hers. With this thought uppermost in her mind, she answered Miss Calder's question with one of her own.

'Was it your afternoon off yesterday, or do you live out?'

Taken by surprise, the servant raised one eyebrow and eyed her suspiciously.

'It was just that I was wondering,' said Rose quickly, 'why you let yourself in with a key. I took that to mean you lived out.' Her words were met with a frosty silence. 'I was a little surprised, that's all, that you didn't live in. I mean, on account of Miss Dewhurst being an invalid.'

There was something of an awkward silence. Rose was painfully aware that she had appeared too inquisitive. If only she had let Miss Calder talk in her own longwinded, gossipy way, she would not have aroused the woman's suspicions, and no doubt would eventually have obtained the information she sought. But she reminded herself that time was of the essence. She must use whatever means were in her power to detain Miss Calder, and ascertain all the woman knew, before the servant learned the true nature of Alec Dewhurst's death, and that Rose was in fact not a hotel employee but an amateur sleuth and married to a member of the British aristocracy.

'If I had not taken a liking to you, I might well ask what business it is of yours if I live in or out,' said the lady's maid, a trifle indignant. 'But seeing as you ask, and I believe you to have my mistress' best interests at heart, I don't see why I may not tell you.' She drew herself up to her full height. 'I live out in the servants' quarters of the hotel, though why a bed couldn't have been set up for me in the mistress' dressing room, I don't know. Why, I even said as much to Miss Dewhurst as –'

The lady's maid halted abruptly in midsentence. Both women had caught the sound of a door being opened and, taken somewhat unawares, they had turned around rather guiltily to stare at the door in question. It is quite possible that they had momentarily forgotten that the woman calling herself Miss Dewhurst was situated not twelve feet from where they were standing. Or else they had been too engrossed in their conversation to consider that she might be disturbed by the sound of their voices in the echoey hall.

Chapter Eighteen

The duchess emerged from her room wearing a white silk *negligée*, over which had been thrown, somewhat hastily, a satin lace dressing gown which trailed on the floor behind her like a wedding train. Had it not been for the fact that her hair was the colour of dark ebony, she would have given every appearance of being a ghost. For the odd, deathly pallor of her face matched the whiteness of her attire, and she uttered not a word, as she took in the scene before her, standing with her back to the door, her hands behind her clutching at the door knob tightly, as if without its support she would fall.

'Oh, ma'am,' exclaimed Miss Calder, rushing forward in a clear state of agitation, worried in case her mistress had overheard her gossiping in the hall. 'Won't you sit down? I'll get a chair for you, for I'm that afraid you'll fall.' She was rather reminiscent of a little black beetle scurrying about in search of a feast. 'Oh, ma'am, I hardly dare tell you, but you're in for an awful shock, so you are,' she continued putting an arm around her mistress' shoulders. 'The sitting room, I think. You there,' she said addressing Rose, 'open the door, there's a dear.' She returned her attention to the duchess. 'I'll bring you a nice cup of sugared tea. Or perhaps you'd prefer a little brandy. As you know, I don't hold with spirits as a rule, but they do say they're awful good for shock.'

The Duchess of Grismere permitted herself to be steered towards the sitting room. Her maid was obliged to leave her for a moment, propped up against the wall, while she hurried into the room to throw open the wooden shutters to allow the sunlight to seep in. Her mistress, still looking a little dazed, took the opportunity to peer more closely at the stranger, who stood awkwardly in the hall.

'You!' she said, as recognition dawned on her. There was no warmth in her voice. 'What are you doing here? I didn't send for you.'

'There, there,' said Miss Calder, returning to her position in the hall. 'This young lady's been ever so kind. She works for the hotel, she does. I'm afraid I didn't catch her name, but –'

'Lady Belvedere,' supplied the duchess, putting a hand up to her head, almost as if she thought she were in some strange dream.

'Lady …? No, I don't think that can be right …' began the lady's maid, looking from one to the other of them, a look of growing consternation on her face.

'This is the Countess of Belvedere,' said the duchess wearily, walking into the sitting room.

'Yes,' agreed Rose hurriedly, fearing an awkward silence. 'I am here at the request of the hotel proprietor, Mr Kettering. I am afraid, your … Miss Dewhurst, you must prepare yourself to receive some very distressing news.'

'Oh?' A note of fear appeared in the duchess' voice. She glanced nervously at her lady's maid. 'That will do, Calder. You may see to my room.'

If the lady's maid was minded to protest, the look on her mistress' face persuaded her otherwise. Instead, she scurried away leaving Rose and the duchess to face one another in the sitting room. The duchess closed the door and waited for a moment, as if she feared her maid might be tempted to sneak back and listen at the door. Satisfied that this was not the case, she turned and addressed her visitor.

'Well, what have you to tell me?' she said, a touch of contempt in her voice. 'Has Lord Belvedere seen fit to write to my husband after all?'

Rose, slightly taken aback by the woman's tone, took a moment or two to answer.

She glanced around at her surroundings, as if looking for inspiration on how best to break the awful news to the duchess of her lover's death. The sitting room was a very pleasant room, though sparsely furnished, with newly distempered walls and pale painted floorboards, over which had been strewn some rugs. The walls were bare save for a couple of framed watercolours of the island. The room boasted only two sofas, which were upholstered in a pale gold brocade. The simplicity of the interior inclined Rose to speak plainly and dispense with pleasantries.

'I'm afraid there has been an accident. Mr Dewhurst … Mr Dewhurst is dead.'

On entering the room, both women had remained standing. The duchess had crossed the floor and taken up a position in front of the marble fireplace. Rose, left to stand awkwardly beside one of the sofas, had felt herself to be at a disadvantage. Having spoken, however, her words, in their abruptness, had the effect of seeming to reverse the positions. Everything that followed afterwards seemed to occur very slowly so that, after the event, Rose could remember each individual movement. First, the duchess took a step backwards and collided with the mantelpiece. Then she put out a hand to steady herself and in the process inadvertently caught the corner of a pale blue glass candlestick. The object fell to the floor and smashed in to a hundred tiny pieces. The woman stared at them, as if oddly fascinated by the damage she had caused. With legs that seemed to be made of heavy stone, Rose moved forward and, taking the woman awkwardly by the elbow, steered her towards one of the brocade sofas. The duchess, her legs seeming to buckle beneath her, sat down heavily, dragging Rose down with her so that the two women found themselves unintentionally sitting side by side. It was a moment before either of them spoke.

'Alec … dead?' The duchess uttered the words as if she were in a daze. 'No … no, he's in his room. That's where he is. He's still asleep.' A strange optimistic note had entered her voice, which sounded strained and hollow. 'I shall ring for Calder and ask her to wake him. You will see.'

Before Rose could stop her, the duchess had leapt to her feet and was stumbling towards the bell-pull, an old-fashioned affair consisting of woven glass beads. She began pulling on it for all she was worth, almost as if her very life depended upon it. The lady's maid appeared at the door looking flustered and a trifle out of breath, not to say put out.

'Wake Mr Dewhurst,' the duchess commanded, without preamble.

Miss Calder, a look of horror on her face, looked desperately from one to the other of the women, uncertain what to do. For Rose's tragic news was still ringing in her ears like the peals emitted by the bell-pull.

It was clear to Rose that the duchess was in no mood to be argued with.

'Do as your mistress says,' she said quietly. 'Go to his room.'

Only with the knowledge that Alec Dewhurst was not in the building was there any hope that the duchess would begin to listen to reason. As it was, it was a fretful wait, though, in actual fact, it was merely a matter of a few seconds before the servant had returned from the task and was informing them that Alec Dewhurst was not in his room.

'And that's not all, ma'am,' she added. 'His bed's not been slept in, neither. And he's not in his study, if you was thinking of asking me to look for him in there. Me and her ladyship are just after going in that room, and such a state it's in as I never did see.' Noting the pained expression that her words had produced on her mistress' face, she added: 'Now, you sit down here and take the weight off your feet. That's right. If you lean back, I'll put these cushions here, like this, and you can rest your head on them. I'd close my eyes, if I were you, and take a couple of deep breaths. You'll feel better for it. You've had an awful shock, so you have.'

It was a few minutes before the lady's maid had completed her ministrations to her satisfaction and could be persuaded to depart the room and leave her mistress to her visitor's care. Though she refrained from commenting, it was obvious from the odd glances she bestowed on Rose, and the way in which she fussed over the duchess in such an exaggerated manner, that the servant was of the view that the girl had handled the situation badly. As it happened, Rose was of a similar opinion and inwardly cursed herself for her lack of tact. She felt no better in the knowledge that the duchess' inherent haughtiness had influenced the way in which she had informed her of Alec Dewhurst's death. Two wrongs did not make a right. She had been too abrupt and had lacked empathy, two failings of which Rose was not usually guilty.

The girl turned and stared rather miserably at the marble fireplace, which in the summer heat seemed remarkably redundant. She had heard tell that in the winter months it was cold on the island; indeed, some years there was even snow. Her gaze dropped to the floor and dwelt for a moment on the broken candlestick. She was thankful that Miss Calder had not spotted this particular mishap; she could only imagine the reproachful glances that would have been cast in her direction if she had. She sighed, thinking that the worst was yet to come. For she had still to inform the duchess of the nature of her lover's death.

Rose looked up and discovered, rather belatedly, that the duchess had been watching her closely. A suspicious gleam had crept into the other woman's tearful eyes, which were now focused unblinkingly upon her. Besides sorrow, Rose was conscious of another emotion emanating from the duchess. It took her a few seconds to identify it as fear. But whether the duchess was afraid for herself, or for what she was about to hear, Rose found it impossible to determine.

'He is dead,' the duchess said in a dull voice.

140

She uttered the sentence as if it were a statement of fact, rather than a question. Certainly, she did not require an answer. The combination of her servant's well-meant but slightly over bearing ministrations and the knowledge that Alec Dewhurst had not spent the night in his room forced her to accept that what she was being told was indeed the truth.

'Yes,' Rose said. 'I'm awfully sorry. I didn't mean to speak so abruptly. It was frightfully unkind of me.' The duchess made no comment on this observation, and Rose hurried on. 'Mr Kettering, the hotel proprietor, asked me to call on you and break the news. He didn't want you to hear it from the servants.' Still the duchess did not speak, though her eyes did not leave Rose's face. With nothing but the prospect of a continuing silence, Rose found herself rambling on. 'It was Mr Kettering who found Mr Dewhurst.'

Still no words escaped the other woman's lips. At mention of the hotel proprietor she had given a little start, and her gaze had left Rose's face to stare down at the floor, as if the painted floorboards held for her an awful fascination. Only her hands showed any real movement. They had been folded neatly in her lap, but they had become restless and started to clench and unclench, the knuckles showing white under the pale skin. On occasion, the duchess took the odd deep breath, giving the impression that she was making efforts to compose herself. Once or twice she lifted her head, as if she were on the verge of speaking, but thought better of it.

'Mr Kettering found him on the beach. Apparently he is in the habit of going for an early morning swim. He found Mr Dewhurst's ... body a little way from the bottom of the cliff.'

The duchess stared at her: 'Alec fell over the edge of the cliff? Is that what you are telling me?' She sounded incredulous and for a moment it appeared she was struggling for breath. A few seconds later, however, and the words came tumbling out of her mouth in a torrent. She did not wait for Rose to answer her question. Instead, she seemed intent on answering it herself. 'I suppose he must have lost his footing.' She got up from the sofa and began to pace the room, her hands still clenching and unclenching by her side. 'If his bed's not been slept in, as Calder says, it must have happened last night.' She gasped and put a hand up to her face. 'He always goes ... went for a walk before turning in for the night. He couldn't sleep otherwise. Of course, I told him how dangerous it was. Wandering over to the cliff edge, I mean. I warned him it wasn't safe. But of course, he wouldn't listen,' she said rather bitterly. 'Men seldom listen to what women have to say.' She produced a silk handkerchief from her pocket and began to dab rather ineffectually at her eyes. 'I can't ... I can't believe he's dead,' she said. 'It seems so awfully futile. It was ... it was all for nothing.'

Surmising correctly that the woman was referring to the abandonment of her husband, Rose waited a few moments for the duchess to compose herself and sit down. While she did so, she took the opportunity to steal a sideways glance at her companion, noting the dark smudges under her eyes and the fine lines around them, which looked more pronounced in the raw morning light without a layer of powder to conceal them.

It is possible that the duchess became conscious that she was being studied, for she looked up and for one unguarded moment her eyes met Rose's. Behind the tears Rose detected a look of anguish and some other emotion she could not put her finger on. The next minute and the duchess had averted her gaze, her fingers pulling at the fine satin lace of her dressing gown. 'Must you tell my husband?' she said.

The duchess' head was bowed, the expression on her face hidden from view, her restive fingers still playing with the fabric of her dressing gown. Rose stared at her. Despite this show of seeming indifference, she had the odd impression that the woman was waiting on her answer with bated breath.

When no answer appeared forthcoming, the duchess said: 'I should like to keep it from him. It won't do any good his knowing the truth.' She gave Rose an imploring look. 'It would be as much for his sake, as for mine. Why, you told me yourself that he was ill and had aged dreadfully. Don't you see? It would be a kindness to him if he never found out about ... about Alec... if you didn't tell him –'

'What would you do?' asked Rose rather sharply, though she knew the answer.

'Well, I'd return to England, of course,' said the duchess. 'There would be no reason for me not to take up my old life. I could think up an excuse as to why I had to leave when I did.'

Rose stared at her. 'You mean you would never tell your husband the truth?'

'No. I daresay you will think it awfully wrong of me,' continued the

142

duchess. 'But you, yourself, suggested that I write to my husband. You were quite right when you said that I was miserable. I have been quite wretched. I didn't know quite what to do. I loved him, you see, Mr Dewhurst. But I never for one moment stopped loving my husband.' She sighed. 'I was not aware of the type of man Alec was until … and then, you see, it was far too late to do anything about it.'

Rose was struck by the woman's candour which, whilst rather splendid in its way, was also frightening. There was a ruthlessness about the woman that she found somewhat chilling. She also experienced a pang of conscience. She had permitted the duchess to prattle on, ignorant of the true nature of her lover's death. In so doing, the woman had inadvertently provided her with a motive for why she might have wished Alec Dewhurst out of the way.

'I'm afraid you should prepare yourself to receive another shock. Mr Dewhurst's death was not an accident.'

The duchess started. A look of puzzlement crossed her face. 'What do you mean?' Enlightenment of some sort slowly dawned on her. 'Surely you're not suggesting it was … it was suicide?'

'No,' Rose said. There was a long pause. She looked at the duchess, wondering if she would supply the word that was on the tip of her own tongue. The woman, however, looked bewildered. Certainly, she gave every impression of not having grasped what was being conveyed to her. 'The doctor who examined Mr Dewhurst's body,' continued Rose, deliberately speaking slowly, 'is of the opinion that Mr Dewhurst was murdered.'

Had Rose produced a pistol and pointed it at the woman, the effect of her words on her listener could not have been more devastating. The duchess dropped her handkerchief. A look of horror lit up her features so that they became grotesquely contorted. It seemed to Rose that the woman recoiled from her, leaning back heavily on the cushions, and looking as if she wished for nothing more in all the world than that the sofa should open up and swallow her whole.

'Murdered?' the duchess said, her voice little more than a whisper. 'No! You must be mistaken. Why … why should anyone wish to kill …?' She stopped abruptly, her eyes widening. Rose could not tell now whether it was disbelief or fear which clouded her face. For a fleeting moment, it looked as if the woman might faint. Had she still been standing, then no doubt she would have crumpled to the ground. 'You're … you're a liar!' the duchess gasped between shallow breaths. Her lips were trembling, but a little colour had returned to her face accompanied by a flash of anger. 'How dare you?' she demanded. 'It is wicked of you, wicked to say such a thing!'

'I'm afraid it's true,' said Rose quietly. 'Mr Dewhurst undoubtedly fell from the cliff as the result of a blow to the head.'

'What?' The duchess looked incredulous and put a hand up to her head as if to feel his wound upon her own skull.

'Mr Dewhurst suffered a blow to the back of his head,' continued Rose quickly. It seemed to her, all things considered, that she had spent a great deal of time with the duchess and Miss Calder. A furtive look at her wristwatch informed her that, in all likelihood, the other guests would by now be in the hotel dining room having breakfast. 'The wound was neither self-inflicted, nor as a result of his fall,' she continued, speaking hurriedly. 'Whether the blow was fatal, or rendered Mr Dewhurst unconscious is not yet known, but the result was the same; it caused him to topple over the edge of the cliff.'

'I … I don't believe you.'

'You needn't take my word for it. You may speak with the local doctor who examined him, if you wish,' said Rose, trying to keep the impatience from her voice. 'He will tell you the same. Mr Dewhurst was murdered. Someone struck him with a blow to the back of his head which, one way or another, caused his death. Lord Belvedere has viewed the body and is of a similar opinion.'

Rose gathered her things together. She had said her piece and now she must leave, but not before she had carried out one last task.

'I would be grateful if you would accompany me to Mr Dewhurst's study,' she said. 'There is something I should like to show you.'

For one awful moment, she thought the duchess might refuse. Rose had given her little reason why she should fall in with her wishes. Indeed, she had yet to inform the woman that she had been engaged by the hotel proprietor to investigate Alec Dewhurst's murder. A quick glance at the duchess, however, revealed that the shock that gripped her was absolute. She was in no fit state to query any command given her. Almost without thinking, and with heavy footsteps that seemed to drag across the floor,

144

she followed Rose out into the hall and stood beside her as Rose threw open the study door. It was only then that she appeared to recover a semblance of her senses. A sharp gasp of breath escaped from her lips as she surveyed the ransacked room. She could not fail to see the desk, with its drawers pulled out and their contents strewn across the floor in such a chaotic fashion.

'When was the last time you were in this room?'

'I?' The duchess shook her head. 'I don't know. It was Mr Dewhurst's room. I seldom had occasion to use it.'

'But you have been in this room before?'

Was it Rose's imagination or did the duchess hesitate for a moment before answering?

'Yes, of course,' she said. 'I had forgotten how untidy Alec kept this room.'

Rose glanced around her at the disorder, at the scattered pages and the books with their ruined spines. It seemed to her that the state of the room was more than just the result of someone's slovenly clutter. She was tempted to say as much but, on reflection, thought better of it. Instead, she crossed to the fireplace and examined the empty hearth. A fire had not been lit in it for months, and yet what appeared to be the charred remains of some letters lay in the grate. It was as if someone had seen fit to put a match to them and had tossed them into the empty grate to burn. She stooped and examined what was left of the singed correspondence. Only a few small fragments remained and, of those, only one small piece contained anything akin to writing. She peered at it closely. To her disappointment, she realised that it was no more than one incomplete word. She returned the scrap of papers to the grate, deciding nevertheless that she would memorise the partial word. 'Ober', she said to herself softly. 'Ober.'

She looked up and discovered that the duchess was regarding her closely. The woman had remained on the threshold to Alec Dewhurst's study, and had no doubt witnessed her studying the fragments in the grate. Aware that her activities might be perceived as rather peculiar to anyone unaware that she was an amateur sleuth, Rose hurried across the room to join her. Ushering the duchess out into the hall, she closed the door firmly behind them.

'Did Mr Dewhurst keep this room locked?' she enquired and then,

145

when she received no answer: 'Is there a key?'

The duchess' thoughts appeared elsewhere for it was a moment or two before she muttered rather distractedly: 'I don't know.'

'Nothing must be touched,' said Rose firmly. 'The room will have to be examined for fingerprints.'

It was difficult to know whether the duchess had heard her for the woman's only response was to put a hand to her forehead and close her eyes. The next minute, she had begun to sway, clinging at Rose's arm to steady herself. The girl steered her back into the sitting room. 'You'd better lie down and rest a while. You've had an awful shock.' Rose looked about her for the lady's maid. 'I expect Miss Calder's just popped out,' she said, wondering how long it would be before the servant came back. She ought not to leave the duchess alone. She looked again at her wristwatch, and then up at the clock on the mantelpiece. Time was marching on and the only two people she had spoken to were the Duchess of Grismere and her maid. Indeed, she was still in the Dewhursts' rooms and likely to remain there for a while. Mr Kettering would be waiting for her in the dining room, impatient to inform his patrons of the tragedy and of the measures he had put in place to apprehend the murderer.

Rose glanced at the duchess. The woman was lying stretched out full length on one of the sofas, her head resting on a couple of cushions. There was nothing agitated about her manner now. Judging from the sound of her breathing, she was almost asleep. Certainly, she had closed her eyes and was lying very still. Rose hesitated, unsure what to do. Though she was reluctant to go before the servant had returned, it seemed to her that there could be no real harm in leaving the duchess alone.

She glanced at the clock again. 'I must go,' she said finally. 'Will you be all right?'

The duchess muttered something under her breath. Though Rose could not make out the words, she construed them as a sign of assent. Her mind was finally made up. Casting one last look at the duchess, she crept out into the hall. As she quietly opened the outer door, she could still hear the faint sound of the woman's breathing. She closed the door to behind her, resisting the urge to leave it ajar for the servant, and set out quietly across the terrace.

It was only later that she admonished herself for not having waited to speak to Miss Calder.

Chapter Nineteen

Ralph Kettering was waiting for Rose at the entrance to the dining room. He was fiddling impatiently with the horn-rimmed spectacles perched on the bridge of his nose. Being rather long-sighted, he required them only for close work, though it was his habit to wear them on occasions when he wished to appear a little older than he was, or to give the impression of being intellectual or studious, personal traits he valued highly, and considered particularly fitting for the proprietor of a respectable, upper class hotel.

He did not see Rose approach and she took the opportunity to study him. There was a striking resemblance between Ralph Kettering and his younger brother, Giles, Lord Belvedere's personal secretary. It gave Rose the odd impression that she was well acquainted with the man, when in fact she was not. The illusion was not dispelled when the hotel proprietor opened his mouth and spoke, for his voice might as well have been that of his brother's, so similar did it sound in both tone and inflection.

'Ah, your ladyship,' said Mr Kettering, spotting her and straightening his spectacles. 'The guests are all gathered in the dining room. With the exception of Lord Belvedere, of course. He is still with the doctor. They are examining Mr Dewhurst's clothes for traces of …' He paused, as if he did not quite know how to finish his sentence delicately. Instead, he said: 'Lady Lavinia was asking after your ladyship and Lord Belvedere. I didn't tell her ladyship anything, of course. I did not consider it my place to do so, and I … I was afraid the other guests might overhear. It appears they are aware that something is afoot, though not what it is, of course.' He took off his spectacles and made a show of polishing them with his handkerchief. While staring at the cloth he said in something of a mournful voice: 'I'm afraid I am not very good at this sort of thing.'

It occurred to Rose then that the hotel proprietor might well be having second thoughts about his decision not to send for the local police to investigate Alec Dewhurst's murder. She regretted having left him alone to reflect upon his decision. While he awaited the arrival of his acquaintance from the civilian city police force, the mantle of responsibility hung heavily on his shoulders. She took a deep breath,

148

steeling herself to help him shoulder the burden, while harbouring various misgivings herself. To the effect of trying to appear confident of her position, however, she bestowed on him one of her most assured smiles, and it was together as a united team of two that they entered the dining room.

Without exception, every head turned to regard them with a great degree of curiosity.

'Oh, there you are,' cried Lavinia, running forward to meet her sister-in-law and launching into a tirade of sorts. 'I was wondering where you were. Whatever kept you?' Her gaze travelled towards the door. 'Where's Ceddie? Isn't he with you? I say, I think it awfully unfair of you to leave me to breakfast all alone. You might have said. Really, it's been most frightfully dull.'

'Do be quiet, Lavinia and sit down,' Rose said quickly, aware that the exchange was drawing curious glances from those seated at the neighbouring tables.

Mr Kettering coughed rather self-consciously and went to stand on the stage which was ordinarily used by the hotel band. Rose accompanied him, aware that various pairs of eyes followed her progress across the room.

For someone not sure of the position he had opted to take, the hotel proprietor took no time in broaching the subject matter.

'I'm afraid,' began Mr Kettering, without preamble, 'that it is my unfortunate duty to inform you of the tragic death of one of our hotel guests.'

This announcement was greeted by a shocked silence, followed by sharp gasps of breath. His audience then took to looking furtively about the room as if trying to ascertain to whom he was referring by determining who was missing.

'Ceddie!' cried Lavinia suddenly, a look of panic on her face.

'No,' said Rose hurriedly. 'Cedric is all right. I say, do pull yourself together, Lavinia.'

She looked about the room at the expectant faces. All seemed to be fearing the worst. Mabel Adler's eyes were red-rimmed and puffy, as if she had already been crying. Father Adler's face was grim, for once free of its benevolent expression, and Ron Thurlow looked considerably shocked. Miss Hyacinth looked distressed, and her bottom lip trembled;

she cast an occasional furtive little glance at her sister, whose face, in contrast, remained resolutely impassive. Only Mr Vickers appeared visibly excited by the news, though Rose thought that even in him she detected a degree of apprehension.

'It's Mr Dewhurst,' said Mr Kettering. 'He ... he has met with a most unfortunate accident.'

'He has been murdered,' corrected Rose, still staring at the faces before her, hoping that her abruptness would bear fruit. For it was perfectly feasible, she reasoned, that in one fleeting, unguarded instant she might detect in one face at least a sign of something akin to prior knowledge, if not guilt.

Out of the corner of her eye, Rose noted that the hotel proprietor looked aghast at such directness. Miss Hyacinth emitted a startled little scream; her hand flew up to her mouth as if to stifle her cry. The others were also decidedly shocked and Mabel Adler had begun to cry. Rose studied their faces closely, trying to ascertain if anyone looked unsurprised by the news that had been imparted. She thought it possible that Mr Vickers looked relieved which, mingled with his air of excitement, made a most unsavoury picture. Ron Thurlow had gone very white, and Miss Hyacinth, having recovered from her scream, now looked as if she was on the verge of joining Mabel by bursting into tears. Father Adler, Rose noted with a degree of interest, made no move to comfort his daughter; if anything, he seemed to withdraw within himself. Lavinia seemed understandably shocked by the news, her eyes wide. A look of anguish had fleetingly crossed Miss Peony's face, before it had returned to its expression of impassive indifference.

Ron Thurlow appeared to be the first to recover. 'I say,' he said, 'how perfectly appalling. Murder, you say? Are you quite certain there has not been some dreadful mistake?'

'Quite sure,' replied Mr Kettering, regaining some of his composure. 'I, myself, found Mr Dewhurst's body earlier this morning a little way from the bottom of the cliff ... I do beg your pardon, ladies ... your ladyship,' he said, nodding in the direction of the Misses Trimble, Mabel Adler and Lavinia, and becoming a little flustered. 'Do forgive me. It is a most shocking business and –'

'Oh, don't mind me, Mr Kettering,' said Lavinia, rallying. 'It isn't the first dead body I've come across and I doubt it will be the last.' She added, with a show of flippancy: 'In fact, I'm really quite an old hand when it comes to murder.'

'Quite,' said the hotel proprietor hurriedly, conscious that Miss Hyacinth looked as if she might faint. 'Naturally, I initially assumed that Mr Dewhurst had met with an unfortunate accident.'

'Toppled over the edge of the cliff, do you mean? said Mr Vickers, edging his way forward towards the hotel proprietor.

'That seemed the most likely explanation,' agreed Mr Kettering, a trifle coldly. 'On further examination, however, it appeared that Mr Dewhurst had suffered a blow to the head which would either have been fatal or rendered him unconscious. Either way, there is no doubt that it was this injury which caused him to fall from the cliff.'

'Think yourself to be a bit of an expert in the field, do you?' enquired Mr Vickers rudely.

'Certainly not,' retorted the hotel proprietor. 'It is not my opinion, but that of the doctor who inspected the ... the deceased.'

'Are you suggesting he was pushed?' continued Mr Vickers, apparently undaunted by the rather lacklustre reception of his comments. 'Couldn't the blow have been self-inflicted? By that, I mean, couldn't the fellow have tripped and banged his head?'

'No,' said the hotel proprietor. 'I put that very question to the doctor who examined his body; Dr Costas. The blow was struck to the back of the deceased's head ... Again, ladies, I feel I must apologise ... this is all very unpleasant for you ...' He paused a moment to remove his spectacles and polish the lenses vigorously with his handkerchief.

'What you are saying,' said Mr Vickers, summing up, 'is that this doctor fellow of yours thinks this blow was struck by a third party, as it were?'

'Dr Costas is very strongly of the view that the ... the injury was not something the deceased could have inflicted upon himself, either by accident or design.'

'So he couldn't have slipped?' persisted Mr Vickers meditatively. A thought seemed to occur to him, for he said: 'Any good is he, this Dr Costas chap?'

'He is a doctor of the very first rate,' replied the hotel proprietor tersely.

'I suppose you'll be wanting us to remain here?' said Mr Vickers. 'Just 'til the police have had a word with us, like. No question of me leaving now, eh?' He gave the hotel proprietor an unpleasant leer. 'Not that I'm very minded to stay, seeing as how you treated me last night. Shocking, that's what I call it. I've a good –'

'That will do, Mr Vickers,' said Mr Kettering. 'I'd be obliged if you would kindly be quiet and sit down. I don't need to tell you that this is a pretty ghastly affair and I don't need you to make it any worse.'

Mr Vickers snorted but made no further protest, instead returning to his table while mumbling something derogatory under his breath.

'I have not contacted the local police,' said Mr Kettering, addressing his guests as a whole. 'Instead I have sent for an acquaintance of mine in Athens, who is in the civilian city police force. Murder is much more in his line.'

'In Athens? Good lord!' exclaimed Ron. 'It'll take him an age to get here.'

'A couple of days at most,' said the hotel proprietor quickly. 'But I'm sure you will agree with me that this is a … a most delicate matter which needs to be handled carefully.'

There was a long pause as everyone reflected on this statement, and then Ron said: 'Look here, Kettering –'

'I do not propose that you all be kept waiting,' said the hotel proprietor hurriedly. 'That's to say that we all just sit here doing nothing. Indeed,' he added before anyone could interrupt, 'nothing could be further from the truth. I have in fact, on behalf of Hotel Hemera, engaged Lady Belvedere to investigate this case in her capacity as a private enquiry agent of very great reputation.'

This statement was met with a startled silence. Even Mr Vickers appeared surprised by the turn of events and began coughing rather violently. Rose found herself blushing. To be described as a private enquiry agent, when at best she considered herself to be no more than an amateur sleuth, was a little too much to bear. Certainly, it turned her cheeks a vivid crimson and for a moment she wished she could do anything but meet the incredulous gaze from the sea of faces before her.

'What a jolly splendid notion,' remarked Lavinia, seemingly coming to her rescue. 'My sister-in-law has really a most remarkable reputation as an amateur sleuth. She's solved simply loads of murder cases; dozens, in fact,' she exaggerated. 'Scotland Yard would be at a complete loss without her.'

'Oh, yes,' enthused Miss Hyacinth, turning to address the younger woman. 'Why, dear Lady Lavinia, you were telling me only the other day how Lady Belvedere is acquainted with the very best detectives, and of course, your ladyship, I have read of your exploits in the newspapers,' she said, turning to address Rose. 'I think it the most marvellous idea, I really do, and I for one would much rather be interviewed by you, dear Lady Belvedere, than by anyone else. Certainly than by one of the local policemen.' She lowered her voice. 'One hears such awful stories, though I daresay there is not a word of truth in them.'

She beamed rather ingratiatingly at Rose. Was it the girl's imagination or, beneath the warm smile, did she detect a faint flicker of something akin to fear? Certainly the little bright eyes seemed to dart for a moment towards her sister, though, if Miss Hyacinth was seeking a sign of reassurance from that quarter, she was to be disappointed. For Miss Peony's face was, to all intents and purposes, little more than a mask. Remarkably so, Rose thought, given the circumstances. It was as if the woman was making every effort to assume an air of indifference.

'Naturally what I have said has been a great shock to you all,' continued Mr Kettering, keen to bring his speech to a close. 'I would not be surprised if some of you wished to retire to your rooms to digest this news. I would, however, ask that you remain here in the dining room. Lady Belvedere, with my assistance, will be speaking to each of you in turn. You may then return to your rooms or continue with the activities that you have planned for the day. I would ask, however, that none of you seek to leave the hotel.'

He stood and waited to ascertain how his instructions were received. Possibly he was of the view that at least one of his guests would protest, and even question his authority to detain them at the hotel. To Rose's surprise, no one, not even the objectionable Mr Vickers, demurred. She had expected that at least one of them would insist that they be permitted to leave the hotel without delay. That no one did so was a cause of interest.

Having concluded his speech, Mr Kettering descended the stage and began to make his way towards the door.

''Ere,' said the ever-vocal Mr Vickers. 'What about Miss Dewhurst? I trust you'll be giving her this little speech, same as you gave us?'

'Yes, indeed,' said the hotel proprietor coldly. 'As it happens, Lady Belvedere has already spoken with Miss Dewhurst, not that I can see it is any business of yours.'

'It's more my business than you might think,' retorted Mr Vickers mysteriously.

'I very much doubt that,' replied Mr Kettering. He took a step or two towards Mr Vickers. 'I should warn you that I will not tolerate you bothering any of my guests.'

'What, threatening me now, are you?' Mr Vickers laughed; it was not a very pleasant sound.

Mr Kettering countered with a few choice words of his own, leaving the man in very little doubt as to the measures the hotel proprietor would take should Mr Vickers be foolish enough to disobey his orders. Rose stole a glance around the room. For a few moments at least, the attention of the others would be on the argument. She walked quickly over to her sister-in-law and spoke quietly in her ear, cautious of being overhead.

'Lavinia,' she said, a note of urgency in her voice, 'if you have anything to tell me, you should tell it to me now.'

'What do you mean?' replied her friend, her eyes widening in genuine surprise.

'When I speak to you later, I shall not be alone. Mr Kettering will be with me.'

'Yes?'

'What I am trying to say is if you have anything to tell me which you would not wish to say in front of Mr Kettering, you must tell it to me now.'

Lavinia raised her eyebrows. 'I don't know what you mean,' she said, making no attempt to lower her own voice to match that of her companion's.

'Ssh!' said Rose sharply, uncomfortably aware that, despite her best efforts, their conversation was attracting a few interested glances. 'I have … I have something that belongs to you.'

'Do you? That sounds awfully intriguing. What is it?' demanded Lavinia.

154

'Oh, do be quiet and listen,' cried Rose in a loud whisper, looking about her apprehensively.'

'Really, Rose. You do talk in the most frightful riddles sometimes,' said Lavinia laughing.

Rose made as if to respond, but it was too late. For Mr Kettering, having finished his rather heated conversation with Mr Vickers, had appeared at her shoulder. She noticed that his cheeks were flushed and that his spectacles had slipped a little way down his nose so that they sat crookedly. It was obvious, even to the most casual observer that he was keen to leave both the room and the quarrel with Mr Vickers behind him. There was nothing else for her to do other than give Lavinia one last warning look and follow the hotel proprietor out of the dining room.

Chapter Twenty

Rose followed Mr Kettering across the terrace and into the foyer of the main hotel. She found herself ushered into a small room positioned behind the entrance hall, which served as the hotel proprietor's office. It was a pleasant room, commanding as it did a fine view of the hotel grounds and having the benefit of being light and airy. It was decorated very much in the guise of a gentleman's study. Fine floor to ceiling oak bookcases, laden with old volumes of the classics bound in calf leather, lined the walls. A capacious oak desk took up a considerable portion of one end of the room, to which three mahogany chairs had been drawn up, as if Mr Kettering was intending to call a business meeting. A couple of Mecca Shiraz oriental rugs of muted colour were strewn about the floor and a Chesterfield sofa in faded leather stood in one corner of the room. Framed oil paintings of hunting scenes hung from the distempered walls. Rose had the odd impression, as she glanced about the room, that a small portion of England had been brought to the island's distant shores. Indeed, that if she were to stand with her back to the window so that the scorching sun and the vivid cornflower blue of the sky were hidden from view, she might be standing in a cottage in one of the English counties.

'This room reminds me of home,' Mr Kettering said with a rueful smile, as if he guessed her thoughts. 'Not very in keeping with the surroundings, I know.' He coughed and cleared his throat. 'I thought we might interview the hotel guests here. That's to say, it seemed to me as good a place as any.'

'Yes,' agreed Rose. 'This will do very well.'

'Hello?' said Mr Kettering, for there came to their ears the sound of hurrying footsteps. A moment later and the door was thrown open and Cedric appeared.

'I say,' the earl said, without preamble, 'we found something rather odd when we were searching Dewhurst's clothes.'

'Oh?' said Rose, interested. 'What was that?'

'The chap's pockets were stuffed with trinkets. Absolutely crammed with them. It must have weighed him down a bit. His jacket would have been quite ruined, even if he hadn't fallen over the edge of the cliff and got covered in sand. The lining was ripped to shreds in places and one or two of the seams were coming undone.' He sighed. 'It makes you wonder why the fellow didn't stuff them into a sack or a case.'

'It does', agreed Rose. 'It also suggests that he may have been in something of a hurry. Where are they now, these trinkets?'

'With Costas. The fellow's awfully thorough. He insisted on cataloguing them. He refused to let me have them until he'd made out a detailed list.'

'That sounds like Costas,' said Mr Kettering, with a note of approval in his voice.

'I made a quick note of the items myself,' said Cedric, consulting a page from his pocketbook. 'Ten pairs of gold cufflinks, some with enamel, others with diamonds or sapphires, and one pair with coral and onyx. Five pairs of gold collar pins; seven gold tie clasps, some with diamonds; four pairs of gold shirt studs and six gold pocket watches.'

Mr Kettering raised his eyebrows. 'I suppose,' he said, 'I should place them in the hotel safe. I would not wish them to be stolen.'

'I should like to examine them before you do,' said Rose, 'particularly the pocket watches.'

The hotel proprietor said, in a slightly lowered voice: 'It seems to me rather strange that Mr Dewhurst should carry such items on his person, and in such a fashion too. You don't think there is any possibility that he stole them, do you?'

'Well, I'm not missing any jewels,' Cedric replied with something of a grin, 'and Father Adler doesn't strike me as the type to wear coral and onyx cufflinks.' He adopted a more serious tone. 'If the man was a thief, he'd have done better to steal the women's jewellery. I know for a fact that Lady Lavinia has brought a string of pearls with her, to say nothing of a rather valuable diamond necklace.'

This did little to alleviate Mr Kettering's anxiety. 'By rights, my lord,' he said, with a worried frown, 'such items should be placed in the hotel safe.'

'They should,' agreed Cedric, 'but I'll leave you to tell my sister that! It's possible she may listen to you; she certainly won't heed me on the subject. But I wouldn't worry if I were you. I doubt very much our man Dewhurst was a thief. These items seem to me just the sort of thing a rich woman might give to her lover.'

Mr Kettering went bright red and seemed suddenly fascinated by the pattern on one of the rugs. 'You are suggesting that these ... these items were presents from ... um, Miss Dewhurst?'

'And other women. It wouldn't surprise me at all to discover that was how Dewhurst made his living, if you can call it that. Didn't Vickers say as much?'

'I suggest we refer to Miss Dewhurst as the Duchess of Grismere now,' said Rose. 'I think there is little use in us carrying on the pretence and calling her by anything else. Not if we want to get at the truth.'

'I agree,' said Cedric. 'Anyway, I very much doubt whether there is anyone among the hotel guests who still believes she is Miss Dewhurst. And if there is, Vickers is probably at this very minute putting them right.' He turned to address his wife. 'Talking of the duchess, did you manage to speak with her? I suppose it was an awful shock for her, Dewhurst dying like that? How did she take the news?'

'Rather badly as it happens,' Rose said. 'That's to say, I thought she did at first.' She gave a brief account of her conversation with the woman. 'Of course, I shall need to speak with her again; she didn't tell me much. I wonder,' Rose pondered aloud, 'if that wasn't her intention.'

'I say, it's a bit much her hoping to return to her life in England as if none of this had ever happened,' said Cedric. 'I wonder what the duke will have to say about that. Still,' he added, 'it suggests that she wasn't too fond of Dewhurst. That's to say, she may have gone off the deep end for him in the beginning, but it sounds to me as if she'd tired of him.'

'Which would have given her rather a good motive for wishing him dead,' said Rose, 'particularly if he did not wish to be thrown over. He may have threatened to blackmail her. There were letters, you know. She told me as much.'

'Good heavens!' cried Mr Kettering, looking appalled.

'Mr Dewhurst,' continued Rose, as if the hotel proprietor had not spoken, 'struck me as the sort of fellow who wouldn't want to have been discarded, not if he thought he was on to a good thing.'

'I say,' said Cedric, 'what if the fellow was blackmailing her already?'

'It would explain something that was rather puzzling me,' admitted Rose. 'That's to say, it would explain why the duchess was persuaded to come to dinner last night when it was very evident that she did not wish to be there.'

'And also why Dewhurst was quite happy to carry on with Miss Adler in front of her,' said Cedric. 'I say, I know one ought not to speak ill of the dead, but the man was an absolute cad. No wonder someone saw fit to bump him off!'

'I don't suppose,' said Mr Kettering in rather a small voice, 'that there is the faintest possibility that the murderer was not one of my hotel guests?'

'I think it highly unlikely,' said Cedric, 'unless someone followed him to this island with the purpose of murdering him, of course, which doesn't seem very likely. For one thing, he was evidently travelling in disguise. Dewhurst was not his real name, you know. Vickers told me he was called Goodfellow. And if you are thinking that the motive could have been theft, I shouldn't bother if I were you. Any self-respecting thief would have taken those trinkets with him, not left them on Dewhurst's body for us to find.'

There was a long pause in which Mr Kettering looked very pale and took a deep breath, as if preparing himself for some terrifying ordeal. Rose looked at him with some anxiety, aware that to his ears she and her husband may have sounded rather glib. In truth, she was as much affected by Alec Dewhurst's murder as the hotel proprietor himself. She was also all too aware of the potentially devastating effect such an incident could have on the future of Hotel Hemera.

'I'm awfully sorry,' she said, 'We didn't mean to be flippant. I do hope you don't regret your decision that I investigate this case?'

'Not at all, your ladyship,' said the hotel proprietor urbanely. 'I feel pretty shaken up about all this, I don't mind telling you. It'll take me a while to get my head around it, that's all. I knew, of course, that we should need to interview the hotel guests, but I suppose it didn't really occur to me that we would be looking for motives for why any of them may have wished Dewhurst dead. There is something rather ghastly –'

'I quite understand how you must feel,' said Rose quickly. 'It's perfectly horrid and too beastly for words, but I'm afraid it must be done. And anyway, it would be too awful for everyone to have to sit and wait for your friend to arrive from the mainland, each aware that they were under suspicion and knowing there was not the smallest thing they could do about it. At least this way they will have a chance to get off their chests anything they may wish to tell us. If nothing else, it will give them something to do.'

'You are quite right, your ladyship,' agreed the hotel proprietor, rallying a little. 'Who would you like to speak to first?'

'Actually,' said Rose, aware that she was treading on thin ice, 'I should like to have a look at the guests' rooms, if you have no objections.'

Mr Kettering looked as if he had a great many objections to this proposal and that he had every intention of putting them into words. Rose held up a hand, before he had a chance to protest.

'I'm afraid it's absolutely necessary that I see the rooms as soon as possible,' she said quickly. 'Certainly before the guests have had a chance to return to them.'

'It would be most irregular,' objected Mr Kettering.

'It is just possible that they may have left something incriminating in their rooms. Really, it is the very first thing the police would do if they were here.'

'Is it really?'

'Yes,' said Rose, with slightly more conviction than she felt. 'And in this particular case, the murderer was no doubt of the belief that Mr Dewhurst's death would be determined an accident. You do see what that means, don't you, Mr Kettering?'

The hotel proprietor looked perplexed.

'The murderer would have thought there was little need to cover his tracks,' explained Rose. 'However, now that he knows we regard the death as suspicious, he will be at pains to rid himself of any bit of evidence which might be considered incriminating or as providing him with a motive for wishing Alec Dewhurst dead.'

'I do see, of course, your ladyship, but it would be most improper,' said Mr Kettering. 'My guests are certain to complain, and I can't say that I would blame them.'

'There's no reason why they should know,' said Rose firmly, 'unless we find some incriminating piece of evidence. Then I think they will have far more to worry about than the fact we searched their rooms.' Noting that the hotel proprietor still looked unconvinced, she added: 'We'll need to do a thorough search, of course, but we shall make sure that everything is put back as neatly as we found it.'

'Very well,' said Mr Kettering rather reluctantly, and somewhat against his better judgement. 'Where do we start?'

'I'd better get back to Costas,' said Cedric, following his wife and the hotel proprietor out of the office and into the foyer. He strode away, intent on examining the trinkets.

Meanwhile, Rose and Mr Kettering began their search of the guests' rooms. After some deliberation, they commenced with Mr Vickers' room, which Rose thought was rather a miserable affair. Not only, she was to discover later, was the room tiny in comparison to all the others, it was decidedly shabby and chaotic, and looked as if it had seen better days. The same could be said of Mr Vickers' clothes, of which there appeared to be only a few. They were heavily darned and frayed in places and draped untidily over a chair. Some had fallen off the chair onto the floor and lay muddled with two pairs of shoes which were badly scuffed.

Mr Kettering raised his eyebrows above his horn-rimmed spectacles but refrained from comment. It is possible that he was at a loss for words to describe his opinion of the state of the room. Rose, meanwhile, acted as if she did not see the disorder and instead focused her attention on exploring every item. With a practised hand, she searched the pockets of Mr Vickers' rather dubious clothes, opened drawers, tore the sheets and pillow case from the bed and even looked under the mattress. She remembered her words to the hotel proprietor about putting everything back neatly; fortunately, in Mr Vickers' case, the place was in such a state of disarray that she thought it unlikely he would realise that a particularly extensive search had been made of his room. However, despite the jumble, Mr Vickers' room was regrettably devoid of personal items.

It was not until Rose looked under the bed that she found the old, faded leather attaché case. With Mr Kettering's help, she pulled it out and discovered firstly that it was surprisingly heavy, and secondly, to her dismay, that it was locked. An anxious look crossed the hotel proprietor's face. She wondered if he was worried she might insist that they force the lock. It was not her intention, however, to do damage. Instead, she turned the case over and found a shallow pocket on the outside of the case. She put her hand inside and withdrew from it a photograph.

Mr Kettering, standing behind her shoulder, let out a gasp.

'It's the duchess and Mr Dewhurst,' he exclaimed.

'Yes,' agreed Rose. 'By the looks of it, this photograph was taken in

Athens for, unless I am very much mistaken, that's the Acropolis in the distance.' She laid the photograph down on the bed. 'It seems we were right to suspect Mr Vickers of being a reporter.' She slipped her hand inside the pocket again and felt right down to the bottom. She had not expected to find anything else, yet her fingers came across another piece of thin card about half the size of a picture postcard. She withdrew her hand. It was another photograph, and of the duchess again, but this time she was standing beside a much older man, whom Rose assumed must be the Duke of Grismere. This impression was confirmed by the informal nature of the photograph. There was nothing very posed about the way the two people were positioned. Indeed, the duchess had half turned to face her husband. There was a broad smile on her face, as if she were laughing at something that he had said. In addition to this, she seemed to be in the act of half bending down to stroke a fox terrier that played at her feet. It was an intimate picture, and a natural one. Staring at the photograph, Rose felt she was intruding on something that had been meant for only the duke and duchess' eyes. Even so, she found it difficult to avert her gaze, for the woman pictured was a very different creature to the cold and anxious one that haunted the rooms of Hotel Hemera. She stared more closely at the background featured in the photograph. It appeared that the husband and wife were standing in a walled garden, abundant with flowers. Behind them loomed a large stone-brick building complete with turrets. They were evidently standing in one of the gardens at Grismere Castle.

'I wonder,' said Mr Kettering, echoing her own thoughts, 'where Vickers got hold of this photograph?'

After a final glance at Mr Vickers' room, they went to search the other guest rooms. These were also to reveal various mysteries of their own, or at least questions which required answers. Only Ron Thurlow's room aroused little interest, being as it was full of the various memorabilia associated with a representative of a travelling agency. There was a work journal of sorts which detailed the young man's impressions of the island. These included the various sights of interest that might be visited by the customers of the travel company which employed him. The names of local fishermen from which seaworthy boats might be chartered had also been jotted down, as well as the names of tavernas which might be persuaded to cater for the British palate. Yet again, there seemed very few personal items in Ron Thurlow's rooms, though what there was appeared to be of a surprisingly good quality for a man of his profession, from the silver-backed brushes to one or two fine tailored suits that hung in the wardrobe.

Rose opened the door to the Trimble sisters' room and found that it was almost excessive in its tidiness, which made a welcome change to Mr Vickers' disordered room. Due to its neatness, it was a particularly quick room to search, much to Rose's relief as she was ever conscious of the hotel residents waiting in the dining room. While she searched, Mr Kettering stood watching, delicately averting his eyes when Rose saw fit to rummage in the drawer that contained the siblings' undergarments. She had not unearthed anything of particular interest, and was just about to leave the room, when out of the corner of her eye she caught sight of something that looked out of place given the orderliness of the chamber.

Rose advanced to the fireplace and stared at the empty bow fronted grate, Baroque in style and of a cast iron construction. The fire basket was supported by a pair of columned standards, which in turn were topped by pinnacle finials, and it was these that drew Rose's attention. For on one of the finials, what appeared to be a piece of material had apparently got caught, giving the odd impression that it had fallen out of the chimney. On closer inspection, the item was revealed to be a small velvet pouch. Rose opened it and felt inside. To her disappointment, it was empty. She turned her attention to the chimney itself and rather gingerly felt up inside, aware all the while that Mr Kettering was regarding her actions with a great deal of curiosity. Her fingers came across a piece of cloth which was bunched up in to a ball. With growing excitement, she withdrew her hand and stared at what appeared to be a folded handkerchief fastened by a length of ribbon. Eagerly she undid the bundle to reveal the contents and let out a small gasp. What was produced was a small silver brooch designed in the fashion of a bow studded with sapphires.

'Good heavens!' exclaimed Mr Kettering, as was his wont when confronted with anything out of the ordinary. So absorbed had Rose been in her task, she had been unaware that he had crossed the room to stand at her side.

The hotel proprietor lowered his voice slightly, though there was no one present to overhear them. 'Of course, some of our guests refuse to use the hotel safe in which to place their valuables. They prefer to keep them in their rooms, though, I admit, it is the first time I have heard of anyone stowing them up the chimney. Really, it is a most insecure place. I suppose they wanted to ensure it was well hidden?'

'Yes,' said Rose, turning the object over in her hands and staring at it, clearly fascinated. 'They would want to keep this piece hidden. It would be important to them that they did.'

'Because it is very valuable, do you mean? Really, I must have another word with the Misses Trimble about using the hotel safe. My staff are quite trustworthy, of course; I pride myself on the fact, but even so –'

'They would not want this brooch to be found,' said Rose, 'because … it is stolen, you see.'

'Stolen?' cried Mr Kettering, looking horrified. 'Good heavens! Are you suggesting the ladies staying in this room are thieves?'

'Yes,' said Rose. 'That's to say, one of them certainly is a thief. They may both be in it together for all we know, but one of them most definitely is a thief.'

The hotel proprietor looked at her inquiringly. Before he could ask her how she knew, Rose said:

'You see, it's mine. It's my brooch.'

They left the Trimbles' room in a gloomy and contemplative silence, and proceeded towards the Adlers' rooms, with Rose wondering whether any more surprises awaited them there. She had slipped the brooch into her pocket, where it nestled with the two photographs taken from Mr Vickers' room. What a motley collection she was accumulating. She stole a glance at Mr Kettering's troubled face. She felt rather sorry for him. Hotel Hemera had been open only a few weeks and already it could number a thief and a murder victim among its guests, to say nothing of the murderer.

She would need to confront the Trimble sisters about the theft, of course. She wondered whether it could have any bearing on the murder, or whether it was some isolated, unconnected incident. She rather hoped both siblings were not thieves. Due to Miss Peony's deafness and tendency to appear dumb, Rose felt that she did not know that woman particularly well. Therefore, if one of the Trimble sisters had to be a thief, she would rather it be Miss Peony than Miss Hyacinth, to whom she had taken rather a liking.

They hurried to the Adlers' quarters, which consisted ostensibly of three connecting rooms. Two of the rooms were furnished as bedrooms, the other as a sitting room-cum-study. A quick search of the latter room revealed very little other than a pile of dusty sermons lying on the writing desk and a well-thumbed copy of a guidebook of the island, from which the vicar had derived his facts about Skiathos, and spouted them to a receptive Miss Hyacinth. The room was oddly one of two halves. The study part was in mild disarray, while the area dedicated to the sitting room was tidy and ordered, and had a feminine feel about it from the vase of fresh orchids residing on the bookcase to the silk cushions in pastel hues which lay plumped up on the sofa.

Rose did not expect the bedrooms to produce anything of particular interest. In this, however, she was to be proved wrong.

Mabel Adler's bedroom was, in many respects, a mirror of the sitting room with regards to womanly taste. It boasted a canopy bed and a kidney-shaped dressing table complete with a drapery of muslin over chintz. A nursing chair reupholstered in floral cotton and decorated with a contrasting valance of a knife-pleated silk frill finished the picture of a light and pretty room. Rose saw this all at a glance. It did not surprise her in the least. What caused her sharp intake of breath, however, was the fact that this room, like Mr Vickers', seemed to be in various stages of disarray. A packing case lay on the bed, some of its contents still intact, the rest thrown in piles over the bedcovers and on the floor.

Rose walked over to the wardrobe and threw open the door. It was empty save for a selection of wooden coat hangers which, without the usual array of gowns and blouses that adorned them, looked strangely bare and forlorn. Rose advanced to the eggshell painted chest of drawers. They were as devoid of possessions as the wardrobe. She glanced at Mr Kettering, who merely frowned and shrugged his shoulders.

'Were the Adlers planning to leave the island?' Rose enquired.

'Not to my knowledge,' said the hotel proprietor. 'That's to say, their plans were not very definite, but I expected them to stay for another week at least. I certainly did not expect them to leave today, if that is what you are asking me.'

They hurried to Father Adler's room to ascertain if it was in a similar state of transition. The vicar's bedroom resembled very much the study section of the sitting room in that it was cluttered with various ecclesiastical books and spiritual readings. Indeed, it showed itself to have an occupant who by nature preferred living in a slightly chaotic and muddled environment. What it did not reveal, however, was a person in the throes of packing. There was no sign of a suitcase, and a cursory glance showed that Father Adler's garments were still hanging up in his wardrobe.

Rose felt distinctly puzzled. She began to pace the room as if she thought it might help to clear her head. Had Mabel Adler intended to leave the island without her father? Outward appearances would suggest she had, and yet something had made her change her mind. For a reason, as yet unbeknown to Rose, the vicar's daughter had decided not to finish packing her things. Rose stopped abruptly. Or perhaps that was not it at all. It was quite possible that Mabel Adler hadn't been packing her possessions in the case. Rather, she had been putting them back and had been disturbed in the act of doing so. Rose found herself standing bedside Father Adler's bed. She had meant to leave the room when her gaze fell on to the beside table on which there was a stub of a candle in a brass candlestick. The candlestick was of the sort used by Wee Willie Winkie. That is to say, it had a round, curved base to catch wax spills, and it was this base that had caught her eye. For a piece of paper, screwed up tightly into a tiny ball, had been placed on it. It was so small that, had she not been standing next to it, she might easily have overlooked it. As it was, there was nothing about the little ball of paper which suggested that it might have any significance to her investigation. However, almost without thinking, she put out her hand and unfolded the slip of paper.

Chapter Twenty-one

For those left behind in the dining room, there was the sense that they were existing in some sort of shared, ghastly dream. They sat dumbfounded, a vague recollection of having been informed of Alec Dewhurst's death on the very edge of their consciousness. If it had not been for the bewildered expressions on their companions' faces which matched their own, it is quite possible they would have considered the memory no more than a figment of their fanciful imaginations. Gradually, however, as the dust settled and the shock subsided, they became less dazed. It was then that the awful truth hit them as suddenly and completely as a vicious blow. Alec Dewhurst was dead. Alec Dewhurst, a fellow guest, who had dined each evening with them in this very room. His life had been extinguished and, what was more, his end had been a violent and unnatural one. Murder. The word had an awful, sinister ring to it. It didn't happen to patrons of an exclusive hotel on a remote Greek island. It was something that happened to other people. These were the thoughts that filled their minds. And if that were not bad enough, they were required to remain in the dining room among the remnants of their breakfast, looking over at Mr Dewhurst's empty seat and picturing his ghost supping there. A shiver went down their collective spines. It really was too beastly for words. What was more, the idea of being summoned in turn and having questions put to them, to have to account for their movements on the previous night … And in the meantime they must wait, with nothing to do but watch the minutes crawl by with excruciating slowness on the face of the Chinoiseries lacquered clock that dominated the mantelpiece.

Without Rose to accompany her, Lavinia had forsaken her feigned attempt at bravado. Instead, she sat staring into the distance, as if the back wall held for her some strange fascination. Ron Thurlow was similarly occupied. Mabel Adler was still sobbing quietly, dabbing at her eyes with one corner of her handkerchief, furtively peering beyond the folds of the cloth to cast a cautious glance at her parent. Father Adler sat in silent contemplation. He had initially expressed the obligatory words of condolence. 'An appalling business; a most shocking affair. Really, I don't know what the world is coming to.' This directed to the Trimble sisters, for it seemed that he had all but forgotten the existence of his own daughter sitting at his table, her head buried in her handkerchief. Miss Hyacinth had for once refrained from responding to his comments. Instead, she had sat hunched and small, a tiny, frightened creature. Certainly, her little black eyes darted with worrying regularity in the direction of her sister, her gaze lingering on her sibling's face. Miss Peony herself was unresponsive. It was quite impossible to believe that she was unaware of the fact that Miss Hyacinth was staring at her and looking to her for a lead. For some reason, known only to the woman herself, Miss Peony chose to be uncooperative. She sat at an angle with her back stubbornly turned towards her sister. She refused to catch the other's eye. Indeed, she might have been sitting alone at the table, so little notice did she take of her companion.

'Peony,' said Miss Hyacinth in a loud whisper. 'Peony.' There was no response. Miss Hyacinth began to tug at her sister's sleeve. At first, she did so tentatively then, when she received no reaction of any sort, she pulled at the fabric more frantically. Her voice rose in volume. 'Peony.'

Miss Peony spun around, regarded her sibling, and scowled.

'Ssh! Be quiet. Do you want everyone to look at us?' Her voice was a rasping whisper. It contained a harsh note which was not lost on Miss Hyacinth, who withdrew her hand and fell silent for a moment. Instead of complying with her sister's instruction, however, she leaned forward, reminded of the question she had asked her sister in the early hours of the morning when it was still dark.

'Where did you go last night? You never told me. Where did you go to at half past two in the morning?'

'Never you mind.' Miss Peony said gruffly. Then, almost as if it were an afterthought, she added: 'It was never as late as that.'

'It was. I remember looking at the clock on the mantelpiece.'

This observation was met with a resolute silence.

'Why were you dressed all in black?' persisted Miss Hyacinth, who proceeded to speak rapidly in the hope that she might receive at least one truthful answer. 'You never said. You told me you couldn't sleep, but you didn't tell me where you went. Where did you go?'

'Oh, do be quiet, Hyacinth,' snapped Miss Peony, losing patience, her voice an urgent whisper. 'It's better you don't know. It's for your own good.'

Miss Hyacinth's mouth opened very wide and her hand shot up to her lips. She sank back into her chair, almost as if she were recoiling from her sister. Her mind worked frantically, each image she conjured up in her imagination more frightening than the last.

'Were you there?' she asked at last in a frightened little voice. 'By the cliff; were you there? Oh Peony, did you see what happened?'

Her sister did not answer but a memory came back to Miss Hyacinth of looking at her sister's hands, which at that moment were clasped tightly together in their owner's lap. Strong, capable hands; she had always thought them. And last night she had thought they looked stronger and more capable than ever. Indeed, it had struck her then that they did not belong to an invalid, or at least to the fragile and demur person her sister portrayed in public. Miss Hyacinth knew all too well what her sister was. Though she loved her dearly, she knew her sister to have a mean and spiteful streak. She remembered that on Miss Peony's return from her nocturnal outing she had taken off her wristwatch and, in so doing, her sister had noticed that her hands had trembled.

Miss Hyacinth started at the recollection. She leaned forward and gingerly put out a hand to grasp her sister's sleeve. Before her sibling could withdraw her arm, Miss Hyacinth's grip tightened. Miss Peony turned and glared at her, her eyebrows slightly raised in surprise. She had a good ear, that's to say one ear that was less deaf than the other. Miss Hyacinth pulled her sister towards her so that she might speak into that ear.

'Oh Peony,' she cried. 'What have you done?'

It took Rose but a moment to read the scrap of paper and digest its contents. She folded it once and put it in her pocket to join the other objects she had accumulated during their search of the guests' rooms. Though she was aware that Mr Kettering had been watching her closely while she was reading the slip of paper, she did not tell him what was written on it. Neither did he ask her, and she wondered whether he was still reeling from the discovery that at least one of the Trimble sisters was a thief.

They made their way back to the hotel proprietor's office, each absorbed in their own thoughts. It was only when they entered the room that either showed any inclination to speak. It was Mr Kettering who broke the silence. It was patently apparent to Rose, from both his manner and his speech, that he was beginning to fret.

'They'll be wondering what has come of us. By that, of course, I mean the guests.' He stared forlornly at the pocket in which Rose had stowed the objects she had found. 'I suppose we shall have to inform them that we have searched their rooms. I mean to say, they will wonder how we came across those … those items.'

'They will assume that we have been talking to the duchess,' Rose said. 'I don't think it will have occurred to them that we have searched their rooms.' She turned to face Mr Kettering in order that she might impress upon him the importance of her next words. 'I shall not necessarily tell them what we have found. Indeed, I do not intend to mention it unless I feel it has a bearing on the murder investigation.'

'But your brooch −' objected the hotel proprietor.

'Just because a person is a thief, it doesn't necessarily mean they are a murderer,' said Rose firmly. 'My brooch has been retrieved and returned to my possession, so no real harm has been done.' She held up her hand as Mr Kettering made to protest. 'It is not as if we found any other stolen jewellery. Now,' she said, raising her voice slightly to indicate that she did not wish for there to be any further discussion on the subject, 'I wonder who we should interview first? Of course, I shall need to speak with the duchess again.' She paused a moment and saw Mr Kettering pale at this somewhat alarming prospect. 'But I expect she is still sleeping and it is probably best to wait a while till she is over the initial shock.'

She was aware that it was on the tip of the hotel proprietor's tongue to say they should see the Trimble sisters first. Her own choice, however, was quite different. Somewhat to Mr Kettering's surprise, she said:

'I think we should see Mr Vickers first. If anyone has anything of interest to tell us, I think it will be that gentleman.'

Mr Kettering raised his eyebrows above his horn-rimmed spectacles but refrained from comment. Instead he picked up the bell on his desk and rang it. The servant who came in response to his ring was promptly dispatched to get the guest, and a minute or two later the gentleman himself appeared.

170

The first thought that struck Rose was that Mr Vickers was highly amused both at having been the first person to have been summoned, and also by the rather strange sight that greeted him on his arrival. For both Rose and Mr Kettering were seated behind the hotel proprietor's large oak desk, almost as if they were sharing equal billing. Mr Kettering, it seemed, did not intend to be hidden away in some discreet corner to take his notes. Rather, he intended to be an active participant in the proceedings.

A chair had been drawn up in front of the desk for the intended occupation by the person being interviewed. Indeed, Mr Kettering indicated as much by way of a curt nod of his head in the direction of the chair the moment Mr Vickers entered the room.

It immediately became apparent, however, that the newcomer had other ideas. Instead of taking the proffered chair, he remained standing and took up a position in front of the fireplace, one elbow propped nonchalantly on the mantelpiece in a gesture reminiscent of an idle young man, rather at odds with his advanced years. Indeed, there was something insolent about the pose he struck and the leer on his face which accompanied it, which was almost grotesque. The hotel proprietor did not beat about the bush in reprimanding the fellow.

'You'll sit down and do as you are told. We'll have none of your ill-manners or cheek here, my man. You'll answer our questions and be done with it.'

Mr Vickers pulled a face. 'That's no way to speak to one of your guests. I'm as good as the next man, I am, and I won't stand for it, do you hear?' He did not allow the hotel proprietor any time to answer, but carried on, wagging his finger at Mr Kettering while he spoke. 'And here's another thing. There's no one here as can say as how I have to sit down, and I won't neither, not if I don't want to,' he said sulkily. 'And as to you asking me questions, well, you haven't any right to, poking and prying into things that don't concern you. Anyway, you can ask your questions all you like, but it don't mean I have to answer 'em, not if I don't want to.' He gave Mr Kettering a sardonic smile. 'Last time I looked, you weren't the police, even if you gives yourself airs and graces what you don't deserve and behave as if you are.'

'That'll do,' snapped the hotel proprietor, keen to stem the tirade that was being flung at him. 'We'll have none of your lip here. If you know what's good for you, you'll answer our questions and be done with it. It'll be better for you if you do. Any respectable man would do so and, if you don't, we'll only go thinking you have something to hide. And you wouldn't want us to do that now, would you?'

Rose found herself wincing slightly at Mr Kettering's condescending tone. To her mind, he was speaking very much in the manner of a headmaster addressing an unruly child. Given Mr Vickers' speech to date, she had expected him to answer the hotel proprietor's reproach with a few choice words of his own. Instead, the man's only response to this admonishment was to scowl ferociously.

'And I'll ask that you keep a civil tongue in your head,' continued the hotel proprietor, getting into his stride and feeling as if he had the upper hand. 'You'll treat Lady Belvedere with the respect she deserves, or you'll have me to answer to.'

All the while, during this exchange, Rose had been sitting quietly, her eyes never for one moment leaving Mr Vickers' face. It seemed to her that the man was a mixture of emotions. He was highly amused by the proceedings, but he was also wary. He was insolent and outspoken, and yet he was also snivelling and subservient. It was difficult to know how best to deal with him. That he was in possession of useful information, she did not doubt. But that he would be reluctant to divulge what he knew, she was also equally certain.

'You are quite right, Mr Vickers,' she said at last. 'I have no right to ask you any questions and equally you are not obliged to answer them. I would, however, be very grateful if you would indulge me and concede to our request.'

'Fancy yourself as a bit of an amateur sleuth do you, your ladyship?' Mr Vickers asked with the same sardonic smile.

Before Rose could answer, Mr Kettering said indignantly: 'I'll have you know that Lady Belvedere has a very great reputation in that field, not that it is any business of yours.'

'I'd say it's every business of mine if you're intending –'

'You are quite right, Mr Vickers,' said Rose quickly, fearing that she was making little progress, and conscious that there was a roomful of guests waiting to be interviewed. 'I am only an amateur sleuth, not a real one. That's to say, it is not my profession.' She paused a moment before adding: 'But I am certain your employer, if he were here, would want you to answer my questions.'

'Eh, what do you know about my employer?' demanded Mr Vickers, clearly rattled. 'I ain't told you what line of work I'm in.'

'You informed me,' said Mr Kettering a trifle frostily, 'when you made your booking. Yes, I have it here.' He selected a piece of paper from his desk and gingerly picked it up by one corner, as if he feared that in some way it might be contaminated. 'Under occupation, you have written 'commercial traveller.' In fact, when you first arrived, you told me some highly implausible story about your holiday being some sort of a reward for procuring the most orders in your region.' He glared at the man seated in front of him. 'Of course, I thought it most improbable at the time. Having become further acquainted with you and the sort of man you are, I now know it to have been a lie.'

''Ere you can't talk to me like that,' said Mr Vickers, jumping up from his chair in his agitation. 'I don't have to stand for it, I don't.'

'You are quite right, Mr Vickers,' said Rose, yet again giving the hotel proprietor something of a reproachful look. 'All the same, I think your employer would prefer you to answer our questions. If he were here, he would, quite rightly, insist that you do.'

Mr Vickers resumed his seat reluctantly and said again: 'What do you know of my employer? You'll tell me. I won't answer any of your questions if you don't. No, and you can't make me, neither,' he added, turning to glare at the hotel proprietor.

'We know you're not a commercial traveller,' said Mr Kettering wearily. 'We know you are a pressman employed by the penny press to write some scandalous nonsense.'

There was an awkward silence and then, much to the hotel proprietor's surprise, Mr Vickers threw back his head and laughed.

'That's what you think I am, is it? One of them reporter fellows?'

'Yes,' said Mr Kettering.

'No,' said Rose quietly. 'I admit I thought you were at first, but I have since changed my mind. It was when I discovered this.' She produced from her pocket the informal photograph taken of the Duke and Duchess of Grismere in their garden. She laid the snap on the desk in front of Mr Vickers.

He started. ''Ere, where did you find that?'

'I think you know very well where we found it,' said Rose.

'You'd no right to search my room, no right at all.'

Rose was of the opinion that she had every right to search the man's room, and, besides, the hotel proprietor as owner of the property had given his permission and been present during the examination. She did not think it worthwhile, however, to argue the point. Instead, she said:

'All the same, we found this in your room.' She spoke firmly. 'If you will just hear me out, you shall have an opportunity to speak. When I found this photograph,' she paused to tap it with her finger for added emphasis, 'it occurred to me that your profession was likely to be very similar to my own amateur one. By that, I mean, I think you are a private enquiry agent and that your employer ... that's to say, the person who has engaged your firm to provide him with information, is the Duke of Grismere. I believe he gave you this photograph from his private collection, so that you might recognise his wife.'

Chapter Twenty-two

Mr Vickers looked considerably taken aback and impressed in equal measure by Rose's pronouncement that he was a professional sleuth. As for Mr Kettering, he seemed to be on the verge of having a nervous fit. His face looked incredulous. Barely conscious of what he was doing, he removed his horn-rimmed spectacles and polished them vigorously with his handkerchief. Only then did he seem to have regained the ability of speech.

'A private enquiry agent?'

'Yes,' affirmed Rose.

From his expression, she wondered whether the hotel proprietor considered such an occupation even more demeaning than that of a newspaper reporter. Though, of course, he would be far too polite to say so aloud, given her own amateur involvement with such a profession.

Mr Vickers looked as if he was fit to burst with pent up indignation, but then thought better of it. Instead he chuckled and said: 'Well, I'll be blowed! Perhaps you are a bit of an amateur sleuth after all. You're right, of course. I am a private enquiry agent as you call it, or as good as. Not a bad one at that, if I says so myself.'

It occurred to Rose that having spoken, the man looked relieved. The veil of pretence had been lifted from his reluctant shoulders, and he could be himself. His natural inclination appeared to be rather verbose and she wondered how much of the drunken hotel bore had been an act.

'Course this isn't my usual line of work,' Mr Vickers was saying. 'Working for the gentry, that is. I've searched for many a disappeared person in my time and, whether they're living on the street or a clerk in one of 'em posh offices, I always says how it makes no difference, not to me it don't. Of course, it shouldn't have been me as come to Skiathos. It should have been Frank. Much better at it, Frank is. With his fancy ways and his handsome looks he'd have given poor old Dewhurst a run for his money, so he would. But he's gone and broken his leg, and Jameson, the chap what owns the agency that employs me, what else could he do but give me the job? Needs must and all that and he knew I'd get there in the end, even if I did ruffle a few feathers in the process, and who's to say it didn't do 'em a bit of good to be ruffled?'

The man paused to give the hotel proprietor a meaningful look. Rose concealed a smile and took the opportunity to interrupt Mr Vickers' monologue.

'You found the duchess and her companion in Athens and came to Skiathos believing she would come here?'

'That's right, my lady. I took a photograph of them in Athens too, though they did their best to keep out of sight. That's to say the duchess did. That young man of hers doesn't like to be kept hidden. I heard about this here hotel opening. Very grand they said it was and it seemed to me just the sort of place the duchess would choose to lay low. Very respectable and all that, with big, airy rooms and the service all proper. Course, I wouldn't know much about that myself, having been given no more than a broom cupboard in which to lay my head, but the duchess had a fine set of rooms for her and her fancy man, I'll say that.'

Mr Kettering looked horrified at such talk, but Mr Vickers had more to say on the subject.

'I won't say it isn't a decent place you've got here, Kettering, but it ain't for the likes of me, I'll tell you that. And why anyone would want to go and stay on the other side of the world, when they can go to Eastbourne, I don't know. I've never been so hot in all my life as I've been here. Burning, the sun is, fit to make you blister. I'll go back home the colour of a lobster, so I will; my missus won't recognise me.'

'Mr Vickers,' Rose said, keen to bring the man's observations to a close and return to the subject in hand, 'am I correct in supposing the Duke of Grismere has engaged your agency to find his wife?' Mr Vickers hesitated a moment before nodding. 'They say the duchess left her husband a letter,' continued Rose. 'Do you by any chance know what was written in that note?'

A sly look came over Mr Vickers' face. 'Wouldn't you like to know, my lady? That's confidential information, that is. Sworn to secrecy we were. I can't just divulge it to anyone.'

'We'll have none of your insolence,' snapped Mr Kettering. 'Answer her ladyship's question.'

'All right, all right. Keep your hair on,' said Mr Vickers somewhat rudely. 'I don't see as how it matters now, what with the chap being dead and all.'

'Mr Vickers, if you do know what was written in that letter, I'd be awfully grateful if you would tell me,' said Rose quietly. 'I'm not saying that it has any bearing on Mr Dewhurst's death, but it would help with my investigation if I were in possession of all the facts.'

There was a long pause while the private enquiry agent considered this request. He passed his tongue over dry lips and gave the impression of an animal caught in a trap desperately trying to decide how best to save its own skin.

'Very well, as you like,' Mr Vickers replied, at last, somewhat grudgingly. He retrieved from his pocket a rather grubby notebook and flicked over the pages until he came to the one he wanted. 'Copied it down, so I did, word for word.' Rose caught the hotel proprietor's eye and indicated that he should do the same. Mr Kettering picked up his fountain pen and sat with it poised above a crisp, blank page of his pocketbook. Meanwhile, Mr Vickers took a deep breath in preparation for reading aloud what he had written down in an untidy scrawl.

'Here, we are.' He coloured slightly before he said: '*"My darling. I ask that you forgive me for what I am about to do.*' He coughed. The words sounded strangely odd uttered as they were in Mr Vickers' rather common accent. *'If there were any other way, then please believe me, I would have taken it, but I have no wish to bring disgrace on you, or on your good name. I ask only that you respect my wishes and do not search for me. I do not wish to be found. Know only that I have loved you deeply and that I could not have wished for a better husband."*'

'Good heavens!' said Mr Kettering, finding himself moved by the expression of such desperate sentiment.

'Yes,' agreed Mr Vickers. 'Not bad. That's to say, I've read a lot worse in my time, I can tell you. If you're going to throw your spouse over for another, you'd do worse than copy what the duchess has written. Proper flowery stuff it is, all right, and though there's some who'll say it's nothing but sentimental drivel, it's a good deal kinder than some of the nonsense I've read. Shocking it is, some of it.'

Rose repeated the words over in her mind. The only comment she voiced was that it made no reference to Alec Dewhurst.

'What can you tell me about Mr Dewhurst? That wasn't his real name, was it?'

'No, it weren't, as I was only after telling Lord Belvedere last night, only he wouldn't listen. Frogmarched me out of the dining room, he did, as if I were nothing but a common criminal,' said Mr Vickers, sounding indignant. 'And there was me only trying to do my job. Can't a man do an honest day's work these days without being accosted?'

'I'm awfully sorry,' said Rose in a conciliatory tone. 'We thought you were a reporter looking for a scoop. We were trying to protect the duchess' reputation. Of course, if we had known the truth …' She did not complete her sentence, allowing Mr Vickers to interpret it as he wished. She paused a moment and then asked rather abruptly: 'Didn't you say Mr Dewhurst's name was really Goodfellow?'

'That's right. You've got a good memory, your ladyship, so you have. Mr Alec Goodfellow, that's him. Been in trouble with the law on account of being something of a petty crook. Preys on rich women a lot older than himself, he does. Some of them are foolish enough to give him gifts. Them as don't he helps himself to a little bit of their money. We're not talking their life savings, just a bit of the housekeeping, like, as you might call it. Course, most of 'em don't say nothing, but one or two of 'em takes a pretty dim view of it and kicks up a stink, as it were. Anyway, he found himself stood in the dock. Put in jug, he was. I daresay it was a bit of a shock to him, not that he didn't have it coming. But usually the women he went after had a husband lurking somewhere in the background and that sort don't want a scandal.'

'Do you think he was above a little blackmail?' asked Rose curiously.

'I can't say as how he was, or how he wasn't. Though, to tell you the truth, I don't think blackmail was much in his line,' replied the private enquiry agent reflectively, rubbing a rather spotty chin with his hand. 'Not for any moral reasons, mind. He'd have done it all right if it were easy, like. But I think he thought it was too much effort and a bit of a risk. When he tired of a woman, or she tired of him, he just got himself another. You met him. He could be quite charming when he put his mind to it and, with those looks of his, he was spoilt for choice. What with women being the silly creatures they are over a handsome man, begging your pardon, your ladyship, meaning no offence, like. But Goodfellow could pass himself off as a proper gent, all right.' He sighed. 'Still, even he must have thought someone was looking down on him and smiling when he bagged a duchess.'

'Where were you last night?' demanded Mr Kettering abruptly. He had finished scribbling down one or two notes concerning Mr Goodfellow's character and had become rather bored by Mr Vickers' endless chatter. Really, he did not know why Lady Belvedere encouraged the fellow. The man could talk the hind leg off a donkey given half the chance.

'You know where I was last night,' replied Mr Vickers, sounding vexed. 'In my room licking my wounds, I was. You took my camera off me and locked it in that there safe of yours. Aye, and I'll have it back, thank you very much or you'll have Jameson to answer to. Stealing, that's what I call it.'

'Where were you last night, say eleven o'clock?' persisted the hotel proprietor.

'Sitting in my room fuming and wondering whether Jameson would accept a written account of the duchess being here on Skiathos instead of a photograph of her as proof.'

'You were in a frightful temper, if I remember rightly,' said Mr Kettering. 'Who's to say you didn't leave your room unobserved and meet with Mr Dewhurst?'

'No one at all,' said Mr Vickers, with an unpleasant leer. 'And no one's to say I didn't creep up behind him and bump him on the head, neither, if that's what you're getting at. But you can't prove nothing.'

'I wouldn't put it past the likes of you to try your hand at a bit of blackmail,' retorted Mr Kettering.

''Ere, that's –'

'Thank you, Mr Vickers, you may go,' said Rose quickly, fearing matters were getting rather out of hand.

She shot Mr Kettering a warning glance. She had expected him to sit quietly and take notes, not to antagonise the witnesses and suspects. She waited until Mr Vickers had made his way to the door before she added, almost as if it were an afterthought: 'I'd be most grateful if you would leave the investigating to us with regard to Mr Dewhurst's murder.'

The private enquiry agent turned and grinned. 'Don't you go worrying your pretty little head about that, my lady. I ain't poking my nose in this here murder. It's more than my job's worth, what with me being employed to find the duchess and all. Jameson will take a pretty dim view of it, I can tell you, if I goes about getting evidence to convict her, what with the old duke employing us, like. He'll not want to believe his wife's a murderess, even if everyone else does!'

'What an objectionable fellow. I wouldn't trust the man an inch, your ladyship,' remarked Mr Kettering, the moment the door had closed behind the private enquiry agent.

Rose nodded, somewhat preoccupied, though it occurred to her that even Mr Vickers could be in little doubt regarding the hotel proprietor's inherent distrust of him. Before she could pass comment, however, the door opened again and her husband entered, carrying a brown leather traveller's bag, which she recognised as his own. He placed it with care on a chair and the hotel proprietor proceeded to give him a detailed account of their interview with Mr Vickers.

'Well I never! A private enquiry agent, you say?' Cedric chuckled. 'I can just imagine Vickers lurking in the shadows spying on some unfortunate victim.'

'I wouldn't put it past that fellow to try his hand at a bit of blackmail,' said Mr Kettering, with feeling. 'I doubt he earns much in the ordinary course of things, not by the look of him.'

'You may be right,' the earl replied, a little cautiously. 'I admit I never took to the fellow.'

'He seems to me just the sort who'd like nothing better than to twist some money out of a scoundrel like Dewhurst,' continued the hotel proprietor with relish. 'He'd probably tell himself the fellow deserved it.' He leaned forward and said in a conspiratorial tone, 'Who's to say he didn't have a quiet word with Dewhurst? He might have said he wouldn't disclose certain information to the duke in exchange for a sum of money.'

'Or alternatively,' suggested Rose, 'he might have threatened to tell the duchess about Dewhurst's past unless he was paid to keep quiet. I doubt very much if the Duchess of Grismere is aware of his criminal record.'

'I say, your ladyship, you might be right,' agreed Mr Kettering enthusiastically, straightening his horn-rimmed spectacles.

'Dewhurst wouldn't have stood for it, of course,' said Cedric, entering into the spirit of the discussion. 'I mean to say, he didn't strike me as the sort of chap who'd permit himself to be blackmailed.' He began to pace

180

the room. 'Vickers and Dewhurst arrange to meet at the cliff edge. They would have chosen a late hour when they could safely assume the other guests had retired for the night. They quarrel and ... no, that won't do. One can make quite a good case for why Dewhurst might have killed Vickers, but not the other way around.'

'Yes,' agreed the hotel proprietor. 'Why would Vickers kill Dewhurst if he saw him as the goose that would lay the golden egg, as it were? It doesn't make any sense.'

'Dewhurst might have threatened him,' said Rose.

'Yes,' conceded Cedric, 'but in a struggle, I'd put my money on Dewhurst winning. Physically, Vickers is a pretty inferior specimen. He's the sort of fellow one could knock down with a feather.'

'But, if you remember,' Rose said, 'Mr Dewhurst was struck from behind. It would have been perfectly possible for Mr Vickers to have aimed the blow, particularly if Alec Dewhurst did not consider that the man posed a physical threat to him.

There was a short silence while each imagined various scenarios involving Mr Vickers in the death of Alec Dewhurst. At length, Rose turned her attention to the stout leather traveller's bag.

'It contains all the trinkets that Dr Costas and I found stuffed in Dewhurst's pockets,' explained Cedric, following her gaze. He proceeded to empty the bag. When he was finished, there was quite a display of jewellery boxes and pouches. 'It's all here,' he said, emptying the contents from the various boxes and pouches on to the hotel proprietor's desk. 'Ten pairs of gold cufflinks; five pairs of gold collar pins; seven gold tie clasps; four pairs of gold shirt studs and six gold pocket watches.'

Rose examined each item carefully, turning them over in her hands, while Mr Kettering hovered at her shoulder observing that it represented quite a haul.

'It certainly does,' agreed the earl. 'If he was prudent, a man could live on the proceeds from this little lot for quite a long time. I suppose a fellow in Dewhurst's line of work would regard it as a sort of pension, to be plundered when times were lean.'

'Are these all the trinkets that you found?' asked Rose.

'Yes. I say, is something missing?' Cedric asked sharply.

'The gold full hunter pocket watch,' Rose answered, 'The one Mabel Adler examined and commented on at dinner last night. There were clusters of diamonds on the outer casing. I remember distinctly because they shone in the candlelight.'

Cedric picked up the various pocket watches. 'These are all gold, all right, but four are half hunters.' He paused to examine closely the two remaining full hunter pocket watches. The outer casing of one was elaborately engraved with a design of entwining leaves and flowers; the case of the other was plain except for a few diamonds in the very centre. 'No large clusters of diamonds on either,' he said, 'I say, is it at all possible that you were mistaken? Dewhurst didn't strike me as the sort of chap to misplace a valuable piece of jewellery. It ought to be here with the rest.'

'It might have been stolen,' said Mr Kettering, looking anxious. He caught Rose's eye. It was evident that the same thought had occurred to both of them. Rose remembered all too vividly the small velvet pouch that had caught on one of the finials of the fireplace in the Trimble sisters' room. She shuddered and said aloud: 'It is quite possible I was mistaken. If we do not find the pocket watch in Mr Dewhurst's rooms, I suggest we ask Miss Adler to scrutinise these pocket watches. She should be able to tell us if any of them is the one she examined last night.'

Rose glanced at her wristwatch, conscious that the hotel guests were still waiting in the dining room and no doubt becoming restless.

'On reflection, I don't see why the others might not return to their rooms or go out on to the hotel terrace,' she said. 'I daresay they are feeling rather bored. We can always send for them when we wish to speak with them. After all, we have done a thorough search of their rooms.'

'Very good, your ladyship' said Mr Kettering. 'I'll inform them myself.' He crossed the room. At the door he turned and inquired who they would be speaking to next.

'I think,' said Rose, 'I should like to have another word with the duchess. She, of all people, should be able to tell us about Mr Dewhurst and whether he had any enemies.'

Chapter Twenty-three

'The Misses Trimble,' said Mr Kettering, as they made their way towards the Dewhursts' suite of rooms. 'Would it not be as well to speak to them now? They may well have the pocket watch on their person.'

'I do not propose that we search each guest,' said Rose, certain that such a request would be met with opposition. 'We shall speak to the Misses Trimble after we have spoken to the duchess. The Duchess of Grismere was undoubtedly the last person to see Mr Dewhurst alive, other than the murderer, of course.' Mr Kettering shrugged, clearly of the opinion that she was making a grave mistake in not speaking with the Trimble sisters immediately.

'I have a suspicion,' said Rose, 'that they will restore the pocket watch to its hiding place in the chimney as soon as they return to their room. It will be easy enough for us to find it there.'

'If they do that,' commented the hotel proprietor, 'they will find that your silver brooch is missing.'

'Only if they unfold the handkerchief in which the brooch was hidden,' replied Rose. 'I was very careful to refold it and put it back where I found it in the chimney. I even retied the ribbon.'

Miss Calder answered the hotel proprietor's knock on the Dewhursts' door. She gave the impression that she had been standing behind it waiting for them and burst into speech almost before the door was fully open.

'The poor dear,' she said, presumably referring to her mistress. 'She's just finishing her second cup of tea. Bearing up quite well, she is, all things considered. Had a little sleep, which has done her a world of good.' She put her hand to her chest and declared for the umpteenth time: 'Awful fond of her brother she was.'

Rose and Mr Kettering exchanged meaningful glances. Even now, it seemed, the lady's maid was ignorant of her mistress' true identity or the real nature of her relationship with Alec Dewhurst.

They followed Miss Calder into the sitting room where the duchess was reclining on one of the sofas, propped up by an abundance of cushions. A thin blanket had been placed over her legs. She made no effort to get up to receive her visitors, or indeed to alter her position on the sofa. To Rose's mind, the woman gave every appearance of being the invalid that Alec Dewhurst had purported her to be.

A quick glance at the duchess' face was sufficient to inform her that the woman was not particularly pleased to see her callers. Rather, she gave the impression that she was mildly irritated by the intrusion.

'You may go, Calder,' said her mistress. 'Close the door behind you. I suppose,' she said, looking at the hotel proprietor, and addressing him in her most haughty voice, 'you have come to pay your condolences. It is not necessary. I should prefer to be left alone.'

'I'm afraid that is not possible, your grace,' said Rose. She sat down firmly on the opposite sofa even though she had not been offered a seat. Mr Kettering remained standing rather awkwardly at the door.

'I informed you earlier this morning,' Rose continued, 'that Mr Dewhurst had been murdered. I should like to inform you that I am now here in something of an official capacity. That is to say, Mr Kettering has engaged me to investigate Mr Dewhurst's death. You may not be aware of the fact,' she said, conscious that the colour was rising in her cheeks, 'but I am by way of being an amateur sleuth.'

This statement was met with a resolute silence, which it appeared Mr Kettering felt it his duty to fill.

'Yes, indeed ... Miss ... your grace,' he said, rather ingratiatingly. 'Lady Belvedere has a great reputation in that regard. She is, in fact, held in the very highest of esteem by Scotland Yard. They have consulted her ladyship on a number of cases.'

'Have they, indeed?' said the duchess, looking from one to the other of them with a degree of contemptuous amusement.

Rose's cheeks, still flushed after so glowing an endorsement from the hotel proprietor concerning her detecting abilities, reddened further under the duchess' mocking smile. For it was patently obvious that the woman was highly cynical of such claims. Faced with such overt scepticism, Rose fought the temptation to inform her of the various cases in which she had played a salient part in solving the murder in question. Instead, she said:

'Mr Kettering has sent for an acquaintance of his, who holds a position in the civilian city police force in Athens. In the meantime, I shall be undertaking my own investigation into this affair. I am aware that this has been a dreadful shock for you.' She paused a moment to consider carefully her next words. 'I am aware also,' she said, speaking slowly, 'that this is a delicate matter. While I assure you that you may rely on my discretion, I shall need to be in possession of all the facts.'

The Duchess of Grismere turned rather pale. Some of her haughtiness left her, but a streak of anger quickly rose to the surface and gave her a flush of colour. She said, in something of a cold voice:

'It seems to me, Lady Belvedere, that you are already in possession of all the relevant facts. Indeed, you and I have engaged in endless conversations where I have done very little else but inform you of all the facts.'

While Rose was of the opposite opinion, she did not feel it worthwhile to argue the point. Instead, she said:

'Will you tell me when you first made Mr Dewhurst's acquaintance?'

'In the spring at some ball or other,' said the duchess, somewhat evasively. 'You needn't bother to ask me any questions about ... about my relationship with Alec. I shan't answer them if you do. Do you hear me? I ... I don't want to go over it; it doesn't do any good.' She put a hand up to her forehead and covered her face. 'Besides,' she added wearily, the expression in her eyes hidden by her hand, 'you ... you know what they were.'

'Are you aware of whether Mr Dewhurst had any enemies?' asked Rose, somewhat frustrated by the duchess' stubborn refusal to answer specific questions, and those she did, not in detail. The girl was determined, however, not to be swayed from asking the questions she had in mind.

'You know the sort of man he was,' replied the duchess, with a note of bitterness. 'He was the type to make enemies. I am sure he had a great many.'

'When was the last time you saw Mr Dewhurst?' continued Rose, feeling that she was making very little progress.

'I imagine it was the same time that you did, yourself, Lady Belvedere,' said the duchess, raising her head to look at her questioner. 'The last time I saw him, I was standing talking to you by the tennis court. Mr Dewhurst was running, hand in hand, with Miss Adler towards the cliff edge. After our conversation ... well, I was upset. I returned to my rooms.'

185

'You didn't see Mr Dewhurst again?' persisted Rose.

'I have just this minute told you that I did not,' replied the duchess, a note of impatience in her voice.

'You might not have actually seen him, but perhaps you heard him return to your rooms?'

'No. I took a sleeping draught. It is a habit of mine. I fell asleep as soon as my head touched the pillow.'

'Were you aware that Dewhurst was not Mr Dewhurst's real name?'

'What do you mean?'

Was it Rose's imagination, or had a note of fear entered the duchess' voice? Certainly she no longer appeared bored with the line the questions were taking.

'Mr Dewhurst's real name was Goodfellow.'

'Oh, yes,' the duchess said quickly. 'I knew that his name was Goodfellow.' She sounded oddly relieved, as if she had feared some other revelation. 'We travelled under assumed names. We thought it would be less … conspicuous. My husband …' She faltered, unable, or unwilling, to continue her sentence.

'His name,' continued Rose, 'was Alec Goodfellow.'

'Yes.'

'Did you also know that he was a petty criminal?'

'I … I don't believe you,' said the duchess, though the expression on her face suggested otherwise.

Rose had the odd feeling that the duchess was playing a part. She wondered if it was for the benefit of the hotel proprietor, who looked decidedly uncomfortable by the turn the conversation had taken. It is quite possible that he felt an obligation to contribute to the colloquy to prevent it from deteriorating any further.

'It really is most unfortunate,' he ventured, somewhat apologetically, 'but I am afraid Lady Belvedere is quite right. That's to say, we have it on good authority that the deceased was a thief who had served a period of time in prison.'

'I see.' The words were spoken wearily, without emotion.

Rose had the odd impression that the duchess had either long ago resigned herself to the fact that Alec Dewhurst was a thoroughly bad lot, or else she was being told a fact which she already knew. She sat in a resigned fashion waiting for one of her visitors to elaborate on Mr Kettering's statement. Remembering the way in which the duchess had vehemently defended her lover's character the previous evening, Rose found herself riled. It had not been her intention to be unkind yet, before she could stop herself, she said: 'He was in the habit of preying on women of wealth. He stole from them.'

Two bright spots of colour appeared on the duchess' cheeks and she swallowed hard. While there was something rather pathetic about her, there was also a flash of defiant anger in her eyes, which was rather magnificent. She said: 'Well, he did not steal from me, if that is what you are inferring.'

'You were in the habit of making him gifts?'

'Well, what of it? I don't see what business it is of yours what I did,' said the duchess, sounding indignant.

'Mr Dewhurst produced a pocket watch at dinner last night. Quite an elaborate affair. Did you by any chance give it to him?'

The duchess hesitated a moment before answering, almost as if she suspected Rose of laying a trap.

'What if I did?' she said finally. 'Why do you ask?'

'For no reason other than that it appears to be missing.' The duchess gave a sharp intake of breath. 'We believe that it may have been stolen,' continued Rose, watching her closely. 'Unless, of course, it is in your possession?'

'No,' said the duchess abruptly. 'I don't have it. Stolen, you say? Isn't it among Alec's things?'

'That is what we shall need to find out.'

Rose was quite sure a look of relief fleetingly crossed the duchess' face, replaced hastily by one resembling concern at the potential loss of a valuable piece of jewellery. For some reason that she could not yet fathom, the duchess appeared pleased by the theft of the pocket watch. For, not for one minute, did Rose believe that it was lying in Alec Dewhurst's rooms among his possessions. It was quite ludicrous to suppose it might be there. Alec Dewhurst would not have laden himself down with numerous trinkets only to leave behind the most valuable one of them all. Though the duchess' reaction to the theft puzzled her, she did not have time to reflect on it further. For there came suddenly into her mind a feeling of absolute certainty that something was amiss. She had allowed herself to become distracted. Even now, as she sat and parleyed with the duchess, events were occurring around her which might adversely affect her investigation.

She had a moment of clarity concerning what these might be and sprung up from the sofa. 'Where is Miss Calder?' she demanded. 'What is she doing? What was she doing before we arrived?'

She did not wait for the duchess to answer, but instead fled from the room, pushing past the hotel proprietor, mumbling: 'I must search Mr Dewhurst's rooms.' She did not need to see the half smile that curled up the corners of the duchess' mouth. Neither did she need to witness the lady's maid appear at the door, rubbing her hands clean on her apron, declaring to anyone who would listen that it was all finished. For she knew only too well that she was too late. The damage had already been done.

With a sickening feeling in the pit of her stomach, Rose strode into the hall and threw open the door to the room that Alec Dewhurst had used as a study. The sight that greeted her eyes confirmed her worst fears. Last time she had been in this room it had been in a state of considerable disarray with the drawers of the desk pulled out and rifled, their contents strewn across the floor. The chair and the wicker waste paper basket had been upturned, and the books on the bookshelves had been pulled out, their spines broken and their pages torn.

The ransacked room was no longer chaotic. It had been restored to an order that in all likelihood exceeded its original condition. To Rose, it looked immaculate. There was no scrap of stray paper on the floor. The chair and the waste paper basket had been righted; the books returned to their original positions in the bookcase; and the contents of the desk either disposed of or put back in the drawers. However, it was not this that Rose found particularly vexing. It was the fact that the room had evidently been cleaned within an inch of its life. Every wooden surface had been vigorously polished so that it shone and the floor had been most effectively swept. It was quite possible, if Miss Calder had found the time, that the lady's maid had also seen fit to peg out the rugs on a clothes' line and beat them.

It would be futile now to examine the room for fingerprints. Rose walked over to the fireplace with heavy steps. There was no sign of the scorched fragments of paper. They had been got rid of as effectively as the grate had been swept and cleaned, in common with the rest of the room. At least, she consoled herself, she remembered the incomplete word that had been written on the scrap of paper. 'Ober', she murmured. 'Ober.'

She was still repeating the word to herself when she marched back into the sitting room. There was no sign of Miss Calder who, having completed her task had evidently disappeared. The hotel proprietor was still standing awkwardly where she had left him, just inside the door.

'Ober?' queried Mr Kettering raising his eyebrows above the frames of his horn-rimmed spectacles, as was his way. 'Ober, your ladyship? I believe,' he supplied helpfully, 'it is short for the German word *Oberkellner*, used to describe a head waiter.'

'I don't think the word I read was referring to a waiter,' Rose replied rather curtly.

There was a long pause as she looked pointedly at the duchess. The woman returned her gaze steadily, but the two bright spots of colour had disappeared from her cheeks, making her face seem very pale. Aware that she was allowing her anger to get the better of her, Rose said:

'Why did you deliberately disobey my instructions? I asked that the study be left as it was, that nothing be touched. I told you it would need to be examined for fingerprints.'

Rose was conscious that her voice had risen as she spoke. Out of the corner of her eye, she could see the hotel proprietor fidgeting with his spectacles, consumed with embarrassment on her behalf. It was quite possible that he thought there would be a scene and she again had the feeling that she was handling the situation badly.

The Duchess of Grismere blinked and raised herself into a sitting position with the aid of the arm of the sofa. She discarded the blanket that had been covering her legs and let it fall, unheeded, on to the floor. It seemed to Rose's impatient mind that the duchess' movements were purposefully slow and laboured, as if she was playing for time. Indeed, she imagined the woman's mind working frantically, considering how best to answer her question. Both women, Rose realised, were preparing for the inevitable confrontation, which seemed to have had its origins in their conversation, among the shadows, the night before.

'I was not aware that the room had been tidied,' the duchess said. She spoke both quietly and slowly, though there was a cold note to her voice, which was not lost on Rose. 'In fact, it is the first I have heard of it. I have been asleep and have only just wakened. Miss Calder must have taken the task upon herself to do. Shall I ring for her so that she might explain to you her actions?' The duchess leaned forward. 'I trust you *did* inform her that nothing should be touched?'

Rose stared at her. There was nothing she could say. If the duchess was complicit in Alec Dewhurst's death, and there was a connection with his death and the ransacked condition of the study, then she had played her hand very cleverly. The girl admonished herself severely, for really, she had only herself to blame. She had told the lady's maid that Alec Dewhurst was dead but had refrained from mentioning that he had been murdered. Miss Calder had commented on the state of the study in her presence, but Rose remembered that she had said nothing about leaving the room as it was. She had left the duchess sleeping, not even sure if the woman had heeded her words. She should have waited for the lady's maid to return from her errand. If only she had thought about it, she would have realised that a woman of Miss Calder's character would have seen it as an act of kindness to her mistress to don an apron and undertake a task normally assigned to a housemaid. There was nothing that could be done about it now, and it was all her own fault. A smile played over the duchess' lips and Rose, aware that her own cheeks were burning and that she was allowing her anger to get the better of her again, said:

'I believe the word on the scrap of paper that I found in the grate referred not to *Oberkellner* but to a person's name.' There was a long pause and she regarded the duchess closely, curious as to how the woman would react to such an assertion. 'You were in the habit of calling Alec Dewhurst 'Oberon', weren't you?'

If Rose had announced that she had killed Alec Dewhurst herself, the effect on her listener could not have been more shattering. The duchess gasped and put a hand up to her mouth, as if to stifle the words she was afraid she might utter. Her face now had a deathly pallor, the dark smudges under her eyes more pronounced than ever. Had she not been seated, she would surely have fainted. Certainly, that was the view of Mr Kettering, who in one swift movement had leapt forward and grabbed at the bell-pull, with its woven glass beads, and pulled at it as if his very life depended upon it.

'I?' spluttered the duchess. 'You are surely mistaken.'

'I think not,' said Rose firmly. 'On several occasions in my presence you have referred to Alec Dewhurst as Oberon, before hastily correcting yourself and saying Alec. I think Oberon was the name that you were used to calling him.'

'Very well, said the duchess slowly, knitting her hands together in the odd gesture that was peculiar to her in times of anguish. 'When I first made Mr Dewhurst's acquaintance he did tell me his name was Oberon … Oberon Goodfellow. I … I believed him. I had no reason to doubt that what he told me was true. It was not until much later that he informed me he was not particularly fond of the name and asked if I would call him Alec instead, which I did.'

'Why should he tell you that his Christian name was Oberon if it wasn't?' asked Rose sharply.

The duchess blushed. 'He … he must have discovered somehow that I had a particular liking for the name. You see, 'A Midsummer Night's Dream' has always been a favourite play of mine and …'

She did not finish her sentence, but instead allowed it to falter, burying her face in her hands. It was in this position that her lady's maid found her, hurrying into the room rather belatedly in summons to the bell-pull. Taking in the scene, she proceeded to tell Rose and the hotel proprietor, in no uncertain terms, that they should be ashamed of themselves for upsetting her mistress like that. Awful wicked, it was, and her brother not even cold in his grave.

They were ushered unceremoniously out of the door, Mr Kettering uttering a spate of apologies, while Rose reflected on the importance of the name 'Oberon' and wondered why the duchess had deemed it necessary to lie.

Chapter Twenty-four

Mr Kettering was very quiet as they made their way back to his office. Rose was of the opinion that he had found the interview with the Duchess of Grismere particularly trying and distasteful. Possibly it was only now dawning on him that they would be required to ask questions that were, by nature, prying and intrusive. It was an inevitable part of a murder investigation, as was the fact that those interviewed were frequently nervous or reluctant to be questioned, often supplying evasive answers.

'If you will forgive me for saying, your ladyship, I had the impression that her grace was not being entirely truthful,' volunteered the hotel proprietor, almost as if he had been reading Rose's thoughts. 'That is to say, I do not believe she has told us everything.'

'In a case such as murder, people very rarely do,' Rose said, with the voice of experience. 'Often they are afraid it will put them in a bad light, or else they do not think the piece of information in their possession is relevant to the investigation.' She paused a moment before adding: 'I agree that the duchess did appear rather reluctant to answer our questions.'

'Do you believe that story of hers about the Shakespeare play?'

'No, but I do believe she was telling the truth when she said Alec Dewhurst told her his name was Oberon. The question is, why did he tell her that when it wasn't his real name? Oberon. It seems rather an odd sort of name to choose.'

'There's something significant about that name, all right,' said Mr Kettering, gaining a little in confidence on discovering that Rose was a receptive listener. 'One had only to look at the duchess' face when you mentioned the moniker Oberon to know that.' He glanced down at the notes he had made in his pocketbook. 'Who would you like to interview next? The Misses Trimble? Would you like to see them together or one at a time?'

'Together, I think. I am not certain Miss Peony ventures anywhere without Miss Hyacinth in attendance.'

Rose might also have mentioned that she was curious to see whether, when questioned, Miss Hyacinth would look towards her sister for reassurance, as she had done in the dining room. She was equally interested to know whether Miss Peony would resume her quite remarkable air of indifference.

Mr Kettering coughed and looked a little uncomfortable. 'The ... the brooch. Do you intend to confront the Misses Trimble on the matter of the theft?'

'No,' said Rose meditatively. 'I am not certain the theft is connected with Mr Dewhurst's death. I would not wish it to muddy the waters.' Rose held up her hand as the hotel proprietor made to protest. 'I agree that there may be some connection or other, but we must focus on the murder, not on the theft. Besides, I would prefer to avoid any unnecessary unpleasantness. Of course, I should like to know for my own peace of mind which one of the sisters is a thief, but I believe I can find that out without the need for a confrontation.'

Mr Kettering appeared somewhat perplexed, but he did not consider it worthwhile to argue the point. Instead, he looked with a degree of curiosity as Rose produced the little silver brooch from her pocket and proceeded to fasten it on to the front of her dress. She took a silk scarf from her bag and draped it rather carelessly about her shoulders, thus concealing the brooch. A smiled played across Mr Kettering's lips, for he had an inkling as to what she intended to do.

The Trimble sisters entered the room with a degree of nervousness, which was hardly surprising given the circumstances. Miss Hyacinth's timorousness showed itself clearly by the expression on her face, while Miss Peony's anxiety was wrapped up in a mask of apathy. The addition of the Bakelite ear trumpet clutched tightly in Miss Peony's hand, and which rested in her lap for the duration of the interview, did little to dispel the feeling that the woman was purposefully preventing herself from taking an active part in the proceedings. Due to the cumbersome nature of the instrument, she was stating, as clearly as if she had said it aloud, that it would not be put to any use. Indeed, it was an effective barrier, reminding those present that Miss Peony was deaf, lest they be inclined to forget the fact. It was almost as if the ear trumpet was a weapon that could be called upon at will to be wielded like a shield to deflect any awkward questions. Certainly, it's very presence removed the necessity for its owner to answer them.

To Rose, the very fact that Miss Peony had seen fit to bring the despised object with her, coupled with her quite bizarre expression of indifference, was an indication that the woman had something to hide. Miss Hyacinth's anxious little glances towards her sister only sought to reinforce this feeling. Both women were on guard, though whether their fear arose from the same source, it was difficult to tell. They had every reason to be concerned. One of them, at least, was a thief and the person they had stolen from was sitting in front of them questioning them about a murder.

Miss Hyacinth gave a nervous little smile. Had the circumstances been different, she might well have accompanied it with a nervous little laugh. As it was, she said: 'Oh dear', 'a most shocking affair' and 'quite dreadful' a number of times.

Rose sought to put the two women at their ease by asking them a few questions about their various travels. Miss Peony, as always, remained resolutely silent, while Miss Hyacinth answered readily enough for both of them. Yes, they had been to Greece before. They had stayed at the Acropole Palace in Athens. Was her ladyship familiar with that particular hotel? Two hundred rooms and one hundred and sixty bathrooms! Every room had running hot and cold water and a telephone; had her ladyship ever heard of such a thing? Yes, indeed, they almost considered themselves seasoned travellers. Why, only in March they had undertaken a twenty-one day pleasure cruise to the Mediterranean departing from Southampton. It really had been a most remarkable adventure. They had visited Greece, Italy and North Africa, not that they would want Lady Belvedere to consider them unduly extravagant. Why, it was only after the death of their dear father that they had ever travelled at all. Before that, their holidays had been confined to the British seaside resorts of Sidmouth, Torquay, Brighton, Weymouth and Falmouth. There was a slight pause because Miss Hyacinth thought she might have forgotten one. Oh, yes, she remembered it now. Bournemouth. Now, what had she been saying? Oh, yes, they had decided to visit the Greek islands because they had read somewhere in the travel literature that the islands were popular for sunbathing and yachting. Of course that was not to say they had been yachting, but it really was very pleasant to sit on the beach and soak up the sun though, had they realised it would be so very hot at this time of year … Anyway, they had read in the same travel brochure that Grecian people were friendly and hospitable, and that most understood English, which really was a most important consideration, didn't her ladyship agree?

Rose, finding that her head was beginning to spin with Miss Hyacinth's endless chatter, sought to put a stop to the woman's gentle rambling. It had served its purpose. Miss Hyacinth, at least, appeared to be at her ease. In fact, she was beaming at Rose in a most kindly manner and had hardly cast a glance in her sister's direction during the entirety of her narrative.

'When was the last time you saw Mr Dewhurst?'

Miss Hyacinth looked somewhat taken aback and not a little put out by the sudden change of subject. Her mind was still lingering on the delights of the Mediterranean pleasure cruise; she did not wish to return to the ghastly business of Alec Dewhurst's death. She was stung also by the abruptness of the question and cast Rose a reproachful look.

'Last night in the dining room,' she said, for her, a trifle coldly. She pursed her lips, lowered her voice and leaned forward in her chair. 'I hardly like to mention it, and dear Peony will think it quite dreadful of me if I do, but I couldn't help noticing that Mr Dewhurst was dancing in rather an intimate fashion with Miss Adler. Really, we felt for the poor duchess, my sister and I, though, of course, she had rather brought it on herself; don't you agree?' Her hand shot up to her mouth. 'Oh dear,' she said. 'Have I spoken out of turn? Ought I to have referred to her as Miss Dewhurst rather than the Duchess of Grismere?'

'It is quite all right,' said Rose, concealing a smile, for Miss Hyacinth, in apologising, had only made matters worse. 'I doubt whether anyone, with the possible exceptions of Father Adler and his daughter, is unaware of the woman's true identity.'

'Oh, the vicar knew all right,' replied Miss Hyacinth, before she could stop herself. 'I told him myself only yesterday. I mean to say, I thought he ought to know the sort of man Mr Dewhurst was, given how dear Mabel seemed to be losing her head over him. And of course, I couldn't tell him about Mr Dewhurst without first telling him about the duchess.'

Rose gave her a sharp look but did not comment. Out of the corner of her eye, she caught sight of Mr Kettering scribbling down this salient fact in his pocketbook.

'You did not see Mr Dewhurst again? That is to say, later in the evening when he had finished dancing?'

There was a slight pause. Was it the girl's imagination, or did she detect again the same faint flicker of something akin to fear? Certainly Miss Hyacinth's little bright eyes were seeming to dart towards her sister, much in the same way they had done that morning in the dining room. 'No, I did not see him again,' she said finally. 'My sister and I do not keep late hours. We returned to our room when Mr Dewhurst was still engaged in dancing with Miss Adler. We went to bed and read for a while, as was our habit, and then we turned out our light.'

'And went to sleep?'

Miss Hyacinth nodded apprehensively. 'Oh, yes, indeed. We are quite heavy sleepers.'

'You did not happen to leave your room again?'

'Certainly not,' said Miss Hyacinth, looking a trifle apprehensive.

'Miss Peony?' said Rose, turning her gaze upon the woman's sister. 'Did you leave your room? Perhaps you decided to take a walk before turning in? It was a fine night.'

Rose was vaguely aware that Miss Hyacinth was sitting on the edge of her seat. The question had been a simple one. What was more, she was quite certain that Miss Peony had heard her ask it. Yet she was greeted with such a blank stare by that woman as to suggest otherwise. But she had not been mistaken for she was certain that the look of bewilderment on Miss Peony's face was feigned. Its intention was to deceive. For she did not doubt for one moment that Miss Peony had been avidly following their conversation. Her face might be devoid of all emotion, but the hands in her lap that clutched the ear trumpet had rarely remained still.

'Oh, no,' declared Miss Hyacinth, answering for her sister. 'Peony didn't go out. It is not the sort of thing she would do. Go out alone, I mean, and certainly not after dark.'

Rose stared at Miss Peony, but she remained as resolutely silent as ever. Rose was half tempted to go over to the woman and pick up the ear trumpet, if only to produce a reaction. Instead, she sat quietly at the table, waiting. The ensuing silence that filled the room had the effect of unnerving poor Miss Hyacinth.

'She would have told me if she had,' she continued rather desperately. 'Left our room, I mean. And besides, I would have heard the noise of the bolts being pulled back and the door being opened.'

Rose did not pursue the matter further. She felt tolerably certain that, having concocted a story between them, the sisters would stick to it like glue and, besides, she had her answer as clearly as if she had received it from Miss Peony's own lips.

The interview was drawing to a close. There was still one task left to do and yet Rose found herself reluctant to complete it for the simple reason, she told herself later, that she had been rather afraid of finding out the answer.

In a seemingly careless movement, her hand brushed the edge of her scarf and, in so doing, it fell on to the desk, a bright blue bundle of silk. Rose was wearing a white summer dress, very simple in style and unadorned except for the silver brooch in the shape of a bow. Both the Trimble sisters' eyes were drawn to it, if only because both the silver and the sapphires caught the sunlight which streamed through the window. The brooch glittered very prettily. Though enthralled by it, only one of the Misses Trimble let out a gasp, her hand going up to her mouth and her face turning white. It was all that she could do to stifle the scream that leapt to her lips and yet, of course, it was too late; she had given herself away.

'Well I never!' exclaimed Mr Kettering as soon as the Misses Trimble had left the room. 'Fancy the thief being Miss Hyacinth! For what it's worth, my money would have been on Miss Peony being the culprit.'

'Yes,' said Rose, rather distractedly, for it had just occurred to her that she had forgotten to arrange for the pocket watch to be retrieved from the sisters' room while they were being interviewed. She admonished herself severely for this oversight, not least because Miss Hyacinth, on realising that her hiding place in the chimney had been discovered, would this very minute either be ridding herself of the pocket watch altogether, or seeking out a new hiding place in which to stow it. Rose advanced quickly to the door and then, for some reason she, herself, could hardly fathom, abruptly changed her mind.

Later, she told herself that it was because she had felt quite certain that, if challenged, Miss Hyacinth would confess to her part in the theft whether the pocket watch was produced or not. Such reflection on her part, however, was yet to come. That particular moment in the hotel

197

proprietor's office, Rose contented herself with listening to Mr Kettering, who had evidently quite forgotten about the existence of the pocket watch. His attention instead had been drawn to Miss Peony's odd behaviour and Miss Hyacinth's claim that neither she nor her sister had left their room after retiring for the night.

'Do you believe Miss Hyacinth was lying, your ladyship?'

'I believe she is holding something back,' said Rose carefully. 'Did you notice how adamant she was that her sister had not left the room?'

'She did not like you questioning Miss Peony,' observed Mr Kettering.

'No. I think she was rather afraid what her sister might say, which leads me to believe that it was Miss Peony, rather than Miss Hyacinth, who took a walk last night after the sisters had supposedly turned in. That is to say, I believe Miss Peony waited until her sister was asleep and then let herself out of the room.'

'To do what?' asked the hotel proprietor. 'Surely you are not suggesting that she went out with the intention of murdering Mr Dewhurst?'

'No,' said Rose, 'but I think it quite possible that she went out in search of him. I am quite certain that something untoward happened. I do not believe it is in Miss Peony's character to look so impassive or unconcerned about the murder of a fellow guest. Her habit is to nod and smile, not to adopt a rigid mask. This morning, in the dining room, she did not seem particularly shocked by the news of Mr Dewhurst's death. Under the circumstances one would expect her to show some signs of being shaken or upset.'

Mr Kettering nodded sagely, remarking that, now he came to think of it, he could quite well imagine Miss Peony striking Alec Dewhurst on the back of his head with that ear trumpet of hers.

Chapter Twenty-five

Mabel Adler entered the room tentatively, the effects of recent sobbing very apparent on her young face. Her eyes were red-rimmed, and her complexion wan and pale. She clutched in one hand a damp handkerchief, rolled up into a ball, her restive fingers picking at the fabric as if seeking for something, anything, to do to distract her mind from dwelling on the awful events that had occurred. The thought struck Rose that the handkerchief would be quite ruined, twisted and pulled out of all recognition. If this thought struck the vicar's daughter, however, it did not stop her from plucking at the miserable square of cotton and rolling it up into an ever tighter ball.

Rose and the hotel proprietor stared, appalled by the rapid transformation that had ravaged the young girl's features. For once Mabel Adler appeared careless about both her appearance and her dress. Strands of hair were plastered to her forehead and the blouse she wore was crumpled and creased as if she had lain down while wearing it. She bore so little resemblance to the Mabel Adler with whom they were familiar, that she might have been no more than a pale and inferior imitation of herself.

Alarmed by her rather pathetic appearance, Mr Kettering hurried forward and ushered the girl into a chair. He poured her a glass of water and regarded her with something of a paternal air as she sipped at the liquid gingerly. After a while she cradled the glass in her hands and her fingers became still. She looked from one to the other of them with wide, scared eyes.

'Is it true?' she asked in a very small voice. 'Is ... is he really dead?' Rose nodded. 'I ... I simply can't believe it,' she said. 'I'm ... I'm all to pieces.'

'It's been a dreadful shock,' said Rose kindly. 'I know it's beastly for you, but I'm afraid we must ask you a few questions.'

Mabel stared at her apprehensively. The knuckles on the hand holding the glass were quite white. It occurred to Rose that, in her present agitation, there was a fair possibility that the girl would break the glass. She leaned forward and took it from her and put it down on the desk out of harm's way. Bereft of clinging to the glass, Mabel returned to pulling at the fabric of her handkerchief.

'Before I ask you any questions about Mr Dewhurst,' said Rose, keen to distract the girl, 'I should first like you to look at these.' She proceeded to remove from Cedric's bag the two gold, full hunter pocket watches which she laid out carefully on the hotel proprietor's desk. 'I wonder if you could tell me whether you have seen either of these pocket watches before?'

The girl's brow clouded for an instant. No doubt she was remembering the pocket watch that she had examined the night before with such childish enthusiasm. She leaned forward and put her hand out towards the objects. She studied each in turn, handling them with a solemn reverence. This time her eyes did not widen appreciatively. Instead, she blinked back tears.

'I thought that one was Mr Dewhurst's,' she said in a voice hardly above a whisper, pointing at the watch which had a few diamonds in the centre of its outer casing. 'But Alec's ... Mr Dewhurst's one had more diamonds. I ... I counted them.' She put a hand up to her eyes, as if she found the recollection too painful.

'It wasn't this one by any chance?' said Rose quickly, pushing forward the other watch. 'It's engraved with entwining leaves and flowers; can you see?'

'Yes. It's ... it's beautiful. But it's not Mr Dewhurst's pocket watch, if that is what you're asking me. His didn't have a design on it as such, just his initials. Only ...' she paused a moment before adding, 'only, of course, they weren't his initials.'

'Oh?' said Rose, trying to keep the eagerness from her voice. 'Whose initials, were they?'

'I don't know. But they weren't Alec's. They didn't begin with an "a". I thought they did at first, because sometimes people write a capital "A" as if it were a large lower case "a", don't they? I know my aunt does. But it wasn't an "a". When I looked more closely, I realised it was an "o".'

'Do you remember what the other initials were?'

'No, I don't. I didn't have time to look at them closely. I was more interested in counting the diamonds. All I remember was that there were three initials.'

'Could the last initial have been a "g"?' asked Rose.

'A "g"?' said Mabel, screwing up her face in concentration as she tried to drag her mind back to the night before. 'Oh no, I don't think so. It had more lines. By that, I mean it was made up of lines like a capital "M", or a "W".'

'You are quite certain that neither of these pocket watches was the one Mr Dewhurst produced at the dining table last night?'

'Quite sure,' said Mabel. 'I am quite certain I should recognise it if I saw it again.'

Rose returned the pocket watches to the bag and looked at Mabel. Some of the girl's natural colour had returned to her cheeks and she had stopped fidgeting with her handkerchief. It seemed to Rose a shame, therefore, that she was obliged to pry and probe into matters that she was fully aware the vicar's daughter would rather not dwell upon.

'When did you last see Mr Dewhurst?' she asked gently.

The colour that tinted Mabel's cheeks now took on a bright, unnatural hue that accentuated the deathly pallor of her skin beneath its thin veil of powder.

'You danced with Mr Dewhurst last night and then you went for a walk with him,' prompted Rose, when no answer appeared forthcoming.

In her mind's eye she saw again Alec Dewhurst taking the girl in his arms and then the couple rushing past her, hand in hand, towards the cliff edge. It was clear that Mabel shared the same recollection, for the girl was now dabbing at her eyes ineffectually with the screwed up handkerchief.

'Yes,' said Mabel, between sobs. 'It was such a lovely walk. It was so beautiful. I … I shall never forget it for as long as I live, not even if I live to be a hundred.'

Rose was tempted to ask Mabel what they had talked about. On reflection, however, she thought better of it. The girl was in a fragile enough state and, besides, it was easy to imagine the general course their conversation had taken. Instead, she said:

'Did you return to the hotel together? Or did you leave Mr Dewhurst at the cliff edge? You must tell me; it is frightfully important that you do.'

'My dear young lady,' said Mr Kettering, addressing the girl before Rose could stop him, 'did Mr Dewhurst do something to frighten you? Perhaps you pushed him away and he fell? It would be quite natural if you did. Took steps to defend your dignity, I mean. I daresay you didn't realise you were standing so near the edge. The courts would take a very lenient view about that sort of thing, I can tell you. But you must tell us the truth. It is the only way we can help you, my dear.'

Mabel stared at the hotel proprietor with her mouth gaping. Her eyes had widened to a frightening degree. Rose was inclined to copy her reaction, so taken aback was she by the hotel proprietor's intervention. Her initial inclination was to object. She was the detective, after all, albeit it an amateur one. She might be acting on the hotel's behalf, but it was up to her, surely, not Mr Kettering, to determine the questions to be answered. Yet, oddly, she found herself loath to interject. There was a certain simplicity and frankness to Mr Kettering's questions. It startled those addressed into making a response, where a more subtle line of questioning might well have produced an awkward silence or barely audible answers.

'You … you think I killed Alec … Mr Dewhurst?' stuttered Mabel. 'How could you? How could you be so wicked as to suggest such a thing?'

With that, she dissolved into a flood of tears. Rose cast a reproachful look at Mr Kettering, who retreated into flicking over the pages of his pocketbook followed by a thorough straightening of the items on the desk before him.

'There, there,' said Rose briskly. 'Mr Kettering didn't mean anything by it. They are the sort of questions we shall be putting to everyone, you know,' she said mendaciously. 'It is merely a matter of form.'

'I didn't kill Alec,' said Mabel, a defiant note of bitterness creeping into her voice. Even if *he*,' she paused to give the hotel proprietor a scathing look which had the unfortunate gentleman again seeking refuge in the pages of his pocketbook, 'suggests I did. He oughtn't to say such things.'

Rose decided that the best way to diffuse the situation was to repeat her original questions. She said: 'Did you return to the hotel together? Or did you leave Mr Dewhurst at the cliff edge? It is frightfully important that you tell us.'

'We returned to the hotel together. I was worried about leaving my father by himself. I knew that awful Trimble woman would be bothering him and Mr Dewhurst was concerned for his … his sister.'

202

Rose gave the girl a candid look. 'You know, of course, that Miss Dewhurst was nothing of the kind? By that I mean she was not really Mr Dewhurst's sister.'

'I didn't know it then, that she wasn't, and I am not sure that I believe it now.' Mabel stuck out her bottom lip, very much in the manner of an obstinate child.

'Miss Dewhurst is in point of fact the Duchess of Grismere. You must have heard of 'The Disappearing Duchess'? It has been in all the newspapers.'

Mabel gave a brief and rather grudging nod.

'And Alec Dewhurst was not really Alec Dewhurst,' continued Rose, watching the girl closely. 'His name was Alec Goodfellow and he was by way of being a petty thief.'

Mabel started violently. Rose thought her surprise appeared genuine. Certainly the words that followed suggested that it was.

'I ... I don't believe you, not about him being a thief.'

This sentence was met with a resolute silence which merely seemed to alarm Mabel further. It was as if she were clutching at little bits of rope that were snapping and breaking in her fingers.

'I suppose,' she conceded finally, 'that there might be some truth in what you say, about Miss Dewhurst not being his sister, I mean. I did rather wonder if she was. She was simply years older than Alec and I know he found her rather trying. It wouldn't surprise me in the least to hear that he had grown bored with her.' A defiant look came into her eyes. 'But I don't believe a word you say about Alec being a thief. Nothing will make me believe that.'

It seemed useless to argue the point. Instead Rose said: 'Your father told you last night that Miss Dewhurst was the Duchess of Grismere, didn't he? I think it would have been after you had returned to your rooms, following your walk with Mr Dewhurst. I daresay he was frightfully angry about that. You would have quarrelled.'

The colour left Mabel Adler's cheeks and she blinked.

'We didn't argue as such, not until ... He said he thought she might be the duchess,' she replied in a dull voice, choosing her words with care. 'But really he was not certain. He did not know quite what to believe. Miss Hyacinth is the most frightful gossip, you know. You always have to take what she says with a large pinch of salt. When Miss Dewhurst appeared at dinner he thought Miss Hyacinth had got it all wrong. Why she couldn't have minded her own business, I don't know.'

'She cares about you,' said Rose gently. 'You might not realise it now, but she endeavoured to save your reputation.'

'What do you mean?' Mabel looked startled.

'Mr Dewhurst asked you to elope with him to Athens, didn't he? I daresay he told you that you'd be married there. Before you judge Miss Hyacinth too harshly, I think I should tell you that he was not the sort of man to marry anyone, and certainly not a girl without a fortune. I'm afraid he'd have thrown you over when he had no further use for you.'

Mabel Adler looked as if she had just been slapped. It occurred to Rose that no one had ever spoken to her so bluntly. Had Rose not been her social superior, she did not doubt for a moment that the girl would have got up and marched out of the room. As it was, she muttered in a voice hardly above a whisper: 'How dare you? How can you be so cruel?'

'I'm sorry,' said Rose. 'But it needs to be said. I daresay that at this moment you hate me like poison. I know I should if I were you, but in time I believe you will accept that what I have told you is the truth. Now,' she said, keen to progress the interview, 'you suggested just now that you and your father did in fact argue. When precisely was that? Was it, by any chance, when he intercepted Mr Dewhurst's note to you?'

Rose produced from her pocket the slip of paper she had located in the base of the Wee Willie Winkie candlestick in Father Adler's room and laid it out on the hotel proprietor's desk.

Mabel bent forward and studied the note. If she was minded to protest at their having read it, she thought better of it. In fact, the girl appeared quite resigned and not a little exhausted. It was quite possible that she had not slept very much the previous night, if at all. Certainly she seemed to wilt before them. All the fight in her appeared to have deserted her. She bowed her head and rubbed her swollen eyes with a hand that trembled.

'Alec gave the note to a servant and instructed him to deliver it into my own hands. At least, that is what he said he was going to do. I suppose the servant didn't listen. Or perhaps he didn't understand. Either way, he gave it to my father instead of to me. Of course,' she said with a note of indignation, 'he shouldn't have read it; my father, I mean. It was addressed to me, but he recognised that it was written in Alec's hand.'

'And you quarrelled?'

'He came marching into my room and found me packing.' She shuddered. 'We had the most almighty row. I have never seen my father so angry. I daresay you think I always get my way and I suppose usually I do. I know Miss Hyacinth thinks I wrap my father around my little finger; I've heard her say as much to Lady Lavinia.'

'But last night he stood his ground?'

Mabel gave a bitter little smile. 'I should say he did! He read me the riot act, as one might say. I … I was quite frightened. I have never known him be like that. He raised his voice to me. He said …' she stopped abruptly in the middle of her sentence. Her hand flew up to her mouth, as if she wished to retract the words.

'Yes?' said Rose. 'What did your father say?'

'I don't want to tell you. You … you can't make me.' Mabel sounded very much like the obstinate, spoilt child again. Rose decided to handle her precisely as if she were a wilful infant.

'It really won't do, Miss Adler. You may sulk and pout all you like, but in the end you will have to tell us what he said. It will be much better for you and your father if you do.' Rose paused a moment, aware that this might not necessarily be true if the vicar was guilty of Alec Dewhurst's murder. 'What did your father say he would do?'

'He said that he was going to find Alec and have it out with him,' Mabel sobbed. 'He said it would be much better for Alec if he didn't find him; that if he did, he didn't know quite what he'd do. He said that in all likelihood he'd swing for him.'

'Well,' said Mr Kettering, as soon as the door had closed behind a tearful Mabel, 'that was a very good act, I must say. Miss Adler is quite an accomplished little actress.'

'You didn't believe she was speaking the truth?' said Rose. She remembered the concerned manner in which the hotel proprietor had urged Mabel Adler to take a seat before she fainted, and the way in which the girl had responded by giving him a filthy look when he had suggested that she had killed Alec Dewhurst by accident.

'Not a word, though she was quite convincing,' said Mr Kettering. 'I'll give her that. Creeping in here all meek and red-eyed and then turning the tables on her father, while all the time pretending it was the last thing in the world she wanted to do.'

To Rose's mind, the girl had appeared sincere. She said, with little conviction: 'I suppose it is just possible that Miss Adler and Mr Dewhurst argued at the cliff edge.'

In truth, she could not imagine Mabel Adler killing the young man. The girl who had run hand in hand with Alec Dewhurst to the cliff edge had been full of high spirits. She had giggled and skipped. Indeed, the two young people had not seemed in the mood for argument, certainly not to enter into a quarrel that would result in one of their party's violent death.

The hotel proprietor, however, was not to be deterred. 'Miss Adler might have slipped out later to warn him that her father had intercepted the note,' he said, picking up the scrap of paper from the desk. 'It says here that they should meet at the usual place. That may well have referred to the cliff. I daresay Father Adler did not know where his daughter and Dewhurst were in the habit of meeting. If he were minded to confront Dewhurst, as Miss Adler told us, he would in all probability have gone to Dewhurst's rooms. That would have given Miss Adler the opportunity to slip out and go to the cliff to warn Alec Dewhurst that her father was aware of their plans and meant to put a stop to them.'

'Yes, but that supposes Mr Dewhurst had gone back to the cliff edge,' said Rose. 'Why would he be there at that particular time? It would have been too early. This slip of paper indicates that Mabel and Alec were to meet at one o'clock in the morning. If the vicar intercepted this note, it must have been delivered at a much earlier hour. According to Mabel Adler, he proceeded directly to her room to confront her and found her packing. I would therefore be very surprised if it was much after half past eleven when they had their quarrel.'

Well,' said Mr Kettering, reluctant to relinquish his theory, 'just for argument's sake, let's suppose Alec Dewhurst did return to the coastal path. It is quite possible he wished to collect his thoughts and considered it as good a place as any. Miss Adler found him there and they quarrelled. If he thought the vicar was going to cut up rough, he might well have blamed Miss Adler. A fellow like that would want to cut his losses. He would most probably have told her that he wanted no more to do with her and a girl with Miss Adler's disposition would have been frightfully upset.'

206

'If they did quarrel, as you suggest,' said Rose, 'I think it far more likely that they rowed about Miss Dewhurst. If you recall, Miss Adler had just made the discovery that Miss Dewhurst was not Alec Dewhurst's sister. It would have been a dreadful shock to her. It is quite natural that she would have questioned Mr Dewhurst's motives for deceiving her and thought the worst.'

Mr Kettering said: 'So we can make out a pretty good case against Miss Adler?'

Rose wondered if that was in fact true. She could picture the girl's distress well enough, for it had been evident during the interview. Indeed, beneath the soft, pretty surface she thought she had glimpsed flashes of the necessary steel required in a person's composition to enable them to undertake such a ghastly deed as murder. Mabel Adler was used to getting her own way. How would a girl like that deal with being thwarted or deceived? As these thoughts passed through her mind, a picture appeared before her eyes unbidden of Mabel, consumed by rage, wielding a heavy object at Alec Dewhurst's head, all the while tears pouring down her face.

Chapter Twenty-six

Father Adler entered the hotel proprietor's study with a degree of sombre dignity as befitted a member of the clergy. Death was not a foreign environment for him. His chosen profession necessitated that he visit the sick and the dying. Indeed, it seemed to him that he was often negotiating the various paths associated with death. He sat beside sickbeds and presided over funerals. He was fully accustomed to death, therefore, but a deliberate, violent killing was beyond the ordinary course of his experience. He was visibly shaken by the recent turn of events. In the dining room he had seemed both withdrawn and aloof. In Mr Kettering's study, in contrast, he was inclined to be verbose, giving voice to the most typical expressions of disbelief as were usually uttered in such circumstances.

'A shocking affair ... a perfectly appalling business ... a most dreadful thing to have happened ...very distressing for all concerned.' The banal phrases tripped off the vicar's tongue. Rose thought that, with very little encouragement, he might be persuaded to continue with his platitudes until he had quite exhausted his considerable supply. In fact, she was rather of the opinion that he wished to do so, that anything was preferable to being asked questions of a distasteful nature concerning Alec Dewhurst's death.

Father Adler had not been given an opportunity to consult with his daughter. He had been unable to ascertain what information she had disclosed during her interview. Rose thought it quite probable that the vicar realised this was intentional, that she had gone to considerable pains to ensure that Mabel did not return to the Adlers' rooms until her father had vacated them. Their paths had not crossed and she knew the vicar had no doubt been left in an awful ignorance. He would be forced to resort to conjecture, a state of affairs which clearly had him rattled.

'My daughter is bearing up very well, all things considered,' he had said quickly, as if he thought it expected of him. 'It has been a dreadful shock for her, as it has for me, of course, what with Mr Dewhurst being in the habit of joining us for meals and the occasional excursion.'

Rose did not speak, thinking it better to remain silent and see where

208

Father Adler's words would lead him.

'How odd it feels to think that only yesterday I was watching him play a game of tennis with my daughter.' He took a deep breath. 'Poor Mabel. She considered him a friend, you know, your ladyship,' the vicar continued. He was apparently of the opinion that it was far better that he raise the subject of his daughter's affection for the murdered man before Lady Belvedere alluded to it. 'Of course, there was no harm in it. She simply could not bear the idea of the young man eating alone –'

'In that case, I am surprised she did not suggest to Mr Thurlow that Mr Dewhurst join him at his table.'

'Ah,' said Father Adler, looking a little flustered. 'An excellent suggestion, of course, your ladyship, but I believe there had been a little … a little falling out between my daughter and Mr Thurlow. Of course, in the ordinary course of events it would have come to nothing, but unfortunately –'

'Miss Adler became rather taken with Mr Dewhurst?' Rose suggested, rather abruptly, eager to progress the interview.

'Quite so. It was … well, it was most unfortunate. I have always considered Mr Thurlow to be a thoroughly good fellow. I'm sure you know the sort, Lady Belvedere? Reliable and pleasant looking without being very remarkable. Mr Dewhurst, on the other hand, though admittedly quite charming was, in my opinion, rather too handsome for his own good. I'm afraid I never took to Mr Dewhurst. I didn't trust the fellow.' He gave Rose a rueful smile. 'Not very Christian of me, I admit, your ladyship, to speak ill of the dead.'

Rose wondered how much of the vicar's view of Alec Dewhurst had been clouded by hindsight. It was tempting to pursue the matter. She thought it quite possible, however, that Father Adler, with his simple, unaffected ways, had never felt quite comfortable in the presence of Alex Dewhurst, with his façade of sophistication. Ron Thurlow was much more his type; if nothing else, the vicar could feel tolerably certain of the sincerity of that gentleman's regards towards his daughter.

'I understand that Miss Adler was under the mistaken impression that the Duchess of Grismere was Mr Dewhurst's sister?' said Rose lightly, keen to evoke a reaction from the temperate clergyman.

Father Adler winced at the mention of the duchess' name. 'We both were,' he said quietly.

Mr Kettering took that moment to look up from his pocketbook and bestow on the vicar a particularly cynical look. Father Adler responded by blinking rapidly and adopting something of a defensive stand.

'We had no reason to suspect otherwise,' he said, a trifle piqued, directing his remarks to the hotel proprietor. How much easier it was to address a man of business than to speak of such delicate matters to a countess of tender years. 'Mr Dewhurst appeared to be a most charming young man. I don't doubt that you thought the same yourself, Kettering, when you first made his acquaintance?' He leaned forward and addressed his next remarks exclusively to Rose. 'His manners, you know, your ladyship,' he said, speaking rather apologetically, 'were most agreeable and Mr Dewhurst was really very interested in my sermons.' He sighed. 'So few people are these days. One tries one's best, of course, but ...'

Father Adler did not bother to finish his sentence. He had reverted to his usual gentle demeanour of absent-mindedness. Rose was aware that she must shake him from the safety of his vagueness, for she needed him to be attentive. The man before her appeared remarkably quiet and unassuming, and yet she remembered Mabel telling her only half an hour before, in this very room, that her father had been out of character the previous night. Indeed, if she remembered the words the girl had used, she had never witnessed him be so angry. What was more, if one were to believe his daughter, the vicar had threatened violence against Alec Dewhurst. It certainly could not be disputed that shortly afterwards the young man had met with a particularly violent death. Rose shuddered. Had she not been warned by a schoolmistress that it was the quiet ones one had to watch? It was the loud ones that were full of harmless bluster.

'I think I ought to tell you, Father Adler, that we are in possession of this note,' she said, handing him the scrap of paper she had shown Mabel Adler earlier. 'It was found in your room. It refers to an assignation arranged between the deceased and your daughter.' She held up her hand as the vicar made vague and ineffectual attempts to protest. 'The truth has a way of coming out in the end, you know. We only want the facts. If you and your daughter are innocent, you have nothing to fear. Besides, Miss Adler has already told us that you intercepted this note and confronted her in connection with its contents.'

'What is more,' piped up Mr Kettering from the depths of his pocketbook, 'your daughter informed us, Father Adler, that, when you went to speak to her, you found her in the advanced stages of packing.'

Father Adler stared at them, clearly mortified by the extent of their intelligence.

'It does no good to protest, I can assure you,' continued Mr Kettering, on a roll. His manner was distinctly condescending. 'We know what happened. You gave Miss Adler a piece of your mind. You spoke to her in no uncertain terms concerning her fondness for Mr Dewhurst. You informed her that the woman purporting to be his sister was in fact his lover, the Duchess of Grismere!'

There was a shocked and awkward silence that lasted a few seconds.

'I am ashamed to say,' said Father Adler at last, rather mournfully, 'I was inclined to take what Miss Hyacinth Trimble told me with a large pinch of salt. In my profession it does not do to be seen listening to what one terms as 'village gossip'. I have developed something of a knack of only half listening to such things, as it were, and focusing my mind instead on something more constructive. But I had heard enough and, when I read the note, my suspicions were naturally aroused. And then when I found my daughter packing ...' he faltered, recalling the awful scene that had followed. 'I suppose it could be said I gave my daughter a pretty severe scolding. I really don't remember quite what I said, but Mabel ... she accused me of lying,' he mumbled, staring into the middle distance. 'My own daughter! I tried to reason with her, but she refused to listen. I ... I couldn't believe a thing like that possible, not with my Mabel. And to discover that she intended to elope with that scoundrel Dewhurst –'

'It would have made any father angry,' said the hotel proprietor, quite oblivious to the unintentional pun, though it brought a smile to Rose's lips. 'We know you flew into a violent rage,' continued Mr Kettering. He had conjured up a vivid picture in his mind and now he ran with it. In fact, so real was it in his imagination, he might have been an unobtrusive observer of the quarrel between father and daughter, watching the events unfold before him.

'Yes' said Father Adler, distractedly. 'I suppose I must have raised my voice.' He gave a wan smile. 'And now I come to think of it, I remember trembling. I put my hand out and discovered it was shaking. Mabel was quite frightened of me and I think even I was a trifle scared. I don't recall ever feeling such anger against a fellow as I did towards Dewhurst that night. I wasn't myself. It was almost as if I was someone else.'

'Miss Adler told us that you threatened to kill Mr Dewhurst,' Rose said quietly.

'Did I?' For a fleeting moment, Father Adler looked surprised. 'I suppose I must have done, if Mabel says I did. Really, I can't recall exactly what I said. I was in something of a daze. I do remember finding myself on the path that runs past the tennis courts and wondering how I had got there.'

'Oh?' Rose said sharply. 'Then you didn't go to Mr Dewhurst's rooms? If you went past the tennis courts, as you say, you must have been making for the cliff path.' She leaned forward a little in her chair, trying to contain her growing excitement. 'Was he there? Did you find Mr Dewhurst standing on the edge of the cliff?'

'Oh, yes,' said the vicar, 'and I meant to give him a piece of my mind, I can tell you.'

'And then,' said Mr Kettering, not to be out done, 'a few hours later he rolled up dead on the beach where I, myself, found him.'

'Are you saying you didn't give him a piece of your mind?' said Rose, as if the hotel proprietor had not spoken. She fervently wished that Mr Kettering would hold his tongue, particularly as it appeared the vicar was on the verge of confessing to the murder of Alec Dewhurst.

'I know I would have done if it had been my daughter he was carrying on with,' continued Mr Kettering helpfully.

'Oh, do you have a daughter?' asked the vicar. 'Is she on Skiathos? I can't say I've ever met her.'

'Father Adler,' Rose said, trying to return the vicar's thoughts to the matter in hand. 'This is terribly important. Did you strike Mr Dewhurst?'

'I felt pretty shaken up by it all, I don't mind telling you,' said the vicar hesitantly, 'I recall being in a bit of a daze and then, suddenly, I wasn't. Mr Dewhurst was standing before me in the distance looking out to sea. I remember I quickened my pace; it is quite possible that I even started running. But, as I neared him, he turned his head slightly to one side and started speaking. It was then I realised that Dewhurst was not alone. He was talking to someone else.'

'Did you see who it was?' asked Rose abruptly.

212

'No. You see, the person must have been standing a little way down the coastal path. If Dewhurst had not shifted his position at that moment, I might quite well have thought he was talking to himself.'

'What did you do?'

'I turned around and retraced my steps,' Father Adler said shrugging. 'The things I meant to say to Dewhurst were intended for his ears alone. I had no intention of having an audience.'

'You returned to your rooms?'

'Yes, though no one saw me. My daughter was in her room, where I had left her. I went into the sitting room and poured myself a whisky. I sat down and contemplated what I was going to say to Dewhurst.'

'Then you still intended to have it out with him that night?'

Rose regarded the vicar with renewed interest. Even Mr Kettering looked enthralled, his pen poised ready.

'Yes. But as it happens, I didn't,' said Father Adler. 'I am not used to strong liquor. I suppose I must have dozed in my chair, because I woke up with a start. I looked at the clock on the mantelpiece and to my horror discovered it was half past three.'

'What did you do?' demanded the hotel proprietor.

'Well, it was obviously too late to speak with Dewhurst. I had no intention of rousing him from his bed and creating a scene. I resolved instead to demand an audience with him after breakfast. The thought occurred to me, of course, that he might have already fled the hotel.' He passed a hand across his forehead, 'I picked up my empty whisky glass, which had rolled on to the floor, and retired to my bedroom. I did not want my daughter to find me asleep in the chair.'

'Did you look in on Miss Adler before you retired to your room?' inquired Rose.

'Yes,' said Mr Kettering, before the vicar could answer. 'If I'd been in your shoes, I would have done. I would have wanted to be absolutely certain that she was in her room and not on her way to the mainland with Dewhurst.'

Father Adler favoured the hotel proprietor with a scowl. 'As it happens, I did look in on my daughter. She was there, all right, sleeping the sleep of the innocent.'

'There's nothing to say Miss Adler did not creep out of the hotel and

213

kill Dewhurst while Father Adler was dozing in the sitting room,' remarked Mr Kettering, as soon as the vicar had departed, the vicar's steps slow and his manner subdued. 'For that matter,' the hotel proprietor added, 'there is nothing to say she was actually in her room when her father returned to the hotel.'

'True,' said Rose, 'but Mabel Adler could not have been the person Mr Dewhurst was addressing on the coastal path, if that is what you are suggesting. She might well have followed her father when he left the hotel, afraid what he might do to Alec Dewhurst when he found him, but she could not have got to the cliff edge before him without being observed.'

'It seems to me,' reflected her companion, 'that neither Father Adler nor his daughter have a very satisfactory alibi. What is more, each had a motive for why they might have wished Alec Dewhurst dead.' He advanced towards the bell-pull. 'Who do you wish to speak to now, your ladyship? I think we ought to partake of some refreshment, don't you? This interviewing business is thirsty work.'

'Lady Lavinia, I think,' said Rose. The hotel proprietor raised his eyebrows above his wire-rimmed spectacles, as was his habit when he was surprised. Rose, conscious of his inquiring look, added hastily. 'It is just a formality, that's all. In fact, you needn't be present.'

Mr Kettering had returned to his chair and sat down. He did not strike her as minded to leave the room before all the interviews were completed. Most probably he would consider it a dereliction of his duties. Rose racked her brains rather desperately. She did not want him there while she interviewed Lavinia, not if she could possibly help it. But how to get rid of him without arousing his suspicions, that was the question.

'As it happens, I have a task for you,' she said finally, with a sense she was clutching at straws. 'I should be awfully grateful if you would call on the duchess and ask her what initials she had engraved on Mr Dewhurst's pocket watch.'

Mr Kettering looked surprised, but distinctly flattered.

'Of course, your ladyship, I should be honoured. Should I also ask her grace about the font?'

'Yes, do,' said Rose hurriedly, ushering him towards the door. The servant materialised and was promptly sent in search of Lavinia. 'Do tell her to come at once,' Rose said. She turned her attention back to Mr Kettering. 'You are far more tactful than I am. I'm afraid I may have been rather abrupt in my dealings with the duchess. I can't tell you how very grateful I would be if you could ask her a few more questions concerning her initial meeting with Mr Dewhurst. Yes, do take your pocketbook with you; it is most important that you write down everything she tells you.'

With the hotel proprietor safely dispatched, Rose waited impatiently for her friend to arrive. She began to pace the room. Whatever was keeping Lavinia? Inwardly she cursed the girl, for she had visions of her sitting at her dressing table applying her makeup. Really, she should have gone to find Lavinia herself. After all, there was no real reason why the interview should take place in this room. Indeed, it would be far more preferable if it didn't and then there would be no fear of the hotel proprietor appearing at an inopportune moment. Why hadn't she thought of that earlier?

'Oh, so this is where you've been hiding yourself, is it?' Lavinia said, appearing at the door. 'Kettering's lair.' She passed a finger idly across the spines of the books on the bookcase and picked up a pewter tankard. She scrutinised the inscription engraved on its polished surface. 'Fancy Kettering being something of an athlete. You'd never think it to look at him, would you? Speaking of the fellow,' she continued, putting the object down on the desk with a thud, 'where is he? Have you sent him to take statements from the servants?'

'Where have you been?' demanded Rose, dispensing with pleasantries. She had no intention of answering Lavinia's fatuous questions. 'I've been waiting ages,' she continued, taking her sister-in-law by the arm and steering her towards the chair, recently vacated by Father Adler. 'We haven't much time.'

'Haven't we?' Lavinia said languidly. 'Speaking for myself, I've all the time in the world ...'

'Well, I haven't. And neither have you, not if you know what's good for you.'

Lavinia's eyes widened in surprise. 'I say, darling, you are being frightfully cryptic. Is that the new line you've decided to adopt when questioning suspects? I can't say I care for it much.' She gave her friend a reproachful look. 'It sounds a trifle menacing, if you don't mind my saying.'

'Lavinia, do be quiet. Now, listen to me. You must tell me the truth. It's frightfully important that you do.'

'What do you mean?'

Was it Rose's imagination, or had a note of fear crept into the girl's voice? Certainly, she was aware that she had Lavinia's full attention at last.

'When did you last see Alec Dewhurst?'

'Why, last night, of course. As a matter of fact, I danced with him after you and Ceddie had retired for the night. It was frightfully early. Why is it that people become frightfully boring and dull when they get married?'

'It really won't do, Lavinia'

'I haven't the faintest idea what you mean.'

'Yes, you have. You're trying to change the subject, and you mustn't.' Rose held up her hand as Lavinia made to protest. She resisted the temptation to take the girl by the shoulder and shake her. 'Look here, I know you were on the cliff path last night. Suppose you tell me how it all happened.'

'I don't know how you can possibly know that.'

'Well, you were spotted, for one thing. That's to say, Father Adler spotted Alec Dewhurst speaking to someone on the cliff path. I think that person was you.'

Lavinia pouted. 'Whatever makes you think it was me? It could have been someone else. Mabel Adler, for instance, was in the habit of walking to the cliff with Alec Dewhurst. Surely you are aware of that?'

'I am. But I also happen to know that at that precise moment Mabel Adler was sitting miserable and chagrined in her room. It won't do any good being stubborn, you know. I know for a fact that you were on the cliff path last night.' Rose bent forward and took her friend's hand. 'Lavinia, you must tell me what happened. It is the only way I can help you. I've sent Mr Kettering on an errand but I expect him back any minute.'

'How did you know I was there last night?' Lavinia said sulkily. A thought struck her and she looked indignant. 'I say, I hope you weren't spying on me. It would have been frightfully rotten of you if you were.'

'Of course, I wasn't,' Rose said, losing patience. She produced from her pocket a gold filigree earring which she passed to Lavinia.

216

'Oh, you've found it! I'm frightfully glad. I was awfully afraid that I had lost it. Wherever did you find it?'

'A little way down the cliff path. I remembered that you were wearing just such a pair of earrings last night at dinner.' Lavinia stared at her but said nothing. 'I was searching the area this morning with Cedric and Mr Kettering. I suppose one could say we were looking for clues. I spotted the earring. I recognised it immediately; I knew it belonged to you.' She paused a moment for her companion had gone deathly pale. 'Before I quite knew what I was doing,' Rose continued hurriedly, 'I picked it up and put it in my pocket.'

'Did ... did anyone else see what you did?' Lavinia asked in a quiet voice.

'No. Is that what is worrying you?' Rose continued, not waiting for her sister-in-law's reply. 'Now, Lavinia, you must tell me exactly what happened.'

It was at this rather inopportune moment that Mr Kettering chose to make his reappearance. Returned from successfully completing his errand, his spirits were high. They were soon to be dashed, however, as he saw the expression on Lavinia's face. Her reservations were shared by her companion, though Rose at least made an attempt to conceal her feelings. Nevertheless, there ensued an awkward silence with the hotel proprietor realising, rather belatedly, that his presence in the study was far from welcome. He found himself to be in something of a quandary, and stared perplexed at the two women.

'I can't,' said Lavinia finally. 'I can't tell you.' She looked beseechingly at her friend. 'Rose, you mustn't make me. It's ... it's too awful.' And, with that, she buried her face in her hands.

Chapter Twenty-seven

Another silence followed this statement. This time it was Mr Kettering's turn to look appalled. He was not good at dealing with weeping women at the best of times. He averted his gaze, apparently fixated by the pattern on one of the rugs on the floor and wondered how the situation should best be handled. Inwardly, he observed that when Miss Adler had sobbed she had not cried with the wanton abandonment of Lady Lavinia. Rather, she had done it discreetly, dabbing at her eyes with the edge of a handkerchief.

Lavinia lifted her head and giggled. The hidden face and heaving shoulders had misled her observers. The hotel proprietor pursed his lips and cast her a most reproachful look. The deplorable girl seemed to be having a fit of the giggles! In contrast, Rose's reaction was one of distinct relief. No need to fear the worst. Not now that Lavinia had laughed in that ridiculous fashion. She could quite easily hazard a guess as to what her friend might be about to reveal. There was no denying that Lavinia had acted somewhat foolishly. But she had not acted criminally. At worst, her character might be slightly tarnished in the eyes of Mr Kettering, but that was all.

'Suppose you tell us what happened,' Rose said, somewhat curtly, annoyed that she had been needlessly anxious about her friend. She also had no wish to prolong the interview, which was likely to prove highly embarrassing for a man of Mr Kettering's sensibilities. Lavinia, she knew, would require little encouragement to play to her audience. Indeed, knowing her friend as she did, the girl would take a great delight in shocking the hotel proprietor with her escapades. If she was to be chided for behaving with little thought to her reputation it would be later and not in Mr Kettering's presence.

'As I told you,' Lavinia said, rather resenting Rose's tone, 'I danced with Mr Dewhurst after you and Ceddie retired for the night.' She leaned forward in her chair and smiled sweetly, her expression rather forced. 'Did I mention that he was the most accomplished dancer?'

'You did not,' said Rose, in the same brusque tone, though she was finding it hard not to smile in spite of herself. Really, Lavinia was quite impossible. 'I suppose it was Alec Dewhurst who suggested the two of you should go for a walk on the cliff?' she said. 'I daresay he commented on it being a very fine night for a stroll?'

'Yes, he did say something of the sort,' admitted Lavinia, a trifle crossly. 'You make it sound so dreadfully sordid, and really it wasn't a bit like that.' She arched an eyebrow and said rather haughtily. 'In fact, if you must know, he was frightfully sweet. He told me that he had been absolutely dying to make my acquaintance but that he didn't dare approach me in company. He didn't think Ceddie would approve, you see. He was terribly upset that Ceddie had taken such an irrational dislike to him.'

'Hardly irrational,' replied Rose.

'Ceddie?' queried the hotel proprietor.

'My brother, Mr Kettering. Lord Belvedere,' said Lavinia helpfully.

'Really, Lavinia,' said Rose, 'whatever were you thinking?'

'Calling Cedric, Ceddie, do you mean?' the girl replied, deliberately misunderstanding her question. She gave a heartfelt sigh. 'I was bored. There's very little to do here and no society to speak of, unless you count us, of course.'

'Lavinia!' Out of the corner of her eye, Rose was aware that the hotel proprietor had stopped writing. 'There's heaps to do here, if you would only apply yourself.'

'We can't all be like you, you know.' There was a long pause, and then Lavinia said: 'I'm sorry, but you did ask. As I've already said, I was frightfully bored and I didn't want to go to bed. I thought it would be rather thrilling to go for a walk in the moonlight with a handsome young man. I daresay I should have given a thought for the duchess, or even Miss Adler, but I'm afraid I didn't. You see, I didn't think there would be any harm in it, and, besides, I've always been rather curious about Mr Dewhurst, haven't you?'

'What happened?'

'Oh, nothing to speak of. That's to say, I suggested we go down the cliff path and take a walk on the beach. I thought it would be awfully pleasant, hearing the waves lapping the shore, and all that. But Mr Dewhurst wasn't very keen. He kept looking in his pockets as if he was searching for something that was not there.'

'His pocket watch?' suggested Rose. 'I daresay he was looking for it and discovered it was missing.'

'Not that lovely gold and diamond affair?' exclaimed Lavinia. 'He had it at dinner, I remember seeing it.'

'It was stolen,' said Rose shortly.

'Was it really? Well I never! But I suppose it might explain why he seemed rather put out. He was awfully keen to finish our walk. I thought it rather rotten of him at the time.'

'I daresay he was anxious because he did not know what time it was. He had arranged to meet Miss Adler at that very spot. It would have been most unfortunate for him if she had arrived while you were there.'

'I see,' said Lavinia coldly. 'Well Miss Adler didn't appear, if that's what you were wondering? I climbed back up the footpath and, as I neared the top, Alec Dewhurst had the sheer audacity to try and kiss me.'

The hotel proprietor looked up from his pocketbook, evidently shocked.

'Oh, you mustn't worry, Mr Kettering, I didn't let him,' said Lavinia, smiling wickedly. 'It was awfully embarrassing really, because, you see, I tried to push him away, but a strand of his hair became tangled on the gold and pearl comb I was wearing in my hair....' She paused to address Rose. 'You know the one I mean? It's frightfully pretty. I was desperately afraid he would break it.' She laughed gaily. 'We must have looked a right old pair because it took simply ages to get untangled and all the time we were trapped there thinking the other was perfectly beastly and wishing we were anywhere but standing there fastened together.' She giggled. 'It was absolutely horrid. We couldn't get away from each other fast enough, I can tell you.' She became reflective. 'I suppose that must have been when I lost my earring. I say, Rose, I'm awfully glad you found it.'

Mr Kettering raised an enquiring eyebrow. Not wishing to explain her discovery of the earring, Rose said quickly:

'Mr Dewhurst was alive when you left him?'

'Oh, absolutely. You should have seen him run back towards the hotel; I swear he was sprinting.' The expression on Lavinia's face became more serious. 'I say, do you think I was the last person to see him alive?'

'Other than the murderer, you mean? Most probably. I don't suppose you saw anyone, did you, on your way back to the hotel?'

'No, I didn't.' Lavinia got to her feet, realising that she was about to be dismissed.

Rose turned and addressed her next remark to the hotel proprietor. 'I suppose we ought to speak to Mr Thurlow now.'

Lavinia had been making her way towards the door but, at mention of the courier, she turned around and said excitedly; 'Oh yes, do. Fancy me forgetting! I know for a fact that Mr Thurlow had a very good motive for wishing Alec Dewhurst dead.'

'On account of Miss Adler throwing him over for the deceased, do you mean?' said Rose.

'No, though I doubt he'd have been too pleased about it. I know I wouldn't, if I'd been him. No,' she paused, her face brightening with excitement as she retraced her steps back to the chair she had so recently vacated and stood behind it. 'He had a proper motive. What would you say if I told you that Ron Thurlow had been to prison?'

Mr Kettering dropped his fountain pen. It occurred to Rose that he must be wondering if his guests comprised entirely of criminals. 'Begging your pardon, Lady Lavinia, but I think you must be mistaken,' he said. 'Mr Thurlow works for a highly reputable travel company. He has the most impeccable references.'

'I heard it straight from the horse's mouth,' said Lavinia, a little put out. 'That's where he first made Alec Dewhurst's acquaintance.'

'Surely Mr Thurlow didn't tell you that himself?' said Rose incredulously.

'Of course not. It isn't something one would exactly brag about, is it? No.' Lavinia put her hand on the chair and leaned forward. 'I just happened to overhear him talking to Mr Dewhurst.' She had the grace to blush slightly. 'They didn't see me.'

'You were eavesdropping, you mean?' Rose said sharply.

'I'm not in the habit of listening to other people's conversations,' Lavinia said, a trifle defensively. 'I happened be on the cliff path, that's all, when they were standing on the edge of the cliff talking.'

'Were they aware that you were listening?'

'No, I've already told you. They were too engrossed in their conversation to notice me. They were quarrelling, you see, and their voices carried. I heard every word.'

Lavinia required very little prompting to provide a surprisingly comprehensive summary of the conversation that had taken place between Alec Dewhurst and Ron Thurlow. Both Rose and Mr Kettering listened with interest, the latter writing down every word in his pocketbook. When Lavinia had finished, Rose said, to herself as much as to anyone else:

'So Thurlow is not Ron Thurlow's real name, any more than Dewhurst was Alec Dewhurst's?'

'It's dashed confusing, isn't it?' said Lavinia, 'I say, I felt awfully sorry for Mr Thurlow, particularly when Mr Dewhurst threatened to tell his employer and Miss Adler that he'd been in prison, if he said anything to the duchess about his past.'

'Mr Dewhurst admitted to being the duchess' lover?'

'I should say! He fair boasted about it.' Lavinia paused a moment. A perplexed expression suddenly crossing her face. 'I say, that's jolly odd.'

'What is?' Rose asked sharply.

'Well, Mr Dewhurst boasted that he was living with another man's wife but, now that I come to think about it, he was quite adamant that she was not the Duchess of Grismere. Mr Thurlow pressed him on the point.'

'That does strike one as rather odd,' agreed Rose. 'One would expect a man like Dewhurst to brag to all and sundry if he had secured the affections of a duchess.'

'Well, he didn't. In fact, he sounded awfully put out when Mr Thurlow put the question to him.'

'It seems to me,' commented Mr Kettering, 'that, if what Lady Lavinia says is true, Mr Thurlow had ample motive for wishing Mr Dewhurst dead. In fact, I would go so far as to say that he has the best motive of the lot of them. First, he was in fear of losing his job. It stands to reason his employer didn't know he had a criminal record. A fellow who'd been to prison would find it awfully difficult to get another place. Second, Miss Adler. Mr Thurlow seemed awfully fond of her and then this Dewhurst fellow goes and woos her from right under his nose for no other reason than out of spite, as far as I can see.'

'Are you going to arrest Mr Thurlow?' Lavinia asked rather breathlessly.

'We ought to see what he has to say for himself, first,' said Rose, thinking that Lavinia was being dreadfully premature in her assumption. Rose was perusing Mr Kettering's notes at the time and did not look up from what she was doing nor hear the exchange that passed between Lavinia and the hotel proprietor, as the latter escorted her to the door.

'It is only a matter of time, Lady Lavinia, before Mr Thurlow is apprehended,' Mr Kettering said quietly. 'Of course, in telling you this I am relying on your absolute discretion. But I see no harm in it, what with your being a relative of Lady Belvedere's, so to speak, and quite as accustomed to violent death as her ladyship, if the newspapers are to be believed.' Lavinia nodded encouragingly. 'Yes,' continued the hotel proprietor, 'I am quite confident of an arrest before the day is out.'

Had Rose heard these words and advised caution, it is quite possible that the events that followed, and the various outcomes, might have been quite different.

A servant had been dispatched to summon Ron Thurlow and, while they waited for the young man to arrive, it occurred to Rose she had quite forgotten to enquire about the hotel proprietor's interview with the Duchess of Grismere.

'Did you find out from the duchess what the initials were that she had engraved on Alec Dewhurst's pocket watch?'

'Indeed I did, your ladyship, though her grace was rather loath to tell me.' Mr Kettering paused a moment to shudder at the recollection of his interview with the peer. He flicked through the pages of his pocketbook. 'Yes, here they are. I made a particular note of it. "O", "E", "G"; all in upper case.'

'Then Miss Adler was quite right about the "O", though she appears to have been mistaken about the last letter,' said Rose. 'If you remember, Mr Kettering, she mentioned it was made up of lines like a capital "M", or a "W".'

'Miss Adler must have been thinking of the middle initial. A capital "E" is made up of lines. She most probably got into a bit of a muddle.''

'I wonder,' said Rose. Something was niggling at the back of her mind. Before she could reflect any further on the matter, however, they were joined by Ron Thurlow, who entered the room in a watered-down version of his usual affable manner. It was apparent that he, like the other guests, had been affected by the recent tragedy. The skin on his cheeks was taut, and he too looked wan and pale.

'I'm sorry you've been kept waiting. It's always rather galling to be last,' Rose said. 'Let's get to business, shall we?'

She began by asking a few perfunctory questions concerning Ron Thurlow's employment as a travel courier, and his stay on the island. The questions had the desired effect and the young man began to visibly relax.

'Can you suggest a motive for why anyone might wish to harm Mr Dewhurst?'

Ron started at the abruptness of the question, which seemed to him to have appeared out of thin air, and he shifted in his seat uncomfortably.

'No,' he said, though the expression on his face suggested otherwise.

There was a long pause. Ron took a deep breath and said: 'Look here, I daresay it's common knowledge that Mr Dewhurst and I didn't hit it off frightfully well. That's not to say we argued. We ... we just didn't take to each other, that's all.'

Rose did not consider it worthwhile to argue this point. Mr Kettering, however, appeared to have other ideas.

'You detested the fellow, didn't you?' he said. 'He took your girl. You quarrelled.'

Ron coloured slightly and said rather cautiously: 'I admit I have an admiration for Miss Adler –'

'You were next door to being in love with the girl, weren't you?' continued Mr Kettering, in his pugnacious mood. He had not forgotten that there sat before him a man with a criminal record masquerading as a thoroughly decent chap. 'When a fellow's in that condition he'll do any fool thing.'

Ron stared at the hotel proprietor open mouthed. He was not used to Mr Kettering speaking to him in such an aggressive manner. 'As it happens, I minded awfully at first,' he said, a note of reproach in his voice. 'But then you get past minding, don't you?'

'Do you?' Rose said.

'Yes, you do.' Ron paused a moment before continuing. 'I'm rather used to it, as it happens. I'm not the sort of man a girl loses her head over.'

'And Alec Dewhurst?'

'Oh, he was just the sort of fellow a girl breaks her heart over.' Ron gave Rose a rueful smile. 'Even I will admit the fellow possessed a certain charm, not to mention being handsome. Women like that sort of thing, don't they?'

Rose ignored the question and said: 'When did you last see Mr Dewhurst?'

'Last night in the dining room. When I left, he was still dancing with Miss Adler.'

'That must have riled you?' said Mr Kettering.

'It did, but I didn't do anything about it, if that is what you are suggesting.'

'You didn't arrange to meet Mr Dewhurst later that night?' Rose asked. 'Or possibly you went for a walk on the coastal path before turning in and encountered him on the cliff?'

'No. I didn't see him, I tell you, not after I left the dining room.' Ron regarded the hotel proprietor's sceptical face and said with asperity: 'Look here, I had no reason to kill the chap. A man doesn't go about murdering every fellow who takes his girl.'

'I ought to tell you, Mr Thurlow, that we have a witness to a conversation you had with the deceased in which he threatened you,' said Rose slowly, watching the expression on the young man's face change to one of apprehension.

'Yes?' he said rather feebly.

'We know you were by way of being friends,' said Mr Kettering, rather nastily. 'That's to say you made each other's acquaintance while in prison.'

Ron looked from one to the other of them. He appeared quite at a loss for words.

'Don't be an ass, for heaven's sake,' said the hotel proprietor exasperated. 'We only want the facts, you know. As her ladyship says, we have a most reliable witness to your quarrel.'

'Very well,' said Ron, in something of a resigned voice. 'But I ask that you hear me out and not interrupt me.' He glared pointedly at the hotel proprietor.

'Of course,' said Rose hurriedly, before Mr Kettering had an opportunity to reply.

'Whatever you may think of me,' began Ron, 'I am not a criminal.' He held up his hand as the hotel proprietor made as if to protest. 'You agreed to hear me out, remember? I admit I went to prison, but for someone else's crime, not my own.'

225

'A likely story,' mumbled Mr Kettering from the depths of his pocketbook, in which he had been hastily scribbling.

'I don't ask that you believe me, but it happens to be the truth,' retorted Ron, 'I got in with a fast set and … well, the girl I was rather keen on at the time stole some money. I didn't know what she had done until the police came to arrest her. She was in a dreadful state and in a moment of sheer madness, or chivalry, or whatever you want to call it, I told her that I'd take the blame. It was a damned foolish thing to do, of course, but there it is. To cut a long story short, I was convicted and sent to prison. There, I met Alec Dewhurst, who, among the sea of rogues and scoundrels, seemed to me rather a decent sort. Anyway, I suppose you could say we became friends after a fashion. Dewhurst wasn't his name then, of course. I knew him as Alec Goodfellow.'

'Did you know that he was a petty crook who preyed on rich women?' asked Rose.

'I knew that women were attracted to him,' said Ron, choosing his words with care, 'and that he was not very particular whether they were married or not. He told me one of them had given him a particularly valuable gift and when her husband, whom she had never mentioned, found out about it he kicked up an almighty stink. He accused Dewhurst of theft and had him arrested. Dewhurst told me that was how he came to be in prison; he was as innocent of the crime for which he was convicted as I was myself.'

'And you believed him?' enquired Mr Kettering cynically.

'At the time, I did,' Ron said, defiantly. 'I had no reason to doubt him. It may sound rather odd to you but, if it hadn't been for Dewhurst, I don't know how I'd have coped with being in prison. My friends deserted me and I didn't have any family to speak of. Dewhurst was released a month before me. I was all for looking him up, but then I found he had been arrested in connection with another theft. It occurred to me then that I had been awfully naïve. He was evidently not at all the man I thought him to be.'

'He threatened to inform your employer that you had been to prison,' said the hotel proprietor. 'In fact, he told you he thought it was his duty to do so.'

'What if he did?'

226

'That would have been a pretty good motive for wishing him dead. A respectable job would be hard to come by for a fellow like you with your prison record.'

'There I beg to differ, Kettering,' Ron said, a flash of triumph in his eyes. 'My employer knows that I've spent some time in prison. What is more, he is fully aware I am innocent of the crime for which I was convicted. That girl I told you about is his daughter. She confessed everything to him and he gave me this job in gratitude for my services to his family.'

'If that is indeed true, Alec Dewhurst had no hold over you to remain silent,' said Rose sharply.

Was it her imagination or did a look of fear fleetingly cross the young man's face?

'I had no wish for Miss Adler to know I'd been to prison,' replied Ron rather sulkily. 'I ... I didn't want her, or Father Adler, to think any the less of me.'

To Rose this seemed rather an inadequate explanation, but she did not press the point. Instead, she said:

'If you cared for Miss Adler, as you claim, you would have warned her about Alec Dewhurst, regardless of the harm to your own reputation.'

'I tried, but she cut me dead. She wouldn't listen to anything I had to say against the fellow,' said Ron bitterly. 'I didn't stop there, of course. I told Miss Hyacinth of my concerns, that I believed Dewhurst to be a thoroughly bad lot. I hoped she would have a quiet word with the vicar. They're thoroughly decent people, the Adlers. I shouldn't have wanted Mabel ... Miss Adler to come to any harm.'

'Very good of you, I'm sure,' said Mr Kettering, sarcastically.

Rose cast him a reproachful look and said hastily. 'That will be all, Mr Thurlow. Thank you awfully for being so candid.' She waited until the young man had advanced to the door and was on the point of opening it before adding: 'Just one more thing, Mr Thurlow, before you go.'

'Yes, your ladyship?' Ron turned around slowly. Again there was the momentary look of apprehension.

'Mr Dewhurst's pocket watch is missing, the one he produced at dinner last night. You picked it up when it fell on to the floor, if you remember? I couldn't help noticing that you examined it closely. Do you by any chance happen to recall the initials that were engraved on the case?'

A look of unmistakable fear crossed Ron's features. Rose had the impression that his brain was working very quickly. Once, or twice, he opened his mouth to speak, and then closed it again. She had asked a simple and seemingly harmless question, and yet the young man was patently reluctant to answer it. She did not doubt for one moment that he was able to do so if he chose, that the initials were as vivid to him now as they had been last night, when he had been staring at the pocket watch.

'From memory,' he said at last, 'I believe they were "A", "E", "G", but, of course, I might be mistaken.'

Chapter Twenty-eight

'Well, he got the "E" and the "G" all right, and in the correct order,' said Mr Kettering, 'I'll give him that. As to the "A", well he made the same mistake as Miss Adler initially did, which is perfectly natural because as the young lady said, some people write a capital "A" as if it were a large lower case "A", which is easy enough to confuse with an "O".'

'Yes,' said Rose, 'and I suppose one could also argue that Mr Thurlow would naturally assume the "O" to be an "A" on account of Dewhurst's Christian name being Alec.'

'And the "G" of course was for Goodfellow, which was the fellow's real surname. The duchess and Mr Thurlow mentioned that the middle initial was an "E" even if Miss Adler didn't recall it.'

''But what I don't understand, Mr Kettering, is why Mr Thurlow was so reluctant to tell us. It was almost as if he was making it all up.'

'Well, I don't trust the fellow myself,' said the hotel proprietor, 'as you know, your ladyship. All that nonsense about him being innocent. To my mind, Thurlow's far worse than Dewhurst because he goes about the place pretending to be all pleasant and honest when really he's nothing of the sort. Still,' he added, 'it'll be an easy enough story to check. That employer of his should be able to tell us whether he's telling the truth or not.'

'I wonder,' said Rose. 'By that I mean, if it is true, his employer might not want to admit it. Don't you see?' she added, as the hotel proprietor looked at her with a rather blank expression. 'He would have to acknowledge that his daughter was a thief who had escaped justice. I doubt any father would care to admit that.'

Before Mr Kettering had a chance to comment, Cedric appeared at the door. 'All done? I daresay you've had quite a day of it. Are you any nearer to arriving at the truth?'

'I can't say that we are,' Rose said, with a shrug of her shoulders. 'It seems to me that practically everyone had a reason for wishing Alec Dewhurst dead. Admittedly some of the motives are stronger than others.' She sighed. 'But really, everyone had an opportunity to do the deed and no one has an alibi to speak of.'

'And some of them are holding things back, you can tell, my lord,' said Mr Kettering, with a worried frown. 'Not that I think we'll get much more out of them. You've got your work cut out for you, your ladyship, if you don't mind my saying, if you're to find the murderer.'

'And yet,' said Rose, 'I've got this niggling feeling at the back of my mind that I've been given a number of clues, if only I could recognise them.'

'Oh?' said Cedric, looking interested.

'The pocket watch, for instance,' said Rose. 'I can't help thinking it's important, but I haven't the faintest idea why it should be, or how it's connected with the murder. Then there's Miss Peony. Her behaviour is very odd. I'm sure she's hiding something, and Miss Hyacinth looks absolutely frightened to death. The duchess is definitely holding something back, and really, it is very strange that she should decide to abandon a husband whom, according to you, darling, she was absolutely devoted to, only to run off with a charming, but fickle young scoundrel. It doesn't make any sense because she doesn't strike me as a stupid or impulsive woman, rather the contrary in fact. And then, of course, there is Mr Thurlow who is quite possibly not the gentleman he appears to be.'

'Good heavens,' said Cedric with a chuckle, 'you certainly seem to have a great many lines of inquiry to pursue.'

'Yes,' said Rose, somewhat distractedly, for she had picked up the hotel proprietor's pocketbook and was flicking through the pages. 'I say, Mr Kettering, would you mind awfully if I were to take this? I should very much like to pore over your notes this evening. It's just possible that they may suggest something or show a discrepancy between the statements.'

'But of course,' said Mr Kettering, making a little bow. 'I'm afraid my shorthand is not up to scratch. I tried to capture the flavour of the interviews, if not every word. Now, of course, if it had been my brother Giles taking the notes ...' His face clouded slightly as a thought occurred to him. 'I do hope, your ladyship, that you can read my handwriting; it's not very neat.'

Rose glanced down at the writing, which seemed to her to have been written in a meticulous hand and laughed in spite of herself. 'Why, Mr Kettering,' she said, 'I do believe you are quite wasted in your profession.

You should have been a calligrapher!'

Following her interview with Rose and Mr Kettering, Lavinia had returned to the Belvederes' rooms in a state of considerable excitement. An arrest was imminent and none of the other guests had the faintest inkling. How delicious it was to be in possession of this tantalising fact and how utterly frustrating to have no one to share it with. Where was Ceddie? He ought to be here. It was absolutely maddening that he wasn't.

She picked up a magazine and flicked aimlessly through the pages, barely affording them a glance. With increasing frequency, she gazed at the clock on the mantelpiece. It seemed to her impatient mind that the hands had stopped or, if not halted exactly, that they crawled forward at the slowest of snail paces; certainly they barely moved. She got up and began to pace the room. It was likely to be simply ages before anyone returned. She couldn't possibly be expected to wait and keep what she knew to herself. It was beyond human endurance. She sat down hard on the sofa. To stay here and do nothing when goodness knew what was taking place in the foyer …

Lavinia leapt up from her seat. After all, there was no earthly reason why she had to remain here. She was not a child that had been banished to its room. There was nothing to stop her wandering over to the entrance hall of the hotel. What could be more natural than that she should wish to study the list of organised excursions that was affixed to a wooden board at one end of the foyer?

The thought had no sooner taken hold than she had sailed out of the room and was crossing the terrace. A moment later and she had collided with the Misses Trimble, who happened to be out for a stroll and were trying to decide, with little success, where to walk which did not involve either the cliff or the beach.

'Oh dear, Lady Lavinia, I was only saying to my dear sister that I don't know whether I shall ever be able to bring myself to stand on the edge of the cliff again. The view is quite spectacular, of course, but I know for certain it will conjure up the most awful images. When one thinks what happened to poor Mr Dewhurst –'

'I shouldn't think about it if I were you,' said Lavinia quickly. 'Much better to come back to my rooms with me and have some tea. I don't know about you, but I am simply famished.'

Before they could reply, Lavinia had rather expertly herded the two Trimble sisters towards the Belvederes' quarters. A quarter of an hour later and they were comfortably ensconced with a good selection of cakes and sipping from fine bone china teacups. Only then did Lavinia impart her news with much made of the fact that she was taking Misses Hyacinth and Peony into her confidence, and really they mustn't breathe a word of what she told them to another living soul.

'Mr Thurlow!' squealed Miss Hyacinth, very clearly agitated. 'Why, surely dear Lady Lavinia, there must be some mistake?' Such a very pleasant young man, always so courteous. I can hardly believe him to be a murderer. And he's spent some time in prison, you say? Dear me, how dreadful ...'

Miss Hyacinth prattled on in a similar fashion for a full five minutes. Her sister, in contrast, remained silent. This, in itself, was not particularly remarkable, Miss Peony being known for saying very few words in company, preferring instead to retreat into the shadows and hide behind her deafness. On this occasion, however, even a casual observer might have noticed that, at mention of Mr Thurlow's imminent arrest, she had turned very pale and the knuckles of her hands, which she clasped tightly together, showed white.

A few minutes later and Miss Peony had claimed a headache which necessitated that she must retire to her own room to rest. No, she did not wish Hyacinth to accompany her. Much better that her sister remain here so that she, Peony, could have some peace and quiet. Besides, it would be much more pleasant for her sister than to tend to the needs of a patient.

Miss Peony set out towards the room that she shared with her sister. Once arrived, she closed the door securely behind her and locked it. Next she drew the thin material, that served as a curtain, across the window. A part of her was even tempted to close the shutters, but she decided that one had to draw a line somewhere. It would have surprised her sister very much to know that Miss Peony's next move was not to take to her bed. Instead, she sat behind the smallest of tables, lit a candle and pulled a sheet of notepaper slowly towards her, all the while contemplating what to write.

How, she wondered, did one address a murderer? One could hardly write "Dear Murderer", but then "Sir" or "Madam" seemed hardly to suffice. After some deliberation, she settled on: "To whom it may concern." She knew the identity of the intended reader, of course, but the fear that her letter might fall into the hands of others, for whom it was not meant, made her adopt caution. Next, she had to decide what to write. That in itself was difficult enough and, after several false starts, she had just completed writing the letter to her satisfaction when Miss Hyacinth came gliding into the room. Miss Peony, hoping the ink had dried sufficiently, hastily covered the sheet of notepaper with a convenient book which happened to be lying on the table.

'Oh, Peony, I thought you'd be sound asleep. You do still look a little bit peaky, you know, dear.' Miss Hyacinth settled herself down on the sofa. She stared inquisitively at the book, for her sister was not a habitual reader. 'I've been having the most splendid little chat with Lady Lavinia. We thought it would be a frightfully kind gesture if we were to give the duchess a little box of sweetmeats. What do you think, dear?'

'I think,' said Miss Peony gruffly, 'that you're beginning to sound a great deal like Lady Lavinia. It will be interesting to see what our little village of Clyst Birch makes of it.'

'We thought it would show the duchess that we were all thinking of her,' continued her sister, not at all deterred by her reception. 'She must be feeling dreadfully alone at this sad time.'

'Stuff and nonsense!' said Miss Peony, with feeling. 'The woman brought it on herself, carrying on with a man that's hardly out of short trousers while she has a husband tucked up in a castle and pining for her.'

'We thought we would sign it "from your fellow hotel guests", though, the way you're carrying on, dear, perhaps we should write "from your fellow hotel guests, with the exception of Miss Peony Trimble."'

Her sister croaked with laughter in the manner that was peculiar to her.

'Really, Peony, dear,' said Miss Hyacinth, standing up, 'you do sound rather like a frog when you make that sound. I do hope you'll never do it in company.' She fluttered about the room. 'But I take it from your laughter that you have no objection to being included among the hotel guests sending their condolences to the duchess?'

Miss Peony gave a snort which might have been interpreted in several ways. Miss Hyacinth chose to interpret it as one of acquiescence. She gave a furtive glance at her sister. Miss Peony looked thoroughly bored by the subject. Well, she would say no more about it. Her sister caught her eye. It is quite possible that it occurred to her that she had been rather churlish because the next minute she said, no doubt pretending an interest she did not possess:

'I suppose it is you who are putting the sweetmeats together rather than that Lady Lavinia?' Her sister nodded, wincing a little at the common nature of Miss Peony's language. Really, anyone would think, listening to her, that she had been born in the gutter instead of being the daughter of a respectable clergyman. 'I suppose,' continued Miss Peony, quite oblivious to her sister's thoughts, 'that you'll be wanting me to tie it up with one of those fancy bows I'm so good at doing?'

'Oh, would you?' exclaimed Miss Hyacinth, clapping her hands together in childish glee. 'It would be awfully good of you if you would.'

'Hmm,' grunted Miss Peony, which Miss Hyacinth interpreted as being a "yes".

Miss Hyacinth, easily pleased, proceeded to sit at her dressing table and apply cold cream to her face while murmuring how drying to the skin the Grecian sun was, and did Peony know that Lady Lavinia applied cold cream to her face at least five times a day?

No, Peony did not know how many times Lady Lavinia applied cold cream to her face each day, and neither was she the faintest bit interested in such a trivial piece of information. Rather, her thoughts returned to the sheet of notepaper concealed beneath the book. After a quick look at Miss Hyacinth, which assured her that her sister was absorbed with studying nothing better than her own reflection, Miss Peony surreptitiously withdrew the sheet of notepaper from its hiding place and hurriedly reread its contents, whispering the words very quietly to herself as she did so.

'"*To whom it may concern. I feel it my duty to inform you that I am in receipt of certain knowledge concerning the murder of Mr Alec Dewhurst. I should like you to know that it was never my intention to reveal this information, indeed that I meant to take it to my grave and would have done so gladly had I not had reason to believe that an innocent person is about to be arrested for his murder. As you will appreciate, I cannot in all conscience stand by and allow this to happen when I am in receipt of the true murderer's identity. I ask that you do not force my hand. It would be much better for you, I feel sure, if you were to come forward and confess your guilt. A Well-wisher.*"'

Chapter Twenty-nine

Rose had mistakenly assumed the other hotel guests would keep to their rooms that evening, and that dinner would be served to them on trays. It had not occurred to her that, having been holed up in their rooms all day, they would be bored of their own company and also that of their immediate companions. It was not that they had been imprisoned, yet they had felt tethered, for most were nervous of venturing too far from their own quarters. The dining room provided a welcome sanctuary and satisfied their craving for company. It also represented a return to some form of normality, albeit a temporary one. For they could dress for dinner, as was their custom, and continue conversations they had begun before Alec Dewhurst's untimely death. Indeed, they could sit at their usual tables and almost pretend that everything was as it had been before the murder cast its awful, rippling shadow.

As she entered the room, Rose nodded to her fellow guests. On first glance it appeared most were already there. Mr Vickers and Mr Thurlow were sitting in their habitual places, two solitary figures, one of them loud and mildly inebriated, the other quiet and reflective. The courier had risen from his seat on her entrance, as had Father Adler, a few tables away, who, up to that moment, had been sitting in a troubled silence beside Mabel. The girl might be physically present, yet she gave the impression of being distant in spirit. Rose wondered idly whether the gulf that existed between father and daughter would ever be truly healed. Cedric, Rose noted with amusement, was glaring at Mr Vickers, who had remained resolutely seated. It did not bother her particularly that the private enquiry agent was discourteous. Rather, it made her want to laugh. She wondered whether she was becoming irrational, the effect of having been cooped up in Mr Kettering's office for hours on end, asking the same questions, prying and probing into others' private affairs in a relentless fashion. At least, she thought, the Misses Trimble appeared unchanged, with Miss Hyacinth prattling on to her sister and the elder Miss Trimble, as always, nodding her head at regular intervals. On closer inspection, however, it appeared Miss Peony was not listening to what her sibling was saying. Indeed, she looked rather vacant, her eyes glazed, as if her thoughts, like

Mabel's, were elsewhere. Wherever they were, they caused her to frown and her eyes to dart about the room in something of a furtive manner, which had Rose intrigued.

Rose was aware that her own arrival had cast a shadow over the proceedings, that she was being viewed with a degree of wariness. It was a situation that was not unfamiliar to her, for she straddled the precarious line between neighbour and detective. While she might sympathise with her fellow guests' predicament, she did not share it. They were suspects and witnesses in a murder investigation, and she was their inquisitor.

Rose's appearance in the dining room that evening may well have caused conversations to falter and stop, but it did not produce gasps or sharp intakes of breath. These reactions were reserved exclusively for the woman who appeared in the doorway a few minutes later. Every head turned, all eyes drawn to look at the figure that hovered on the threshold of the dining room. She suffered their penetrating gaze without flinching. The woman had drawn herself up to her full height and observed her fellow guests without expression. Only her hands betrayed that she was anxious, her fingers clutching tightly at a little beaded evening bag. She did not move from her position by the door. Having arrived, she gave the impression that she did not know what to do. Should she venture into the room, or turn back and retrace her steps? It is quite possible that it occurred to her that she had made a ghastly mistake. She was a figure of interest and fascination. She could not enter the room without her every movement and expression being scrutinised. Perhaps it was preferable after all to remain in her own rooms with only the well-meaning, but insufferable, Miss Calder for company. On reflection, she thought it was, and was on the very point of retreating when Cedric, the first of those present to collect his senses, advanced forward to greet her.

'Good evening, your grace. Won't you join us?'

He did not wait for the duchess to reply, but instead turned and beckoned to a servant to lay another place at his table. With little choice but to remain, if she did not wish to appear churlish, the Duchess of Grismere walked into the room and took the seat beside Rose.

After a few moments of fascinated silence, conversations resumed. At the Belvederes' table, however, colloquy was rather stilted, and might have been absent entirely, had Cedric not taken it upon himself to

236

continue a predominantly one-sided conversation that required little input from anyone else beside the occasional nod. Rose found herself at rather a loss as to what to say, the various uncomfortable interviews she had held with the duchess weighing heavily on her mind. Even Lavinia who, with her reputation for frivolous chatter, might have been depended upon to perpetuate the conversation with very little effort, was oddly quiet. This, in itself, was so remarkable an occurrence that it drew from her brother a few concerned glances.

Rose considered it fortunate that her husband was ignorant of his sister's dealings with Alec Dewhurst, of which she knew he would have heartily disapproved. She had caught the girl's eye twice that evening and knew that, if nothing else, Lavinia was ashamed of the levity she had displayed during her interview.

To Rose's mind, the duchess appeared listless and distracted, turning her head to look from one table to another. It was possible that she feared she was an object of discussion. Certainly she seemed apprehensive and the little, quick movements of her head were erratic.

'I shouldn't have troubled you,' she said abruptly, while Cedric was in the middle of a sentence. 'I intended to keep to my rooms.' She took a deep breath, as if the very act of speaking was an effort. 'If … if it had not been for the basket of sweetmeats, I should have done.'

'Basket of sweetmeats?' said Cedric puzzled

'Oh,' exclaimed Lavinia brightening. 'I say, did you like them? We thought you would.'

'Was it your idea?' enquired the duchess, unable to keep the note of surprise from her voice, though her eyes showed a new interest in her companion.

'No, not entirely,' replied Lavinia, reddening slightly. 'But I thought it was a jolly good idea when Miss Hyacinth suggested that we should give them to you.'

At mention of her name, Miss Hyacinth looked up inquisitively.

'We were just talking about the basket of sweetmeats,' Lavinia explained brightly.

'Dear Lady Lavinia and I wanted to do something for you, your grace, on behalf of all the hotel guests,' Miss Hyacinth said in a very gushing fashion, her voice carrying across the room.

'Pah!' muttered Mr Vickers into his drink.

'That … that was very kind of you,' said the duchess, lowering her eyes. She looked a little embarrassed by the sudden rush of attention that her comment had generated.

'We thought you must be perfectly miserable,' said Lavinia, feeling that some of the glory had been taken from her, 'and, speaking for myself, I always feel frightfully hungry when I'm upset, don't you? We thought sweetmeats would be just the thing. When one is distressed, one often doesn't feel like eating a full meal, just something sweet.'

'And I knew that Mr Kettering had the most delightful little silver Georgian sweetmeat basket,' said Miss Hyacinth, advancing towards the Belvederes' table. 'It's kept on the sideboard.' She beamed at the duchess. Her smile was reciprocated with a rather pale imitation. Lavinia looked slightly put out. Miss Hyacinth wondered whether she should have remained at her own table. 'It occurred to me it would be just the thing to use,' she said rather desperately, addressing her remark to Rose, who alone seemed receptive to her commentary. There was an awkward pause. Miss Hyacinth knew that she should return to her table and yet, for some reason, her feet refused to obey this simple command. Instead, she stayed standing rather awkwardly beside the Belvederes' table.

It was evident that the duchess felt obliged to show a little more polite interest. 'Was it you who decorated the handle of the basket with the bow?' she said.

'No, that was I,' croaked Miss Peony loudly who, it appeared, felt her presence was also required at the Belvederes' table, if only to retrieve her sister. It is also possible that the woman, so often ignored, wished to be congratulated for her efforts.

The sound of her voice, so infrequently heard, made everyone start. Miss Hyacinth herself visibly winced and glanced anxiously about her. Really, Peony was too much. Why had she used that awful voice, which she usually reserved for when they were alone? On the rare occasions she talked in public, she spoke quietly. What had come over her? And was it Miss Hyacinth's imagination or had Father Adler actually spilt his wine? To say nothing of that awful Mr Vickers, who was positively beside himself with laughter. Well, she would certainly be having words with her sister that evening when they returned to their room.

Miss Peony, if she was aware of her sister's verminous thoughts, appeared quite unperturbed by them. 'It was I who arranged the sweetmeats in the basket,' she said, in the same loud croak that carried.

'Yes,' said Miss Hyacinth quickly, crimson with embarrassment on her sister's behalf. 'And it was very prettily done, dear.' She took her sister by the elbow and steered her back to their table. 'Why were you using that voice?' she hissed. 'Really, I think you did it just to spite me, I really do.'

'You've spilt your wine,' remarked Mabel to her father. She stared transfixed at the crimson stain, which appeared to be spreading across the white linen, and turned very white.

'Oh dear, how clumsy of me,' said the vicar, dabbing hastily, but rather ineffectually, at the damaged tablecloth with his napkin.

Mr Vickers sidled over to Ron Thurlow's table and leered. 'Fancy giving sweetmeats to a murderess,' he remarked. 'Whatever will the old biddy think of next?'

Ron, who had been staring down at his knife and fork, looked up. 'You can go to the devil!' He spoke with such unexpected ferocity that Mr Vickers shrugged and shuffled back to his own table muttering: 'Wonder what's eating him?'

Ron Thurlow sat back in his chair, aware that his outburst had not gone unnoticed. A few curious looks were cast in his direction. Admonishing himself severely, he flung down his napkin, rose from his table, and wandered out into the night.

'Hyacinth, I have a headache,' said Miss Peony.

'Have you, dear?' said her sister, with a remarkable lack of sympathy.

'I must go to bed.'

'What a good idea,' replied Miss Hyacinth.

'You must come with me. It ... it isn't safe to remain here.'

'What utter nonsense,' said Miss Hyacinth. 'If you will insist on being in one of your ridiculous moods, I, for one, won't be a party to it.' With that, she got up purposefully from the table. 'Now, if you have no objection, I think I'll take my coffee with the Adlers.'

Miss Peony watched as her sibling joined the vicar and proceeded to help him in his futile efforts to dab at the wine stain. With various misgivings, Miss Peony got up from her own chair and made for the door. Once there, she hesitated. It was no good. She didn't have the necessary courage to return to her room by herself. But she could hardly sit alone at her table, so very obviously snubbed and abandoned. Besides, Hyacinth had no doubt mentioned to Father Adler that she had retired to her room with a headache. It would appear odd, therefore, if she were to remain in the dining room. She crossed the floor to the French windows and went out on to the terrace. She would stay here a few moments and gather her thoughts. She was certain she was trembling, but on the terrace she could come to no harm. She was merely a stone's throw from the dining room. Even so, her legs felt very weak. She pulled up one of the white cast iron chairs that occupied the terrace, and sat down. Her deafness muffled the sound of the music played by the band. The soft, sombre notes drifted out to her, soothing her troubled mind and lulling her into a reverie of sorts. She dozed.

She awoke with a start. It was dark. She was sitting on the terrace and it was dark. The band had ceased playing and the dining room lay behind her in darkness. Everything was shrouded in darkness. She had fallen asleep and now she had woken she found herself quite alone. Fear entered her bones and she stumbled to the French windows. She tugged desperately at the handle. They were locked. Mr Kettering employed very diligent servants; she had said as much to Hyacinth. Miss Peony rattled the handle of the window to make quite certain it wouldn't open. It made a degree of noise, and this, together with her own deafness, meant that she did not hear the footsteps that crept up behind her. She had resorted to banging on the window stupidly with her fists, when the blow struck.

Chapter Thirty

'She told me it wasn't safe to remain in the dining room. She said we must leave, but I ... I wouldn't listen,' sobbed Miss Hyacinth bitterly. 'I ... I shall never forgive myself, never.'

'You couldn't possibly have known what would happen,' said Rose gently.

Flanked by Cedric and the hotel proprietor, Rose had sat in a respectful silence watching the dawn rise from the centre of the window where the curtains did not quite meet. They were in the Trimble sisters' room, and a full hour had passed since the discovery of Miss Peony's body on the terrace.

'My last words to her were uttered in anger,' cried Miss Hyacinth, dabbing at her eyes with one corner of a lace handkerchief. 'I accused her of being in one of her moods.' She wrung her hands with renewed anguish. 'Oh, if only I hadn't been so angry with her, I might have noticed earlier that she was not here when I returned. You see, I purposefully refused to look in the direction of her bed. I thought she might still be awake and I didn't want to catch her eye. I wanted her to know how annoyed I was.'

'What made you realise she was missing?' enquired Rose curiously.

'I woke with a start. I had an awful feeling that something was wrong. All of a sudden I knew what it was. It was too quiet. You see, I couldn't hear Peony breathing.' She leaned forward in her seat, as if she was about to communicate some highly confidential fact. 'I had often accused her of snoring.'

'And that is when you roused the hotel?' said Cedric.

A makeshift search party of sorts had been quickly assembled, comprised of Mr Kettering and a few servants. It had not taken very long for them to discover Miss Peony's body. The hotel proprietor, though beside himself, had acted quickly. Notwithstanding the hour, he had immediately summoned the Belvederes. As they sat in Miss Hyacinth's room now, they were wearing clothes that had been hurriedly pulled on, and their hair had not seen a brush.

Rose glanced around the room. Her gaze took in Miss Peony's bed, which had not been slept in, lingered for a moment on the empty fireplace and drifted towards the waste paper basket. Something caught her eye. She leaned forward. The basket contained a few balls of paper that had been hastily screwed up; indeed, some were coming undone. It took her but a moment to cross the room and retrieve the topmost paper. She unfolded it and read its contents with growing excitement. It was a draft of Miss Peony's letter to the murderer. She gasped and, without a word, Cedric and Mr Kettering crowded round her so they might peer over her shoulder. When they had finished reading, Rose passed the sheet of paper to Miss Hyacinth, without a word. The woman glanced at it and emitted a startled cry.

'Peony was writing something when I came into the room yesterday. She tried to stuff it under a book before I could see what she was doing. It must have been this.' She waved the creased piece of paper frantically in the air. 'Why, oh why, didn't she tell me what she was doing? I would have stopped her.'

'Did you know that she had seen the murderer?' Rose asked rather sharply.

'I ... I knew that she had been out that night ... the night Mr Dewhurst was killed,' Miss Hyacinth replied hesitantly. 'She woke me up when she returned. She told me to go back to sleep. I ... I knew she was upset about something but she refused to talk about it.'

It was on the tip of Rose's tongue to say that they should have told her, that they had lied during their interview and obstructed her investigation. A look at the distraught expression on Miss Hyacinth's face, however, persuaded her to do otherwise. Instead, she said:

'Do you think it might have been to do with the pocket watch? Was Miss Peony trying to return it?'

If she had suddenly announced that every one of the hotel guests had been murdered, the effect could not have been more tremendous. Miss Hyacinth turned very white and buried her face in her hands. Rose could barely decipher the words that she uttered through heartfelt sobs.

'It's ... it's my fault ... If I hadn't taken it ... none of this would have happened.'

Rose did not have time to comfort the woman. Instead, she said abruptly: 'Where is it? Do you still have it?'

Miss Hyacinth was too upset to reply. Rose marched over to the fireplace and thrust her hand up the chimney and felt inside. It took her a few seconds to locate the hiding place where she had found her brooch. Her fingers closed over a small velvet pouch, the same pouch she had discovered caught on one of the pinnacle finials of the grate. She withdrew her hand and, with trembling fingers, withdrew from the little sack a gold and diamond object. Had she been her husband, she might have whistled. Alec Dewhurst's pocket watch looked up at her in all its jewelled glory. For a moment Rose stared at it stupidly. Then the engraved initials caught the light. "O, "E", "W", she murmured. 'They're "O", "E", "W".

Having arranged for Miss Calder to sit with Miss Hyacinth, who stubbornly refused to leave the room she had shared with her sister, the others had returned, weary and shaken, to their own quarters. Rose had been persuaded to go back to bed to snatch a few hours' sleep before another endless round of interviews commenced. Even as she undressed, she was tolerably certain that they would prove fruitless. There would be no convenient witnesses or alibis. Miss Peony had been killed at a time when both hotel guests and servants had been asleep. The hour, Rose acknowledged, somewhat bitterly, had been well chosen by the murderer.

She awoke barely an hour later, her mind racing. With a blanket wrapped around her, she crept out of the bedroom she shared with her husband and padded across the hall in bare feet to the sitting room. Sleep was now furthest from her mind and in here she might sit and think without fear of waking Cedric. Ensconced in the blanket on the sofa, she stared at the pocket watch and Miss Peony's note, both of which she held in her hands like two sinister trophies.

She studied the pocket watch first and murmured: 'There's no "G". She sighed and turned her attention next to Miss Peony's note. She wondered idly what the murderer had done with the original. She doubted it differed in many respects from the draft she held in her hand. Indeed, if it had not been for the fact that there were two large ink blots on the sheet she was reading, her copy might well have been the one given to the murderer.

Miss Peony, she noted, had taken the precaution of not signing the document with her own name. Instead, she had written "A Well-wisher".

Given that it was highly improbable that the woman had handed the letter to her murderer, she wondered how the murderer had found out Miss Peony's identity. Had she been spotted delivering the letter? Rose thought it unlikely that Miss Peony would have slipped the letter under the murderer's door. She would have had to cross the terrace where there was every chance she would have been observed from any number of windows. It needn't have been the murderer who had seen her either, for anyone might quite innocently have remarked to the murderer that they had seen her deliver the note. Rose was quite sure Miss Peony would never have trusted a servant to deliver it for her, for there would always have been the fear that it would fall into the wrong hands.

She thought it far more likely that the woman would have left the note somewhere where the murderer was certain to find it. The dining room was the obvious choice, for everyone sat at their assigned tables in their allocated seats. The note could quite easily have been slipped under a napkin or placed on a chair. But it would still have involved a degree of risk. Miss Peony could quite easily have been observed doing the deed. Rose put a hand up to her head, which was throbbing, because of course she *had* been observed, which was how the murderer had discovered that it was Miss Peony who had written the letter.

The more she thought about it, the more certain she was that Miss Peony had placed the note in the dining room for the murderer to find. Any other day, that would have ruled out the duchess being the murderer but for the fact that she had eaten in the dining room last night. Though, of course, Miss Peony could not have known that she would, or indeed where she would sit. Still, the fact remained that every one of the hotel guests had been present in the dining room that evening, and a few hours later Miss Peony had been murdered on the terrace, not a stone's throw from the room.

Now the question was, had anyone appeared particularly upset? Rose had just arrived at a recollection of Ron Thurlow marching out of the room with a scowl on his face while dinner was still being served, when the door opened and Lavinia entered the room. One look at the girl's pale face told her that Lavinia was aware that something frightful had occurred. If there was any doubt Lavinia's next words confirmed the fact.

'What is the matter? What has happened?'

'Miss Peony is dead,' said Rose quietly. 'She has been murdered.'

Lavinia sank down beside her on the sofa and pulled some of the blanket towards her. As she did so, her eyes fell on Miss Peony's letter and, before Rose could stop her, she had picked up the sheet and was reading it. 'Did ... did Miss Peony write this?' she asked, her eyes widening. Rose nodded. 'Is ... is this why she was murdered?'

'Yes. That's to say, I believe it was the reason she was killed. Of course this is only a draft. We can't be absolutely certain what she wrote, or even that the murderer ever received the letter.'

'But you think it very likely?'

'Yes, I do,'

Lavinia burst into tears. 'It's ... it's all my fault,' she sobbed.

In answer to Rose's look of astonishment, she proceeded, in tears, to give an account of her encounter with the Trimble sisters on the terrace and the conversation that followed over afternoon tea.

'You told them Mr Thurlow was about to be arrested for Mr Dewhurst's murder?' Rose exclaimed in disbelief.

'Mr Kettering told me he was,' Lavinia said, on the defensive. 'I didn't think there would be any harm in my telling Miss Peony and Miss Hyacinth. How was I to know that Miss Peony was going to feign a headache and return to her room to write that stupid letter?'

Inwardly, Rose cursed both Mr Kettering and Lavinia for their stupidity. Aloud, she said: 'I suppose you weren't to know what she would do.'

'No,' agreed Lavinia heartily. 'It was jolly stupid of her not to tell you. About the murderer, I mean. She was just asking for trouble.'

'She was trying to protect the murderer,' Rose said, more to herself than to her companion.

'The only person I can imagine Miss Peony ever wanting to protect would be her sister,' Lavinia observed, 'and she'd hardly write a letter to Miss Hyacinth, would she?' She yawned. 'I don't know about you, but I'm going back to bed.'

'I will stay here,' said Rose. 'I should like to sit and think for a while. Yesterday I felt certain I possessed all the clues I required to solve Alec Dewhurst's murder, if only I could assemble them in the right order.'

'Well, I daresay Miss Peony's death has made a mess of things,' Lavinia remarked.

'I wonder,' said Rose.

'Will you and Ceddie be going to breakfast this morning?' asked Lavinia sleepily. 'I shan't want to sit at the table by myself.'

Rose felt a flash of irritation. Only a few minutes ago Lavinia had been claiming she was to blame for Miss Peony's death. Now the girl's thoughts seemed to be preoccupied with food.

'Why must you insist on calling Cedric, Ceddie?' she said testily. 'You know he hates it when you do it in public. It's a ridiculous name.'

Lavinia stared at her open-mouthed, and Rose immediately regretted her outburst.

'I've always called him Ceddie,' Lavinia said tersely, 'ever since we were children and I have no intention of calling him anything else. And, if you must know, I've never liked the name Cedric, I can't for the life of me think why my parents chose to call him such a stupid name.'

With that, she flounced out of the room, closing the door behind her with a very loud bang.

Feeling she had been suitably rebuked, Rose lay on the sofa, her back propped up by cushions, the thin blanket draped over her legs. It was becoming quite a habit of hers, she mused, to sit quietly and evaluate her various observations and findings, sifting the wheat from the chaff, the material facts from the insignificant ones.

She thought back to Alec Dewhurst's sudden arrival at the hotel with the duchess, which had drawn gasps and sharp intakes of breath from the other guests. Her pulse quickened. She knew now that Ron Thurlow had recognised the young man, while the others had identified his companion as the 'Disappearing Duchess'. She closed her eyes. She held in her hand Miss Peony's letter. There had been another letter too, the one the duchess had left for the duke to read, after she had abandoned him. She had made no mention of Alec Dewhurst, only that she did not wish to bring her husband disgrace. They were considered a most devoted couple and yet the duchess had left the duke for a fickle and worthless young man. The duchess' words came to her out of the darkness. 'I am not quite the awful woman you suppose me to be,' she had said, 'and Alec is not the man you think he is. You judge us both too harshly. If you only knew the truth …'

What, Rose wondered, was the truth? The duchess had been at pains to keep it concealed from her. It had something to do with the name Oberon

246

.. She remembered an instance in the dining room when the duchess had been met with a steely glare by Alec Dewhurst because she had called him by that name, and then there was the scrap of paper in the ransacked room.

Her mind then drifted to the conversation Lavinia had overheard between Alec Dewhurst and Ron Thurlow, which struck her as decidedly odd in a number of ways. Her thoughts floated to the previous evening in the dining room. There had been talk of sweetmeats and the vicar had spilt his wine. Mr Vickers had said something to Ron Thurlow and he had stormed out of the room.

Rose supposed she must have dozed, though she was hardly conscious of the fact, for it seemed to her that her mind had kept active, turning over the pieces of the jigsaw, trying to fit them together to form a coherent picture.

Yet when Cedric woke her a couple of hours later, she felt as if she was coming back from a very long way off. She had been sunk in the depths, but now she was floating to the surface. She clutched at her husband's hand for a full three minutes as the truth slowly dawned on her. At last she turned to him and said, in a voice hardly above a whisper: 'I know who did it. I know who killed Alec Dewhurst and Miss Peony. I know, but I haven't the faintest idea how I can prove it!'

Chapter Thirty-one

Rose had summoned Mr Kettering and informed him she knew the identity of the murderer, much to that gentleman's astonishment. She had refused to provide him with any particulars, but requested that he make an announcement to the other hotel guests at breakfast.

'I should like you to advise them of Miss Peony's death,' Rose had said. She had glanced at her wristwatch and added: 'Ask them to assemble again in the dining room at half past eleven. Tell them I wish to speak to them on a matter of great importance.'

'And the duchess?' the hotel proprietor had asked tentatively. 'Should I ask her to attend?'

'I should like everyone to be there, Mr Kettering, even Miss Hyacinth.'

Next Rose had sat down at her writing table, picked up her fountain pen and written a few sentences on the hotel's headed notepaper. Like Miss Peony before her, she had made several attempts before she was satisfied. 'Concise and to the point,' she had whispered to herself. 'I say, I wonder if it will work?'

She had placed the letter in an envelope and put it in her pocket along with Miss Peony's letter and Alec Dewhurst's pocket watch. It was then that she had glanced at the clock on the mantelpiece and noted there was still a full hour before her presence was required in the dining room. She had paced the room and then sat down at the writing desk again. She took up her pen. She might as well scribble down the salient points of the case she had constructed. If nothing else, it would give her something to do while she waited. She had just finished making her notes when Cedric entered the room, his face drawn.

'It's a ghastly business, all right,' her husband said, without preamble. 'I thought it was appalling seeing Dewhurst's body stretched out on a slab. But it was a hundred times worse seeing Miss Peony's.' He sunk on to a chair and Rose came over to him and put her arms around him. They remained like that for a few minutes before Cedric made an effort to pull himself together. He spoke in the same strained voice in which he had commenced.

'I can't tell you how small and pathetic she looked,' he said. 'It was awful. Costas says she was struck on the back of the head in a similar fashion to Dewhurst, but that, in this instance, the blow definitely killed her; there's no doubt about that. The only small blessing is that there were no defensive wounds of any kind. With any luck the poor woman never knew anything about it; she was deaf after all.'

Rose nodded. It seemed to her that there was nothing else she could say. She did not doubt the image of poor Miss Peony's body would haunt her husband's thoughts to the end of his days. It filled her with increased resolve. She had felt a degree of sympathy for the murderer of Alec Dewhurst, for she could not help thinking that the deceased had contributed to his fate by his own actions. The murder of Miss Peony, however, she viewed very differently. It was a heartless, desperate act, brought about by the murderer's selfish desire for self-preservation.

She entered the dining room with Cedric by her side. The hotel proprietor was already there, his expression anxious. The hotel guests, who, as one, turned to stare at her, looked similarly apprehensive. They were all present, even the duchess, who sat at a little distance from the others with an air of detachment. Miss Hyacinth, her eyes puffy and red-rimmed from continuous weeping, sat at the Adlers' table, Lavinia beside her, holding her hand. Mabel, her cheeks tear-stained and her eyes wide with fright, stared straight ahead of her, a handkerchief held up to her trembling lips. The vicar sat between Miss Hyacinth and his daughter and cast concerned glances at each in turn. Mr Thurlow looked quite ghastly, as if he had suffered a terrible shock. Even the disreputable Mr Vickers appeared strangely quiet and subdued.

Rose made her way to the front of the stage. She wished, with a sinking feeling, that it was all over and done with, that she was not about to accuse someone of murder and ask that they confess and face the consequences of their actions. She slipped her hand into her pocket and felt for the letter she had written. Its presence gave her reassurance and for a moment she held it tightly between her fingers. She cleared her throat and launched into a prepared speech of sorts.

'As you are aware,' she began, 'I was engaged by Mr Kettering, on behalf of the hotel, to undertake a private investigation into the death of Mr Dewhurst.' She paused a moment before adding: 'My investigation was extended, of course, to include Miss Peony's death.' She heard Miss Hyacinth stifle a sob. She hesitated a moment before adding: 'I have now concluded my investigation.'

Her words were met with a series of gasps and sharp intakes of breath Miss Hyacinth gave a startled cry.

Before anyone had an opportunity to speak, Rose continued in a clea voice. 'This has been a particularly difficult and puzzling case. Most o you had very good reasons for wishing Alec Dewhurst dead, and none o you had any alibis to speak of.' She paused again for a moment, aware that one or two of the guests were shifting in their chairs uncomfortably 'The case was further complicated by the fact that Alec Dewhurst was not the man he purported to be.'

She was aware that she had the full attention of her audience now. 'Before I elaborate any further on that point, it is perhaps worth noting that Alex Dewhurst was a young man who incurred a great many enemies. He had a reputation for preying on rich women and pilfering their money and trinkets.' She paused to cast a look in the duchess' direction; the woman was looking into the middle distance with steely resolve.

'I believe,' Rose continued, 'the murderer intended Mr Dewhurst's death to be mistaken for an unfortunate accident. The deceased was in the habit of walking along the edge of the cliff before turning in for the night. He might, quite easily, have stumbled in the dark and toppled over the edge.'

'You talked about motives,' piped up Mr Vickers. 'I hadn't any motive for wishing the fellow dead.'

'Hadn't you?' said Rose. 'You are a private enquiry agent employed by a firm engaged by the Duke of Grismere to find his wife. On the night of Mr Dewhurst's death, you had an altercation with the deceased in the dining room and your camera was confiscated. It is quite possible that you wanted revenge. Who is to say you were not above a bit of blackmail?'

''Ere, that's a lie!' interjected Mr Vickers, jumping up from his chair. 'You've no right saying such things. I've a good mind to —'

'Be quiet and sit down,' ordered Mr Kettering. 'You'll hear what her ladyship has to say.'

'If you were minded towards blackmail,' Rose continued, holding up her hand as Mr Vickers again made to protest, 'you were well placed to carry it out. All you had to do was threaten to disclose the duchess' whereabouts to her husband unless a certain sum was paid. You had the

250

necessary photographic evidence.' She paused, before adding: 'Mr Dewhurst did not strike me as the sort of man who would allow himself to be blackmailed. I daresay he would have put up quite a fight.'

'Pah!' said Mr Vickers.

'Speaking of blackmail,' Rose said, turning away and walking towards the travel courier's table, 'Mr Dewhurst was not above a bit of blackmail himself. Indeed as you are aware, Mr Thurlow, we have a witness who overheard a conversation between you and the deceased in which Mr Dewhurst threatened to disclose to both your employer and Miss Adler the fact that you had spent some time in prison.'

Unlike Mr Vickers, Ron Thurlow remained silent. He merely bowed his head in acknowledgement and stared down miserably at the tablecloth. This was perhaps fortunate, for Father Adler and Mabel were both regarding him with eyes wide in disbelief. Rose strolled towards their table.

'Both of you had very good motives for wishing Mr Dewhurst dead,' she said quietly. Father Adler attempted to make a feeble protest, while Mabel merely stared at her, some of the colour returning to her cheeks.

'You, Miss Adler, were in love with Mr Dewhurst. Indeed, you were planning to elope with him on the night he was murdered. You were in the very act of packing your cases when you discovered that he had deceived you. Mr Dewhurst's companion was not his sister, as he had led you to believe. Indeed, Alec Dewhurst had gone to considerable pains to ensure that you believed his lie, even arranging for the duchess to join you and your father at dinner to give credence to his story. Having become aware of his dishonesty, you no doubt realised that Mr Dewhurst's intentions towards you were hardly likely to be honourable.'

'How dare you!' cried Mabel, covering her face with her hand. 'He … he loved me.'

'Father Adler,' Rose said, turning her attention to the girl's parent, 'on discovering Miss Mabel intended to elope with a man you regarded as no better than a scoundrel, you flew into a rage so ferocious that you frightened your daughter. You told me yourself that you set off to tackle Mr Dewhurst, and we only have your word for it that no such confrontation took place.'

'Yes,' mumbled the vicar sadly.

Rose returned to the stage. 'All perfectly reasonable motives for

251

wishing Alec Dewhurst dead,' she said slowly. 'But, right from the beginning, it seemed to me that one person, above all others, had a particularly strong motive. Only one person had forsaken everything to be with Mr Dewhurst. That, of course, was you, your grace.' She turned abruptly to face the duchess. 'You had abandoned your husband, your reputation, your position in society and even some of your wealth. And then you made your awful discovery. You had sacrificed it all for a man quite unworthy of your affections.'

The Duchess returned her gaze without flinching.

'Not only was Mr Dewhurst a petty criminal,' continued Rose, 'but he made no secret of the fact that he had become bored of you and was quite taken with Miss Adler. It is quite reasonable to surmise that this made you feel both miserable and desperate. A person in that state of mind might be capable of anything.'

The duchess sat motionless. It was almost as if she was quite oblivious to what was being said.

'Let us suppose,' said Rose, 'that you learned that Alec Dewhurst intended to leave the island with Miss Adler. You quarrelled. I daresay you would have begged and pleaded with him to stay, but he refused to listen. Alec Dewhurst's mind was quite made up; he was desperate to be gone. Let us picture it. He quickly stuffs his pockets with the hoard of trinkets that he has amassed and heads off towards the cliff. Unbeknown to him, you follow him. He starts to descend the path. You will not permit him to abandon you. You have forsaken everything to be with him. You decide there, on the cliff edge, that if you cannot have him, there is only one thing to be done and that is ...'

Rose left the sentence unfinished and regarded the duchess, who now returned her look with an odd flicker of amusement. 'You are quite wrong,' she said, in a voice that carried across the room.

'Yes,' agreed Rose quietly. 'I am quite wrong because your conduct does not make any sense.' She began to pace the room, collecting her thoughts as she went. 'Why would a woman, who was neither stupid nor impulsive, decide to abandon a husband, to whom she was reportedly devoted, to run off, on a whim, with a thoroughly worthless young man?' No one answered her. 'You left your husband a note,' she said, glancing first at the duchess and then down at Mr Kettering's notes, which she had picked up from the stage. "*'If there were any other way, then please believe me, I would have taken it.'*"

'No!' cried the duchess, putting her hands over her ears. 'I ...I don't want to hear ... I don't want to hear what I wrote.'

"*'Know only that I have loved you deeply and that I could not have wished for a better husband,*'" continued Rose relentlessly. 'That does not sound to me like a woman who is no longer in love with her husband.'

'I ... I told you. I still cared for him.'

'And Alec Dewhurst, did you care for him?'

'Yes, but –'

'But not in the same way that you loved your husband?' suggested Rose.

The duchess nodded. Some of the colour had returned to her face.

'It was clear to me that Mr Dewhurst had a particular hold over you. At first I wondered if he was blackmailing you. However, you appeared genuinely shocked when I put forward the suggestion. It occurred to me then that any hold Alec Dewhurst might have over you was of your own making. That is to say, you were partially, if not fully, complicit. But it did not explain why you made no objection to his growing attachment to Miss Adler. For you do not strike me as the sort of woman who would permit a man to make a fool of her, particularly in public. The only explanation was that your relationship with Mr Dewhurst was not what it appeared to be on the surface. I could not forget what you had said to me during our first conversation. 'I am not quite the awful woman you suppose me to be, and Alec is not the man you think he is. You judge us both too harshly. If you only knew the truth.' But what was the truth? And then it suddenly dawned on me. Alec Dewhurst was not your lover! And yet you had abandoned your husband, whom you loved dearly, to be with him. Who could have a greater claim on your heart than your husband?'

'My son,' cried the duchess. 'Alec Dewhurst was my son!'

Chapter Thirty-two

'Alec Dewhurst was my son,' repeated the duchess, though this time when she spoke, her voice was barely above a whisper, as if the sentence had escaped her lips unwillingly.

Her revelation had been met with a shocked silence. Rose looked quickly about her. The faces of the other hotel guests, without exception, bore signs of having been violently startled; one or two of them looked as if they could hardly comprehend what they were being told. They were vaguely aware that the whole complexion of the investigation had changed.

Having delivered her devastating piece of news, the duchess appeared quite spent. She leaned back heavily in her chair and closed her eyes.

'Begging your pardon, your grace,' said Mr Kettering apologetically, 'I hope I am not speaking out of turn, but I'm afraid that I don't quite understand. By that I mean why the need for secrecy and … and deception, if I may be so bold? I do not understand, not if the deceased was your son.'

'Only a fool would ask a question like that,' snapped the duchess, rather nastily. There was a long pause. She sat up sharply in her chair, opened her eyes and said rather grudgingly: 'It was a youthful infatuation. I was young and foolish. It was before I had made the duke's acquaintance.' She stared at her audience, her eyes bright. She appeared to be willing them to comprehend her, while challenging them to condemn her if they dare. The vicar, Rose noted, looked suitably appalled, as did Miss Hyacinth. 'Was I expected to have my life ruined by one foolish mistake?' asked the duchess. 'A man can have many indiscretions and his reputation remains untarnished, a woman has only one and her character is ruined.'

'It's awfully unfair,' agreed Cedric, from the far corner of the room.

'My son was well provided for,' said the duchess, 'I made certain of that. And of course I exchanged letters with his guardian, though I was careful never to see him, or him me.' It seemed that, now she had spoken on a subject that for so long she had kept hidden, she could not stop. 'Having given him up as a baby, barely a week after his birth, I did not hink I would pine for him. But in that I was wrong. I missed him dreadfully. Perhaps if I had been blessed with other children ...' The duchess paused a moment to compose herself. 'I did not intend that he should ever discover the details of his parentage, but I suppose he must have found out somehow. But when he came to me for assistance after a piece of bad luck, I ... I couldn't turn him away.'

Rose cast a furtive glance at Mr Kettering. The hotel proprietor looked thoroughly taken aback by the duchess' remarkably candid answer to what he had considered was a perfectly innocent question. It occurred to Rose that, in all probability, he heartily regretted having spoken.

The duchess leaned back in her chair again. If Rose thought the woman's mind was elsewhere, she was to find herself mistaken. Barely a minute elapsed before the duchess said, in a voice that was both sharp and clear:

'I don't suppose even you, Lady Belvedere, will accuse me of having murdered my own son?'

'No,' said Rose, 'I should not accuse you of that.'

'Look here,' interjected Mr Vickers, sounding aggrieved. 'This is all very well, to be sure, not that I know how you're going to put it to the duke, if you don't mind me saying? Not that it's any of my business. But what about this 'ere inquiry of yours?' he said, glaring at Rose. 'You said as how you had finished your investigation. I took that to mean as how you knew who the murderer was.'

'I do know who the murderer is,' said Rose quietly.

'Well, if you do, you've got a funny way of going about telling it,' Mr Vickers replied quickly, still in his objectionable tone, though his eyes looked alert. 'Why you were wanting to go around the houses like that, I don't know. Telling everyone as how they had a motive for murdering the fellow, to say nothing of the poor lady, and telling everyone all of our secrets we'd rather keep hidden.'

'You are quite right, Mr Vickers,' Rose said. She held up her hand to Mr Kettering, who looked about to give Mr Vickers a piece of his mind. 'The problem is that I don't quite know where to begin. In the ordinary course of things, I would of course commence at the beginning. But today I think I will start in the middle. You see, if it had not been for Miss Peony, I should not have known with absolute certainty who the murderer was. It seemed to me that it could quite easily have been one of two people.'

'Start with Miss Peony, before you lose me,' said Mr Vickers, looking perplexed.

'Very well. I have here,' Rose paused to retrieve from her pocket Miss Peony's letter, 'the draft of a letter written by Miss Peony, the original of which I believe she gave to the murderer. Before I say anything more, I should like you all to read this letter.'

There ensued a lull in the proceedings as the document was duly circulated and read by the hotel guests amid a number of gasps and shrieks.

'You will have noticed that Miss Peony took the precaution of not signing the document with her own name. Instead, she had written "A Well-wisher". In light of the contents of this letter, one may be forgiven for assuming that Miss Peony had been spotted delivering her letter and had been killed by the murderer to prevent her from revealing his identity. This, however, was not the case.'

'You're surely not suggesting there were two murderers?' cried Mabel, clutching at her father's arm in alarm.

'No,' said Rose. 'There was only one murderer. What I meant was Miss Peony was not spotted delivering the letter.'

'Then how did our murderer know it was her that wrote it?' asked Mr Vickers.

'Because she told him,' Rose said abruptly, 'though really I should say her.'

'Her?' said Mabel, glaring at Lavinia in a most unfriendly fashion, as if she suspected the girl of being the murderer.

'Yes. You see, the murderer was you,' she said, pausing to address the killer, her finger pointing towards the Duchess of Grismere.

'What utter nonsense!' retorted the duchess.

'And yet, I ask that you hear me out,' Rose said firmly. 'Miss Peony's conduct in the dining room on the night of her murder was very odd. That is to say, it was out of character. As a rule, Miss Peony was quiet and withdrawn. Yesterday, she was willing to step forward and speak in the loud, rather hoarse voice that she usually reserved for when she and Miss Hyacinth were alone.'

'Why?' piped up Lavinia, who thought she had been unusually quiet,

256

and really ought to say something, if only one word.

'Because she was afraid the murderer would think her sister was the author of the letter.' Miss Hyacinth gasped and burst into a fresh flood of tears.

'Miss Peony had been faced with the problem of how to give her letter to the murderer without being seen,' Rose continued. 'She believed she had arrived at the ideal solution. Miss Hyacinth and Lady Lavinia had decided to present the duchess with a basket of sweetmeats on behalf of the hotel guests. Miss Peony offered to tie the bow to the handle of the basket. This provided her with the perfect opportunity to hide the letter at the bottom of the basket.'

'I still don't see how you could possibly have known Miss Peony had written that letter,' said Lavinia. Her remark was directed to the duchess who, after her initial outburst, had maintained a steadfast silence.

'She didn't,' said Rose. 'Not at first. It had not occurred to Miss Peony that, on receiving the letter, the duchess would decide to have her dinner in the dining room. She needed to find out who had prepared the basket of sweetmeats, you see. If you remember,' she added, glancing at Lavinia, 'she mentioned to us that she had received them and that was why she was there.'

'I say,' exclaimed Lavinia, 'I told her that we thought she should like them and she asked me whether it had been my idea. I thought at the time she looked at me curiously.'

'You told her it had been Miss Hyacinth's idea,' said Rose.

'Well it had been.'

'I told her we had wanted to do something for her on behalf of all the hotel guests,' Miss Hyacinth said in a very small voice. 'Oh, if only I had kept quiet, my sister might still be alive!'

'Miss Peony made a point of telling the duchess that it had been she who had decorated the handle of the basket with a bow and she who had arranged the sweetmeats in the basket,' Rose said. 'She wanted to let the duchess know, beyond any doubt, that she was the author of the letter, not Miss Hyacinth.'

'You have no proof that is what happened,' said a voice. The Duchess of Grismere had got to her feet and was moving across the floor. 'It's conjecture, that's all. There is nothing to say this woman did put that letter in my basket of sweetmeats. She could just as easily have slipped it under the murderer's door or quite possibly, and in my opinion quite probably, never delivered such a letter at all.' The duchess advanced towards Rose. 'Besides, you said yourself that you would hardly accuse me of murdering my own son.'

'And I stand by my word,' Rose said. 'I should not accuse you of murdering your own son. But I would accuse you of murdering the man who pretended he was your son.'

'What ... what do you mean?' cried the duchess.

She had halted abruptly and her hand pulled at the fabric of her dress. Rose was vaguely aware of a mixture of reactions from the other hotel guests. A moment later, and there was a deathly silence, where Rose was quite certain she could have heard a pin drop.

'Alec Dewhurst was not your son Oberon. It was not until the night of his murder that you realised you had been deceived. When Mr Vickers was being escorted from the dining room, after his altercation with Mr Dewhurst, he remarked that the deceased's real name was Goodfellow, not Dewhurst, and hinted that he knew him to be a man of low morals'

'Ay, that's right,' affirmed the man in question.

'Later that same evening, I had a conversation with you in the grounds of the hotel,' continued Rose. 'If you remember, Lord Belvedere came to fetch me and you slipped into the shadows. He happened to remark to me that Mr Vickers insisted Alec Dewhurst was in fact a petty thief who went by the name of Goodfellow. Knowing what I do now, I don't doubt you overheard our conversation.'

'I believe you returned to your rooms to seek out the truth among Mr Dewhurst's papers and belongings. It was you, your grace, who ransacked the room that Alec Dewhurst used as his study. You were in search of evidence that the man you had believed to be your son was nothing more than a cheap imposter.'

'And the pocket watch?' enquired the hotel proprietor. 'If you don't mind my saying, Lady Belvedere, you always seemed most curious about the initials on Mr Dewhurst's pocket watch.'

'Thank you, Mr Kettering, I had quite forgotten the pocket watch,' Rose said. She addressed the duchess. 'You gave Mr Dewhurst a gold full hunter pocket watch, which had his initials engraved on it. He produced it at dinner on the night of his death.'

258

'Well?'

'You told Mr Kettering that the initials were "O", "E", "G"; all in upper case. He made a particular note of it in his pocketbook.'

'What of it?' demanded the duchess, though there was a note of fear in her voice.

'You were lying.' Rose produced from her pocket Mr Dewhurst's pocket watch.

'You told me it was missing,' cried the duchess.

'It was, but it has since been found,' said Rose. She deliberately did not look at Miss Hyacinth. 'The initials you had engraved on Mr Dewhurst's watch were your son's initials. "O", "E", "W". There is no "G" among them. You did not know then that the man who purported to be your son went by the name of Goodfellow. I'll wager your son's surname begins with a "W". When I first interviewed you, you told me that you had always been aware that Mr Dewhurst's real name was Goodfellow. But you could not possibly have known that on the date that you gave Alec Dewhurst this pocket watch; the presence of this letter "W" proves otherwise. Alec Dewhurst also happened to mention to Mr Thurlow that you did not know his real name. As I have already said, it was not until the night of his murder that you discovered Alec Dewhurst's surname was actually Goodfellow. At the time of his death you knew full well that Alec Dewhurst was not your son, though you may pretend otherwise.'

'And suppose I did,' said the duchess. 'You have no evidence to show that it was me who murdered Mr Dewhurst. All you have against me is that I might possibly have lied to you concerning his identity. That is to say, that I pretended that he was my son rather than a petty criminal who preyed on wealthy women. It is perfectly possible that I felt ashamed for having been taken for a fool.'

'I should like you to make a full confession of your guilt,' said Rose bluntly. 'If nothing else, you owe it to Miss Peony.'

The duchess laughed. It was not a very pleasant sound.

'You beast!' cried Miss Hyacinth, making as if she meant to tear the duchess to pieces, which it was quite possible she might have done, had she not been prevented from doing so by the intervention of Father Adler and Cedric.

'Before you give me your final answer,' said Rose slowly. 'I should like you first to read what I have written in this letter.' With that, she took the last object from her pocket and handed it to the duchess, who tore open the envelope with a degree of curiosity.

No one stirred as the duchess read its contents. It was merely a few scribbled lines but it obviously intrigued her, for she read it again and again, as if she were finding it hard to digest its contents.

'Is it true?' she murmured, her eyes widening. 'Is what you have written true?'

Rose nodded slowly. The duchess took a deep breath. 'Very well,' she said solemnly, in a loud voice. 'Then I confess to the murders of Alec Dewhurst and Miss Peony Trimble. Where would you have me sign? Here?' Rose handed her a pen and she scribbled her signature and made hastily for the door. No one tried to detain her. At the doorway she turned and said again: 'Do you promise?' Rose nodded. The duchess turned to Miss Hyacinth and said: 'I'm sorry. It was never my intention to harm your sister.'

With that, she was gone. The others sat in a stupefied silence, not quite certain what they had just heard or witnessed. Only Rose was running across the floor and between the tables until she drew level with Ron Thurlow. Bending forward she said in an urgent whisper:

'Quick. You must go to the duchess. There really is very little time.' Ron turned and regarded her with a dazed, uncomprehending look. 'Quick,' repeated Rose, taking the man by his shoulders and shaking him gently. 'You must go to the duchess and tell her the truth. You must go to her and tell her *you* are Oberon!'

Chapter Thirty-three

'I should very much like to know how you guessed I was Oberon,' said Ron Thurlow, who had taken up a position in front of the fireplace.

'Yes, do tell us, Lady Belvedere,' said Mr Kettering, turning in his chair to regard Rose, who was seated beside him. 'I have been wondering myself how you arrived at that conclusion.'

They were in the hotel proprietor's study. Three weeks had elapsed since the duchess had confessed to the murders of Alec Dewhurst and Miss Peony, and the dark atmosphere that had hung over Hotel Hemera like a creeping miasma was beginning to dissipate.

'I suppose it was a number of things really which, if viewed individually, did not appear very odd, but when looked at collectively raised a number of questions in my mind.' Rose smiled at Ron's bemused face. 'I'm afraid I am explaining myself very badly, Mr Thurlow. It is rather difficult to know exactly where to begin. Perhaps I should mention them in the order that they occur to me now?'

Ron nodded. He left his position by the fireplace and seated himself in one of the chairs that faced the desk.

'When we undertook a search of the guests' rooms,' Rose began, 'it struck me that your personal effects were of an unusually good quality for a man in your profession.'

'I say, did it really?' said Ron, with a note of surprise in his voice.

'Then there was the matter of Alec Dewhurst's pocket watch. When it slipped out of Miss Adler's hand and rolled on to the floor, I could not help noticing how very quick you were to get out of your chair to retrieve it. At the time, I supposed you were just curious to determine, like the rest of us, whether it had been damaged or broken in the fall. But later I wondered if you had seized the opportunity to examine the initials engraved on the case.'

'You're quite right,' said Ron. 'It gave me a bit of a turn, I can tell you, when I saw my own initials.' He smiled. 'Oberon Edwin Winslow at your service, my lady; quite a mouthful, I'm sure you'll agree?'

'You'd had your suspicions concerning Alec Dewhurst, hadn't you?' Rose said astutely. 'That he might be pretending to be you, I mean?'

'Well, it seemed a bit too much of a coincidence that a man whose brief acquaintance I had made in prison should take it upon himself to run away with a woman who just happened to be my relation,' Ron said. 'Besides, just before that incident with the pocket watch, my ... my mother,' he paused for a moment and blushed, 'called him Oberon. I can't tell you what a start it gave me, hearing her say my name like that. And then when I saw the look Dewhurst gave her, well, I suppose I realised the truth. The game had rather been given away.'

'Yes.'

'I have always rather detested the name Oberon,' confessed Ron, a little sheepishly. 'That is why I shortened it to Ron.' He chuckled. 'I suppose most people assume Ron is short for Ronald; it usually is.'

'For me, that was one of the final pieces of the jigsaw,' said Rose. 'Lady Lavinia insists on calling my husband by a pet name, even in public. It is quite a ridiculous name, but she gave it to him when they were children and I suppose the name has stuck. It struck me that Oberon was quite an unusual name and somewhat old-fashioned. If a person were called Oberon and did not like the name, I wondered what he could shorten it to. It came to me all of a sudden that it could quite easily be shortened to Ron.'

'And then you realised that I must be Oberon?'

'Everything fell into place if you were. Not just your clothes, or the fact that you had picked up the pocket watch to examine the initials on the casing, or even that Alec Dewhurst did not wish to be referred to as Oberon in public. There were other things too, like why you lied about the initials on the pocket watch.'

'Right from the start I suspected that my ... my mother had killed Dewhurst. If she had assumed Alec Dewhurst was her son and then had discovered he had deceived her ... I had no reason to suppose anyone else had a motive for wishing the fellow dead.'

'Except for yourself, of course,' Rose said quietly.

'Yes,' said Ron with a rueful smile. 'I can see why you might have thought that.' He got up and began to pace the room. 'When I discovered I was the son of the Duchess of Grismere, I hated her like poison for abandoning me. It never occurred to me I should ever meet her.' He gave a bitter laugh. 'We moved in rather different circles. I never wished to lay eyes on her but, when I did, I found I couldn't bring myself to tell you my suspicions concerning her guilt. I suppose in a way I wanted to protect her. That was why I told you that stupid lie about the initials on the watch; it was very clumsily done.'

'It was your conversation with Alec Dewhurst that first put me on the right track,' Rose said. 'I didn't hear it myself, of course, but I believe Lady Lavinia remembered it pretty much word for word. One thing struck me at once. Why was Mr Dewhurst so adamant that his companion was *not* the Duchess of Grismere? One would have expected a man like that to have boasted if he had secured the affections of a duchess. The answer, of course, was that it was essential to his plans that you be kept in ignorance concerning his companion's real identity. For, if you knew, what was to stop you going to the duchess and informing her of the truth? That was why he tried his hand at blackmail. He was not to know that your employer already knew of your criminal record.'

'But how did Alec Dewhurst know that the duchess had a son born out of wedlock?' piped up Mr Kettering, feeling that it was high time he contributed to the conversation.

'Mr Thurlow told him, didn't you?' Rose said gently, turning to Ron, who nodded sheepishly. 'I daresay you confided a great deal to him while the two of you were in prison. You told us yourself that you struck up quite a friendship with Mr Dewhurst in the mistaken belief that he was a decent fellow.'

'If only I had gone to my ... my mother as soon as I discovered Dewhurst's little ruse,' said Ron glumly. 'If I had not been so reluctant to speak to her, then –'

'You are not to blame for what happened,' said Rose quickly. 'It must have been a terrible shock for you to realise that your mother was staying at the hotel.'

'But I might have saved poor Miss Peony's life,' protested Ron. 'I don't care a jot about what happened to Dewhurst; he brought it upon himself, but Miss Peony ...' he faltered.

'I have often wondered why Miss Peony sought to protect the duchess,' reflected Rose. 'The only conclusion I have reached is that she knew the real reason why she killed Alec Dewhurst.'

'Are you suggesting that she overhead their quarrel?' said Mr Kettering.

'Yes. That's to say, in a manner of speaking. It is pure conjecture, of course, but I believe Miss Peony crept up to the Dewhursts' rooms with the intention of returning the pocket watch. No doubt she intended to place it beside the door, or somewhere near, where it was certain to be found. I think she peered in at the window and witnessed some of the quarrel. I believe it quite possible she could read lips, on account of being deaf. Anyway, I think she was able to make out enough of the row to understand the gist of what was being discussed. I daresay she was still wondering what to do with the pocket watch when she saw Alec Dewhurst set off towards the cliff and the duchess go after him a minute or two later. I have no doubt that the duchess' manner was furtive; she would have kept to the shadows for fear of being seen, and I think Miss Peony was sufficiently intrigued to follow them.'

'Are you suggesting that Miss Peony saw the duchess kill Mr Dewhurst?' exclaimed Mr Kettering, with a shudder. He looked appalled at the idea.

'Yes,' said Rose. 'If you remember, Miss Hyacinth told us her sister was awfully upset when she returned.'

There was a long pause, during which Rose caught Mr Kettering's eye. Interpreting the look she gave him correctly, the hotel proprietor made a hasty excuse and left the room. Ron Thurlow barely waited for the door to close behind Mr Kettering before he turned to face Rose and said in a quiet voice, full of emotion:

'Will you tell me, your ladyship, what was written in that note you passed to my mother?'

'Yes,' said Rose. 'I wrote that there was a strong possibility that her son would be arrested for the murders and that, if she cared for him, she should confess to the crimes.'

'But that wasn't true!' cried Ron. 'The very fact that Miss Peony wrote to the murderer when she thought it likely that I would be arrested proves that.'

'Possibly,' agreed Rose, 'but without the duchess' confession we had no real evidence that the letter had actually been delivered, and certainly not to whom.' She held up her hand as Ron Thurlow made to protest. 'I believe the letter was conveyed to the murderer in the way I described, but I had no proof, and besides a very good case could be made against you,

you know. You have admitted yourself that on the night of Alec Dewhurst's death you had realised he was impersonating you. Who is to say you didn't quarrel on the edge of the cliff?' Ron made a face. 'You see,' said Rose gently, 'it was necessary for the duchess to confess her guilt as much to protect the innocent as to punish the guilty.'

There was an awkward silence and then Ron said:

'Was that all you wrote?'

'No,' said Rose quietly. 'I told her that, if she confessed, I should send Oberon to her.'

'I see,' said Ron. 'Did you know ... did you know what she was going to do? Did you know that she would take an overdose of her sleeping mixture after I left her?' He gave a start. 'But of course you did! You told me to be quick, that there was very little time.'

'I did not know for certain, of course,' replied Rose, choosing her words with care, 'but I thought it very likely. I knew she had the sleeping mixture and that she would not want the scandal of a trial.'

It was quite a long time before Ron Thurlow spoke; then he said:

'She told me that she had never stopped loving me. She even wrote to the duke before she took the sleeping draught to ask him to do what he could for me.' Ron's face brightened a fraction. 'I met the duke in Athens. He sent for me. He was terribly cut up, as you can imagine. Really, he is the most remarkable man. He was awfully frail, but quite determined to see me. He told me he had loved my mother very much and that he intended to fulfil her last wish. I rather got the impression that he plans to treat me like the son he never had. I shan't inherit the title, of course, but I shall be very well provided for.' He lowered his head and said quietly. 'Not that I deserve it, of course.'

'I can't think why not,' said Rose. 'It was a very selfless act you did, Mr Thurlow, going to prison in place of another. I can't think of many people who would have done that. I think the duke will be very fortunate to have you for a son.'

'Darling, I daresay you won't believe me,' remarked Lavinia to her sister-in-law, as she reclined on one of the bentwood and wickerwork chaises on the hotel terrace, 'but I think I am rather going to miss her.' She sighed. 'I suppose I had grown rather fond of the woman in a strange sort of way.'

Rose regarded her companion and smiled. Lavinia was referring to Miss Hyacinth, who had left the hotel some half an hour before. They had accompanied her as she made her way down the cliff path to the beach, and had stood on the sand and waved at her as she had climbed into the boat, which was to take her to Athens to begin her return journey to England. The Adlers had gone with her, Mabel complaining loudly that the sea looked jolly rough and that she hoped she was not going to be sick, while Miss Hyacinth fussed over her like a mother hen. Mr Vickers had already been seated in the boat, a broad grin on his face. Not only was he returning to good old Blighty, but he was a far richer man into the bargain. For the duke had taken the precaution of paying the private enquiry agent a substantial amount to ensure his silence concerning the tragic events that had occurred on the island.

'I do hope Miss Hyacinth will be all right,' continued Lavinia. 'When she returns to Clyst Beech I mean, or whatever that awful little village is called where she lives, and that she could never stop talking about. It sounded dreadfully dull. I do hope she won't be terribly lonely without her sister.'

'Clyst Birch,' corrected Rose, 'and you needn't worry. Miss Hyacinth is going to stay with the Adlers.'

'For a few weeks, perhaps,' said Lavinia, 'but she will have to go home eventually.'

'I should be very surprised if she ever returns to Clyst Birch,' said Rose.

'What do you mean?' Lavinia forced herself into a sitting position with the aid of her elbow so that she might better view her companion. It took a moment or two for enlightenment to dawn on her. 'Surely you're not suggesting ...?' She faltered, unable to continue her sentence, her eyes bulging at the very thought.

'I think Father Adler and Miss Hyacinth will make a very good couple. They are most ideally suited.'

'But matrimony at their age,' protested Lavinia, making a face.

'Even you will be Miss Hyacinth's age one day, Lavinia,' said Rose, leaning back on her sun lounger. 'There is little doubt in my mind that they shall be perfectly happy.' She closed her eyes, only to open them quickly at the sound of Lavinia giggling.

'I've just had a thought. Poor Mabel. Fancy having Miss Hyacinth for a step-mother! She'll fuss around her dreadfully. You saw what she was like on the boat. The poor girl won't have a moment's peace.'

'I think Miss Hyacinth's ministrations are just what Mabel Adler needs,' said Rose. 'Her father adores her, of course, but he has allowed her to become rather spoilt and rather too used to getting her own way.'

She put a hand up to her mouth to conceal a smile, for she might as well have been talking about her friend. Fortunately Lavinia did not appear to see any similarity between herself and the vicar's daughter, and carried on talking in a similar vein. Rose, well used to her friend's idle chatter, listened with only half an ear, her thoughts returning to the moment when Miss Hyacinth had made her farewells.

'I can't thank you enough, dear Lady Belvedere,' Miss Hyacinth had said, in a voice barely above a whisper. 'My poor, dear sister would thank you too, if she were here with us today ...' her voice had faltered. Rose had thought the woman was on the verge of tears and had smiled at her compassionately.

'If only I hadn't taken –'

'You won't believe how many people have told me that it was all their fault that the deaths occurred,' Rose had said, rather firmly. 'But really there is only one person to blame for what happened, and that is the murderer. I should like you to promise me that you will remember that. You were a very good sister to Miss Peony. I think she was jolly lucky to have had you for a sibling. Now, dear Miss Hyacinth, I should like you to think about yourself.'

'You are too kind, really you are.' Miss Hyacinth had bent forward and lowered her voice. 'You were frightfully good about your brooch and Mr Dewhurst's pocket watch. I ... I should like to tell you that I shall never take anything again, I promise you, not for so long as I live. It has always been rather a weakness of mine. I always returned them, always. Father and Peony found it dreadfully embarrassing. I suppose that was why I was encouraged to stay at home and keep house. I always said to dear Peony it would be quite different if only I had one fine piece of jewellery of my own that I could sit and admire.'

'Then I should like you to have this,' Rose had said, producing from her pocket the small silver brooch designed in the shape of a bow. The sapphires had caught the light.

'Oh no, I couldn't possibly,' Miss Hyacinth had protested feebly.

Rose had pressed the brooch into her hand. 'I should much rather you have it, dear Miss Hyacinth. I think it will look much nicer on you than it does on me.' Miss Hyacinth had smiled, though there were tears in her eyes, and Rose had squeezed her hand.

'I suppose we could invite Miss Hyacinth and Mabel for a visit,' Lavinia was saying. 'To Sedgwick Court, I mean. I'd simply die to see Mabel's face when she sees the extent of the house and grounds. Wouldn't you? It rather puts this hotel to shame, don't you think? And Miss Hyacinth would simply adore Sedgwick village. I daresay she'd get on frightfully well with your mother. I say, Rose, you look a bit peaky. Are you all right?'

'I just feel a little sick, that's all. I don't think I ate enough breakfast.'

'You felt ill yesterday morning too,' said Lavinia. She was just on the point of lying back down on her chaise, when she sat bolt upright, struck by a tremendous thought. 'I say, Rose, you don't think you could possibly be –'

'Lavinia, you mustn't say a word to Cedric, promise me,' said Rose quickly. 'I am not going to tell him until I am quite sure.'

'I shan't breathe a word,' exclaimed Lavinia, though her excited tone suggested otherwise. 'Oh, wouldn't it be exciting if you were? Of course, I should never want to have children myself. They're absolutely horrendous for one's body, not that I suppose you'd care, but I should absolutely hate to be fat. One hardly ever gets one's figure back, you know. I suppose Ceddie will want a boy, to inherit the title and all that, but I should absolutely adore it if you had a little girl. I have always wanted a niece. I say, do you think there's any chance she'll be just like a little version of me?'

'Heaven forbid,' Rose said laughing. 'I shouldn't wish that on any child!'

ACKNOWLEDGEMENTS

I am extremely grateful to Thomas Cook for permitting me to consult their collection of archive travel material and, in particular, I would like to thank Paul Smith, their Company Archivist, who provided me with invaluable help and assistance.

35702604R00160

Printed in Poland
by Amazon Fulfillment
Poland Sp. z o.o., Wrocław